INTRIGUE

Seek thrills. Solve crimes. Justice served.

Wyoming Ranch Justice
Juno Rushdan

Mississippi Manhunt
R. Barri Flowers

MILLS & BOON

DID YOU PURCHASE THIS BOOK WITHOUT A COVER?
If you did, you should be aware it is **stolen property** as it was reported
'unsold and destroyed' by a retailer.
Neither the author nor the publisher has received any payment
for this book.

WYOMING RANCH JUSTICE
© 2024 by Juno Rushdan
Philippine Copyright 2024
Australian Copyright 2024
New Zealand Copyright 2024

First Published 2024
First Australian Paperback Edition 2024
ISBN 978 1 867 91769 0

MISSISSIPPI MAN HUNT
© 2024 by R. Barri Flowers
Philippine Copyright 2024
Australian Copyright 2024
New Zealand Copyright 2024

First Published 2024
First Australian Paperback Edition 2024
ISBN 978 1 867 91769 0

® and ™ (apart from those relating to FSC®) are trademarks of Harlequin Enterprises (Australia) Pty Limited or its corporate affiliates. Trademarks indicated with ® are registered in Australia, New Zealand and in other countries.
Contact admin_legal@Harlequin.ca for details.

Except for use in any review, the reproduction or utilisation of this work in whole or in part in any form by any electronic, mechanical or other means, now known or hereafter invented, including xerography, photocopying and recording, or in any information storage or retrieval system, is forbidden without the permission of the publisher, Harlequin Mills & Boon.

This book is sold subject to the condition that it shall not, by way of trade or otherwise, be lent, resold, hired out or otherwise circulated without the prior consent of the publisher in any form or binding or cover other than that in which it is published and without a similar condition including this condition being imposed on the subsequent purchaser.

All rights reserved including the right of reproduction in whole or in part in any form. This edition is published in arrangement with Harlequin Books S.A..

This is a work of fiction. Names, characters, places, and incidents are either the product of the author's imagination or are used fictitiously, and any resemblance to actual persons, living or dead, business establishments, events, or locales is entirely coincidental.

MIX
Paper | Supporting
responsible forestry
FSC® C001695

Published by
Harlequin Mills & Boon
An imprint of Harlequin Enterprises (Australia) Pty Limited
(ABN 47 001 180 918), a subsidiary of HarperCollins
Publishers Australia Pty Limited
(ABN 36 009 913 517)
Level 19, 201 Elizabeth Street
SYDNEY NSW 2000 AUSTRALIA

Cover art used by arrangement with Harlequin Books S.A.. All rights reserved.

Printed and bound in Australia by McPherson's Printing Group

Wyoming Ranch Justice

Juno Rushdan

MILLS & BOON

Juno Rushdan is a veteran US Air Force intelligence officer and award-winning author. Her books are action-packed and fast-paced. Critics from *Kirkus Reviews* and *Library Journal* have called her work "heart-pounding James Bond-ian adventure" that "will captivate lovers of romantic thrillers." For a free book, visit her website: www.junorushdan.com.

Visit the Author Profile page
at millsandboon.com.au.

DEDICATION

For all the first responders. Thank you for your service.

CAST OF CHARACTERS

Matt Granger—A military hero turned part-time rancher and campus chief of police at the Southeastern Wyoming University, where a killer is hunting victims.

Hannah Delaney—A strong-willed detective who goes undercover as bait to catch the university killer. Will the secret she's hiding threaten her ability to do her job?

Erica Egan—This journalist will cross any line for a scoop and to see her name in the byline.

Kent Kramer—Not the biggest fan of Hannah Delaney's, this detective is willing to help catch a killer.

Nancy Tomlinson—FBI profiler out at Quantico.

Victor Starkey—A sergeant with the campus police department.

Prologue

He'd waited as long as he could, holding back the urge until it took control. Tonight, he would sate the dark hunger gnawing at him and find some sense of relief.

Watching her, he licked his lips, excited and eager for their hookup. He had it all planned. Everything was in place and ready. The SUV. The syringe. The intimate hideaway where they'd have lots of privacy and time for him to play. She looked stronger than the others. Maybe she'd last more than a day or two. He had high hopes for this one.

Jessica logged off the computer in the university lab and began packing up her things.

Now. He threw a book in his backpack, slung it over his shoulder and hurried to beat her to the door without looking like he was rushing. The key to pulling it off, he'd learned the hard way, was in the timing. If he left behind her, then she'd be on the defensive, wondering if he was following her.

Leaving the place first—whether the lab, the café, the rec center—and then luring his prey to come to him had consistently been easier than shooting fish in a barrel and always got him his quarry without fail.

He pretended to hobble on the foot he'd Velcroed into the immobilization boot on his left leg. Shoving through the front door of the Southeastern Wyoming University computer lab, he stepped out into the cool late-night air. No worries about leaving his fingerprints; the seamless flesh-colored gloves solved that problem. He bent his head away from the camera and lowered the bill of his cap pulled over a shaggy ginger-colored wig.

Plenty of traps everywhere, but he was vigilant. He was prepared.

Making his way to the SUV he kept prepped for these special nights, he slowed down when he heard her leave the building and the door clicked shut. Anticipation slithered through him.

She was only a few feet behind him, drawing closer. He limped to his vehicle parked at the far end of the lot, near the alley she liked to use as a shortcut to the bus stop, where she was headed now, rather than take the long way around the block.

Dropping his bag and decoy keys on the ground, he swore loudly. He bent over and feigned struggling to pick up his keys, which he had slid beneath the car with his foot.

"Oh, man." Another curse flew from him as he glanced around, catching her eye. "Hey." He gave a quick wave with his right hand, ensuring she could see his other arm tucked in a sling like a broken wing, and she slowed. "Would you mind helping me a second?" he asked, and she stopped. He pushed the nonprescription glasses up on the bridge of his nose and limped a couple of steps, giving her a clear view of the medical boot. "If I get down there, I might not be able to get back up." Flashing a gentle smile, he fought the impulse to scratch the top of his lip, which itched from the fake mustache. He was anxious to shed the disguise. Even the colored contacts irritated his eyes.

Jessica glanced from side to side, then looked between the sling and the immobilization boot, deliberating.

She was perfect. Precisely his type. White. Slim. Blond. Dark eyes. High cheekbones. Pretty mouth. Only twenty-years-old. Easygoing. Not too wary.

He'd considered a few others, but she was his top pick for his next hookup. This was going to be his lucky night.

"This is what I get for trying to ride my bike

more and do my part to save the environment," he said lightly, raising the sling. "Someone not paying attention hit me. I'll owe you one."

With a nod, Jessica headed toward him, making the mistake of thinking he wasn't a threat. "I'm the same. Even though my parents offered to help me buy a car, I either bike or take the Secure Ride," she said, referring to the public transportation bus service offered by the university.

Little did she realize that she'd never make it to the bus tonight.

"I would've taken the Secure Ride myself," he said. "But at the closest stop, there isn't a bench, and I'd have to stand while I wait for the bus. The doc told me to keep pressure off my foot." As she drew closer, he pulled the grin wider. His excitement over the risk of grabbing her was liquid fire in his veins. The burn was good. "I appreciate you helping me." He hid his right hand behind his leg, and the sling covered most of the other. Up close, someone could tell he was wearing gloves if they looked carefully. "Can I pay you back with a coffee or something at the Wheatgrass Café?"

Stepping within his reach, she flicked her hair over her shoulder, kicking up the sweet scent of her perfume. The smell reminded him of a previous hookup.

"No need." She narrowed her eyes at him for a second. "Hey, I know you. You're in my Mythology 101 class. I nearly knocked you down the other day." Her shoulders immediately relaxed. A smile tugged at her rosy lips.

Another key to success was to pick one of their classes. The larger, the better, where he could blend in, disappear. Simply sit in once or twice while in disguise. Orchestrate a meeting where they bump into him or vice versa. That first connection, the initial spark, made this moment when he snatched them so much easier because once they remembered him, it lowered their guard.

"Oh yeah," he said, filling his altered voice with pleasant surprise. "I didn't recognize you." The truth was, he'd memorized her face, the shape of her body, the way she moved. Fantasized about tonight a hundred times. "By the way, I'm Theodore Cowell. Just call me Theo." Introductions put them further at ease.

"Jessica Atkinson."

His next steps flew through his mind. *Take hypodermic needle from sling. Dose the girl. Grab her. Quick tussle*—they always fought and lost. *Pop trunk. Toss her in the vehicle. Handcuffs. Leg irons. Gag. Drive.*

He could do it in under a minute. His best record was twenty-two seconds. None had ever gotten away. By the time he got behind the wheel and sped off, the ketamine would hit her system, keeping her quiet for several hours. Once she woke up, then they'd party.

"Thanks again." He smoothed his palm over

the slight bulge of the compact handgun tucked in the pocket of his lightweight jacket. He only carried it for insurance. Not that he had a problem killing an animal or a person by pulling the trigger—he was a hunter in every sense of the word and was even a long-range deadeye, capable of hitting a target one mile away. But using a gun to wrangle his prey would be cheating.

"Sure. No problem." She got down on her hands and knees and reached under the car for his keys.

Always worked like a charm.

Time slowed to a crawl. He looked around, sweeping the area once more, ensuring no witnesses lurked nearby. It was just the two of them. His heart throbbed with anticipation as he pulled out the hypodermic needle.

Chapter One

Hannah Delaney got off the Secure Ride bus operated by SWU, surprised it had arrived four minutes ahead of schedule. Hitching her backpack on her shoulder, she headed for the computer lab to work on a project.

At least, that was what she wanted people to believe.

Her police chief had given her the undercover assignment at the last minute after the University Killer suddenly resurfaced ten days ago, taking the life of twenty-one-year-old Madison Scott. For nearly the past decade, the murderer had struck on and off, always claiming three lives within a month, using the same MO before disappearing again.

Hannah had pored over the routines of the previous victims, zeroing in on things they'd had in common, and tried to recreate their lifestyle.

She'd moved into on-campus housing, enrolled in a myriad of classes, frequented the Wheatgrass Café, rode the Secure Ride bus at night, hit the gym at the Sweetwater Recreation Center, biked during the day to downtown, shopped at the farmers market and caught live music at the local bar, the Watering Hole.

She still hadn't had a chance to swing by the computer lab at night on a regular basis like some of the victims had done in years past. Fall semester had only been in session for less than three weeks. With all the new student events and socials, where a predator might be lurking, there simply hadn't been enough hours in a day to cover everything. She had to prioritize. The lab wasn't high on the list, since Madison Scott had never been there. Quite honestly, Hannah didn't understand why many students would use the campus computer lab these days when most had a personal laptop.

Time was running out. The killer was going to snatch his next victim soon. Only twenty days left for him to claim two more lives. Hannah only hoped she was doing enough to catch his eye. She'd do anything to spare someone else from being violated and murdered. Stopping monsters was her life's mission, the only way for her to atone and silence her demons. It drove everything she did—why she got up in the morning, became a detective, even why she kept everyone at a distance.

You'll find him. You have to.

Dressed in jeans, an open flannel button-down with a tank top beneath it, hair in a high ponytail to make her appear even younger, she blended in with any other student. The only thing to set her apart was the concealed gun in her inside-the-waistband holster at the five-o'clock position between her back and hip, and the small knife that was a part of her belt buckle.

She took the alley, a shortcut to the lab. There was no way for her to know for sure if any of the other victims had ever used this same route at some point leading up to their murder. It was smarter and safer to walk around the block to get to the lab, using the well-lit sidewalks, where a passerby might see something. Yet young people, not considering the fragility of their lives, tended to trade security for convenience.

People showed you who they were in subtle ways by their choices and preferences, which were almost as telling as a Myers–Briggs personality test if you watched someone for weeks on end. Whether they were cautious or carefree. Skeptical or trusting. Selfish or caring. Predictable or impulsive.

All the slain women had been described as kind, thoughtful, naive. Somewhat of a loner. Most importantly, creatures of habit.

Despite being the right physical type, this was where Hannah was at a disadvantage. Less than ten days wasn't long enough to establish a consistent routine, a pattern the University Killer could rely on. He not only chose his victims for their appearance, but she suspected he also stalked them to know precisely when and where to strike.

Two more women were going to die soon if she couldn't lure him in as the bait.

A soft scuffling sound came from the other end of the alley near the outskirts of the computer-lab parking lot. Whatever it was, it was bigger than a rat.

Hannah's gut tightened. She picked up her pace down the alleyway, sticking to the shadows of the wall. Straining to see in the dim light, she caught sight of a dark SUV, the back end of the passenger's side.

The trunk door popped open.

Someone grunted. More scuffling noises.

"What are you doing?" a woman asked, her voice frantic.

Two people stepped into partial view, but the dark SUV partly obscured them. A man wrestled with a blond woman, possibly in her early twenties. The man hit the blonde in the face, dazing her, and hauled her to the back of the vehicle.

Dropping her backpack, Hannah rushed forward. She drew her weapon from the holster.

"Police!" Hannah called out, holding the Glock in a two-handed grip, sighting down the barrel.

He whirled, pulling the woman up in front of him like a shield, one arm locked under her chin, pressed against her throat. With his other hand, he wrenched one of the blonde's arms clutched behind her back. An empty arm sling swung back and forth along his side. His gaze darted to the open trunk, and Hannah realized how close he had come to getting the young woman inside it.

"Let her go!" Hannah ordered. "Right now!"

Keeping the woman held tightly in front of him, he scurried backward around to the driver's side, dragging her along with him. Her nose was bloody. Her eyes were wide with fear. She clutched the arm over her throat, her feet shuffling in the direction she was being forced.

Easing around the rear of the vehicle, Hannah glimpsed inside the trunk. A chill ran through her. The interior of the cargo compartment was padded. A plastic tarp was laid out. Handcuffs and leg irons each dangled from a chain that had been bolted to either side of the trunk. On the breeze, the biting scent of bleach hit her. No license plate.

She rounded the back side, coming face-to-face with him. One clean shot was all Hannah needed.

"Release her, or I'll shoot." A complete bluff.

Although an excellent markswoman, she didn't have a clear shot with the blonde being used as a human shield.

Between the shaggy hair, mustache, glasses and the way he hid his face behind the young woman's head, Hannah couldn't make out enough details to identify him, much less find the clearance to pull the trigger.

Yanking the woman another foot or two toward the driver-side door, he released the arm wrested behind her back and pulled something from his pocket. A semiautomatic pistol. "Drop your gun," he demanded, pressing the muzzle to the young woman's side. "Or I'll shoot her."

Hannah held her ground, keeping her weapon aimed levelly. "This isn't what you want," she said, taking a calculated risk. Killing his victims slowly after raping them was his MO. Taking her life in an impulsive act wouldn't satisfy him. Not only that, but he'd also lose his only leverage. "I don't think you're going to pull the trigger and kill her."

He eyed the car door. "Who said anything about killing her?" He jammed the muzzle into the woman's side so hard that she winced. "Drop it, or I start putting bullets in her."

Hannah hesitated. The need to put this monster down and end his nine-year-long killing spree was an ache in her soul. She might not get another opportunity if he slipped through her fingers now.

"The first one goes in her stomach," he promised.

Getting this woman out alive was the only thing that mattered at the moment. Hannah glanced over her shoulder at the dumpster near the entrance to the alley. If he tried to shoot at her, she could make it there and duck for cover. She raised her palms with her gun vertical, barrel pointed up. Slowly, she set it down on the ground, never taking her gaze off him and the girl.

"Do you think I'm stupid? Kick it under the car."

She did as instructed, sending her weapon sailing beneath the SUV, only deepening the nasty twist in her gut spiraling into fear. Fear for the life of the young woman.

"Open the door," he snapped at the blonde, tightening his arm over her throat.

No matter what, Hannah wasn't going to let him get away with another victim. Worst case, if he managed to get the girl into the car, she'd pull her backup weapon from her boot and blow out his tires. He wouldn't make it far.

With a shaking hand, the young woman grabbed the handle and opened it. Her eyelids grew heavy, and she swayed in his grip.

Was the hold on her throat choking her, cutting off her airway?

"Let her go!" Hannah took a tentative step forward. "She can't breathe."

"Don't you move. Not another step." He backed up, using the woman's body to block him. His arm loosened around her throat as he climbed into the vehicle, keeping the gun pointed at her side.

The woman swayed again, her head bobbing like she was going to keel over any second.

She'd been drugged. He must have dosed her with ketamine already.

The car engine roared to life while he kept the gun pointed at his hostage. "You'll have to choose. Me or her."

Choose? What does he mean?

He pulled the trigger, shooting the blonde in the side, and peeled off.

No!

The young woman staggered and slumped to the ground. The SUV sped across the parking lot, hitting the street. He turned the corner and sped away, tires squealing, as Hannah raced over to the young woman, knelt beside her and checked the wound.

Thankfully, the bullet had missed her stomach, but it had struck her just above the hip. The woman's brown eyes fluttered closed—a combination of the drugs and shock.

Hannah took off her shirt and applied pressure to slow the bleeding. "Hang in there. You're going to make it." She whipped out her cell phone and called 911.

Once she heard sirens approaching, she wondered which campus officers would arrive on the scene.

She'd readily deal with any of them except for one—the SWU police department chief.

Matt Granger.

Chapter Two

Behind the wheel of his pickup truck, Matt Granger sped to the university campus with his teeth clenched. Since waking up that morning, he'd had a familiar tingle prickling his spine that forewarned him to prepare for trouble. It was his day off from the SWUPD. The bad feeling niggling him had made him consider going in, but he had coordinated a full load of work on the ranch with his cousins. Before he could relax with an ice-cold beer, a sergeant had called with news he'd been dreading.

A young woman had been shot during an encounter with a man they suspected to be the University Killer, and somehow a detective had been on the scene.

Trouble indeed—a subject in which he had plenty of experience. Truth be told, he was drawn to it…or rather, trouble was drawn to him. Good at seeing it coming and neutralizing it, a talent that had served him well during his time in the army as a Special Forces Operator. His job had been training and planning for the worst and then making sure it happened—to the enemy. After seeing too much carnage, he'd returned to his family's ranch, set between Laramie and Bison Ridge. The transition to the Laramie police force and later to campus law enforcement felt natural, even easy. He'd mistakenly thought that in the two small towns, where neighbors helped one another and everyone was so welcoming with open arms, things would be slower, quieter. Safer. Instead of bloodshed and loss, he'd finally find peace.

But whether he was in the army, with the LPD or the campus police, there was no escaping trouble and the death that always followed.

Matt pulled up to the headquarters of the SWUPD, located on the west end of campus, threw his truck in Park, and hurried inside. The department occupied five thousand square feet of the first floor of a parking garage, providing a modern, spacious facility for the law enforcement agency. He nodded hello to a couple officers.

One looked him over with raised eyebrows, making Matt consider how he must appear after sixteen hours of hard manual labor.

It had been his idea to expand his family's sources of revenue by designating a modest portion of the property to big game hunting. He'd taken the lead on building small cabins that could be rented to those looking to hunt or simply relax. Earlier, he and his cousins had been working on Sheetrock and wall texture since the wiring for the electricity had been finished.

Taking off his dark brown cowboy hat, he wished he'd had time to shower, or at least had the foresight to change his sweaty shirt, wash his face and grab a sandwich for the ride over.

Sergeant Lewis stood in Matt's office, talking to a woman—presumably the detective—seated in a chair that faced the desk. Lewis looked up, catching sight of Matt, and opened the office door for him.

"Evening, boss," Lewis said.

The woman pivoted in the chair, glancing over her shoulder at Matt and meeting his gaze. He swallowed a sigh.

Lewis gestured to her. "This is Detective—"

"Hannah Delaney," Matt interrupted, letting the spike of annoyance leak into his voice. The woman was the walking, talking epitome of trouble.

"Oh, you two know each other," Lewis said, surprise stamped on his face.

"Yeah." Hannah gave a curt nod to the officer while keeping her stare leveled at Matt. "We worked a case together before he quit being a detective with the LPD to hide out and play cop over here."

Matt tamped down a retort. He'd been through this rigmarole before, where a cop—usually a detective—hurled an insult at him for taking this position and he, stung by the icy disdain, inevitably went on the defense.

Little good it ever did him.

For some reason, when it came to Hannah, all her taunts teased in a way that reminded him he was not only a cop but also a man. "I forgot you could be so…" He let his voice trail off, realizing that finishing his statement wouldn't help the situation.

"Candid?" she offered.

He measured his words to mitigate the tension in the room. "I was going to say *blunt*. Hard-hitting." *Like a sledgehammer.*

He had no idea why he found that kind of sexy.

Lewis stood still and quiet, shifting an uncomfortable glance between them.

"Would you excuse us, Sergeant?" Matt guided Lewis to the door and closed it behind him. "What are you doing on my campus?" With Hannah, there was no telling. He crossed the room and dropped his hat next to his computer. Leaning on the edge of his desk, facing her, he noticed bloodstains on her white tank top. "And how are you involved in tonight's shooting?"

Sergeant Lewis had given scant details, as he hadn't had a chance to interview Hannah yet before he'd called Matt.

"For the past ten days," Hannah said, crossing her lean legs, "I've been on campus, pretending to be a new student named Helen Davis, in an undercover op to catch the University Killer."

Undercover? He had not seen that one coming.

"I'd been following the routines of the previous victims," she continued, "and came across him attempting to take his next. According to her student ID, she's Jessica Atkinson." Hannah ran through the events leading up to her 911 call.

The student was now being treated at the university hospital. Over the phone, Matt had instructed Lewis to send an officer to watch over her while she recovered.

"Where's your partner?" Matt asked.

"I'm solo on this."

The benefits of having her assigned to a case like this with a partner were obvious and numerous. So why was she working without backup?

He stiffened, hoping she hadn't gone rogue, taking it upon herself to do this outside official channels. If he had to describe Hannah in one word, it would be *firebrand.* And true to that nature, she was incendiary.

The only reason they had been put together on a case was because no one else wanted to work with her and he had lost his previous partner. To this day, he blamed himself for his death, even though the inquiry had found him not guilty of any wrongdoing.

"Why did they pick you?" He folded his arms across his chest. "And why alone?"

She narrowed her eyes at the questions.

Not that he meant them as an insult. One thing he didn't question was Hannah's extensive experience working undercover. If anyone could immerse themselves in a different world, become a different person—quickly—it was her. Yet something else about her that made him uneasy.

"The chief picked me," she said, meaning the chief of the Laramie police department, Wilhelmina Nelson. "She thought I would make the perfect bait."

Now that she mentioned it, Hannah did fit the profile of the previous victims—blond, trim, petite, dark eyes. Although she was twenty-eight, the right clothes, combined with her girl-next-door look and small stature, would make most guess she was no older than twenty.

"You should've notified me about your undercover operation." Matt scratched at the stubble on his jaw. "It's called *professional courtesy*."

"Wasn't my decision not to notify you. Only following orders. If you have a problem with that, take it up with Chief Nelson."

The not-so-polite suggestion was only made to irk him. They both knew he wasn't going to go crying to anyone about this. "Any idea why you were given an order to cut me out of an op on my campus?"

"Three different campus police chiefs have tried and failed to catch this guy."

"And the LPD assumed I'd be the fourth?"

She gave him a one-shoulder shrug. "The University Killer has stayed two steps ahead of your department and evaded capture for almost a decade. There's a reason for that."

"What exactly are you implying? That the perp could be someone in the campus police department?"

"I didn't *imply* anything. I merely stated a fact. You have personnel who have worked here for ten-plus years. Three sergeants and a dispatcher. Everyone else in your department either attended SWU or has lived locally long enough to be a suspect. Have they been investigated?" she asked pointedly.

He flicked her an impatient glance, not caring for the second implication belying her tone. Did she think he was incompetent? "Of course they have, including the support staff."

Ten women had been violated and murdered over the years. The killer hadn't bothered to wear a condom when he'd raped his victims, leaving behind his DNA, and had put a queen of hearts playing card with the eyes scratched out on their corpses.

Matt had only recently taken over as chief. Still, the department's failure to find the killer weighed heavy on him. He'd hoped that the killer would be dead by now or too old to resurface. But as soon as the body of Madison Scott had been discovered—the first under his watch—it had taken him a week to investigate every single person in the department.

"I took the added precaution of getting everyone to take a polygraph test." It wasn't admissible in court and wasn't foolproof, but merely asking them to take it told him a lot if any refused. Mostly it gave him another opportunity for someone to slip up. As a detective, he'd even had a suspect confess once when questioned about how nervous he'd been during the test. "All their alibis have been checked, but two officers didn't have one," Matt admitted.

Hannah narrowed her eyes to slits. "Who are they?"

Hesitant to share that information, he knew not disclosing it would only further raise her suspicions.

"Officer Laura Jimenez," he said, and the tension in Hannah's face eased slightly at the mention of a woman. "And Officer Carl Farran. He would've been twelve at the time of the first murder, and he readily agreed to DNA testing when he didn't have to." Matt had cleared every other employee in the SWUPD. "I realize Chief Nelson suspects there are bad apples in every department, but I hope you don't share the same tainted view." He was willing to make an exception for

Chief Nelson. She'd been brought into the Laramie Police Department for the express purpose of cleansing it of all the corrupt officers, and there had been plenty buried deep. More than enough to require help from the division of criminal investigation—the DCI—under the Wyoming State Attorney's General Office. No one was prepared for the vile things that case brought to light, such as a crooked lieutenant who sold the personal information of every officer in the department, endangering families, putting the lives of kids at risk. The worst part was, the seller had never been tracked down. "My officers aren't dirty, and they're certainly not serial killers."

"My, my, Matt, you seem a bit touchy regarding the subject."

To say he was sensitive on the issue would be an understatement. Not only had he worked for the LPD and had friends who had turned out to be crooked, but his cousin, Holden Powell, had gone through a scandal after his boss, the previous sheriff, turned out to be the worst of the worst when it came to corruption. For a long time, Holden had to deal with people gossiping, giving him the side-eye, wondering if he was guilty by association or how he could be so blind as to miss it.

It lit a fire under Matt to ensure his department was above board. "A dirty cop, much less a murderer hiding behind a badge, is a subject that should make any officer worth their salt touchy."

Her jaw hardened. "The campus police have turned up no leads, no solid suspects and no matches to the DNA the killer left behind. He just keeps slipping through your fingers like grains of sand."

Frustrated by the same thing, Matt had submitted the killer's DNA to a publicly accessible genetic-genealogy-testing service. More than one hundred users had matched as a distant relative, possibly as close as a third cousin. It would take four to six months of research to narrow it down to a pool of people who could be the University Killer. He had a retired investigator from the DCI working on it, unbeknownst to anyone in his office. He was keeping this information on a need-to-know basis. Eventually, the murderer would be caught; it was simply a matter of time, which he didn't have.

"You're not faring much better on your own," Matt said. "He slipped through your fingers tonight, didn't he? You're always the daredevil, but this was reckless. And what do you have to show for it besides a wounded victim?"

She jumped to her feet, still not coming eye level even with him sitting on the edge of the desk. Putting her hands on her slim hips, she drew closer, grazing his knee with her thigh. "Better wounded than dead. That's what she'd be if I hadn't been here undercover. This op was dangerous, sure. Not reckless. Maybe you've been playing cop too long on campus to remember the job can be hazardous."

He took a breath, not wanting to argue with her, especially when she had a legitimate point: Jessica Atkinson was alive and safe thanks to Hannah. "If you'd had backup, we might have him in custody."

"Backup would've meant a partner tailing me. This guy is really good. His setup was sophisticated. The fake arm sling and leg boot. Padded trunk to muffle noise. Handcuffs and leg irons. Which were just an added precaution because he drugs his victims before he even gets them in the vehicle. And the trunk reeked of bleach. A sign he's careful not to leave behind DNA in the vehicle. He would've spotted a partner. Maybe even sensed I was undercover as bait to trap him if someone had been shadowing me."

Hard to disregard Hannah's instincts or the fact that she had gotten more details about the way this guy operated than anyone else had in nearly a decade. Not that he liked how Chief Nelson had made Hannah bait, left to fend for herself with no backup, and had cut him out of the loop about an op on his campus. But whether it had been reckless or clever for her to be out there alone, he was no longer so sure.

"The killer never used a gun before that we

know of," he said, looking for a way to get on better terms with her. "Thanks to you, we'll have ballistics."

"If only I'd had a little more time to lure him in," Hannah said, the regret in her voice palpable. "I'm sure he would've gone for me."

Half of him hoped that wasn't true despite the need to put an end to the killings. No victim had escaped the University Killer. Until tonight. The idea of this twisted psychopath setting his sights on Hannah, regardless of her training, had unease stirring in his blood. When they'd worked together and he'd seen firsthand the cavalier risks she took, which had ironically also made her successful, it'd triggered his protective instincts. Something she had made clear she didn't appreciate.

Not that he could help it or was sexist in any way. The military had programmed him to protect his country, his teammates and those in need, and to be merciless in that endeavor.

He got up and went around to the other side of his desk, putting ample distance between Hannah and himself. "Well, your cover is blown now since he got a good look at you. I trust you're not going to request to be taken off the case."

Her honey-brown eyes sparkled with a definite challenge. "You'd trust correctly."

One of the things he admired about Hannah was her spirit, her *never back down no matter what* attitude. It also worried him because one day it might get her killed.

He dropped into his chair, physically exhausted while adrenaline kept his mind sharp. "My department is going to continue investigating as well," he said. "To avoid wasting resources and duplicating effort, it only makes sense to work together from here on out. We'll make better headway faster. Besides, you could use a partner on this."

"Don't you mean, *campus police* could use a detective?"

Swallowing another sigh, he grinned. "My *advancement* to chief doesn't make me any less of a detective."

She rocked back on her heels, her face wary. "I hope you're not suggesting that you and I work together."

In his mind, there was no question about it. "As a matter of fact, I am. Is there another officer in my department who you think is more qualified? Who can keep up with you?" *Who won't let you run roughshod over them?* "Or who you can trust to have your back despite your brash risk-taking tendencies?"

Averting her gaze, Hannah smoothed a hand over her ponytail.

That was the first time he'd ever seen her speechless, and he relished being the one to have caused it. "What do you say? Unless you need to get permission from your chief before you can decide."

Straightening, she looked up at him. "I'm authorized to do what's necessary to get this guy, but I think it would be better if it was me and another *full-time* detective working this case."

Three irksome implications in one conversation. She was really trying to strike a nerve. Getting close, too. Maybe she wanted him to concede and turn over the case to the LPD.

Never one to shirk his duty, no way that was happening. The killer was targeting women on his campus, making it his responsibility. Detective Delaney would just have to deal with him.

"I'm not rusty." He'd been in the position of campus police chief for only a year. "I'll have Sergeant Starkey, my number two, manage the day-to-day stuff here, and then you'll have me all to yourself full-time," he said, knowing it was the last thing she wanted.

Her eyes flashed with annoyance, but a slight flush colored her cheeks.

Did he get under her skin the same way she did his?

For a few seconds, she just stared up at him. "The less time I spend with you, the better."

As he suspected. He wished he could say the feeling was mutual. She was a tough nut to crack. But the more she gave him a hard time, the more he itched to break past her shell to understand her better.

Being around her had him questioning whether he'd gotten it wrong. Maybe he was attracted to trouble.

"I get I'm not your first choice, or even on your list of choices." He wondered if anyone would make the cut on who she'd want to work with. She was such a loner. "But I thought we made a pretty good team on the cartel case."

A branch of a notorious Mexican cartel had set up shop practically in their backyard, processing and distributing fentanyl and methamphetamine. They had managed to find it and shut it down. No easy feat, with both of them nearly dying in the process, but she couldn't deny they'd been effective.

Hannah frowned. "Yeah, I suppose we did," she said, as if agreeing to eat a bowl of broken glass.

Good thing he didn't have a fragile ego. "I want this guy as badly as you do." Probably more. Every woman taken from his campus, violated and murdered, was one more to keep him up at night. "I think we can stop him. One more case together?"

After a long moment, she nodded her acquiescence. "Fine. I guess we're partners again. Stuck together for the sake of the greater good."

Could she look any less enthused?

Then again, of course she could. This was Hannah Delaney.

"Lucky me." His voice was thick with sarcasm. "Look, the sooner we catch this guy, the sooner you can go back to working solo."

"Just the way I like it." She stuffed her hands in her pockets. "But let's get one thing straight— I'm not following your lead or playing it safe this time."

As if she had before. Refraining from rolling his eyes, he gave his head a little shake in disbelief.

"To nail him," she said, her demeanor turning steely, "we have to do it my way."

Why was he not surprised? "I would expect nothing less."

But following her lead didn't mean he was going to abandon his good judgment.

This time around, he'd make sure they compromised and acted like partners. It was the only way for them to avoid another close call with death.

Chapter Three

Wednesday, September 18
6:00 a.m.

For the past several hours, he'd been unable to sleep. Unable to eat. All he could think about was Jessica. Her sweet mouth. Her pretty face. Her perky breasts. Her lean legs. He pictured her stripped of all her clothes and having his way with her.

But he'd lost her because of that devious cop. She'd ruined his hookup. And he'd needed it so badly.

Anger and frustration ran riot inside him, tangling and swelling into a seething mass until he trembled from the force it. He'd been denied his satisfaction. The release he craved.

Swearing, he pounded a fist on the wood railing of his front porch and stared at the flames in the firepit. His head was throbbing. Maybe he should call in sick today and lick his wounds, even though it was better to stick to a routine the day after nabbing one of his dates.

Tried *to nab but didn't quite make it.*

Last night was a mere setback. Not defeat. He was not a loser, and he would not sulk.

He was going to fight for what he wanted. Take it with no remorse.

But missing a painstakingly planned hookup stirred other emotions inside him, ones he knew for certain he shouldn't dare entertain. Like finishing what he'd started with Jessica.

No, no. No! Too risky.

He had to focus on the next step. Moving forward.

But this growing need could destroy him if he didn't do something—and soon.

His mind careened back to the cop. The slender blonde. With dark eyes. Curves in all the right places. The one who had been undercover, acting like a student. He'd noticed her. How could he not? She stood out. But he'd had others on his carefully cultivated list.

Yes, the list. Stick to the others already chosen.

He'd take a different girl. With everything going on around campus, this week was best. The timing would be perfect.

But what about the pesky cop?

He had to teach her a lesson. Punish her for the sin of disrupting his process. Toy with her. Torture her.

Then he'd kill her, too.

Smiling, he walked down the porch steps, over

to the firepit, and squeezed more lighter fluid onto the flames. The fire roared higher. Smoke curled around him. He picked up the disguise he'd shed from the ground and tossed it into the blaze.

Sometimes less was more, anyway. Glasses and contacts weren't necessary. One thing he was good at—had always been quite skilled at, even as a child—was becoming a chameleon. Though the loss of the sling and orthopedic boot hurt. He'd grown accustomed to using them to lure in his prey.

He'd gotten lazy. Complacent. Now he'd have to come up with a new way to capture his birdies. He went back up to the cabin's porch.

Settling back in a rocking chair, he stared out over the woods that ringed the edge of his property. He loved the forest. Being out here alone never failed to calm him, to steady his thoughts. Rocking in the chair, taking in the green landscape, he considered the best way to achieve his goals.

Cops hated losing. Getting bested by the enemy. He smiled, now knowing exactly how to proceed.

Not only would he beat that harpy at this sport, but he was also going to humble her, break her, make her wish she had never messed with him. The thought of it gave him such sweet satisfaction.

First, he had to figure out who the hell she was. Wouldn't be hard.

With no idea that he was coming, it'd never occur to her that she should be the one hiding from him.

Chapter Four

Regret flared inside Hannah as she watched the forensic artist finish a drawing of the University Killer. Last night's events replayed in her head. Bleach. Handcuffs. Plastic tarp. How close she had gotten to stopping him but had ultimately failed.

Now that psychopath was still on the loose, looking for his next victim.

The forensic artist turned the sketch pad around to show Jessica Atkinson. "Is this him?"

"Yes, that's what he looked like," the young woman said from her hospital bed, staring at the sketch of her attacker. "You got all the details right." A shiver ran through Jessica, and she pulled the blanket up to her neck with a wince.

According to the surgeon, if the bullet had hit her two inches higher, she might not be alive. Once she recovered, and after some physical therapy, she'd be able to walk without a limp. In her bloodwork, they'd found the drug GHB, gamma-hydroxybutyrate, also known as liquid ecstasy. Not only was it a common, illegal date-rape drug, but it was also the same one that had been found in Madison Scott's system. Now they knew the University Killer used GHB in the abduction of his victims as well as throughout the time he held them captive up until he murdered them.

The forensic artist, who worked freelance for local law enforcement, lowered the sketch pad. "You did great, Ms. Atkinson. I only drew what you described."

Hannah took a quick picture of the drawing with her phone.

"You can drop it off with Sergeant Starkey at the station," Matt said to the artist. "I want to get his image out there for everyone to see before noon."

Little good it would do them. "It's a disguise," Hannah said to Matt, keeping her voice low. "He's only going to change it."

Jessica grimaced at the comment.

Hannah sighed. Guess her voice hadn't been as low as she thought.

Cupping her elbow, Matt ushered her off to the side of the room. His grip was firm, and the heat of his palm seeped through the sleeve of her blazer. She gritted her teeth to keep from squirming.

Across the room, the artist uttered something comforting to the young woman that made her nod, her eyes brightening with hope.

Hannah couldn't remember the last time she'd *felt* hope, much less inspired it.

Once they reached the window, she jerked her arm free of his hand.

At six-five, Matt stood a foot taller than her. Dark haired. Overly muscled. A rough-looking part-time cowboy.

They'd worked together when he was a distinguished detective with the Laramie Police Department. Although they'd solved a tough case, he'd rubbed her the wrong way the entire time.

Two words described him best. *Too much.* Too big. Too tall. Too broad. Too self-righteous. Too smart and shrewd to be a university campus cop.

Even his energy was too disquieting. His blue eyes too piercing. All that bundled in a package that was simply too handsome.

There was no denying the last part, no matter how hard she tried, but even thinking it made her skin prickle.

Matt Granger's perfect facade was infuriating.

Too good to be true. Everyone around him believed it was real. Not her. At fourteen, she'd learned that sometimes the devil pretended to be a saint. The pretense so convincing, so calculated, that even those closest couldn't see the evil lurking within.

"Yes, it's probably a disguise," Matt said. Wearing a black T-shirt that was too tight—the only reason he purchased that size was to show off his physique—blue jeans, badge clipped on his top, walkie-talkie hooked on his utility belt and a dark brown cowboy hat, he glanced down at her with one of those disapproving looks she'd grown to despise. "But it'll take some thought and maybe a day or two for him to change it. In the meantime, not only do we have his current disguise but also his MO. We'll make sure every student will be wary of anyone wearing an arm sling or a walking boot or even asking for physical assistance."

Something was better than nothing. Hannah nodded. "We should also encourage a buddy system of some sort."

"When I took over as campus police chief, there had been an uptick in thefts and sexual assault. So I helped the university form a student organization to promote safety. I'll call an emergency SAV meeting, and we can talk to them about it. They'll spread the word quickly."

"'SAV'?" she asked, vaguely remembering seeing a flyer with the acronym.

"Students Against Violence."

"Good idea—forming the organization and talking to them." Maybe he *was* making a difference on campus. Still didn't change the fact that he could make an even bigger one working for the LPD.

He flashed a wry grin. "Did you just pay me a compliment?"

Not on purpose. Her guard had slipped. She had a tendency to go soft around him and usually overcompensated for it by turning more surly than normal. "Don't let it go to your head. I'm undercaffeinated. I had expected a delicious flat white from your fancy, expensive-looking espresso machine when I showed up this morning." Clearly, his department had a healthy budget.

"Sorry about that. It's on the fritz. My office manager is working on getting it fixed."

She'd spotted Dennis Hill fiddling around with the machine. He hadn't really seemed like he knew what he was doing. Not that she was an expert in the handyman department.

"I'll buy you a cup of coffee in the cafeteria on the way out," he offered.

She needed a triple shot of espresso at this point, but if he was buying, then she'd even take the mediocre java from the hospital.

Matt took out his phone. "I better send Sergeant Starkey a text letting him know the sketch is on the way and what I want him to do with it."

The artist finished packing up his things and waved on his way out of the room.

Hannah went over to Jessica's bedside. "I know talking about all this is difficult, but it's important. We only have a few more questions for you."

After Jessica nodded, Hannah proceeded. "Do you have a personal laptop?"

"Yeah. Of course."

"How often did you go to the computer lab?" Hannah asked.

Jessica pressed a palm to one of her bruised cheeks, resting her face in her hand. The bandage over her swollen nose—at least it wasn't broken—tugged at her pale skin. "Every Tuesday, Thursday and Saturday."

Matt stepped closer, coming up alongside Hannah. "Why only on those days?" he asked.

"I started going the first week of school. On the days when I have my engineering class—Tuesdays and Thursdays. I go on Saturdays now, too, to keep up with the workload."

Hannah made a note in her pad. "Why did you use the lab at all since you have a laptop?"

"Modeling software the university paid a license for is loaded on the computers in the lab. To use it on my personal laptop, I'd have to buy it. Costs a small fortune. Besides, my computer doesn't have the gigs to run it without the software glitching, anyway. The ones in the lab are a lot more powerful. And they offer free printing but don't advertise it. Those who know go there all the time just for that. I had planned to print out a paper for my Comm. 1 class." Tears welled in her eyes. "But I ran out of time because I wanted to catch the bus."

"You're slated to graduate next spring," Matt said. "Most students take Communication 101 during their first year. Why did you wait so late?"

"I wanted to balance some of my more challenging coursework with easier classes. Thought it would be less stressful that way."

"Which one were you enrolled in?" Hannah asked. Comm. 1—as most students on campus called it—was offered twice that quarter: either Monday, Wednesday and Friday for an hour at three p.m. or Tuesday and Thursday for an hour and a half at nine a.m. The registrar's office was going to email a copy of Jessica's class schedule to Matt before noon, but the more ground they could cover now, the better.

"The one that's three days a week," Jessica said.

A chill slithered down Hannah's spine. They'd been in the same Comm. 1 class. Hannah didn't remember seeing Jessica, but the auditorium had been packed with students, many of them blond females.

"Besides the supposed bike accident, what else did you talk about before you were attacked?" Matt asked.

Jessica shrugged. "I don't know. Everything happened so fast. One second, he was helpless and nice. Kind of sweet. Like a wounded puppy. The next thing I knew, I felt the pinprick of the needle before I was even upright from the ground, and then he snatched the keys from my hand."

Victims sometimes had trouble recalling information, not wanting to relive the trauma of the assault. "We need you to try to remember anything else that he said or did that might help us." Hannah held her watery gaze, her heart breaking for the woman and all the others who had been killed. "Any detail, no matter how small or insignificant, could be the key to stopping him before he has a chance to go after someone else."

Jessica nodded miserably and closed her eyes. A moment later, she said, "He offered to pay me back for helping him."

"Pay you back how?" Matt asked.

"With coffee at the Wheatgrass Café."

Hannah and Matt exchanged a look. She turned back to Jessica. "Did you go to the Wheatgrass often?"

"I usually grabbed lunch there. Since it was a short walk from the quad, it was convenient." Jessica's eyes flew open. "There is something else. Last night, while I was talking to him, I recalled running into him once before. I mentioned it to him."

"Do you remember where?" Hannah asked. "And when?"

"Mythology 101. But what day?" She shrugged. "Honestly, I don't know. Maybe when we had the lecture about the Titans. Last week, Tuesday or

Thursday. I can't say for certain. But the class was from four to five."

"Are you sure you were the one who remembered him and not the other way around?" Matt asked.

"Yeah. I'm positive. He claimed not to recognize me."

A blatant lie after stalking her for days, weeks—who knew for how long. "To get you to lower your guard," Hannah said, thinking out loud.

"It worked." Jessica closed her eyes again for a second, just long enough for a shudder to shake her. "That's when he introduced himself. Told me his name was Theodore Cowell."

An alias, surely, but Hannah wrote it down anyway. Once they dug into the name, it might lead to something if they got lucky. She turned the page in her notebook, quickly going over all the places the other victims frequented. "Did you ever use the Sweetwater Rec Center?"

The fitness center was popular among the students. Those who took at least six credit hours a quarter received free membership.

"My first year. I took a tour and the HOPES class."

"'HOPES'?" Hannah asked. She'd seen a brochure about it but had been focused on other things.

"It stands for Healthy Options for the Prevention and Education of Substances," Matt said. "They teach students to make healthy choices."

"The class wasn't preachy or judgmental at all." Jessica rubbed her arms. "I learned a lot."

"Do you remember who gave you the tour or who led the class?" Hannah asked.

"It was the same person—Perry Slagle."

Hannah made a note. She remembered the guy. He had approached her, offering to give her a tour, but she had declined. Perhaps that had been a mistake. "How often did you go back to the rec center?"

"I go swimming once a week. Great pool. Nice facility. But I honestly use the rec center more to decompress. I make appointments a couple of times a week to use the relax-wellness pod or the massage chair."

"Appointments online?" Hannah asked, writing it all down.

"Sometimes. You can also go to the Athletic Training Room the same day to see if they have any openings. Other than that, I bike everywhere during the day to keep the pounds off. At night, I always used the Secure Ride shuttle. I heard it's supposed to be safer."

The service was separate from the normal school bus, which ran a preplanned route on campus. Secure Ride only operated on weekdays from six p.m. to two a.m. and all day on the weekends. Students could also use the Secure

Ride app to be picked up or dropped off at any location within the town limits during those hours.

"It is safer and has cut down on the number of DUIs and alcohol-related accidents," Matt said. "My department highly advises all students to use the free service."

"How long has the university had the program?" Hannah asked.

Matt met her gaze. "About twenty years."

Hannah arched a brow at him with a knowing look. They needed to investigate the drivers. He nodded in silent agreement.

Jessica wrapped her arms around her midsection. "Do you really think the guy who attacked me is the University Killer?"

"Yes." Hannah gave a solemn nod. "We do."

"I can't believe I fell for his act." Jessica's shoulders sagged as tears fell from her eyes. "How could I be so stu—"

"Hey, don't do that to yourself," Matt said, cutting her off, his voice warm and soothing. "What happened wasn't your fault. This guy is a predator. A cold-blooded killer who preyed on your kindness."

Hannah recognized the guilt swimming in Jessica's glassy eyes. She knew better than most how easy it was to allow an encounter with darkness to snuff out your own light. "Is there anything else you can remember?"

"No." Jessica sniffled, and Matt handed her a tissue. "I'm sorry."

So was Hannah. "You should seek counseling on campus. Talking to someone about what you went through could help you heal and move forward."

Therapy had helped Hannah make sense of her past. Of discovering her father was a monster. But no amount of counseling had stopped her from building walls around her heart. Or had changed her mind that love was a game for the foolhardy.

Matt scrubbed a hand over his jaw with a distant look like he was thinking about something. Hannah made a mental note to follow up on it. He wasn't the type of partner to withhold information, but it could slip a person's mind to mention it.

"I'll have an officer posted outside your door twenty-four-seven until we catch this guy. We'll keep you safe," Matt said. He had assigned campus cops to stand guard in twelve-hour shifts, from nine to nine.

"Try to focus on rest and recovery." Hannah pressed one of her cards into Jessica's cold hand. "If you remember anything else, please give us a call."

On their way out, the assigned officer, who was seated in a chair beside the door to the room, jumped to his feet. Carl Farran.

"You don't have to get up every time I pass you," Matt said.

Farran stood ramrod straight at attention. "Yes, Chief."

Hannah and Matt made their way down the hall.

She slipped her notebook into her blazer's pocket. "I don't think it's a good idea to have him on guard duty until his DNA results come back officially clearing him."

"Duly noted," Matt snapped, and the know-it-all hotshot kept walking without a glance at her.

"That's it? You're not pulling him?"

"No. I am not." As she opened her mouth to protest, he raised a hand, silencing her. "When the first victim was murdered almost ten years ago, Carl was twelve and weighed ninety pounds soaking wet. I know that because I checked with his former pediatrician. Does that sound like the rapist and murderer of a grown woman? Or one with the knowledge to cover their tracks?"

She looked back at Officer Farran over her shoulder. He had sat down and was watching them walk to the elevator. Lanky and unassuming and baby faced, he didn't look like a twisted killer. But neither had her father. "No, it doesn't, but you're the one who likes to keep everything clean. Having a suspect, who hasn't been formally cleared guarding our witness is messy. Not to mention reckless." She'd been itching to throw that word back in his face. It had hurt when he'd called her that.

With anyone else, their insults and judgments didn't bother her. For some reason, only Matt got to her. She hated that he thought she wasn't good at her job and wasn't a smart detective.

"Label it what you want," he said, not looking the least bit fazed. "Carl is not a suspect. He's a person of interest at most, and even that is a stretch. I've got to use my people efficiently. In order to prevent this guy from snatching another woman, I need my most experienced officers patrolling campus. Not babysitting."

"You agreed to do this my way."

Stopping short, he pinned her with a stern look and nudged the brim of his cowboy hat up with a knuckle. "I did. And I will. But on this, don't push me. We've got plenty of reasons to fight. A common-sense decision shouldn't be one of them."

Matt was a stickler for the rules and playing things by the book. His motto was *No such thing as too careful*. This approach was out of character for him. Then again, she'd never seen him in charge of a team or a department with people to manage. Either way, she wasn't going to push this, since Farran was too tall—only a couple of inches shorter than Matt—to be the man she had encountered last night. The guy they were looking for was between five-ten and six-foot, possibly five-nine. Footwear could alter height an inch or two. "We need to see if there's surveillance footage of the Mythology 101 class."

"Not sure how much help it will be, since he was wearing his disguise, but I'll have Starkey look into it, along with a list of drivers working when Jessica and Madison Scott rode the Secure Ride," Matt said.

"Our perp mentioned the Wheatgrass Café for a reason. All ten victims frequented the place." She'd made an effort to swing by the café twice a day while undercover.

"Might just be because it's familiar to everyone on campus, but I think we should check it out, too. Let's grab coffee there instead of the cafeteria," he suggested.

"We also need to speak to the Comm. 1 professor," Hannah said. "Every victim took the same class."

"Right along with every other student. It's a prerequisite to graduate, regardless of your degree."

"Even more reason to talk to him."

"The only problem is that over the past nine years, the instructor has changed four different times. Other than the syllabus, the classes have nothing in common."

Frustration bubbled up in Hannah. "Great." Bye-bye to a possible lead.

"Except for one thing." Matt pressed the call button for the elevator. "The location."

"Go on," she said, gesturing for him to elaborate.

"The auditorium is right across the hall from where Dr. Bradford Foster has held his classes for the past eleven years. He teaches two popular courses. Psychology of Crime and Justice and Psychology of Serial Killers. That's not all—one of the victims from the last time the University Killer surfaced was a student of his."

"His field of expertise would enable him to know how to be a serial murderer without getting caught."

"My thoughts exactly."

The elevator chimed.

"When we were wrapping up with Jessica, you got that look in your eye," Hannah said.

"What look is that?"

The doors opened, and they stepped on.

"Like you found a piece to the puzzle."

He shook his head. "I wish. After that poor girl almost blamed herself for what happened, I thought about how different serial killers go after their victims."

Hannah hit the button for the lobby. "There's more to it than that." She could tell by his strained tone that he was filtering his ideas. "I hate it when you hold back." Only his thoughts. Not his criticism.

"It's nothing, really. A few nights ago, I streamed a movie about Ted Bundy. I was thinking specifically about him. The ruses he used to lure his victims to the vicinity of his vehicle. A plaster cast on a leg. A sling on one arm. Sometimes hobbled on crutches. Then he asked for assistance in carrying something to his vehicle. Our guy did practically the same thing. Almost as though he'd watched the movie and had taken notes."

"You're right." Hannah's mind churned over what Matt had said. "His MO is pretty similar." She took out her cell phone.

"What is it?" Matt asked.

"You might be on to something," she said, typing into the search engine. She hit Enter, pulled up the page she was looking for and scanned it. Two paragraphs down, she found it. "That son of gun." She turned her phone so Matt could see the page. "Ted Bundy was born *Theodore* Robert *Cowell.*"

"The name he gave Jessica."

The elevator stopped, and the doors opened once more.

"This is some kind of game to him," she said, getting off the elevator with Matt. "He puts the queen of hearts playing card on the body of his victims." She kept her voice to a whisper as they headed for the outer doors. "He is bold enough to rape them without a condom, leaving behind his DNA."

"He's not afraid of getting caught. Brazen. Must be confident that he's not in any database."

"Not yet, anyway," Hannah agreed. "But the amount of bleach he used in the vehicle is a sure sign he didn't want to leave DNA there. On his victims is fine, but not in the car. Why?"

"Control, is my guess. The body he discards, while the car is his domain, a part of his hunting ground. He spends a lot of time in it and wants to keep it clean. Hence, the bleach."

She was impressed by his insight. "Makes sense." Further proof he was wearing the wrong badge. Working with him had been a challenge on multiple levels, but they had closed one of the toughest cases of her life. Maybe together they could do it again.

With a whoosh, the outer doors opened, and they stepped outside into the brisk morning air. She shivered against the crisp breeze and glanced at Matt's bare arms. "You're not chilly?"

"I run hot."

"Why does that not surprise me?" Everything about the guy was hot. Matt Granger definitely had raw physical appeal.

Shake it off, she mentally chided herself.

"You're one to talk," he said with a smug expression. "All I get from you is fire or ice."

She couldn't deny it and wouldn't apologize for it. "We all deal with stress differently." Even the stress of sexual tension, but her current source was about this case. "I feel like there's this clock in my chest, counting down to when our guy makes his next move." They only had twelve days left in the month for him to claim his next two victims. "He's been so slippery for so long." She was terrified of failing yet again.

"I bet he didn't plan on firing his gun. He only did it because you surprised him. It was a mistake. Ballistics will be back tomorrow. It might turn up something."

The murderer using the university as his hunting ground strangled his victims, which wasn't quick or easy. The act was personal and didn't leave ballistics traces.

Matt put his hand on her shoulder, giving it a light squeeze, and she found his touch reassuring even though she wished she didn't. "No matter what game this sicko is playing, we're going to make sure that in the end, he doesn't win."

Chapter Five

As Matt opened the door to the Wheatgrass Café, his cell phone buzzed. He took it out of his pocket and glanced at the caller ID. "It's Starkey," he said to Hannah. "Order me a large black coffee with two pumps of vanilla syrup."

She made a gagging face over the amount of sugar. "I thought you were buying."

He whisked out his wallet and tossed it to her. "What's up?" he said, answering the phone and walking away from the entrance.

"Flyers with the University Killer's likeness have been made and printed."

"You included the warning at the bottom in bold, red font?"

"I read the text you sent, Chief. It's done. The flyers are being put up all over campus as we speak, starting with the quad since it gets the most traffic. I sent a copy to the news station.

It'll air within the hour and from there around the clock. I also emailed a copy to Erica Egan."

Matt's blood pressure spiked at hearing the name. "I don't want my department dealing with her. She only writes sensationalized articles with flagrant disregard for the feelings of innocent people." The woman had written stories that had wounded members of his family. Mostly his cousins Holden and Sawyer and his new wife, Liz. "My department doesn't do her favors. You got it?"

"Sorry. But we wanted a copy to go the *Laramie Gazette*, right?"

"To the *Gazette*. Not to Egan. Send it to the editor in chief next time."

"She slipped me her card one day and said if I had anything for the paper that it should go directly to her. What's the problem?"

Pinching the bridge of his nose, Matt shook his head over the sergeant's naivete. "Did she slip it to you one day or one night over drinks while she was cozying up to you in a bar?" Dead silence on the other end of the line was the only answer he needed. "May I remind you that you are a married man? With kids?" Granted, they weren't little, but even at eighteen and twenty, they'd feel the impact of an affair. "Don't mess up a good thing."

"I didn't go home with her. Only a little harmless flirting," Starkey said, but Matt knew there was nothing harmless about that viper. "She's nice."

Matt huffed out an annoyed breath. "And pretty. And sexy." The kind weak men found irresistible. "And willing to cross any line to break a story and see her name in the byline below the headlines. Stay away from her. Do we have an understanding?"

"Sure do. I'll get the flyers disseminated."

"Hold on. I need you to find out if there are any surveillance videos of the Mythology 101 class last week on Tuesday and Thursday. I want to know if there's any footage of our guy interacting with Jessica Atkinson. Also, get with transit services about the Secure Ride app. We need them to give us a list of drivers who picked up or dropped off both Atkinson and Scott."

"Roger that."

"Where's Dennis?" Matt asked, needing his office manager to handle something for him.

"He's still tinkering around with the espresso machine."

"I want him to call everyone on the SAV contact list and set up an emergency meeting at six o'clock in the lobby of the Student Union." Most of them would be done with their classes by that time, and the building was adjacent to the quad, making it easy to get to the dorms for those who lived there.

"I'll tell him."

"And I want of stack of flyers waiting for me there so I can pass them out at the meeting."

"We'll make it happen, Chief."

Matt disconnected, tucked his phone in his pocket and headed back inside the café. Hannah was at the counter with two large to-go cups and a couple of protein bars in front of her, notepad out, and talking to the manager, a woman in her fifties or sixties.

"Ma'am." He tipped his hat at the manager and read her name tag: Barbara S.

"This is my partner, Campus Police Chief Matt Granger," Hannah said.

"I'm aware." Barbara offered a pleasant smile. "The school paper did a wonderful piece on you. As I was telling Detective Delaney, you're looking at my usual crew. They work flex hours between them Monday through Friday, five a.m. to six p.m. I work at the register on the weekends. It's a lot slower when classes aren't in full swing. Other than that, they fill in when they can." She gestured to her staff.

Matt looked over at the workers. Four of them—two girls and two boys. They were barely twenty years old. One guy had braces, and the other—at two hundred pounds and five-five—didn't meet the physical description. "How long have they worked for you?"

"A couple of them since last year," Barbara

said. "The other two are new hires that started right before the quarter began."

"Does anyone run deliveries for you?" Hannah asked.

"We only deliver to the university hospital and the campus police department. Otherwise, I'd need a dedicated runner. As it stands right now, I send one of them to make the deliveries and I handle the register while they're gone."

Matt picked up his cup and a protein bar. "Thank you for your time."

Sipping her coffee, Hannah strolled out of the café ahead of him. Her long blond hair was loose, swaying a bit as she walked and catching the late-day sunlight when she stepped outside.

On the sidewalk, he faced her. She wore a navy blazer over a fitted V-neck tee, jeans, booted heels, her badge clipped to her belt and her gun holstered on her hip. Even though she still had a dewy glow to her complexion and appeared younger than her age, without the ponytail, there was no hint of a girl. Standing in front of him, she looked formidable—all woman.

He held up the protein bar. "Is this supposed to be a power lunch?" he asked, wondering what happened to the woman who loved hearty meals.

"More like a power snack. I remember you need sustenance every couple of hours, or you get cranky. And trust me, I prefer it when you're not cranky." With a hint of a grin, she handed him his wallet. "I'm surprised you trusted me with it."

"Why?" He took the leather bifold and slipped it back in his pocket.

"Who simply hands over their wallet?"

"You're my partner, not a stranger. It's not as if you're going to steal my credit card number. Plus, I don't have anything to hide." He opened the protein bar and bit into it.

Tipping her head to the side, she studied him for a long moment.

"What is it?" he asked, her silent scrutiny making him uneasy.

"Nothing. Just trying to figure you out." She took a sip of coffee and put her bar in her pocket. "Peel beneath the *perfect* outer layers."

Perfect? The way she'd uttered the word didn't sound like a compliment, but he was the first to admit that he wasn't without flaws. "I could say the same."

A quirk of a smile played around one corner of her mouth. "If you want to know me, you're wasting your time. There's nothing more to me than this—a woman with a badge and a gun, determined to put the bad guys away no matter the cost to myself."

How grudgingly she let go of bits of herself. "Maybe that's all you *want* there to be, but there's more." *A lot more.* And he was going to do some peeling of his own.

"Believe what you want." She threw on a pair of sunglasses and looked away. "I say we speak to Slagle next."

"The Sweetwater Rec Center is only three blocks over," Matt said. "Want to walk and stretch our legs?"

"We may as well. I need to burn off some energy. Besides, the College of Arts and Sciences building is right across the quad from the fitness center."

Matt ate his protein bar and finished his coffee on the fifteen-minute walk. He chucked his trash in the waste receptacle near the front doors of the rec center. "Do you know what this guy looks like?"

"Buzz cut. Dark hair. Brown eyes. Clean shaven every time I've seen him." She opened the door, and he walked in behind her. "Lean and wiry. Easy to tell he works out a lot. A bit under six feet. Looks like he could be in his late thirties. Real chatty. I found it off-putting. And he's very enthusiastic."

The facility had been renovated and expanded a few years back. At twenty-thousand square feet, it was massive and state-of-the-art. If Matt had time to indulge, he'd use the equipment here, but plenty of work on the ranch kept him fit.

"Can I help you?"

He turned his attention to a woman sitting at the reception counter behind a stack of towels.

Hannah flashed her badge. "We need to speak with Perry Slagle. Is he around?"

The woman's smile faltered as she looked at the badge prominently displayed on Matt's shirt. "Sure." She picked up the phone and pressed a button. "Hi, Perry. The police are here to speak with you." She listened for a moment. "Okay. I'll let them know." Hanging up, she glanced at them. "He's about to get someone set up in the Cryo-Lounge Recovery Chair. He'll come out front as soon as he's done."

"Will he? How nice of him," Hannah said. "Where can we find him?"

"In the Wellness Room." She pointed over her shoulder. "Back through there."

Hannah stalked off like she knew where to go.

Matt trailed along, his gaze darting around. Glass, mirrors, sleek equipment and sweaty bodies as far as the eye could see.

They passed a large sign that read *Wellness Room*. It didn't take them long to find Perry standing beside a student the size of football player, who was reclining in what appeared to be a comfortable space-age lounge chair.

"I've got it programed to gradually decrease the temperature since it's your first time, buddy. But trust me," Perry said, talking a mile a minute, "you're going to feel incredible afterward and even better over the next few days. Say goodbye to muscle fatigue. This is just as effective as an ice bath, without the inconvenience of getting wet."

Hannah sighed. "What did I tell you?"

"Maybe he'll talk himself into a confession."

"Perry Slagle," Hannah said, and the guy turned toward her. She held up her badge. "We need a word with you."

"After thirty minutes, you'll be good to go." Perry patted the student on the shoulder. He came over to them with a pleasant smile, his eyes bright and sparkling with energy. "I told Mindy I'd be out front in a sec." No hint of an attitude in his friendly tone.

"We didn't feel like waiting," Hannah said, guiding him out into the hall.

"What can I do for you?" Squinting, he stared at Hannah. "I know you. You refused to take a tour last week. Didn't even want to see the fifty-two-foot rock wall. Everyone wants to take a gander at that thing, even if they don't ever climb it. I thought you were a student."

"I'm Detective Delaney. This is Campus Police Chief Granger. We're investigating the murder of a student, Madison Scott."

"Oh yeah. I read about that in the *Laramie Gazette*. So sad."

"Did you know her?" Matt asked.

"We weren't friends, if that's what you mean, but I remember her. Talking to her. Seeing her here."

Hannah took out her notepad. "Did you happen to give her a tour?"

Perry shrugged. "I don't know. It's possible. We don't keep records of tours, but I give them all the time. I love getting people excited about the facility and fitness."

"Do you know if she took your HOPES class?" Matt asked.

"As a matter of fact, she did. Last month. Sweet girl. She also brought along her roommate. I encourage the more, the merrier for my HOPES class. Unlike some substance abuse–prevention programs that rely on a fear-based approach and promote a *just say no* message, HOPES takes a more positive approach and focuses on harm reduction. I recognize that college students are young adults, who have the intellectual capacity to make responsible, informed decisions about their substance use. Heck, I've an eighteen-year-old enrolled here myself."

Hannah looked up from her notes. "Do you keep records of who attends those classes?"

"We have to. The class is mandatory for all first-year students, as well as those who transfer in with less than sixty credits and those who are twenty-one years of age and younger."

Matt and Hannah exchanged a quick glance. That would've been every victim.

"The gym is open from five in the morning

until ten at night," Matt said. "What's your work schedule?"

"I'm usually here during the weekday from nine to three, but I also do personal training outside of those hours. I'm off on weekends, unless I have a one-on-one class."

"Must be nice to have such a flexible schedule," Hannah said.

Grinning, Perry folded his arms, his T-shirt exposing rock-solid biceps and powerful forearms. "My wife certainly appreciates it. She's a nurse at the university hospital. Works nights. I pick up the slack with the kids. And when Tina is off, I get extra me-time."

"'Kids'?" Matt asked. "You only mentioned you have a kid going to SWU."

"He was our surprise baby when we were seniors here ourselves. We decided to wait to have more. Our other son is twelve and our daughter is ten."

Three kids. Sounded stressful. "Where were you eleven nights ago, on Saturday the seventh, between twelve thirty and one thirty in the morning?"

They didn't know the precise time Madison Scott had been taken, but they did have a time of death.

Perry's gaze darted around as he thought about it. "That was Labor Day weekend. My wife took the younger ones to Boise to visit her parents.

On Saturday, I was home, watching the football game. SWU versus Las Vegas. Started at eight forty-five. Didn't end until almost one in the morning. Went into overtime. Good game. Our star quarterback, Linder, is going to be a first- or second-round draft pick—mark my words."

"Did you watch the game alone?" Matt asked.

"Yeah."

Hannah finished writing. "Where were you last night between ten and eleven p.m.?"

"I was home with the kids. My wife was at work."

"What time do they go to bed?" Matt asked.

"Eight thirty, if they've got school the next day. Otherwise, ten."

"Are your children good sleepers?" Matt gave an easy smile to keep the guy from getting guarded. "Any trouble with them getting up in the middle of the night asking for water? Nightmares? That sort of thing?"

"I'm lucky. I've got sound sleepers. I cut off liquids one hour before bed. And don't tell my wife, but if one is acting restless or cranky, I give them a kiddie sleep gummy."

No alibi for Scott's murder, and he could've easily snuck out last night while his kids had been asleep. Now for the hard part. "Would you consent to giving us a DNA sample?"

Perry's smile fell. "Why? I'm not a suspect, am I?"

"We're looking at common connections between the victims," Hannah said, "and you happen to be one of them. The sample would take thirty seconds. A buccal swab. We brush a Q-tip on the inside of your cheek. That's it. Then we can cross you off our list."

Perry nodded, unease glinting in his eyes, his jaw tightening. "Yeah, yeah. That makes sense. But kind of sounds invasive, too."

"It would be really helpful," Matt added.

"I want to help. I do. I've got nothing to hide, but I still don't see how I figure into the equation."

"Of course you don't, and the sooner we don't have to look in your direction, the better for everyone. How about you come by the station after work today?" Matt asked. "It'll only take a second. I promise."

"I can't." Perry lowered his head, his gaze shifting around. "Today isn't good." He looked up at them. "I think I might want to talk to my wife and a, um, a lawyer first. Is that okay with you?"

They'd lost him. He would never voluntarily give a DNA sample after speaking with a lawyer.

Hannah stiffened, probably sensing the same. "Sure."

"Am I free to go now?" Perry asked.

Matt nodded. "You are. If we have any additional questions, we know how to find you."

Perry hurried away down the hall, not glancing back at them.

"All the victims have the HOPES class in common. They have *him* in common." Hannah pointed at Perry.

"Not to mention he had opportunity with Scott and Atkinson." It was difficult to ask people to recall where they were two to three years ago, much less nine.

"Maybe we give him a couple of days to squirm. To worry. I doubt he'll talk to a lawyer and certainly not his wife. Raising the subject with her could cause marital strife. Then, when he doesn't think we're still looking at him, we speak to him again. Lean harder—and next time we'll bring the buccal-swab kit with us."

"Let's go talk to Dr. Foster." Matt turned for the entrance. "We might have better luck with him."

Chapter Six

At the College of Arts and Sciences building, Dr. Foster's class was still in session.

"What time does it end?" Hannah asked, staring at one of the SWUPD flyers that had already been taped on the wall.

Along with the drawing of the suspected University Killer was other pertinent information: Male. White. Approximate height. Medium build. His use of medical devices and request for assistance as a ploy. The vehicle driven, a dark SUV—possibly a Chevy Tahoe or GMC Yukon, after she had reviewed plenty of makes and models and had narrowed it down.

At the bottom, in bold, red text, was a warning:

Be advised that the suspect is most likely wearing a disguise and his physical appearance may change. Stay alert. Use the buddy system.

"Two thirty," Matt said.

Hannah glanced at her watch. They'd have to wait forty-five minutes.

She spun around and faced the large auditorium doors across the hall. "His class ends right before Comm. 1 begins. He could easily watch students flowing into the room. It's usually packed. I'd say two hundred, maybe more. Fifty-three percent of the student body is female." Hannah fished out her notebook and flipped through the pages. "The Mythology 101 class that Jessica took was Tuesday and Thursday at four p.m. Do you know if Dr. Foster has a class at that time?"

"Easy enough to look up." He grabbed his phone and did a quick search of Foster's classes. "He doesn't teach on those two days this quarter."

Pivoting on her heel, she eyed the doors to Foster's room. There were two ways to approach it. Wait until the doctor was finished with his class and then catch him off-guard. If they went in now, they'd lose the element of surprise—but by the same token, their presence might rattle him. "Why don't we sit in and listen to his lecture? We might learn something."

"It's your call."

On the walk over, to keep the chitchat with Matt to a minimum, she'd read the professor's bio, getting up to speed on him. Divorced. Two kids. Both attended SWU. He'd written a couple of books, worked as a consultant for the Seattle Police Department before he relocated from Washington to Wyoming. Now she was ready to see him in action.

She pulled the door open and crept inside. Matt followed behind her into the dimly lit room. Unlike the auditorium across the hall, this one was much smaller, seating fewer than fifty.

Dr. Bradford Foster was at the front of the room, standing before his presentation as he clicked on to the next slide. His gaze flickered up to Hannah and Matt as they found seats in the top back row.

"The making of a serial killer is never clear, and every case won't fit inside the same box," the professor said. "Many factors can lead a person to become a violent adult, from causality to mental illness. There is so much variation between each serial murderer, one cannot generalize them beyond the simple definition that they have killed at least two victims with a cooling-off period between those murders, ranging from hours to years. With that being said, there tends to be common characteristics that can be found in the psychopath personality disorder. Lack of remorse and empathy. A strong impulsivity. The need for control." Foster walked around the front of the room, using lots of hand gestures. "Not every psychopath is a serial killer, but rather, various serial murderers present some psychopathic traits. A charming personality. Pathological liar.

Like to think of themselves as all-knowing. Have great self-esteem but also some antisocial traits." He brought up the next slide. "Now, let's look at causality before we dive into today's notorious killer."

The students were absorbed in his lecture, their gazes following his every movement more than looking at the slides. Most seemed to be recording the class on their phones and laptops rather than taking copious notes.

Hannah had to hand it to him—Dr. Foster was an engaging orator. He had a fluid way of dissecting the minds of psychopathic killers, identifying their uncontrollable urges, anger, excitement or the need for attention as the drive for the offender's behavior. His style lessened the danger and with that, the degree of fear one should have regarding a brutal monster.

"I like to alternate between examining serial killers of the past with those more recently brought to light. Last time, we looked at Jack the Ripper. Today, Edward Ressler."

Hannah stiffened in her seat, her blood going cold.

Dr. Foster clicked onto another slide, bringing up a picture of her father. Suddenly, it was like all the air had been sucked out of the room and she couldn't breathe.

Matt leaned over, bringing his mouth close to

her ear, putting a gentle hand on her forearm. "Are you all right?"

Frozen, she couldn't immediately respond. Matt must have sensed or seen her distress but didn't know the cause. No one knew Hannah's real identity, that she was Anna Ressler, the daughter of a serial killer. Not even Matt.

She stared straight ahead at the image on the screen, right into the familiar dark eyes, and nodded.

"Sure?" he whispered, the concern in his voice tugging at her heart.

Hannah cleared her throat. "Yeah. Fine." She was anything but fine. She wanted to run from the eighteen-by-twenty-four picture enlarged on the screen, out the auditorium, through the front doors of the building and keep going until she forgot she was the spawn of pure evil.

"Even though he targeted mostly women in his county in Colorado, he was known as the Neighborhood Killer. He tortured and murdered more than forty people," Foster said, a burning ache building in Hannah's chest. "Ressler was known as an upstanding pillar of his community, who attended church weekly. A good husband. A devoted father."

Hot bile rose in her throat. It was all true. Before he was caught, her childhood memories had been fond ones. Standing on his toes and twirling around in the living room, listening to folk-rock music. Hiking in the Rocky Mountains. Church on Sundays. Weekend fishing trips. Grilling in the backyard.

Heart-wrenching images flooded her, and she struggled to push them away. She tightened her hands into fists, her nails digging into her palms.

"His wife, Mary-Beth, was married to him for twenty years and claimed she never suspected a thing. After he was arrested, he later admitted that when he got married, he stopped killing for a while—that cooling-off period—because of his wife. He was able to bury his alter ego. You might be asking yourselves, *Then what happened to make him start up again?*" A dramatic pause for effect. "He became a father," Dr. Foster said with a chuckle.

Some of the students laughed along with him.

But the words were a blistering hot knife in Hannah's chest. She'd heard it all before, but each time, the emotional wound reopened as though it had never healed.

"Ressler claimed the stressors of parenthood drove him to release his rage and thirst for blood once again," the professor said. "Ironically, it was his daughter, Anna, who led to his capture and arrest."

Sweat rolled down Hannah's spine. Her heart raced with dread. To have her father, her life— *her misery*—dissected like a lab rat, the intestines picked at and examined under a microscope as a lesson for these kids who had no concept of what it meant to live with and love someone truly evil.

Finding it hard to breathe, she pressed her fingertips to the base of her throat. Her pulse thrummed under her skin. Unwelcome fears of betrayal and loss tangled together and curled around her chest like choking vines.

Dr. Foster pivoted and glanced at the clock on the wall. "Okay, guys, we're going to stop here today because we're out of time."

The class groaned in unison while Hannah exhaled a breath of relief.

Foster went to the wall and turned on the bright lights. Hannah squinted against the harsh glare. Students began packing up their things.

"Are you sure you're okay?" Matt asked, putting a palm on her knee. "You're pale as death. Look like you've seen a ghost."

What were the odds that Foster would lecture on her father today?

Hannah unclenched her hands. "I'm nauseous." That was putting it mildly. She wanted to puke. "Probably just low blood sugar." Another lie.

"Well, that's because you didn't eat that four-course lunch you bought us with my money," he said, joking about the protein bar. "You want to eat before we talk to Foster?"

Unable to stomach anything, she shook her head. Better to get this over with and then get some fresh air. "Come on." She gave his shoulder a tap, got up and headed down the stairs, passing the students filing out.

Once she reached the bottom of the stairs, a thought filled her with dread. What if Foster recognized her? Who she really was? Anna Ressler, spawn of the Neighborhood Killer.

The pictures of her in the media were of a four-teen-year-old girl. Surely Foster had refreshed his memory, going over everything about her father before the lecture.

She slowed, letting Matt walk ahead of her.

Matt gave her another concerned glance before approaching the professor. "Excuse me, Dr. Foster, we'd like a word with you. I'm Campus Police Chief Matt Granger, and this is my partner, Detective Hannah Delaney."

She would've preferred it if Matt hadn't mentioned her first name, even if it had been slightly changed. She went by her mother's maiden name, and *Hannah* was close enough to *Anna* for Foster to piece it together if she looked familiar to him.

Searching Foster's eyes for a reaction to her name, she spotted a flash of recognition, but then it was gone. It must've been nothing.

"Good afternoon, Officers." Bradford Foster switched off the projector. "What can I do for you?"

The professor stood around five feet, ten inches tall and, for a man of fifty-two, was extraordinarily fit. His polo shirt hugged firm biceps and a trim waist. He had a full head of thick hair feathered with gray. His smile was gleaming white and friendly, his teeth straight.

"We'd like to speak to you about the resurgence of the University Killer," Matt said.

"Really?" Foster grabbed a blazer hanging on the back of his chair and pulled it on. "Would you like to take a look at the case and consult? I did a little freelance work for law enforcement in Seattle before I took the job here. They found my insight invaluable."

Another wave of nausea swamped her, and she put a hand on the side of the desk to steady herself. "We're aware of your freelance work—but no, that's not why we're here."

"Then what is it?" Foster asked, his face tanned and glowing like he invested in good skincare products.

Hannah took out her notepad. "Did you know Madison Scott?"

A slight frown crossed his face. "The young lady who was murdered a few days ago? No, certainly not."

"She took the Comm. 1 course right across the hall from this room," Matt said. "You may have seen her in passing, in between your classes. May have even spoken to her."

Foster straightened. "If so, I don't recall."

Matt reminded him of the date of her death.

"Where were you that night between two and four a.m.?"

"I was home. Asleep. Alone," Foster said in an arrogant tone, like it was a challenge.

"Did you know Isabel Coughlin?" Matt asked.

Isabel had been the University Killer's last victim almost three years ago. Thirty months, to be precise.

Foster considered the question. "The name rings a bell."

"It should," Matt said. "She was one of your students before she was murdered. You gave her a C in this course."

"I can't remember everyone. Perhaps she should have paid closer attention to my lectures." Foster closed his laptop and tucked it inside his leather messenger bag. "I do my best to empower my students with the tools necessary to spot psychopathic tendencies and avoid danger."

Hannah tightened her grip on her notepad at his callous tone.

Matt mentioned the day and time of Isabel Coughlin's death. "Do you recall your whereabouts?"

"I do not. It was a long time ago."

She hadn't bothered to jot down any notes because she could tell how this would go. "What about last night? Where were you between ten thirty and eleven?"

"Why? Was another woman abducted or attacked? If you let me take a look at the case file, I'm sure I could be of help."

Matt pulled on a tight grin. "Just answer the question. Where were you?"

"Home. Watching TV."

"Alone?" Hannah asked.

"As a matter of fact, yes." His confidence didn't waver for a second.

Hannah put her notepad away. "What were you watching?"

"A cooking show." Foster flashed a self-assured grin. "I think I'll try making the beef Wellington with truffle mashed potatoes and pairing it with a nice Bordeaux. More than enough for three. I could have you two over, and we could discuss the case like colleagues while I give you input."

A hard pass on dinner with this smooth talker. She wasn't sure she'd be able to stomach a meal with him.

Matt stepped closer, invading his personal space just a bit. "What vehicles do you own?"

"I drive a light blue BMW Z4. Why?"

Winters in Wyoming must be tough for the professor with a Z4. Next to impossible to drive through more than five inches of snow. Accumulations of ten to fifteen inches or more for a single storm weren't uncommon. Most people around there who had a little sports car also had a second vehicle, something a bit more rugged.

"Would you consent to DNA testing?" she asked. "Simply to rule you out so we can move on to real suspects."

"I think not." Foster picked up his messenger bag and slung the strap on his shoulder. "The idea of my DNA sitting in a database makes me uneasy."

She bet it did, but she also reminded herself that even innocent people were cautious.

"How about letting us take a look at your vehicle and where you keep it?" Matt suggested. "I'm sure it's a beauty and you like to park it in the garage."

The point was to get in the door with consent and then push the boundaries of their exploration a bit to see what they might find.

Foster chuckled, showing his pearly whites. The smile was more feral than friendly. "How about you get a warrant, and then you can take a look?"

Hannah heard the bitter defensiveness in his tone and knew then that it was time to pivot.

The professor brushed past them, going toward the stairs.

"We didn't mean to offend you," Hannah said, starting after him. "We're just following procedure." He kept walking. "On second thought, discussing the case over some wine and beef Wellington sounds like a good idea."

She still didn't want to break bread with the

man, but the idea of having access to his home and getting a sample of his DNA was appealing.

Foster stopped on the steps and turned around slowly. "So one of you can tiptoe off to my bathroom, find my comb and put some of my hair in an evidence bag? Or pocket a fork I used?" He shook his head. "Do you take me for a fool, Detective Delaney? The opportunity to graciously accept my assistance is gone."

Matt came up alongside Hannah. "Only a guilty person or someone with something to hide wouldn't cooperate with us," he said.

"Au contraire. If a person is innocent, there is no obligation to prove it to the police. Every smart citizen should take this approach. Trying to convince the authorities to reverse their suspicions only exposes a person to considerable risk with little to no benefit. It's one of the things I teach in my Psychology of Crime and Justice course. You two should enroll. I guarantee you'd both learn plenty."

Hannah stepped closer to Foster, drawing his smug gaze. "You don't have an alibi. Probably because of your antisocial traits despite your great self-esteem. Charming?" She didn't think he was, but his students seemed to. "Check. All-knowing? Check—at least, *you* think you are. Need for control? Check." She didn't mention *pathological liar*, but given enough time with him she could probably check that one off, too.

They stared at each other until his face turned from cocksure to uncomfortable.

"My students love my charm and wit, and my controlled nature has served me well," Foster countered. "I see no reason to apologize for being an expert in my field. Yes, apparently, I knew one of the victims, and another took a class across the hall from where I teach around the same time."

"All the victims took a class across the hall from where you teach," Matt said.

Foster didn't bat an eyelash. "Coincidence. Nothing more. Yes, I have no alibi for Madison Scott's murder or for whatever related incident might have happened last night that you're also investigating. But what about motive? Let's say for argument's sake that I am the University Killer. What would have angered me or enticed me to kill after all this time?"

Another challenge. Testing them.

"Last month, you were passed over for tenure," Matt said. "I heard you didn't take it well."

Foster's expression went deadpan.

Hannah gave him a small smile. "Sounds like a motive to me."

"I'm an esteemed professor and was given assurances that I'd make tenure next time. If that's all you've got, let's see how you two fare getting a warrant." Foster took a couple more steps, stopped again and looked back at them. "You local cops, regardless of what city or small hick town, are all the same," he said with disdain. "Never recognizing when you're out of your depth, outmatched and outsmarted. Or when you could use assistance from an expert. Not working with me is your loss. But let me give you a piece of advice, not that your egos will allow you to take it—you could use help from a profiler. Otherwise, he's going to kill two more women and then go quiet again for a few more years. And when he does, you'll wish you had accepted my initial proposal for me to provide input." He hurried up the steps and out of the auditorium.

Matt folded his arms and leaned back against a chair. "What's your assessment of him?"

"Even if he's not the University Killer, I don't like him. He has this air of superiority. Too controlled, with that all-knowing smugness, which, by the way, are characteristics of a serial killer that he listed."

"Agreed."

"And the last bit about recommending we use a profiler felt twisted. Like he was using reverse psychology. Make us feel inadequate so we double down and prove that we can catch this guy without any outside assistance." *I see you, Bradford Foster—and your little mind games.*

If only they had a profiler on the Laramie PD. She'd go straight to them with the case file.

"Agreed," Matt said again.

She looked at him in disbelief. "Come on,

you've got to have more thoughts than that. I can see it on your face that you do."

"Am I that easy to read, or have you made studying me your hobby?"

He wasn't easy to read. Not one little bit. "Your thoughts?"

"I think since he lives on campus, I'm going to have an officer tail him in plainclothes. May as well rifle through his trash while we're at it and get a sample of his DNA to be on the safe side."

Sometimes there were moments, such as this one, when they were in perfect sync instead of in opposition, and she wanted to give him something more affectionate than a high five or fist bump.

"I also think that, reverse psychology or not, the professor was right." Matt took out his cell phone. "We need a profiler."

Once again, they were of like mind. "You say that while you're dialing as though you have one in your contacts list."

By way of admission, he smiled and gave a small shrug.

This man never ceased to amaze her.

Chapter Seven

Wednesday, September 18
3:10 p.m.

"Thanks, Liz. You're the best. Tell Sawyer I'm looking forward to seeing you guys at Thanksgiving." Matt hit the disconnect button and met Hannah at the top of the steps in the auditorium.

While he was on the phone, she had done laps around the room, going up and down the steps countless times. The woman had boundless energy. But he'd noticed she still hadn't eaten.

"Well?" she asked him as they pushed out the doors into the corridor.

"Success."

Once they got outside the building, he explained. "My cousin, Sawyer Powell—"

"One of the four cousins you live with out on the Shooting Star Ranch?"

"Sort of, kind of." That had come out of left field. "Anyway, Sawyer recently married Liz Kelley."

"The famous FBI agent who was out here help-ing him investigate?"

Sawyer and Liz had been in the news almost every day during their investigation "The very same."

"She profiles serial killers?" Hannah asked.

"No. Would you listen?"

They strolled across the quad, headed back to his car.

"Sorry. My mind is racing a mile a minute. I thought doing stairs while you were on the phone would help, but it hasn't."

He understood that problem. Working until you were bone-tired—as a police chief and on the ranch—solved that issue for him. "Eating might help," he suggested, but she shook her head. Something was still off with her. "Sawyer and Liz are out in Virginia. She works at Quantico."

"Home of the profilers. She called in a favor for you." Hannah glanced at him. "Oh, sorry. Please continue."

"That's it exactly. She put me on hold while she squared it all away. Nancy Tomlinson has agreed to look at our case file because of the urgency of the situation since we know our guy is going to try and kill two more women soon. We just need to send her what we have and keep her apprised of all updates. No matter how small."

Hannah raised her palm and waited for a high five.

So help him, he wanted to wrap her in a big hug and give her a kiss. Instead, he gave her a high five.

"Okay, now elaborate on the *sort of, kind of* part," she said, and he gave her a puzzled look, wondering what she was talking about. "Your living situation. I'll admit, I've been curious since we worked together."

Curious about where he sleeps? "We don't all live under one roof. My aunt and uncle live in the main house. Logan moved into the apartment above the garage once Sawyer moved out. Holden lives with his wife in a house his parents built for them on the property. Monty also lives in a house on the ranch, but alone."

She quirked an eyebrow. "Also built for him?"

"Yep."

"What about your parents?"

Where were all these rapid-fire questions suddenly coming from?

The last time they'd worked together, she wanted to know as little as possible about him. "My dad lives in the bunkhouse. My mom…" He shrugged, annoyed. Not at Hannah. At the topic of the woman who had abandoned her family. Abandoned him.

"And you?" she asked, not pressing the matter of his mother.

Talking about himself was never easy. Talking about himself in regard to his family was, well...tricky. "The majority of the ranch will be passed down to whichever Powell son decides to run the place. But my aunt Holly wanted me to have something." To assuage her guilt. Although she had nothing to feel guilty about. The person responsible for the harm done to him and his father was his mother, Holly's twin sister. "They let me pick a parcel of land, a couple thousand acres, where I built my own house." Put his sweat and blood into that place.

"What?" Hannah stopped in her tracks. "How big is the ranch?"

"Sixty."

"Sixty thousand acres?" she said slowly, in an astonished voice.

He nodded with a grimace because he knew what was coming next. "And no, I'm not rich. Holly and Buck Powell are. Yes, I accepted the land they gave me." Albeit located as far from the rest of the clan as he could get, almost living in Bison Ridge. And only to stop his aunt from blaming herself for the pain and suffering he'd experienced as a child. "But I am paying for it." In more ways than one. "I'm creating another source of revenue for the ranch on the land."

"For the Shooting Star Ranch, on *your* land?"

Matt's jaw tightened. "It's complicated."

Her eyes were serious yet soft as she studied him. This time, it didn't make him uneasy. "This is your thing, isn't it? We've all got one. A soft underbelly. This is yours."

She was exactly right. His family, his mother, his relationship with the Powells—it was indeed his soft spot. His weakness. And his strength.

Alarm bells went off in his head. She'd been acting strange since Foster's lecture, and after they'd questioned the professor, she'd only gotten worse. Nonstop moving. Not eating. The sudden interest in him, asking a ton of questions about his living situation of all things.

Deflecting from herself.

"What's your thing?" he asked.

She rocked back on her heels, her body tensing.

"Come on, Hannah. Tit for tat."

"It's the same as yours," she said grimly. "Family."

He frowned at her honest answer, which didn't tell him anything more than he already knew.

His cell chimed in his pocket. He took it out and read the text message from Starkey.

Transit wants you to swing by to discuss your request in person.

"What is it?" Hannah asked, in that frosty, distant way of hers, putting the wall back up between them.

Matt sighed bitterly, his elation over getting help from a profiler now gone. "We need to go to Transit Services to get the names of the Secure Ride drivers."

"Then what are we waiting for?"

IN THE LOBBY of the Transit Services center, Hannah hung back while Matt strode up to the front desk.

He introduced himself. "I'm here to speak with someone about an official request for information my department made earlier today."

The person at the front desk nodded and picked up the phone. Matt glanced over his shoulder at her, sporting an inquisitive expression, but she averted her gaze.

Hannah had gone from firing a fusillade of questions at him to being brusque, all in a sloppy effort not to overshare.

Foster's lecture had left her on edge and raw, and combined with Matt's uncanny way of getting her to lower her guard—simply by being himself—she was in danger of spilling secrets she'd kept half her life.

A man with rosy cheeks and a receding hairline, wearing glasses, left one of the back offices and came into the lobby. "I'm Otis Ortiz, the supervisor."

Matt shook his hand. "Chief Granger, and this is Detective Delaney."

Now he omitted her first name.

Sweat beaded Otis's forehead and upper lip.

"I received your request for information, and I wish I could be of help, but we have a policy not to give out information about our employees."

"We're investigating the murder of Madison Scott and the attempted abduction of another student last night. The information I requested is vital. I'm sure if you fully understood the gravity of the situation, you wouldn't deny the request and subsequently obstruct justice."

Otis glanced around the lobby and met the prying gazes of the employees seated behind the front desk. "Why don't you come on back into my office?" Spinning on his heel, he hurried down the hall.

Matt and Hannah followed him into the office.

"Close the door," Otis whispered, and Hannah shut it. "Sit down."

Exchanging a glance, they both took seats, facing the desk.

"I already have the information you wanted printed, but I had to make a big show out there of not complying."

"Why is that?" Hannah asked.

Otis wiped his forehead with the back of his hand. "I'm in good health and I want to stay that way."

Matt's brow furrowed. "I don't understand. Care to explain?"

"Oh yeah, I was getting to that," Otis said in an exasperated way. "I cross-referenced the times

Madison Scott and Jessica Atkinson used the Secure Ride with our drivers. Two names came up." Otis picked up a couple sheets of paper. "Bobby Evers and Shane Yates. Bobby has been in the hospital for the past four days. Since you mentioned an attempted abduction last night, I take it you probably don't still want his information."

"Why is he in the hospital?" Hannah asked.

"Appendicitis. They had to operate. He should be out in a day or two."

"Then you suppose right that we won't need his information," Matt said. "But that still doesn't explain your little act in the lobby."

"Yes, yes." Otis took a deep, shaky breath. "That brings me to the second driver and the reason for my ruse. Shane Yates," he said in a whisper.

"Is he here?" Hannah asked. "Are you afraid he'll overhear you speaking about him?"

"He's not in right now. Shane was supposed to work tonight, but he called in sick again. He does that whenever he feels like it."

Irritation ticked through Hannah. She pushed for a clear explanation. "Then why are you whispering?"

"I don't want any of the other employees to hear and then run back to him, saying I was a snitch."

Matt heaved a sigh, undoubtedly annoyed as well. "And you're afraid of him because…"

Otis stared at them like the answer was obvious. "Because snitches get stitches."

"If he's threatened or assaulted you in some way," Matt said, "we can write up a report, and it would be grounds for dismissal."

Pushing his glasses up the bridge of his nose, Otis shook his head. "I can't do that."

Matt took off his hat and ran a hand through his hair. "Why not?"

"Shane is with the biker gang."

Hannah pinned him with a glare, wishing he would simply tell them what they needed to know. "The Iron Warriors?"

That didn't sound like something their leader, Rip Lockwood, would allow. The guy was prior military and kept a tight leash on his men. He never made trouble for law enforcement. A tough guy for sure and undeniably hot if one was drawn to an edgy, bad boy on a motorcycle, but from what she knew of him, he didn't permit harassment and intimidation.

"If only." Otis shook his head. "I know Rip, the president of the Iron Warriors. We went to high school together. He even served in the Marines for a while. Good guy. Decent. He finally cleaned up the club, though it caused a big rift. All the guys doing illegal stuff broke off and formed a new club under Todd Burk. The Hellhounds."

Other than Todd Burk being a scumbag, the

rest was news to Hannah. "When did this happen?"

"Last month."

"They've kept it pretty quiet," Matt said, clearly uninformed as well.

"They don't want to draw any unwanted attention." But Hannah was surprised she hadn't seen any new biker cuts around. Maybe she'd been too busy to notice.

"Where does the new gang hang out?" Matt asked.

Otis sat back in his chair with a grim expression. "Rip gave them the clubhouse of the Iron Warriors."

Whoa. The clubhouse was a single-story building that took up almost half the length of a city block. Rumor had it that every member had his own bedroom there so when they partied, they each had a private place to crash. It was her understanding that they had a bar, game room, armory, conference room, gym and dance area, complete with stripper poles. Handing over control of the facility was no small matter. "Why on earth would he do that?"

"To prevent bloodshed, I guess." Otis shrugged. "Todd didn't want to form a new club, and he didn't want to abide by Rip's rules," Otis said. "A lot of threats were made. Rip gave the Hellhounds the clubhouse to make the transition a peaceful one from what I've heard."

"And you're afraid to report or fire Shane because you think the Hellhounds will cause trouble for you if you do?" Hannah asked.

"Heck yeah, I'm afraid. And I don't *think*. I *know* they will."

"Then we'd bring them in," Matt said. "You'd press charges, and we'd put them away."

Otis flattened his lips into a grim line. "They would send a couple of prospects looking to earn their patches, wearing hoods, to bust the windows of my house and harass me. Even if you did catch them, the Hellhounds would make the next punishment even worse. It's just easier to keep Shane, not let anyone know I snitched and spare myself the misery."

"Give us his home address," Matt said.

Otis handed them the paper he was holding. Not only did it have Shane's address but also his schedule and his picture at the top of the page.

"Yates didn't work last night," Matt murmured.

Hannah stood. "If anyone asks whether you gave us any information, simply tell them you were forced to comply with a court order, and you'll be fine."

Otis's demeanor told her he was unconvinced. "For my sake, I hope so."

Matt took out a business card and grabbed a pen. "I'm giving you my personal cell number." He scrawled on the back of the card. "Call me day or night if you get any blowback on this." Putting his hat on, he stood and walked over to the door. "Thank you for your assistance."

They left the office and strode toward the lobby. Matt handed her the sheet on Shane Yates. She folded it and put it in her pocket.

One of the employees behind the desk eyed them as they pushed through the double doors, exiting the transit center. She looked over her shoulder and spotted the guy picking up the phone, his stare still glued to them.

"It's a good thing we drove over here," she said, headed for his campus police SUV.

"Why is that?"

"Because I have a sneaking suspicion that if we have any chance of catching Yates at home, we'll need to hurry."

Chapter Eight

Wednesday, September 18
4:05 p.m.

As Matt turned down Blackberry Lane, the street where Shane Yates lived, a motorcycle went roaring past them, the rider wearing a Hellhound biker cut, with long, curly hair flapping in the wind.

"Do you want to bet that's Yates?" Matt did a U-turn, tires screeching.

"No need to bet." Hannah glanced down at the picture of their suspect. "It's him, all right."

"How did you know he was going to bolt?" Matt asked. Hannah was good and had great instincts, but that bordered on clairvoyance.

"I saw the employee at the front desk that you spoke with make a call while he was watching us leave."

Matt pressed down on the gas pedal, speeding after Yates. "Might've been nice of you to mention it."

"Hey, I told you we needed to hurry over here."

She had, but still… "Full disclosure would've been better."

"Duly noted," she said, with an underlying tone of displeasure.

He could always tell when she disliked something he'd said to her. This time around working together, calling her *reckless* and uttering *duly noted* were on the list.

Yates glanced back at them and picked up his pace. He took the next corner hard and fast.

Whipping the steering wheel to the right, Matt stayed after him. "I'm sorry I called you reckless. You *can* be—" no doubt about that "—but you weren't last night. To go undercover, alone, to catch the University Killer was gutsy." Still, it irked him, but he couldn't question her bravery or commitment. "And I shouldn't have used such a harsh tone with you when I said 'duly noted' about Farran back at the hospital. I can be overly protective of my people." He took another sharp turn and gunned the gas pedal to keep up with Yates.

Matt flicked a glance at Hannah.

She'd shifted in her seat, facing him, eyes wide, she gaped at him.

He looked back at the road and at Yates. "What? Shocked I'm capable of apologizing?"

"Actually, no. You're the type who would. You care enough about other people. You're empathetic and believe an apology can make a difference. I'm just surprised you noticed those things bothered me."

"I'll make you a deal," he said. "I'll try harder to be less offensive if you try to be less passive aggressive." Yates turned into the parking lot of the Hellhound's clubhouse, and Matt cursed.

Hannah turned to see what had made him swear. "Oh, great. Instead of questioning one Hellhound, now we'll have to deal with all of them."

Yates had parked his bike and ducked inside the building by the time Matt pulled into the lot. He put the SUV in Park, killed the engine and grabbed the handle to open the door.

Hannah placed a hand on his bare forearm, stopping him, her fingers warm against his skin. "I'm sorry, too. For being passive aggressive. When you called me reckless, all I heard was you saying that I was a lousy detective."

"Far from it." He gave her a half grin. "You're the best I've worked with." He thought about Joe, the partner he'd lost, and a pang cut through him. Shoving it down, he got out of the car.

Hannah climbed out and popped some gum into her mouth. She offered Matt a piece, and he declined, not in the mood for bubblegum.

They strode toward the front door, but before they reached it, Todd Burk pushed through, stepping outside, along with two other Hellhounds carrying shotguns.

Todd had been in trouble with law enforcement since they were in high school together, and Matt wasn't too proud of a period when he'd hung out with some of the Iron Warriors. But even as a teenager, no charges had ever stuck to Todd.

The Iron Warriors had given him the fitting nickname Teflon.

"I believe you're lost." Todd gave a Cheshire cat grin, his black hair slicked back, looking every bit the part as leader of an outlaw motorcycle gang. He checked out Hannah, his gaze sliding over her with a sleazy look, and then licked his lips. "It'd be best if you got back in the vehicle and got off our property."

The other two men leered at her as well. Her face and body were lean and honed, but with enough curves to turn heads.

"Not lost." Matt put his hands on his hips. "Here to speak with Shane Yates."

"Don't know anyone by that name," Todd said. "Do you, boys?" He turned to his buddies, and they shook their heads.

"Knowingly lying to a law enforcement officer during an investigation is a Class 1 misdemeanor, punishable by up to twelve months in jail and a $2,500 fine," Matt said. "You might want to reconsider your answer."

Todd smirked. "I don't even bother to contact my lawyer unless it's a felony charge. Mr. Friedman is way too expensive. And if you haven't learned by now, I don't do jailtime. It's not conducive to my social life."

Matt tipped up the brim of his hat. "I saw Yates run inside through the front door less than sixty seconds ago. I need him to come out and answer a few questions. It's not even about club business. That's all."

With a sneer, Todd shook his head. "You Powells may run this town but not my clubhouse."

Matt took two steps forward. "I'm not a Powell."

"Keep telling yourself that." Todd winked at him. "Now, you look, high and mighty campus police chief, you've got no authority here. Scurry on back to the university before I make you leave. Go on. Get gone."

The other two Hellhounds pumped their shotguns.

Hannah laughed. A great, big, loud chortle rolled out of her as she came up alongside Matt. "That is the most impressive display of testosterone I've seen since the last time I watched *WWE SmackDown*." She pushed back her blazer, unclipped her badge from her belt and held it up to Todd's face. "I'm Detective Delaney, and I *do* have authority here. Send Yates out. Now."

Todd hiked his chin up. "Or what?"

Hannah blew a bubble with her gum, letting it expand in his face until it popped.

She was good. Really good. As they were getting out of the car, she had expected things to be difficult and planned this little bit of fanfare.

"Or," she said slowly, with that piercing stare of hers that had a way of dissecting someone layer by layer, "I'm going to haul your two sidekicks into jail for obstruction and intimidation of law enforcement officers. And I'm not going to bother with you directly, since you'll simply wiggle out of trouble, as you're prone to do. But I will be back. With lots of other officers. And even if we get to speak to Yates at that point, I'm going to hold a grudge for all the extra effort and paperwork you made me go through. Then it's going to be my mission in life to make things miserable for you and the rest of the Hellhounds." As usual, her voice and mannerisms were clear and direct. Her husky tone was not dulcet, but strong and razor sharp, like barbed wire. "There are going to be raids. Lots of them. When you're riding around, cops are going to pull your guys over if you are this much—" she held her thumb and index finger apart one inch "—over the speed limit. We will invent reasons to search your vehicles, especially those vans that come in and out of this lot. And let's not forget that nettlesome little law that we usually turn a blind eye to—since it *is* the Cowboy State we're living in—that forbids a felon from possessing a firearm. We'll be shining a bright spotlight on you hence forth."

Hannah took Matt's breath away. She was glorious.

One of Todd's buddies, a burly guy with a beard, set his shotgun on the ground and backed up with his palms raised.

Matt loved watching her work—a sight to behold.

"I don't take kindly to threats." Todd stepped up to her, and Matt put his hand on the biker's chest, making it clear he wasn't allowed any closer. "I might have to send a tantamount warning in return."

Hannah lowered Matt's arm and eased forward, going toe to toe with Todd. "It wasn't a threat. It was a promise. And here's a fun fact about me—warnings don't scare me off. They only make me angry."

"You've got spunk, I'll give you that." Todd smiled. "Because I like you and I'm feeling generous, you can have ten minutes if we happen to have anyone inside by the name of… What was it again?"

"Shane. Yates." Hannah gave him a lopsided grin.

"Okay." Todd jerked his head at the man who

had dropped the shotgun. The guy with the beard hustled inside the clubhouse.

"And we want to speak to him alone," Hannah said.

"That can be arranged. But only for ten minutes. Not one second longer."

The clubhouse door opened. Shane trudged outside with his head bowed, puffing on a lit cigarette.

Yates fit the basic description of who had attacked Jessica Atkinson in terms of height and build. White. About five-ten. Matt guessed the guy weighed around one-ninety. Pinpointing his age could be difficult. Might be in his early thirties and had simply lived a hard life with too much booze and smoking too many cigarettes. Or he was as old as he looked, late forties. But since the assailant had worn a disguise, his true age was anyone's guess.

"You stay safe out there, Detective Delaney," Todd said with a smirk. "The streets can be rough. Especially for a woman." The Hellhound turned to Matt. "See you around, Powell."

Matt clenched his jaw at the veiled threat to Hannah and being called a Powell. A nasty retort was on the tip of his tongue, but he swallowed the words. The dirtbag wasn't worth it.

"Nice to meet you, Shane." Todd put a hand on the guy's shoulder. "Don't say anything incriminating."

Once Todd and his henchmen were inside, Matt snatched Shane up by the collar with one hand, bringing the biker to the balls of his feet. "Why did your buddy at the transit center need to warn you that we were coming to ask a few questions?"

Shane shrugged. "Just looking out for me, I guess."

"Say we believed that—why the need to run?" Hannah asked.

Another shrug. "I don't know. Because cops don't like bikers."

Matt sniffed around the guy's head. "I smell a lie. Do you smell it?"

"Sure do." With a frown, Hannah waved a hand in front of her nose. "Quite the stench. The next answer you give us better smell a whole lot better, or we're going to continue this conversation down at the LPD. Do you want that?"

Yates shook his head. "No."

Matt let him go. "We've got two questions for you."

"Three," Hannah amended. "For starters."

"Get on with it." Shane took another puff from his cigarette. "What do you want to know?"

"Where were you last night between ten and eleven?" Hannah asked. "And don't tell me it was in this clubhouse, because I won't trust a Hellhound for an alibi."

His shoulders sagged as he squeezed his eyes shut for a second. "I can't tell you where I was."

Better than a blatant lie. But Matt suspected this was where the incriminating part would come in. "Well, you had better, or you're about to become our number one suspect in the university murders."

Yates looked up then, his eyes wide, almost bulging out of their sockets, his face turning pale. "I didn't kill anybody."

Hannah gave a one-shoulder shrug. "Make us believe it."

"What if I was doing something illegal?" He took another drag. "Not anything like murder or rape."

Hannah's gaze slid over to Matt, and he nodded.

"Provided that's true, you've got little to nothing to worry about. Spill it." She glanced at her watch. "*Tick, tock.* We don't have all day."

"I was making my usual *drops*. On campus. Okay?"

Narrowing his eyes, Matt snatched him up again. "Drugs? You're dealing on my campus?"

Yates raised his palms. "They're not kids. They're all adults. Pay in cash. Good customers. They ask me for it. I'm providing a service."

"Let him go, Matt." Hannah put a hand on his arm, coaxing him to comply, and grudgingly, he did.

"Prove it," she said to Yates. "Show us your texts."

If he was dealing and making drops on campus, there would be a digital trail.

Yates took out his phone, unlocked it and showed them his text messages from last night.

It was all there: the requests. Messages that he was on the way. Announcements that he had arrived with their order. The usage of slang and emojis for hydrocodone, oxy, amphetamine, cocaine, Adderall, marijuana, mushrooms, ketamine and GHB.

"You've been selling date-rape drugs on my campus?" Matt asked. "To who?"

"The frat boys, mostly. Who do you think?"

"'Mostly'?" Hannah's brow furrowed. "Has anyone—a guy, older than your usual customers—purchased GHB? Maybe more than once?"

"Uh. Now that you mention it…" Yates nodded. "Weird guy. Real creepy."

That was saying a lot, coming from a drug dealer who associated with the dregs of society.

Hannah pulled out her phone and brought up the picture of the sketch the forensic artist had drawn. "Is this him?"

"Yeah." Yates pointed to the image. "That's 666."

"Why do you call him that?" Matt asked.

"He calls himself that. Wiped out my entire

stash of GHB a couple of weeks ago, and before that I hadn't seen him in a while. It's been years."

Shane Yates provided the University Killer with the drugs he used to abduct his victims.

Matt's stomach roiled. He looked at Hannah. "I can't have this guy dealing on my campus."

Alarm swept over the biker's face. "If I don't deal because I talked to you, they'll know I told you, and they'll kill me."

"And we'll promptly arrest them for your murder," Matt said.

"You'd never even find my body. You wouldn't even care if I went missing."

"Don't worry." Hannah patted Yates's cheek. "You'll keep dealing."

"What?" Matt stared at her in disbelief. "No way."

"As my confidential informant," she continued. "You're my new inside man."

Yates shook his head *no*, with a terrified look.

The doors of the clubhouse flew open. Hellhounds began filing out.

"You will," Hannah whispered. "Because if you don't, Chief Granger will shut down your operation and I'll make your buddies believe you're a snitch anyway."

The message was clear. Either way would be a risk to his life.

The Hellhounds mounted their motorcycles—

at least ten—cranked their engines and revved them up to a fierce growl. The noise was almost deafening.

Their time was up, and the conversation was over.

Hannah tipped her head in a silent question to Yates, and he gave a subtle single nod.

But neither the biker nor Matt was happy about it.

Chapter Nine

Hannah couldn't believe she was still arguing with Matt. They had been over it, through it and around the issue ad nauseam.

"This is why no one will work with you," he said, his eyes ablaze with anger. "Because you go rogue."

"I prefer to be on my own because of blowback and grief like this. And others don't want me as a partner—which I'm good with, by the way—because I don't play politics. I simply don't care whose feelings get hurt, so long as I get the job done."

But she couldn't run from the fact that she did care about Matt's feelings and his opinion of her. She hated that he was furious, and she hated even more that she was the reason.

"I knew you were trouble," he said, the word stinging her in an unexpected way, like the lash of a whip. "But I didn't think teaming up with you would be trouble for this campus. Do you understand that I'm responsible for the safety and welfare of these students?"

The SAV members had started to arrive for the emergency meeting and were huddled together in the lobby of the Student Union, watching them.

She tipped her chin up at him. "I do understand." Looking around, she took him by the arm over to a corner that afforded them more privacy. "Keep your voice down. This discussion could get a man killed."

"And that man is slowly killing kids at this school." Cheeks red, he huffed out a breath. "You decided to make that guy your CI with flagrant disregard for my job or the position it would put me in."

"That's not true."

He cocked his head to the side. "What are you going to say next? That day is night, the sun is the moon, the sky is purple—"

"And pigs can fly," she said, attempting to lighten the mood, but he only glared at her. "I did take you and your position into consideration. If we stopped that biker from dealing on campus, he would only be replaced by another using different methods. With him as my CI, he's under my thumb. I can make sure that, at the very least, he doesn't sell date-rape drugs on campus anymore. And as my inside person, we might finally be able to take down Burk's entire operation. Put an end to all their drug running and dealing in this town. In the meantime, you can make sure students, like those waiting for us over there—" she pointed to the SAV kids "—are aware that their drinks might be roofied. If I can do something, anything, to limit the sexual assault on campus, I will. I get that you don't agree with my methods, but you did say you'd do this my way. I never guaranteed you'd like it. We're on the same side, fighting for the same thing. I promise you."

Matt drew in a slow, deep breath. "You're right. I don't like it. But they would simply get someone to replace Yates after they killed him for giving up information. He's nothing more than an interchangeable LEGO block to them."

"He's scum for being a dealer, but I protect everyone I work with. Even my informants. Once he sees that and trusts me, I can turn him against the Hellhounds. Against Todd Burk."

"You do realize that you put yourself in Burk's crosshairs, don't you?"

How sweet that he cared. She was touched. "He's not man enough to come after a cop himself. He'll send some prospect when he thinks I'll least expect it."

Little did the Burks of the world know that she always expected the worst to happen and could handle anything they might dish out.

"It's easy to think that because we're cops,

we're untouchable," he said. "We're not. Dirt-bags like Burk can still reach out and hurt us."

No one could ever hurt her more than her father already had. Not with punches and kicks—but he'd bruised and damaged her all the same.

"I know," she said. "I'll be more vigilant. Scout's honor."

He eyed her with mock wariness. "Were you a Girl Scout?"

She smiled. "No, I wasn't. If I had been, I'm certain I would've been kicked out for mouthing off to the troop leader."

"For that or not selling enough cookies. But for sure, they would've booted you out."

They chuckled, and it was nice. Making peace with him. Seeing a sparkle in his eye rather than anger when he looked at her. He had a nice laugh, rich and full and deep. Sexy. But beneath the grin and the light amusement, she saw a sadness in him, lurking behind the perfect facade. Something dark and painful that felt familiar.

And that's what scared her about him. The part of himself he kept hidden.

Looking down at her face, he brushed a lock of her hair behind her ear, stilling her. Gently, he cupped her chin and ran his thumb along her jaw, and she flinched.

Coming to her senses, she pulled away.

He considered her for a long moment. "I get it now," he said, his voice low and solemn.

She wasn't sure if she should ask or even wanted the answer, but the words slipped out anyway. "Get what?"

"That you're more likely to flinch at tenderness than at pain."

It wasn't a question. Simply a bold, insightful statement.

One she couldn't deny.

"Chief!"

They turned in the direction of the voice that had called for Matt and spotted Dennis Hill, looking frazzled, holding a stack of flyers and waving his Stetson at them.

"We should get the meeting started," Matt said to her.

"There's no *we* in this. This is your meeting. I'm just a humble spectator."

The corner of his mouth inched up in a grin.

They went over to Hill, who was wearing a black polo shirt with *SWU Police* stitched onto it and khakis—the same as the other members of the support staff she'd seen earlier.

"Doing okay, Dennis?" Matt asked.

Hill was winded. His cheeks were flushed, his sandy-brown hair, which was long enough in the front to brush his forehead, was disheveled and beads of sweat coated his face. "Sergeant Starkey," he said, catching his breath, "had me running around campus, putting these up everywhere." He lifted the remaining flyers in his hands. "By the time I remembered you needed some for the meeting, I was clear on the other side of campus and had to run all the way over."

Matt clapped him on the back. "Good exercise."

Not quite out of shape but with a bit of a belly, Hill wasn't fit, either. Though he had a full head of hair, it was thinning at the top and flecked with silver along the edges.

"That's what I kept telling myself all afternoon." Wiping his brow, Hill smiled. Laugh lines formed around his weary eyes.

"I'll go ahead and get started," Matt said. "While I'm speaking, hand out a few flyers to everyone. Okay?"

"No problem, Chief."

Matt welcomed the SAV attendees, a decent crowd of about forty students. She wished there had been more, but the meeting had been called at the last minute. Although the towns of Laramie and Bison Ridge were small, the university was quite large, drawing almost ten thousand students from Wyoming, across the country and from abroad. Tuition was on the lower end, but the students poured thousands of dollars into local businesses.

Someone cut through the gaggle and put down a one-step stool.

Matt stood on it, and everyone's gaze was on him as he towered over them. He had what Hannah could only describe as *presence*. Any room he walked in, she'd bet everyone would not only notice but also stare a second or two.

A rather distracting trait.

She backed up and leaned against a column as she listened to him speak while Hill handed out flyers for the students to give to others, spreading awareness.

From a distance, Matt didn't lose any of his appeal. Even if it was too much. It certainly had been minutes ago, when he'd touched her. The thought sent another frisson of heat through her, which was silly, considering he'd only caressed her face.

"Don't underestimate the seriousness of this threat," Matt said. "The University Killer has already claimed the lives of ten young women, and we believe he will try to take two more before the month is over. Thus far, he has been targeting petite blondes between the ages of eighteen and twenty-two, but that doesn't mean he won't get desperate and go for a different type. Tell everyone you know. Everyone you see on campus. The more attention and awareness we can bring to this, the better."

Late-day stubble made a shadow of scruff over his cheeks and square jaw. Everything about him was hard yet enticing, from his scruples to his sculpted muscles.

A young redhead raised her hand.

Matt pointed to her. "Go ahead."

She held up the flyer. "If this is a disguise that he's wearing, how are we supposed to know what to look for?"

"A man with his height and build. Possibly asking for assistance or using a different ploy to draw you close to his vehicle, where he can drug you and toss you inside."

Bleach.

Handcuffs.

Leg irons.

A shiver ran down Hannah's spine.

"If you get an inkling that you're being followed, get somewhere safe, with lots of people, immediately. If you find yourself in a situation that feels off in the slightest, get out of there. Above all, use the buddy system. No female student should go anywhere alone, especially at night, until we get this guy. In fact, staying inside your dorms and apartments at night would be best."

"Never going to happen, Chief," said a guy wearing a university hoodie. "This is rush week."

Recruitment week for the fraternities and sororities on campus. Hannah's gut clenched.

Dennis Hill finished passing out the flyers and circled around to her. "This is the chief's first rush week," he said in a whisper, and she recalled Matt had left the LPD in October last year, right after their assignment together, to take the position at the university. "He probably didn't realize because he's been focused on the murder. I'm surprised Sergeant Starkey didn't remind him."

The redhead raised her hand again.

"Feel free to share," Matt said.

"He's right. There's going to be a ton of parties. Everyone goes, whether joining or not. It's the biggest event on campus. Most people I know aren't even planning to attend class on Friday."

Hannah swore under breath. The University Killer went after girls with only a few friends, easier to isolate. It was doubtful he'd go for someone in a sorority. But most kids attended a party or two in college, and apparently, the ones occurring this weekend would have a huge draw for all types. This was going to be a nightmare.

"Then again," Hill said to her, leaning closer and keeping his voice low, "the sergeant is probably still peeved he was passed over for promotion to chief. This is the third time."

She turned to him, and the office manager nodded with a grimace.

"Why are they planning to skip class?" Matt asked.

The same kid in the hoodie laughed. "They'll be hung over, man. The parties kick off tomorrow night."

"Thursday is the new Friday," another student called out.

Nothing good happened after midnight. The

kids were dewy-eyed optimists, unaware of the dark side to college parties, which had real consequences. Overdosing. Sexual assaults. Arrests. Blacking out. Driving under the influence. Getting roofied. And too many more dire things she didn't want to consider.

"In the office, we call rush weekend 'the blitz,'" Hill said. "Because it gets crazy with the parties, and the students get quite intoxicated. *Blitzed.* Get it?"

"Yeah." The dread inside Hannah deepened, wrapping around her. "I get it."

"Which reminds me," he said, "I need to get the espresso machine fixed ASAP."

"You might want to call a professional," Hannah suggested.

"I figured out the problem. Needs a new gasket. I'm picking up a replacement on my way home." Hill glanced at the clock on the wall. "I better go before the store closes. Also, I need to get home in time for dinner, or my wife will have a conniption. If she took the time and effort to make the meal, the least I can do is eat it while it's hot. Anyway, you can look forward to an espresso in the morning."

She pulled on a half smile. "Goody."

"There's something else that's come to my attention," Matt said to crowd. "Some of the students, some in fraternities, have been purchasing date-rape drugs. It's easy to slip into your drinks. I'd prefer you to stay home this weekend."

"Not going to happen," someone called out.

Fear of missing out was driving them to attend, when fear of murder should be keeping them in their rooms, playing video games.

Matt sighed. "Only drink what you have poured for yourself. Never leave your cup unattended. If you do, consider it trash and don't drink from it again. For a party, go in groups and leave in groups. There's safety in numbers. Designate someone to stay sober and to account for everyone. This is not the time to trust strangers or to start dating. Spread the word to as many as you can. Let's close the meeting with everyone repeating what I tell you every time."

"Stay alert, stay safe, stay alive," the students said in unison and then began to disperse.

A handful of pretty ladies, including the redhead, stopped Matt, demanding his attention. From the twinkle in their eyes and adoring smiles, they didn't seem to think his brand of appeal was too much. They were fearless in their flirtation.

Did that make her a coward?

Snap out of it, Delaney.

Once he finished speaking with them, Matt made his way over to her.

"You've got quite the fan club," she said, seeing how those girls could be in awe of a handsome campus police chief. A big difference, compared to the college boys.

He shrugged nonchalantly, not showing the slightest interest. "I guess so."

"Most men aren't capable of resisting that. Young, cute, eager to please." For some reason, she was glad he wasn't like most men.

"I sense a compliment buried in there somewhere. But just in case I read that comment wrong, let me set the record straight. If I wanted young, cute and eager to please, I'd get a puppy." His expression turned grim.

Hannah could see the same concern she'd felt earlier, thinking about the upcoming parties, heavy as a boulder in her chest on his face.

"I can't believe I forgot it's rush week," he said.

"You've been dealing with bigger issues, but someone in your office could've reminded you." She wasn't sure if this was the right time to bring up what Dennis had told her.

"It's going to complicate things. I don't know how I'm going to keep these kids safe. Especially this weekend." He ran his hand over the back of his neck. "I need to pop into the office and email Liz's contact, Agent Nancy Tomlinson, what we have so far. Afterward, why don't we grab dinner and hash over the case?"

"I can't. I need to clean out my dorm room and move everything back to my place. For someone who likes to travel light, I can't believe how much stuff I brought." She'd needed more creature comforts than she realized, and then she'd needed things a real college student might've had.

"How about this? You leave your mini SUV—"

"Crossover," she corrected. At least he didn't tease her, calling it a baby SUV like he had last year.

"Leave your *crossover* at the station. We'll take my pickup to the dorm, pack everything in, go to your place, unload it and discuss the case over pizza. Or Chinese. Really anything that delivers."

It had taken her two trips to haul all the stuff. She kept half the cargo space in her trunk filled with emergency supplies. Getting stranded in the middle of nowhere, with limited cell coverage and no essentials—such as bottled water, flares, extra ammo, MREs, blankets, a medical kit, portable charger, two spare tires and her 'go bag' with clothes and toiletries—was never happening to her.

"What about my car?" she asked.

"I'll swing by your place in the morning and pick you up on my way in."

She mulled it over.

"You need to eat," he added.

She did.

"And with rush weekend starting tomorrow…" He shook his head.

The blitz. "Okay," she said. "Since you're providing free labor, I'm buying."

Chapter Ten

"Maybe you could speak with university administrators," Hannah suggested, seated on the carpet in her living room, resting her back against the sofa. "Explain the gravity of the situation and have the rest of rush week canceled."

If only it was that simple.

Sitting next to her, Matt swallowed the pizza in his mouth and washed it down with a swig of the beer he'd been nursing. His limit was half a beer if he knew he had to drive. "Canceling rush is one thing, which they won't do. Quite another thing to convince students to cancel parties. That's the real draw, not recruitment. The festivities, the music, the alcohol—probably the drugs, too." His gut burned again as he thought about Shane Yates dealing on his campus. But Hannah had made valid points.

The biggest being, this could lead to stopping

Todd Burk, the Hellhounds, and their drug trafficking once and for all.

"What if you made it known that you were going to have cops circulating undercover and anyone caught drinking underage would get arrested? I can't think of a better buzzkill. Parties canceled. One problem solved."

She was thinking like an LPD cop, not one working for a university. "After I accepted this position, my limitations were made painfully crystal clear to me. One of the things I'm here to safeguard is the university's reputation. If the school became known as one that uses a campus resource to give students criminal records, enrollment will plummet. Then there's the practicality of executing such a thing. I'd have to arrest eight out of every ten students. I don't have the manpower, enough space in cells—then there's the logistics, overwhelming the court system." He shook his head. "It isn't feasible."

Hannah grabbed another slice of pepperoni pizza from the open box on her coffee table and picked off the pepperoni before taking a bite. "What about the reputation of having a murderer on campus? They can't be pleased with that. Get them to institute a curfew."

"I don't have enough to justify it yet. The administration is resistant to change."

"What more do you need? Another girl dead?"

He hoped not. "They view this as a failure on

my part to do my job. They want this guy caught with minimal disruption to the campus, to the administration and to student life."

She rolled her eyes. "Unbelievable."

"This is my fault, not being prepared for some of the biggest parties of the school year. I should've kept my eye on this while trying to catch the killer. I shouldn't have let it slip through the cracks."

"Hey, there's plenty of blame to go around. I say share it. With Sergeant Starkey." She took a sip of her beer. "He's been with SWUPD for years. He's aware of the parties on rush weekend. Do you know your department even has a name for it? They call it 'the blitz.'"

No. He hadn't heard about "the blitz."

"What was Starkey's alibi?" she asked.

Not this again. "Okay, he didn't bring the parties to my attention, but that doesn't make him a murderer." But it did make him a lousy second-in-command.

"Starkey knows that young women will be extremely vulnerable while there's a killer on the loose. He could've taken steps to mitigate the problem and chose not to. Why?"

"That's a good question."

"Did you know he was passed over for your position?" she asked, eyebrows raised.

"I'm aware."

"Three times."

That, he didn't know. "How are you so well-informed?"

"I'm a good listener." She grinned at him, and he wanted to caress her face, but he also didn't want her pulling away again. "What's his alibi?" she pressed.

"His wife," he said. "She swears they were home together the night Madison Scott was murdered. She has no reason to lie for him. We need to take a closer look at Dr. Foster."

"There's no way he's getting through the winters here in a Z4. Not with all the snow we get." Hannah tipped her beer up to her lips and took a swallow. "I've got an idea, but it's a tedious one."

"Let's hear it."

"We get the DMV records for every dark-colored Tahoe and Yukon that's at least five years old registered in the area. The vehicle had wear and tear on it. Comb through the records and see if he has a second vehicle he neglected to tell us about that matches the description, or if anyone else affiliated with campus does. It's a two-for-one. While checking on him, we might get a lead on a different suspect."

"Do you have any idea how many people drive those vehicles around here and how long it will take to cross-reference whether they have an affiliation with the campus? 'Tedious' is right. I'll need to dedicate an officer to do it. Then I'll need another to tail Foster to ensure he's sitting at home alone and go through his trash when the opportunity presents itself. I barely have enough to patrol and now cover the campus parties, too." Man power was a serious issue.

She set her beer down and angled toward him, their knees grazing. "I might be able to help with that."

"How so?"

"Chief Nelson told me that whatever I need to get this guy and close the case, I can have. I'll ask for Kent Kramer to keep an eye on Foster."

The guy was a good detective. One of the few to survive the LPD purge of corrupt cops.

"If I can figure out how to be sweet and ask nicely, the chief might even give me an officer for the tedious task of going through DMV records."

Matt put his arm on the sofa behind him, easing closer. As he leaned toward her, his thigh brushed the holstered gun on her hip. "You're sweet. You just don't like to let it show."

"That proves how little you know about me."

He was trying to remedy that. "You have a softer side." He'd seen glimpses of it. "One I find sweet."

She chuckled. "Name one sweet thing I've done."

"You rescued a stray cat we found outside a meth lab and gave it to your elderly neighbor because hers had just died."

"Purely self-serving. Giving her the cat stopped

her from knocking on my door whenever she saw my car parked in the driveway and striking up a conversation about drivel because she was lonely."

Hannah lived in a quaint, quiet neighborhood a short drive from the center of town. In stark contrast to the Shooting Star Ranch and its vast acreage, with no neighbors to be seen for miles, the houses on her street were within spitting distance.

"You keep me fed," he said. "You didn't *have* to get me that protein bar from the café." Some liked saccharine, cloying and in-your-face. He preferred the subtle, nuanced sweetness of Hannah Delaney.

"Once again, I was thinking about myself. I made the mistake of not feeding you later in the day, and you nearly tore my head off in the Student Union over Shane Yates."

He had gotten cranky, as she liked to put it, and had snapped at her. Said things he regretted. "I wanted the pepperoni pizza, so you ordered it, even though you clearly don't eat pepperoni." He gestured to the pieces she had picked off and tossed inside the box.

"You're reaching, Granger. Getting two pizzas would've been wasteful. I'm not sweet. I'm trouble. Remember?"

"You can be both. And some trouble is worth getting into."

She grinned at him. "I think that's the best non-apology I've ever gotten."

He met her honey-brown eyes. Amusement faded from her face, uncertainty taking over. As he took her in, really looked at her, the uncertainty in her expression mixed with awareness, and his throat grew thick.

Like earlier, in the Student Union, they were connected on a different level. Slowly, he grasped her chin and brought her mouth closer. She wasn't beautiful in the classic sense but nonetheless captivating. There was something about her features—the lines and curves of her body, the fierceness of spirit—that lured him in.

He drew closer, stopping a hair's breadth from kissing her. "Sweet trouble," he whispered, aching to taste her.

A soft sigh left her mouth, her bottom lip trembling. "I could use some water." She pulled away, jumped to her feet, and took a step back, both physically and emotionally. "Do you want—"

A crash outside—the sound of glass shattering—had her spinning toward the window and Matt leaping up off the floor.

He looked out the window. Flames danced over the hood of his truck, like someone had thrown a Molotov cocktail. "Stay here," he said, moving toward the front door.

"Like hell I will. This is my house." She cut

in front of him, reaching the door first, opened it and stormed outside.

He was right behind her when he heard a rustle coming from the bushes that flanked her doorway.

Whirling at the noise, he faced a man, pouncing from the darkness. The guy charged him, wrapping his arms around Matt's waist, hitting him in the midsection with his shoulder, trying to bulldoze him down. But Matt braced, taking the full force with a groan, grabbed him by his biker cut and tossed him to the lawn. On the top rocker of the leather cut was a Hellhounds patch. The rest was blank. He was a newbie, not a full-fledged member.

From the corner of his eye, he saw a second guy lunge for Hannah. No way for her to stop the tackle; checking a larger, stronger assailant was tough.

At lightning speed, she flowed backward with the blow—using the momentum and his mass to her advantage—and drove her knees up into his abdomen as they hit the ground and flipped him over with her legs.

Before Matt had a chance to be impressed, the other guy charged him again. The same maneuver—head down, shoulder lowered, hitting Matt squarely in the stomach. This time the biker knocked him flat on his back. His attacker landed on top of Matt's chest. The guy got to his knees, quickly sat upright and hit Matt in the face with his fist.

"Nobody messes with the Hellhounds!" he screamed.

Hannah grunted as though she'd been struck hard.

Blocking the incoming blows, he glimpsed Hannah tussling with the other one. Her opponent managed to scramble on top of her and pin her down. She lifted a knee into the man's midsection, which made him gasp and gag. Hannah clubbed her hands together and smashed them against the side of his head, driving him off, and she rolled away.

The wannabe member of the motorcycle gang on top of Matt leaned back, reaching for something in his waistband, but he was having trouble, like it was stuck. Instinctively, Matt realized it was a gun, and if that man succeeded in getting the weapon out, he would die.

Matt reached for the holster on his hip, drew his Glock first and aimed at the biker's center mass. "Hands up!"

A gun fired, the explosive sound of the shot stilling his heart.

Hannah!

"Give me a reason not to put a hole in you," she yelled, and he exhaled in relief. She was okay.

"Get face down on the ground with your hands behind your head, and if you so much as twitch, I'll shoot you."

Matt grinned, but a pang in his cheek made him dial it back. "You heard the woman. Down on the ground."

Chapter Eleven

Thursday, September 19
1:30 p.m.

"Thanks for agreeing to do this." Hannah stood in Matt's office in the SWUPD, sneaking glances through the top half of the wall that was glass, across the hall at Matt as he spoke with Sergeant Starkey behind closed doors.

"I didn't agree," Detective Kent Kramer said, sitting in a chair, holding a cappuccino from the espresso machine Dennis had fixed. Instead of wearing his typical frumpy suit, he was dressed down in jeans and a sweatshirt. Good attire for a stakeout or tailing someone. "I'm only following Chief Nelson's orders."

Between doing the paperwork on last night's events in front of her home, getting her request for additional man power approved, persuading her contact at the DMV to assist and reaching out to the homicide division at the Seattle PD—with the time difference, she was waiting on a call back—she'd spent the morning at the Laramie PD with Matt.

"Well, thanks anyway." She handed him a copy of Dr. Bradford Foster's schedule and glanced back over at the other office.

The conversation appeared to be getting heated, at least on Matt's part, as he was doing most of the talking, while Starkey sat looking bored, giving short responses and plenty of shrugs.

"That's quite the shiner you've got there," Kent said, shifting her attention, and he gestured to her bruised face.

The Hellhound had gotten in a few solid punches before she'd been able to draw her gun. Matt had insisted she put ice on the bruise. In fact, he had gotten the chilled compress himself and placed it on her face. And for a few seconds, she'd let him, accepting his tenderness—a vulnerability she didn't let others see. But despite the ice, no amount of makeup was going to hide her black eye. So she hadn't even bothered to try.

"You should see the other guy," she said. "Believe me, it's worse." She gave better than she had gotten, but she could use a couple extra hours of sleep and some more painkillers.

Kent sipped his cappuccino. "I heard those two 'acted'—" he threw up air quotes "—on their own accord and you can't charge Burk."

"You heard correctly." Their lawyer, Mr. Friedman, had miraculously arrived at the station about ten minutes after she and Matt had hauled them in. "Their story is that no one gave them any order to attack me in exchange for becoming full members."

"Don't you mean *kill* you?" Kent asked with a raised eyebrow.

She gave a one-shoulder shrug. "You say potato, I say potahto."

He wrinkled his nose. "I'd like to know how they got your address."

"They conveniently and cleanly had a ready-made answer for that," she said with a wag of her finger. "Found it on the dark web. Sure enough, there's a site out there with my information."

"Anyone else's from the department as a result of the breach, thanks to the dirty former lieutenant?" Kent asked.

"Oddly, no. Only mine. I guess we now know who bought the information." Todd Burk. "Just can't prove it." She couldn't wait to see that man rotting behind bars, right along with most of the town.

Movement across the hall caught her gaze. Matt was up on his feet. Then so was Starkey. Matt had a good four inches on him, but Starkey was solid, with a runner's build.

Kent sighed. "You know, if you throw a frog into boiling water, those suckers just jump right out. But if you place them in a pot full of water that's room temperature and slowly turn up the heat, the frog doesn't notice the temperature change until it's nearly at a boil. And by then… well, it's too late for the poor guy to jump free."

Looking back at the senior detective, Hannah considered what he said. "Am I supposed to be the frog here?" And was the increase in temperature the toll the job took?

He tipped his head to the side with a noncommittal expression.

Hannah appreciated his wisdom but never imagined she would suffer such a fate. "I'll know when the time comes to get out."

"Are you sure about that? By the look of your face, I don't think you do. We all believe we'll know when it's time. Here I am, still in the pot, too, when I probably should've gotten out a couple years back."

The door across the hall swung open, hitting the wall with a clatter. "Why don't you see how well you do without me helping you? Ungrateful SOB." Sergeant Starkey stalked out of the office, no longer wearing his badge or service weapon.

"I think that's my cue to leave." Kent finished his cappuccino and tossed the disposable cup into the waste bin. "It looks like the professor has office hours today." He stood. "Should be simple enough."

Matt came into the office. "Hey, Kent. It's good of you to help out by keeping an eye on Dr. Foster."

"Not really," the older detective said. "I wasn't given much of a choice. The chief told me to come. So here I am. Can I get a map of the campus?"

"Sure." Matt went around his desk and grabbed one. "Here you go. Also," he said, reaching over and getting something else, "this is a permit that'll allow you to park in designated faculty-only spots. By the way, Foster drives a light blue BMW Z4." He gave Kent the license plate number.

Hannah's cell phone rang. She took it out and looked at it. "Seattle area code." She answered, putting it on speaker. "This is Detective Delaney."

"Hi there. I'm Detective Trahern. I got your message about Dr. Bradford Foster. How can I be of assistance?"

"Yes. Thanks for returning my call. I'm here with two colleagues, SWU Campus Police Chief Granger and Detective Kramer. It's my understanding that Dr. Foster helped your department catch the Emerald City Butcher."

"That's not quite how I'd put it," Trahern said. "His assistance did lead to the arrest and conviction of a suspect, Sam Lee. But something felt off to me about the case."

Hannah glanced at Matt and Kent. "Like what?" she asked.

"We never linked Lee's DNA to any of the victims."

Matt scratched at the stubble on his jaw. "Then how did you get the conviction?"

"Trophies taken from the victims were found in Lee's house. He swore he'd never seen them and didn't know how they got there," Trahern said.

"What kinds of trophies?" she asked.

"Their ID cards, jewelry, sometimes underwear."

Matt folded his arms. "Do you think he was framed?"

"No prints were found on any of the trophies in his house. Felt strange to me, but at the time, we just wanted it to be over. I don't know. Sure hope not. If so, that's on me and my partner," Trahern said, his voice rueful. "That brings me to the next thing that hasn't sat well with me. The vast majority of repeat murderers will spill the beans in custody because of their ego—or definitely in prison because if you're a big, bad killer, life behind bars is easier. I've kept tabs on Lee all these years. To this day, he maintains that he's innocent."

"Foster published a book about his work with your division," Matt said, "and takes a great deal of credit."

"I'm well aware. Whenever I see a copy of it, I get sick and want to burn it."

"But the murders did stop once Lee was arrested, didn't they?" she asked.

"Yeah." Trahern blew a heavy breath over the line. "They did. But another way of looking at it is that they also stopped when Foster left Seattle."

Kent shook his head with a grimace. "Were any of the Butcher's victims raped?"

"They were," Trahern said. "But the perp used a condom, and they had all been killed by blunt force trauma to the head. Though there were ligature marks around their wrists, ankles and throats."

"Sometimes these serial killers who have been at it for a while evolve." Kent's mouth twitched. "Get more violent. More sophisticated. Bolder."

"Does this relate to a case you're currently working?" Trahern asked.

"The University Killer has struck on and off for the past ten years," Matt said. "Each time, he abducts three women. All blond and young. Rapes them and strangles them to death."

"The Butcher's victims were young, too—late teens to early twenties—but not all blond. How is Dr. Foster involved?"

Hannah stifled the groan rising in her throat. "He's a person of interest. The murders started a year after he began teaching at the university, at least one victim was a previous student of his, he's come in close proximity to all of them and he doesn't have an alibi. When we questioned him, he tried to flip the script on us and get us to enlist his help working the case."

"That's one slippery, shady dude," Trahern said. "Did you get any DNA from the victims?"

"We did," Matt said. "Our guy didn't use a condom."

Trahern swore. "Then your University Killer isn't the Emerald City Butcher. We found the killer's hair on one of the victims. You would've gotten a match in CODIS."

CODIS, the Combined DNA Index System, was a national database of DNA profiles from convicted offenders, unsolved crime scene evidence and missing persons.

"Even if you clear Foster for your murders," Trahern said, "I would never work with that pompous, self-aggrandizing jerk ever again."

Her thoughts exactly. "Thanks for speaking with us. We won't take up anymore of your time."

"No problem. If you have any other questions, don't hesitate to reach out." Trahern disconnected.

Hannah slipped her phone in her pocket, her mind spinning. Whether or not the professor was their guy remained to be seen. "My gut tells me we're doing the right thing and should still look into him."

"Agreed," Matt said.

"I'll stick to him tighter than a Rocky Mountain wood tick," Kent said, then turned to Matt. "Hey, I never did get a chance to congratulate you on the new job. One day, you were in the office.

The next, you were gone. We didn't even get to throw you a going-away party."

Matt shook his head. "Parties are for retirements and promotions."

Kent extended his arms. "This is a promotion. One worth celebrating." He patted Matt on the back, and Hannah rolled her eyes with a sigh.

"Not to everyone." Matt lifted his head, his gaze meeting hers.

Kent waved a dismissive hand in her direction. "Don't let this sourpuss rain on your parade. She doesn't know how to be happy when it comes to herself. Unrealistic to expect her to be happy for others. Delaney will find the one dark cloud in the sky on the sunniest of days."

Wow. Could his opinion of her be any lower? "I'm standing right here. Where I can hear you," Hannah said. "And for the record, I know how to be happy." She just *hadn't* been in a very long time.

"Sure, you do. You wouldn't know happiness if it kissed you on the lips, Delaney. You'd shoo it away, mistaking it for a threat."

She put her fists on her hips. "I believe the phrase is 'If it hit you in the face'."

Kent chuckled. "A Hellhound hit you in the face last night. Did it feel like love? *Poor thing.* Love isn't supposed to hurt."

Yet it did for her. Worse than anything else.

Kent looked back at Matt. "Give me a call one night, and drinks will be on me, Chief Granger. Well, I better get cracking." Kent left as quietly and subtly as he had entered.

"I see your chat with the sergeant didn't go well," Hannah said, desperate to change the topic. Starkey had called him in to show him the surveillance footage of the Mythology class right as Kent had arrived, and things took a turn.

"I'll get to that in a minute." Matt closed the office door and leaned against the desk, crossing his arms as he regarded her steadily. "Kent made a good point. I've worked hard to get to where I am. Why do you begrudge this promotion that I earned?"

Taken aback, she stiffened. "I don't."

"You do. Every chance you get, you undercut it. Imply that I'm some kind of coward for taking it. You literally accused me of *hiding out*."

Dropping into a seat, Hannah pressed her palm to her forehead. This was a conversation she'd rather not have, but if he insisted, then so be it. "You're the best detective I've ever worked with. Patient and dispassionate when necessary. Shrewd. Gifted at lasering in on perps in a way that I've never seen before. Like you sense the threat. That's exactly what we need out there in the streets. To take down the Burks and the cartels poisoning this town." She looked up at him.

The paradox of Matt Granger was eating away at her. "You're a war hero. The most decorated detective in the Laramie PD. What are you doing here if *not* hiding out?"

Chapter Twelve

Thursday, September 19
2:45 p.m.

This time, Matt was speechless. He had no idea she regarded him so highly. *The best detective she'd ever worked with?*

The answer to her question wasn't easy or simple and, now faced with it, wasn't one he was fully prepared to give. He sat in the chair beside her. Tipping his head back, he stretched his long legs.

"I was Special Forces. The job involved a lot of killing and seeing buddies die and others wounded. The job was necessary, and I was very good at it, but it took a toll on me. When I came back home, I joined the LPD. I still wanted to make a difference. Always. And I thought, as a cop here—not like in some major city with a seedy underbelly—that there'd be less bloodshed. That I wouldn't have to lose anybody I cared about to the job anymore."

"And then you lost your partner," she said, her voice soft.

He looked at her and nodded. "We shouldn't have split up. But we did, and a perp got the drop on him. When I got to him, he was still alive. I held his hand and watched him slip away while hearing the ambulance only a few blocks from us. I had to explain this to his wife and his children."

She placed her hand on his arm. "I'm sorry."

"I thought I could push through it—that's what I had been trained to do. But that loss hurt more than the others. Not because he meant more than other brothers-in-arms who died. But I can't shut off my emotions any longer. I lost the ability to go numb. Then we got paired up on the cartel case, and you came so close to dying."

Tightening her grip on him, she rubbed his arm with her thumb, and he appreciated the comfort she offered, knowing it was rare for her.

"I didn't want to go through that again. When this job opened, I jumped at the chance to take it. Because I thought it would be safer. Quieter. No chance of losing anyone else I cared about." Hearing the words out loud, he could no longer deny the truth. "I guess you're right. I *am* hiding out. Or at least, I was trying to. With the University Killer back, I suppose the joke is on me. There's just no escaping the darkness and death." For so long, he'd kept everything bottled up inside, unable to unburden himself. He couldn't talk to his family, and he'd figured he'd never share it with anyone. Until Hannah.

She moved her hand to his cheek. "Not everyone is cut out for this kind of work. But we are. It isn't easy and takes sacrifice. We pay a heavy price for it so that others get to look up at the sky on the sunniest of days without seeing any dark clouds."

That's when it occurred to him: Hannah Delaney had accepted not being happy, probably thinking it was simply a drawback of the job. Plenty of depressed, alcoholic cops to substantiate that belief, but it saddened and angered him at the same time to know that she would deny herself love.

"I was wrong about you taking this job," she continued.

"How so?"

"Yes, you're hiding out, but you didn't have to stay in law enforcement. You could've easily become a full-time rancher," she said, and he had considered it. "Instead, you were drawn to the position because a threat that has eluded everyone else for nearly a decade was coming back, and I think you sensed it. This is where you're supposed to be, right here, right now—to stop the University Killer."

He had been compelled to apply for the job, but he hadn't thought of it that way. Could she be right?

Her gaze slid from his to where her palm caressed his cheek. She dropped her hand, like she just realized that she was touching him, got up and moved away, breaking the connection yet again.

She deserved so much more than she was letting herself have. If only she could see it.

"Was there anything useful on the surveillance video?" she asked.

Shoving down the raw emotions he had allowed to surface, he pulled himself together. "Not really. There was no footage inside the class to see him interacting with Jessica Atkinson—only of him in the hall, hobbling in and out of the room."

She picked up a bottle of water and offered it to him, but when he declined with a shake of the head, she twisted off the cap and guzzled half of it. "What happened with Sergeant Starkey?"

He blew out a long breath. "We got into it after I brought up how he neglected to mention it was rush week, knowing another young woman could easily be taken with all the parties that are going to happen. There was a lot of back-and-forth finger-pointing I'm not proud of, but it became clear that he wants me to fail at this job."

"Did you fire him?"

Matt shook his head. "Nope. He took a leave of absence, effective immediately. Not that I approved it, but he's got a ton of vacation days saved up."

"Better that he's gone."

"This is an all-hands-on-deck kind of situation. The more officers, the better. Now I'm down one."

She finished off the bottle of water. "You don't want to hear this."

"Then don't say it."

"I'm obliged. If it's him, we don't want him to know where officers are going to be placed and what areas will be vulnerable."

"He already has some idea. But I don't think he's the killer. A jerk? Sure. What about his alibi? His wife swore he was home."

Hannah lightly touched her cheekbone and winced. "A person can be home with someone without them actually being home."

"How do you mean?" He got up, grabbed a bottle of painkillers from a desk drawer and tossed them to her.

She caught it. "Boils down to perception. Right? Maybe he was home, at first. They had dinner together. Then he decided to go to the garage and work on a car or into the basement or attic to focus on some hobby, in whatever space he's carved out as his alone. A sacred place. Not to be violated. And while he's in there, no one is to disturb him. Easy enough to turn on a radio or television to mask the fact that he snuck out.

Perhaps used a secondary vehicle that he kept parked down the block and killed someone. The entire time, the wife thinks he's home."

He sat back down and stared at her. "That was very, very specific. Alarmingly so."

Averting her gaze, she opened the medicine bottle, popped a pill in her mouth and swallowed it dry. "Just a supposition that came to me. Anyway, it's possible. Don't you think?"

"Sure. It's possible. Crazier things have happened."

"He's got a hobby, something he's into. Doesn't he?"

Most folks did. "Watching baseball." Nothing suspicious there.

"Games can last late into the night, can't they?"

The latest game he was aware of had gone into eighteen innings and hadn't ended until four a.m. "They can, but she told me that they went to bed together."

"Is that what she said? Or was it more general, more vague? Sort of like, they had dinner, he watched some baseball and they went to bed. That could mean she had dinner with the kids. While he ate in front of the television in the space that's his, where he doesn't like to be disturbed, and she went to bed. When she woke, he was beside her, and she simply assumed that he joined her shortly after she fell asleep."

He honestly couldn't remember the exact wording from any of the statements he'd taken, but he recalled the gist, and Starkey's wife was confident he had been home. "Don't forget, he passed a polygraph test, too."

She shrugged. "Maybe he knows how to beat one. They're not one hundred percent reliable," she said, and he agreed. "Being passed over three times and forced to help the person who has the job you've coveted is a lot."

"'Coveted'? You don't hear that word often outside of church."

"Before you got him riled up, you should've asked him to take a DNA test."

"Not helpful." He shook his head. Unfortunately, Matt would have difficulty getting a warrant for a DNA test at this point since Sergeant Starkey had passed a polygraph *and* had an alibi *and* there was no evidence to justify it. "Maybe we can get Kent to go through his trash, too."

"I'll send a text, asking." She took out her phone and started typing.

"There's something that you should know. I submitted the killer's DNA to a couple of those big, publicly accessible genetic-genealogy-testing services. About a hundred users matched as a distant relative, possibly as close as a third cousin." An ideal match in an ancestry search was a parent, sibling, half sibling or first cousin. It was the DNA equivalent of hitting the mother lode. "Logan Powell, my cousin who works for DCI, connected me with one of their retired investigators to research it, but it could take up to six months to narrow it down to a pool of people who could be the University Killer." The further back the matches went, the more branches on a family tree that would have to be built out. "No one else in the office knows about this. I wanted to keep it quiet. When this guy first started killing women, law enforcement wasn't using the public genetic-testing companies to track down suspects. Now, if our guy got wind that we have tracked down relatives somehow, he might bolt and disappear."

Something close to hurt flashed in her eyes. "But why didn't you tell *me* sooner?"

He didn't really have a good reason. It wasn't anything personal. She could be trusted with the information. "Everything has been happening so fast, one thing after another. Besides, we need to stop this guy before he kills two more women in a matter of days. Does it matter that I'm telling you now?"

Looking away, she shook her head. Her phone chimed, and she looked at the text. "Kent says he'll do it—but wants us to know no one has seen Foster for a few hours. Some students have been waiting to talk to him during office hours, but he's been a no-show. One kid claims he takes off sometimes to go fishing near Gray Reef or the North Platte."

"Have Kent check Foster's house," Matt said.

"Already on it. He's headed that way now." She set her phone down. "As for tonight with the parties, we should do something unexpected."

"What did you have in mind?" he asked, his curiosity piqued.

"Can you call in a favor with your other cousin?"

She would have to be more specific. "Which one?"

"Holden. In the sheriff's department. Nelson can't afford to commit any extra officers to this case. But maybe Holden can spare a couple of deputies tonight. We put them in plainclothes and have them circulate some of the parties."

"That's a good idea." Tonight, they needed as much help as they could get.

Chapter Thirteen

Thursday, September 19
6:10 p.m.

The tempting aroma of a hamburger and fries from the Wheatgrass Café wafted through the car. Parked down the street from the university hospital, where cameras couldn't capture him on surveillance footage, he tugged his gloves back on and pulled the top off the to-go cup of the fountain drink. Cola. He squeezed in a few droplets of tetrahydrozoline hydrochloride, decongestant eye drops easily purchased almost anywhere. In case the cop guarding sweet Jessica didn't drink soda, the water bottle in the take-out bag was his backup method of delivery, which he had already spiked. The top had been opened, but he doubted the officer would even notice.

If he had gotten the dosage right, the cop would only get sick—very sick—rather quickly, sending him to the bathroom to vomit. On the other hand, if he had used too much…

Coma. Seizures. Or even death. None were part of his plan.

Although he'd have to forego his hookup with Jessica, a necessary sacrifice, she was still his prey. Claiming her life was essential. The first punishment for the undercover cop.

Detective Hannah Delaney.

He was going to teach her the hard way—his way—that once he had decided to take something, it was his. The only lives she could save from him were those he chose to forfeit.

Her interference would not be tolerated. And would not go with impunity.

He reached over and opened the glove box. Taking out the small envelope, he smiled.

Since he would not be able to enjoy Jessica in his usual way, she would never be one of his queens. Therefore, he couldn't leave his signature calling card.

Instead, he had something special, unique, just for the detective.

He slipped it into the inside pocket of his thin jacket, which already held the syringe with the lethal dose of GHB.

His cell phone rang. He glanced over at it in the cupholder and groaned. He'd never answer right before a kill, but he recognized the number and needed to take it. "Hey, kiddo."

"Hey to you, Dad. How are you doing?"

"I'm well." He scanned his surroundings. "You

excited for your first rush weekend as a full-fledged fraternity member?"

"Yeah, can't wait," his son said. "So much better than being a newbie, jumping through recruitment hoops. But Mom is driving me crazy. She keeps calling, telling me not to drink and that I'm not at school to party but to learn."

"Give your mom a break. She loves you and just wants you to stay safe, that's all."

"Why can't she be cool about this like you?"

"Moms and dads are different. I trust you to make good choices. You'll find a balance between getting an education and having fun. Only you can figure it out for yourself. We can't do it for you, as much as your old mom might wish we could."

"Talk to her. Tell her that. Get her to back off."

"I can't get her to stop loving you or make her not worry."

"Just wish she'd keep it to herself." Liam groaned. "Are you coming to my frat's parents' weekend?"

"Sure am."

"I'd prefer it if Mom skipped it."

"That's between you and her. I am not getting in the middle."

Another groan. "It's the last weekend of the month."

"I've got it marked on the calendar. I wouldn't miss it for the world."

"Great. I've got to go, Dad. I volunteered to be a sober brother tonight, keeping an eye on things, but first I have to go to a safety meeting called by the council."

"What are you talking about?"

"The campus police chief contacted the council because he's concerned about the safety of the students, specifically the girls," Liam said. "The council asked for volunteers to be sober brothers—watch dogs, really—circulating the party, keeping an eye on things, making sure everyone stays safe."

"Really? Interesting."

"Yeah, and they're beefing up the police presence on fraternity row this weekend."

Good thing he was already ahead of the game. No stopping him. Not tonight. He smiled. "I'm proud of you for stepping up to look out for others. You're a fine young man. Have fun this weekend. Love you, kiddo."

"Me too, Dad."

They ended the call, and he refocused on the task at hand. He needed to get back into character.

Looking in the rearview mirror, he checked his new disguise. He pressed down on the beard, ensuring it wouldn't budge, raked down the hair of the mousy-brown wig over his forehead and tucked down the bill of his cap. Patting his augmented fake belly, he made sure it was secure.

"Here you go," he said, practicing his altered voice. Not quite right. Needed a stronger hint of a Southern accent and to be an octave lower. He cleared his throat. "Here you go, Officer."

Perfect.

He got out of the car and locked the door. Lowering his head in case he passed any cameras on the way, he strolled to the hospital.

In the lobby, he breezed up to the front desk. "Hi there. I've got a delivery order for the SWU police officer on guard duty," he said, holding up the to-go drink and a bag with the words *Wheatgrass Café* written across it.

The attendant smiled. "One moment." She typed on the computer. "Room 411."

"Thanks."

Keeping his head down, he went to the bank of elevators and stepped onto a car behind an elderly gentleman. "Four, please."

The older man nodded and hit the button for him.

When it had reached the fourth floor, the elevator dinged, and the doors opened. He stepped off and got his bearings. Slowly, he walked down the hall, taking note of any rooms that appeared unoccupied. He passed the nurse's station and angled his face away. A few doors down, he spotted the cop, sitting in a chair, preoccupied with something on his phone.

"Evening, Officer. Here you go." He handed

the guy the drink and the bag. "Dinner, courtesy of your friends at the SWUPD."

The cop's face lit up like a light bulb, and he smiled. "Thanks. This is better than eating hospital food again."

"Enjoy." He turned and retraced his steps.

Three rooms shy of the elevator, he glanced over his shoulder. The cop had taken the straw from the bag and was inserting it into the fountain drink.

Just as he had hoped.

He ducked into a room that looked empty and slipped inside the bathroom. Keeping his gloves on, he pulled out the clothes he had concealed under his shirt that had been strapped to his body. He slipped scrubs on over everything else he was already wearing, along with a white lab coat. The ballcap, he discarded in the trash. Brand new and purchased while wearing gloves, none of his DNA was on it. He raked down the wig once more.

In a few minutes, the tetrahydrozoline hydrochloride would kick in right around when the hospital would begin their shift change and personnel would be distracted. Timing wasn't just key; it was everything.

Then he'd pay sweet Jessica one final visit.

Chapter Fourteen

Thursday, September 19
7:17 p.m.

With a heavy heart, Hannah stepped off the elevator onto the fourth floor of the hospital with Matt beside her. Officer Carl Farran had been admitted for severe vomiting, blurred vision, difficulty breathing, elevated blood pressure and tremors. Something he'd ingested had most likely been poisoned. He was on the same floor, in room 424.

Hannah and Matt each showed their badge to a hospital security guard who stood outside Jessica Atkinson's room, controlling access as they'd instructed when they got the devastating call about what happened. The guard noted both their names in a log that tracked everyone coming and going. They stepped past him.

The room was so still, quiet as a grave. Hannah went over to the bed and stared down at Jessica's lifeless face. Her brown eyes open, frozen in death.

How?

Hannah gritted her teeth. How had she let this psychopathic killer get to her? Did Jessica know what was happening before it was too late?

There were no signs of a struggle. He must have pretended to be a doctor or a nurse and had injected her arm or the IV bag.

Guilt welled up inside Hannah, making her nauseous. She looked Jessica over, her gaze landing on a small white envelope that had been placed on her stomach.

Hannah glanced around for latex gloves. Matt already had some and handed her a fresh set. She slid on a pair, and he did the same.

As she carefully picked up the envelope, her hand trembled. That monster had rattled her nerves. Deeper than she'd realized.

They examined both sides of the envelope. The back flap hadn't been sealed. With a finger, she lifted it, revealing the edge of a piece of paper tucked inside. Not a playing card, as she had anticipated. Delicately and slowly, she slid the paper free, watching to see if anything fell out along with it, like a hair or anything else. But there was nothing. Only the slip of paper.

On it, three lines had been typed in all caps. It read:

DRESSED TO REVEL, HAZE AND RUN AMOK
CAN'T WAIT FOR SITTING DUCKS LINED UP
NO PALINDROME PALADIN DISRUPTING MY NEXT HOOKUP

"This psycho had the nerve to write a poem?" Her stomach turned, disgust filling her.

"A tercet," Matt said, and she looked at him in confusion. "A poem with three lines."

"A haiku?"

He nodded, staring at the paper. "A haiku is an example of one, but this isn't that." His lips moved like he was counting. "Each line has seven words but a different number of syllables."

She scrutinized the words. "Revel, *haze*, run amok. He must be referring to the parties for rush. He's planning to take his next victim this weekend, maybe even tonight, and he's taunting us with it."

"Look at the last line. I think it's about you," he said, with concern in his voice. "Your first name is a palindrome, spelled the same backward as forward—and technically, you're a paladin. A guardian. A protector. A warrior."

A wave of anger and frustration rushed over

her. "This message *is* for me. He's gloating. Even though I saved her, he still managed to get her in the end. He wants me to feel ashamed that *I*, a paladin, failed to protect her after I promised that I would."

And he had succeeded.

Tears stung her eyes. She swallowed the sudden lump in her throat and placed the poem and envelope in an evidence bag.

"I'm the one who promised." Matt put a steady hand on her shoulder. "This monster got through one of my officers, and that's on me. Not you. Don't you dare think it's your fault."

"That's how it feels." She stared at the poem again. "The way he phrased the last line about me. He's expecting me to fail. He's confident that no matter how hard I try, no matter what I do, somehow, he's going to be two steps ahead of me and grab another woman."

Her nerves tightened at the prospect of that happening. *Not another.* She couldn't bear to lose another one.

"Why didn't he leave a queen of hearts playing card?" Matt said, thinking out loud.

She clenched her jaw, cursing the cruel animal behind all this. "The poem is so much more effective, don't you think?"

"No, what I mean is, why didn't he leave the card along with the poem?" He stared at the paper, and she could see the wheels spinning inside him.

"Almost as though he doesn't consider this to be one of his ritualistic three kills."

Hannah's gut twisted as her heart sank. "Then he only went through the trouble and effort of poisoning a cop and murdering her in her hospital bed, risking exposure and possibly getting caught, just to make me pay for saving her? Because I *disrupted* his *hookup* with her?"

Sweat formed at the base of her spine. Her mind flashed back to the adrenaline-fueled moments when she had stumbled upon him trying to take Jessica. In the hours after the attack, she had replayed the attempted abduction over and over. How she had fought not to let him get the young woman into the car.

All to what end?

She stared at Jessica's cold, pale body. "He's going to rape and murder two more women."

"No. We're not going to let him." He slid his hand from her shoulder to her back. "Do you hear me?"

"What if we are out of our depth, outmatched, outsmarted?" There was no hiding the fear in her voice.

Over the years, she'd learned that a good detective kept their emotions in check no matter how bad, how scary, how deadly things got. She never let anyone see her squirm. Instead, she had always done whatever she needed to do to hold it together and deal with it later, in private.

But standing there with Matt—looking at the woman she'd failed to protect, holding the murderer's provocative message written to mess with her—she couldn't conceal the feelings bubbling over inside.

"This guy isn't as smart as he thinks," Matt said. "We'll get him. One way or another."

She nodded, knowing that it was only a matter of time because the killer had been overconfident and made the mistake of leaving behind his DNA for the past decade. But that sick poem had her second-guessing herself, questioning her next moves.

How was she going to prevent him from taking two more lives?

"While we're here, let's find Nurse Slagle and chat with her about her husband."

"Sounds good." Hannah left the room and went up to the nurse's station. "We're looking for a nurse who works here, Tina Slagle. Can you tell us where to find her?"

"I know Tina," one of the nurses said. "She's off today. My guess is, she's at home, getting in quality time with her kids."

"Thanks," Matt said. As they walked away, he turned to her. "Notice how she said quality time with 'the kids' instead of *the family*?"

"I did. We don't have much time before the meeting with everyone to prepare for the parties tonight. But I think we should make some to swing by the Slagle residence," she said, her thoughts still twisting and churning over that sick tercet.

Dread gnawed deeper at her.

"Hey." Matt caught her by the arm. "Did you hear what I said?"

She shoved the three lines of the poem from her head. "About what?"

"We can have hospital security drop off the surveillance footage at the station. It'll save us enough time to speak to the Slagles." He steered her toward the middle of the corridor to the wall. "I can see that poem is messing with you," he said, and she sighed, unable to deny it. "Last night, you said that I didn't know you well. But there's something about me that you need to understand." Matt drew her gaze and held it. "When I set my sights on accomplishing something, I take dead aim and systematically go over or through everything in my path until I have reached my objective."

She appreciated his efforts to reassure her but was rattled by the idea that Atkinson's death was her fault. "Have you ever been in a battle you didn't think you'd win or survive? And fear wanted to curl you into a ball and try to wish the fight away? You ever felt that?"

"Plenty of times, in the military."

This was a first for her. To not only lose but to also have her nose rubbed in it. "What did you do?"

"Kept my finger on the trigger and my focus downrange, and fought through it. The same way you will now. You're not alone. We'll stop him. You and me, together. I need to hear you say it like you believe it, Delaney. Don't let him into your head. Don't allow him to undermine your self-confidence. Don't let him strip away one of the best parts about you. Your strength. Your will. The way you fight for justice. Because that's what he wants. For you to doubt yourself. You figured out something about him. Enough to run right into him. You did it once. You can do it again. We will stop him."

The other night she had been out on her own. This time, she had a partner. One who'd proven she could rely on him. One she trusted to help her get the job done, even if they had to go into hell and battle the devil himself. "You and me. Together."

As MATT PULLED up to the Slagle residence, which was an easy walk to the university hospital and less than a five-minute drive, Hannah opened one of the buccal DNA test kits that they had in the truck. She tucked the sealed glass vial containing a swab in her jacket pocket.

"Remember," he said, "we'll get more flies with honey."

Hannah grinned. "Well, you said I've got a sweet side. I'll try to tap into that."

Then they went up to the front door. Matt knocked.

A few minutes later, a woman with a messy black bob opened the door. She wiped her hands with a dish towel and slung it on her shoulder. "Hello. Can I help you?"

"Tina Slagle?"

"Yes?"

"I'm Chief Granger." Matt indicated his badge. "This is Detective Delaney. Is your husband home? We'd like to speak with him."

"Actually, he just got back." She opened the door and waved them in. "Come inside."

Hannah offered a small smile. "Back from where?"

"Movie theater. On my days off, I try to give him a few hours of me-time since I'll get mine when everyone else is asleep." She closed the door. "Perry! The police are here." Turning back to them, she said, "May I ask what this is regarding?"

"We're investigating the murders at the school linked to the University Killer," Hannah said as Perry entered the room. "We're examining any possible connections between the victims and trying to eliminate any that we can."

Tina narrowed her eyes. "I don't understand what that has to do with Perry."

"Uh, all the victims had to take my HOPES class," Perry said quickly. "That's all. Nothing to worry about."

"Perry, where were you earlier, between six and seven?" Matt asked.

"Today?" He raised his eyebrows. "I was at the movie theater. Why?"

Hannah flipped to a new page in her notepad. "What did you watch?"

"That silly new action movie," Tina said. "I can't stand the franchise. So Perry always goes without me."

Her husband nodded with a tight grin. "Yeah."

Matt noticed the man wasn't nearly as at ease as he had been at the fitness center, or as talkative. "Were you alone?"

Perry nodded. "Yep."

"Can we see your ticket stub?" Hannah asked.

The guy tipped his head back and to the side. "Uh, you know what? I threw it away with the receipt. After the movie."

A telephone rang in the back of the house. "Elijah! Would you answer that please?"

"Sure, Mom."

Matt smiled. "That's okay. You can pull up your bank account information right now to show us the charge. These days, it pops up like that." He snapped his fingers.

"I can't." Perry stood a little straighter. "I paid in cash."

Tina chuckled. "You never use cash. When did you go to the ATM?"

"Mom, it's the hospital! I think they want you to cover for someone."

Tina sighed. "Excuse me." She left the living room.

Glancing over his shoulder in the direction his wife had gone, Perry stepped closer and then looked at them. "What if I didn't buy the ticket? What if I wasn't alone and I don't want my wife to know?"

"A lot of *if*s." Hannah slid a sideways glance at Matt. "Who were you with?"

"It's a student. I'd rather not say who."

Matt folded his arms. "We need to know so this person can verify your whereabouts."

Perry shook his head. "There has to be another way. Without getting Tina or the student involved in this."

"Unbelievable," Tina said, coming back into the room. "I have to cover for someone. Her boyfriend almost died, and she's an emotional wreck. He's a cop. One of yours, I think." She pointed to Matt. "Apparently, he was poisoned at the hospital, and a woman was murdered." Her eyes got big. "Is that why you're here? Asking where Perry was earlier?"

"We are here to confirm that your husband wasn't involved." Hannah put away her notepad. "Since you can't prove you were at the movies," she said, looking at Perry, "one simple option is to allow us to test your DNA. No one else needs to be involved, and when we speak to the media, we'll be able to say right up front that you aren't a suspect once we have the test results."

Perry glanced at Tina.

His wife shrugged. "Why not? You haven't done anything wrong."

"Sure." Shoulders sagging, he hung his head. "I'll do it."

"Great." Hannah pulled on gloves and opened the vial, and after Perry opened his mouth, she swabbed the inside of his cheek before resealing the swab in the glass tube.

"That's it?" Perry asked.

"That's it," Matt said. "We'll send it off to the lab, and you can get on with your life." For now.

Hannah and Matt left, and they hopped into his truck.

She held up the vial between her fingers. "I've seen perpetrators agree to a DNA test only to run as soon as they're out of our sight. We'll need to get this analyzed as quickly as possible, just in case."

STANDING BY THE large whiteboard at the front of the conference room, Matt was leading the briefing while Hannah sipped on her fifth espresso of the day. He didn't know how she could handle so much caffeine, but she'd shaken off her earlier self-doubt. At least outwardly.

Two of his officers who had worked earlier

in the day had agreed to stay for an extra shift, four more cops were scheduled for the evening and Holden had come through with the sheriff's department, providing three deputies in plainclothes. Nine, not including Hannah and himself, was nowhere near enough, but they'd have to make it work. They had no other choice.

"As you know, Officer Carl Farran has been hospitalized, and Jessica Atkinson, the young woman who was attacked, has been murdered. The ME is examining Atkinson's body to determine the cause of death. Doctors have managed to stabilize Carl and are running blood work on him, but they suspect food poisoning. Detective Delaney and I—" he gestured to Hannah "—reviewed the hospital's security footage, and this is what we found."

Matt played the surveillance video on the screen to the right of the whiteboard.

Everyone watched as the University Killer, wearing a new disguise, walked onto the fourth floor of the hospital, handed Officer Farran a drink and bag of food, and then ducked into an empty room. Minutes later, Carl ran to the bathroom in the hall, and the killer then emerged and entered Atkinson's room, wearing scrubs and a white lab coat, and closed the door.

"He timed this to occur around the shift change for hospital staff. The nurses were unaware of what was happening. Less than one minute later, the killer left Atkinson's room. This leads us to believe he injected a drug in her IV."

Hannah stood and held up a photocopy of the poem. "He left this for us instead of his usual calling card." She handed it to the closest officer. "Take a look at it. He's taunting us, telling us that he plans to take his next victim this weekend, perhaps tonight, mostly likely from a party. We need to show him, even though he has been two steps ahead of us, how good we are at playing catch-up."

The law enforcement officers in the room nodded, giving verbal affirmations.

"Ballistics came back on the bullet the killer fired Tuesday night. We got a print but no match to it. This weekend, starting tonight, is another chance to get him. The sororities aren't hosting any parties," Matt said, "but six fraternities are. I've spoken to the Interfraternity Council, four young men who 'govern' the frats. Although they refused to cancel, they want to be a part of the solution. They've agreed to mandate that each fraternity must have five sober members, keeping a close eye on things. Now, I'm a realist. These are kids, not trained cops. I'm not expecting much, but any extra vigilance on their part is appreciated."

The council had also pledged to find out who was using date-rape drugs and put a stop to it, but

Matt wasn't holding his breath. Instead, he was going to trust Hannah to do as she had promised.

"Okay, now we're going to go over the game plan and where I want everyone stationed along fraternity row. This is going to be a long night. Parties have been known to last until four in the morning." Groans echoed around the room. "Everyone needs to be fully caffeinated and laser focused."

The conference room door opened, and the junior officer working the front desk poked her head in. "Chief! There's a reporter asking for Detective Delaney's side of the story regarding an incident at her house, and she'd like a statement from you about the murder of Jessica Atkinson."

Before he asked the question, he knew the answer. "Who?"

"Erica Egan."

His pulse spiked. "Tell her 'no comment.'"

The duty officer frowned. "Miss Egan told me to tell you that if you responded that way, I should inform you that you'll want to hear her questions to understand in what light her stories will be framed. She has to submit her story within an hour, and she wants you to have the chance to defend yourselves."

Defend? "Give us a minute," he said to the others in the room.

Matt and Hannah left the conference room.

Her phone chimed. She read the text. "Foster

still hasn't gone home yet. Kent has no idea where he could be, but guess what?"

"Tell me."

"Today is trash day for Foster. Kent collected some samples before the waste-management trucks got to it."

"I'll take any good news I can get. I'll ask Logan to get it from Kent. Have the DNA fast-tracked at the DCI."

"But they're notorious for their backlog."

"The governor increased their budget, and DCI recently hired more people so they could handle time-sensitive requests such as this."

"Finally. It's about time. I'll let Kent know." She fired off a quick text to him and shoved her cell phone back in her pocket.

They entered the lobby, where Erica Egan was waiting. The reporter was perfectly groomed, with her hair swept back from her angular face. She wore a low-cut, formfitting sweater the color of ripe mango, tight jeans, high heels and an eager smile.

"How do you know about the incident at Delaney's house?" Matt asked, disgusted.

"Reports of shots fired by the detective during an altercation with two members of the Hellhounds motorcycle club," Egan said, not actually answering the question. "According to the leader of the Hellhounds, Mr. Todd Burk, you instigated the incident after harassing members and trying to coerce them at their clubhouse by issuing unwarranted threats not within your authority. Would you care to give your side of the story?" She shoved a voice recorder forward.

Hannah leaned in, getting her mouth close to the recorder. "No comment. That's Hannah with two h's. Do you need me to spell Delaney for you?" She smiled then, and it wasn't nice.

He hated Egan, but he loved Hannah's style.

The reporter pursed her mouth hard, and lines marred her face. "Don't say I didn't give you an opportunity to set the record straight, Detective."

"'Straight'?" Matt spat the word, full of bitterness. "You slant record, regardless of quotes, and spin stories to influence the public, who you love to claim has a right to know."

"They do." Egan's mouth pressed tight, seemingly offended. "And I'm an objective reporter."

"Cut the bull. All you care about is the number of subscribers."

"My editor cares about subscriber numbers, which have only increased, not only for the paper but online as well since I joined the *Gazette*. Controversy and spice sell, and it keeps getting me bonuses. If you don't like it, take it up with the system." She shoved the recorder in Matt's face. "Chief Granger, would you care to comment on your failure to safeguard Jessica Atkinson, a student who your department was 'protecting'," she said, using air quotes, "and why the University Killer continues to evade capture?"

Matt swallowed the angry words on his tongue. "The University Killer poisoned a police officer, making him violently ill, and murdered a young woman in cold blood. My department, along with Detective Delaney, will not rest until this serial murderer is stopped."

"Is it true that you're unprepared to keep the student body safe during the blitz of rush because you were unaware this is one of the biggest party weekends of the school year?"

He had hoped that Starkey hadn't gone running to the reporter, but her use of the term *blitz*, was making that seem less likely.

"My officers and I are prepared," he said, "and we will be taking added precautions over the next several days."

"Are you saying that no other students will be abducted and murdered this weekend because of the safeguards you're putting in place?" Egan asked.

"I can't get into the specifics of the measures we're taking, but we'll do our best to keep everyone safe."

"Two women slain thus far with you as chief. Do you think your best is good enough? Are you willing to stake your job on it? If the University Killer strikes again and goes quiet once more, should you resign?"

"We're not gamblers," Hannah said acidly. "We're police officers. Don't forget, the University Killer has eluded other campus police chiefs."

"Yes, that's true." Egan gave a sly grin. "But eventually, they all resigned or were fired from the position. I'm merely asking because readers will want to know if it will be resignation or removal for the current chief."

Matt didn't intend for it to be either.

Hannah's mouth tightened, and her eyes were stone cold. "You're assuming it will be one or the other. We're endeavoring, tirelessly, for a different outcome."

"Chief?" Egan's gaze slid over to him. "Care to add to that?"

"My sole focus at this time is on stopping this murderer and bringing him to justice. That's all I have to say."

Egan switched the voice recorder off. Her smile was feline. "Be sure to read my article. It'll be hot off the presses at three a.m."

Based on previous experience and the way Egan had treated his family in the press, nothing she printed would be good for him, Hannah or the university. "I'll be waiting for it, with bated breath, to use it as kindling for a fire."

Chapter Fifteen

Friday, September 20
3:59 a.m.

The night had gone better than he'd planned. *Flawless.* He had never intended to infiltrate a party and take his prize from there.

Sticking to the list meant choosing a birdie who would be predictably at home. And she had been, too. Her roommate was out, no doubt enjoying the festivities of rush. But he had not expected to find another young girl asleep on the sofa. Taking the blonde without waking the other had been impossible.

Complications were always a possibility. Fortunately, he had been prepared, as always.

He squinted as he scanned the headline of the *Laramie Gazette*. He was bone-tired. But sleep wasn't on his agenda anytime soon. Still too much to do before the sun rose, and then he had a full day ahead of him.

Chuckling, he flipped to the next page of the

Gazette. They were the fastest with new stories, so he always started with their paper. The timing had given him the chance to get one, along with a coffee, from the last gas station on his way out of town. He needed to go up to the cabin in the woods and drop off his knocked-out cargo for safekeeping.

He glanced over his shoulder and grinned, his mouth watering in anticipation of the hookup to come.

There was time enough for him to take a break. Enjoy his coffee. See what the lovely Erica Egan had to say about him. Then he'd finish making his way to the woods, only to come right back to town. His busy, busy day was just getting started.

He perused the article, wanting to give that sexy crackerjack of a reporter a kiss. Not only had she covered his handiwork at the hospital so eloquently, but she had also bashed Granger and Delaney with electric writing that carried a powerful punch. He pumped his fist in the air.

Laughing, he couldn't wait for Blondie to take a gander. He'd given her a good blow with his poem, and this article would be a hefty bit of salt in the wound.

He sat a little straighter, invigorated, and stopped reading at the bottom of page four. The article delved into a skirmish outside the detective's house, where she had discharged her weapon at 720 Sagebrush Drive.

His jaw went slack. One didn't see that every day.

A police officer's home address printed in the newspaper! A detective's, no less.

Was this luck or serendipity or karma?

No. It was *fate.* He was becoming a true believer in it.

This presented a new opportunity. He cracked his knuckles, thinking. Debating.

Only a fool would pass up a once-in-a-lifetime opportunity like this. He glanced at the red numbers of the clock on the dash. If he was going to do this, in such an unexpected manner, he needed to hurry, even though he much preferred to take things slowly, drawing out his gratification.

But this would be worth it.

Throwing the gear into Drive, he was set on his chosen course. He pulled out of the gas station parking lot and headed back to town.

Chapter Sixteen

Friday, September 20
6:25 a.m.

Hannah was wiped out and running on fumes. "Thank goodness the night was uneventful," she said as they lumbered back to his office after finishing their after-action debrief with the rest of the officers.

"That we know of." Matt entered his office. "At least on fraternity row."

She followed him inside. "You don't sound pleased by it."

"I am, it's just...when we were out there patrolling, checking on the parties, I kept getting this tingle along my spine. Usually means trouble. Something bad is about to happen."

"No news is good news." They'd even had a couple of security guards posted at the computer lab and rec center as an extra precaution.

"Having the sober brothers circulate the parties turned out to be a good idea by the council.

They kept two girls from getting roofied, and the boys who tried drugging those ladies will face charges." He sat at his desk and turned on his computer. "I need to send an update to Agent Tomlinson about Carl Farran and Jessica Atkinson. Once I'm done, want to grab breakfast?"

"I'm starving." She rolled her shoulders and stretched her neck. "Hash browns, scrambled eggs, bacon and toast would hit the spot. Then I need four hours of sleep. Maybe I can get by on two."

"Sounds good. The part about the food," he said, clacking away on the keyboard. "Why not place an order at Delgado's? Then we won't have to wait for it."

She took out her cell phone and called it in. "It'll be ready in ten minutes. The person who took the order recognized my name and kindly put a rush on it since it was law enforcement."

"Ah, the little perks of the badge."

A giant yawn made Hannah's jaw ache. "I'm tired."

"Me too." Matt was still typing at his computer with a slow, methodical rhythm.

He looked bright eyed and professional and not tired in the least.

A newspaper landed on his desk. The morning duty officer stood, glaring.

"What?" Matt asked.

"You're both in the paper."

"We expected to be," Matt said.

"You won't expect what was printed," the officer said in a singsong voice. "Page four, bottom right."

Matt's face tensed.

Hannah snatched up the paper. For a moment, she wondered what awful things the reporter had written about her, especially if the woman had referred to Todd Burk as *mister*. She flipped to page four, looked down at the paragraph on the right and felt the blood drain from her face.

"How bad is it?" Matt asked.

"Worse," she said, her voice barely a whisper. "Way worse than what you're thinking."

Rage spilled over. She fought the senseless urge to tear the paper into shreds and then go find Egan so she could pummel her into oblivion.

"I want to…" She swallowed the rest of the words: *kill that woman*.

First, her address had been posted on the dark web for every creep and criminal to find. Now, this violation. Making it public knowledge for everyone.

Calmly, Matt took the paper from her clenched hands and read it, but his jaw went tight and his eyes blazed fury. "She needs to be fired."

"The editor signed off on it. Allowed it. Printed it. Because the system sucks." She ran her tongue over her teeth. "The paper will hide behind the

First Amendment. They can even say it was already posted online."

"That was the dark web." His eyes still flickered with anger. "Doesn't give them the right to pull a stunt like this."

"Egan is a menace."

Matt looked back up at her. "I wanted to talk to you about this anyway. Hannah, you can't stay at your place. I was worried before, with your information on the dark web, but this ups the ante. Every scumbag in town will be prowling around your house, waiting for a chance to do only goodness knows what."

"I'll hang a Welcome sign and set up a lemonade stand. Maybe I can make a few extra dollars."

"I'm serious, Hannah. You have to find a new place to live. Today."

"Not that anyone is asking for my opinion," the duty officer said, "but the chief is right. Ms. Egan painted a bull's-eye on you—or rather, your house. You get what I mean."

Matt nodded. "Yeah, we do."

"Got a genie in a bottle who can snap his fingers and make that happen? I can't just find a new place out of thin air that fast."

"You can stay with me until you do."

She grinned. "If this is your sly way of getting me into your bed, cowboy, it won't work."

He frowned. "I have a spare room."

"My job here is done," the duty officer said.

"Thanks for the heads-up," Matt said as the guy left.

"I can't stay with you."

"Why not?"

"It crosses a line. Or *blurs* one." The truth was that if she stayed with him, she'd be tempted to break her own rules: Never sleep with someone she worked with. Never spend the night. Never get personal. No strings. Ever.

She'd already gotten way too personal. And she came dangerously close to kissing him when they'd been at her place, discussing a case and eating pizza. And worse, she had wanted to kiss him. Imagined what his lips would feel like, how he'd hold her. She still did.

Dangerous.

"You've got a choice—my place or my family's ranch," Matt gritted out. He shut off his computer. "Let's pick up breakfast and swing by your house so you can pack a bag. End of discussion."

She shoved to her feet, not wanting to discuss it, knowing deep down that he was right.

Her face ached as she climbed into his truck, but she was careful to make sure Matt didn't see her discomfort. They'd been pretty attached at the hip during this investigation. She'd left her car at her house, and they'd been using his truck, which had sustained minor damage from the Molotov cocktail the bikers had used to draw her out.

After they grabbed their order from Delgado's,

they went straight to her house without bothering to eat. Seeing her address publicized had a way of suppressing her appetite. Must've had the same effect on Matt, because he hadn't reached for the to-go bag on the center console between them.

He pulled up in her drive and parked. "You should follow me in your vehicle. Don't leave it here."

"I guess I need to decide where I'm going." She tipped her head back against the seat. "Are you sure your family wouldn't mind putting me up? I don't want be an imposition."

He frowned, casting his gaze down like that wasn't the choice he was hoping for. "Positive. Plenty of rooms. My aunt and uncle would put you in a separate wing from theirs."

"A *wing*? Is *main house* a euphemism for mansion?"

Clenching his jaw, he flattened his lips.

That underbelly was softer than she'd realized. "Why does your dad sleep in the bunkhouse instead of the main house?"

His fingers tightened on the steering wheel. "Because he's the help. He works there."

"But he's also family, right?"

"It's not what he wants," Matt snapped.

"If you don't want me to go to the Shooting Star, then say so."

"I don't want you to feel like I'm twisting your arm to stay with me. I don't want to make you uncomfortable. The Shooting Star is a good option. It's just…"

"Just what?" Hannah studied his face, trying to understand.

"I hate asking my aunt and uncle for anything. I hate being beholden to anyone. For the job is one thing, calling in a favor to save a life. And I'd do it for you." He glanced over at her. "To make sure you're safe."

Something inside her cringed at putting him in such a position.

"Any man who tries to twist my arm will find it gets broken. And you don't make me uncomfortable." Only nervous. And terrified of making a mistake. "No worries about either. You offered your spare room. I'll kindly take it."

He didn't have to care. He didn't have to offer. But he did. What she wouldn't do in the face of that generosity and selfless kindness was insult him by asking him to call in a favor from his family on her behalf.

They climbed out of the truck and went to her front doorstep. She unlocked the door and stepped into the house. It was chilly inside. Had she forgotten to adjust the thermostat?

"Do you mind if I use the bathroom?" he asked, shutting and locking the door behind him.

"No, go right ahead. I'll throw a few things in a bag."

He headed for the half-bath in the hallway. As

she made her way toward her bedroom, she noticed a draft in the house. Passing the guest room, she rounded the corner to get to her room and stopped.

Her bedroom door was closed. She'd left it open yesterday. She was certain of it.

She drew the service weapon from the holster on her hip. Raising it, she crept down the hall. At the door, she listened. A slight *whoosh, whoosh* whispered on the other side, in the room. She grabbed the knob, twisted slowly, took a breath and threw the door open.

A crisp breeze slapped her in the face, and the curtains rustled from the window, which had been pried open.

In the center of her bed lay a young blond girl, spread eagle, her body bare and pale and bruised, her eyes closed. Ligature marks around her neck. A queen of hearts playing card with the eyes scratched out on her stomach. The decorative quilt had been ripped from the bed and the body on top of disheveled sheets, as though he had raped her here. In Hannah's house. In her bed.

Her skin crawled and her stomach clenched. She leaned back on the doorjamb, looking away from the corpse, her heart lodged in her throat.

Near the front of the house, the toilet flushed.

She took one deep breath, fighting against the shock and horror, the sheer revulsion. And then another.

The bathroom door opened in the hall.

"Matt," she called out, her voice steady but not sounding like her own.

"Yeah?" Footsteps hurried in her direction. "What's wrong?"

He came around the corner, and she stepped aside so that he could see.

"NO SIGHTINGS OF the SUV?" Hannah asked an officer with the Laramie PD over her cell phone.

"We put out a BOLO as soon as you called in the attack on Atkinson. We also went through all the street cameras in your area once we heard about the next victim, but it's limited," he said, and she gritted her teeth at the truth of that statement. Unlike major cities such as New York, Los Angeles and Seattle, which had thousands of traffic cameras, their town and the surrounding area had the bare minimum. "There's no sign of the vehicle. He must know where the cameras are and is deliberately avoiding them."

"Let me know as soon as—"

"Of course, Detective."

"What about the officer cross-referencing the records from the DMV with those of the university?"

"He's creating a list. He worked sixteen hours yesterday and has been back at it since five this morning."

"Okay. Thanks." Hannah disconnected.

The corpse of Kyra Adams being wheeled out of her house in a body bag. She and Matt had found her student ID card on Hannah's bedside table, along with a second one for a Zoey Williams.

They'd stayed at the crime scene for hours, watching bag after bag of evidence collected and removed.

A crime scene. That was exactly what it was now. Not her home, not anymore. The University Killer had taken that away from her. She didn't want the monster to take anything else.

Hannah paced back and forth while Matt was on the phone with the SWUPD. The waiting clawed at her insides.

"Okay. Thanks." Matt disconnected. "Sergeant Lewis finished speaking with Kyra's roommate, who had been out at one of the frat parties all night. They shared a first-floor apartment on campus. Apparently, Kyra and Zoey had been paired in the Student Support program. It's designed to ease the transition of new undergraduates. The system pairs an older second-or third-year student with a new one. Zoey is only sixteen. She graduated from high school early. According to the roommate, Kyra and Zoey really hit off. Kyra got her into a fantasy tabletop role-playing game and would let her sleep over on the couch if they played late so Zoey didn't have to walk back to her dorm alone at night. Zoey is confirmed missing. Cell phones for both girls were discovered in the apartment, along with their wallets."

That poor girl. To be caught in this sick game of cat and mouse that a psychotic killer was playing.

"Why would he take the other girl?" she asked. "She's not his type." From the picture on the student ID, Zoey had deep-olive skin and dark brown hair.

Matt shook his head. "I don't know. Maybe he was desperate. Didn't want to risk having to go through the trouble of kidnapping another girl later with us searching for him. A two-for-one, and he was willing to make do with a brunette."

Another idea came to Hannah. "Or maybe while he was taking Kyra, Zoey woke up and he had to make a choice—kill her there, subdue her or take her—and he preferred option three." She swore under her breath.

"Since he didn't kill her at the apartment, she's probably still alive. There are usually days between the time when he takes them and takes their lives." Matt put a comforting hand to her back, and she moved away from his touch.

She didn't want to be soothed. Holding tight to fury, frustration and control kept her sharp as a switchblade. And kept her from falling apart. "Tell that to Kyra Adams. She died within hours. Because of me. He saw a chance to do this." She pointed at her house. "To rape and murder another woman I failed to protect in my own home."

This was torture. The way he was terrorizing her by using these women like pawns in a game. One designed to hurt her.

Matt stepped around her, and she looked over his shoulder to see why. He was blocking her from the newspaper photographers taking pictures. "This isn't your fault. It's Egan's. If she had never printed your address in the *Gazette*, Kyra Adams might still be alive. Come on. We need to let Forensics analyze the evidence and the ME examine the body. Standing here, giving the papers more fodder when we're exhausted, isn't going to help anything. Or anyone. Least of all Zoey Williams. We need to refuel and recharge. Let me get you out of here, okay?"

He was right. Yet again. The last thing she needed was to be provoked and pushed over the edge to the point where she hit a photographer.

"You lead the way," she said. "I'll follow."

Chapter Seventeen

Friday, September 20
9:30 a.m.

Matt showed Hannah into his house. To call it a *humble abode* would've been accurate. "Look around, and make yourself at home."

She dropped the 'go bag' that she'd taken from her trunk, on the floor near his living room since she couldn't take anything from the crime scene that was at her place and did just that, explored. "Anything off-limits?"

"Nope." He hung up his Stetson.

"Not even the drawers of your nightstand? Trusting me with your wallet is one thing. This could be something else."

A grin pulled at one corner of his mouth. He decided to view her curiosity as interest. "Knock yourself out."

The two-story cabin was simple. The front door opened to a spacious living room, which flowed into a dining room and kitchen. No walls separating the spaces. It was a large, open floor-plan, with the exception of an office, powder room and a little den in the back. Upstairs was his bedroom with en suite. Two more bedrooms shared a Jack and Jill bath.

He'd built it not really thinking about the *why* behind the design. Until Aunt Holly had pointed out it was the perfect layout for a family. Maybe he did have a deep-buried hope—one he'd kept secret even from himself—to one day marry and have kids. Part of him wanted to. He just didn't know how to accept the constant state of vulner-ability having a family would put him in.

All he knew was, this place was his, far from everyone else.

But after what had happened to Hannah, he was reexamining the exposure of this location. The one thing about the Shooting Star Ranch was its high degree of safety. The area with the main house, bunkhouse and where his cousins lived was practically a compound, with security cameras and every ranch hand armed.

No one was able to break in and leave a dead body there.

Out here in the boondocks, isolated and far from the Powells, was another story. His aunt and uncle had cautioned him about the choice. Warning him that the Powells had enemies and, by extension, so did he. Cautioning that a law en-forcement officer would draw even more threats.

At the time, when he'd picked the parcel of land, he'd dismissed their concerns, only focused on his ego. His determination to stand on his own two feet. His need to carve out something separate from them.

There's safety in numbers.

He'd even advised as much to the SAV group, but here, he was not practicing what he preached.

Hannah waltzed down the steps into the kitchen, where he set out the food. "Nice digs. I wonder what the main house looks like."

"Nothing like this."

"I bet." She took off her blazer and tossed it on top of one of the chairs that faced the kitchen island. "Got anything to drink?"

"Where are my manners?" He went to the fridge, opened it and pointed to orange juice, a pitcher of iced tea and beer.

"Anything stronger around here? I need a proper drink."

"I need a shower, and you need food before I show you where I keep the whiskey."

"Pretty certain I could find it if I looked hard enough, but I'd like to get cleaned up, too. So once I'm done with my drink, I can just crash for a couple of hours. Can we both shower at the same time?" she asked. "Any issues with water pressure?"

"None, if we're using the same shower," he said, half joking, half testing.

She gave him a soft smile in response, her gaze not leaving his.

"Beyond that?" He shrugged. "I guess we'll find out. I've never had anyone stay over."

"You? Never?"

"Why so skeptical?

"Have you looked in the mirror, Granger?"

He chuckled. "Sure. But what do you see when you look at me?"

Her smile spread wider, and she averted her eyes. "I expect a tumbler of whiskey waiting by the time I'm done upstairs."

He appreciated a woman who knew what she wanted. "Yes, ma'am."

They both hurried through their showers. To his surprise, his was a pleasant one. The water pressure and temperature had been fine.

When she came down to the kitchen, wearing a tiny pair of shorts that exposed a tempting amount of skin, a tank top—sans bra—and with her hair damp and loose, he had built a fire in the living room and poured a drink for her.

"You clean up good," she said, picking up her glass, and he found it hard not to stare.

He gestured to his lounge pants and T-shirt. "If you say so." Then he poured himself a drink.

She eased closer and leaned against the counter. "I do."

"You never did tell me what you see when you look at me."

"A hot guy." Her eyes heated, and his heart turned over. "Who is overtop in the sex-appeal department."

That was unexpected.

He took a step toward her, testing boundaries. She didn't move away, holding her ground, but he could see her pulse flutter at the hollow of her throat. At her side, her free hand flexed and clenched, and he came to an astonishing realization: he made Hannah Delaney nervous.

"You should eat something. Drinking on an empty stomach can impair your judgment faster and could lead to regrettable consequences."

"I'm not hungry," she said dryly. "At least, not for food." Tipping her head up, she regarded him evenly. "Did you really want me to join you in your shower, or were you playing around?"

The moment stretched as he considered a response. Then he decided actions spoke louder than words. With one last single step, he erased the gap separating them. He slipped his hand around her neck, his fingers sliding up into her hair, and kissed her.

She wrapped her arms around his neck as she lifted onto the balls of her feet and kissed him back.

A shudder ran through him, as much from relief as release. It had been a while since he'd held any woman this way, tasted her lips, soaked in the sweet surrender of her response, and he'd wanted to do this with her for days. Careful of her bruised face, he kept it lighter, more tender than he wanted, much shorter than he wished.

Fighting against the coiled want in his gut, he ended the kiss but kept her close in his arms. "I wasn't sure if you wanted this. You've pulled back from me a couple of times."

She pressed her forehead to his chest, her arms curled around his waist. "Sorry."

The word left her so heavily that he drew back to look down into her face. "Why did you?"

Her gaze lifted, those honey-brown eyes glittering with desire as she smiled at him, a heart-rending curl of her lips. It was like he'd been sucker punched.

"Because I didn't want to be attracted to you, to *want* you. But I am and I do."

Her response was ego-boosting and concerning all at once. "Why didn't you?" he asked.

"There are so many reasons." She sighed. "I don't know where to begin."

He stroked her back. "Start with the easy ones."

"I have rules. No sleeping with a coworker. No spending the night. No strings attached. But I realized that once this case is over—and it *will* end because we're going to catch him," she said, having regained her indomitable, confident balance, "you won't be a coworker. But you seem like the type of man who cares deeply. That you would for a lover, anyway. It would mean waking up in your bed and lots of strings attached, and things would be messy."

Gently, he cupped her chin between his thumb and index finger. "Messy can be worth it. Sort of like the right kind of trouble." He ran his hand over her hair. "You're a good judge of character, because that's exactly how I'll be with you." No supposition. No doubt. Only affirmation. Flings and casual sex never held much appeal for him. "I'm not looking to take the edge off here. When I'm with a woman, I'm with her. In a relationship. I give as much as I take, but I also expect as much as I give."

He didn't know how to be any other way. Once, things had gotten serious for him. His ex had wanted marriage, and the idea had terrified him. He couldn't commit. At the time, he thought he wasn't the marrying kind because of his mother and the damage of her choices. But holding Hannah, he didn't want to let her go. Funny thing was, he felt like he knew her better, trusted her more than he ever had his ex.

Hannah pulled back a bit. "Here goes the not-so-easy part. I'm not a good judge of character. I'm the absolute worst—in my personal life, anyway. And I've been dreading that you're hiding something. That everything I see isn't what I'll get."

In a weird way, she was proving how well she

was able to read him. "I want to work through that. How do we solve it? What do you need from me?"

"Show me yours, and I'll show you mine," she said, and he understood that she meant his soft underbelly. "What's the deal with you and your family? With your father? And the Powells? Why does the subject stress you out and cause you pain?"

This was not a *stand in the kitchen* type of discussion. He grabbed his drink, took her by the hand and led her to the sofa. They sat close, with their thighs touching and her hand on his leg and his palm on her soft, bare knee.

Talking about his family, about the past, wasn't something he did. Easier to keep it locked away. But if he wanted this woman, he'd have to risk the very thing he feared most: being vulnerable.

"My childhood wasn't picture perfect. Things had always been dysfunctional to some extent, with my parents fighting a lot. But my father had been head over heels in love with my mother. No matter the argument or how bad, he made amends, kept the family together, until one day he couldn't. They'd kept the truth from me—that my mom was a gambling addict. She had blown through everything, putting the ranch in so much debt, it was worthless. Then she took off. With another man."

Hannah's eyes softened with pity. "How old were you?"

"Seven. Happened a few days before my eighth birthday." He drew in a deep breath, hating the pain that still surfaced when he thought of it. "Loan sharks showed up. Threatened my father. He offered them the cattle since it was all he had left. They told him that if he didn't get the money to cover my mother's debts, they would kill him and take me as payment. That I'd work for them for the rest of my life. So we left Texas. We ran in the middle of the night. Came here with no place else to go." He took a swallow of his whiskey, embracing the smooth burn down his throat. "My father was a broken man after that, ashamed—a ghost of himself, really." His mother had ripped out his dad's heart and thrown them both away like they were trash. "My aunt Holly took on some of the shame since my mother was not only her sister but also her twin."

"Identical?" she asked.

He gave a curt nod.

"I can't imagine how hard that must've been to be taken in by a woman who looked exactly like the one who abandoned you."

That was it exactly. "Same face. Similar figure. Almost the same voice. But completely different mannerisms and personalities. My mom had been flighty, temperamental, selfish. While Aunt Holly is fierce in her devotion, nurturing, steady, selfless. Her love and affection were a blessing and a curse for that very reason. Made it hard on my dad, too, to be around her. He refused to live in the main house. Grateful that they made him the cattle manager, he chose to live in the bunkhouse, like an employee, and forced me to live with my aunt and uncle in their house, being raised alongside their sons. In a way, he gave me to them and has held himself at a distance ever since."

"How awful." Her voice was thick with sympathy. "Seeing him but not being with him."

"Aunt Holly and Uncle Buck treated me just like I was their son. Anything my cousins got, I got, too. Sometimes they gave me more. Like giving me a parcel of land when only one of their boys will inherit the rest. That's why I'm developing an extra source of revenue—to pay for it in a way." Thinking of how much they'd done for him, given him, made him shake his head with remorse. "I was a fool for not appreciating their love. Instead, I grew up angry and hurt and resentful." If he was honest with himself, he'd admit he was still acting out by choosing to live so far from them.

"I think it's understandable," Hannah said, "considering the circumstances."

"Understandable for a seven-year-old, maybe. Not a teenager. Looking back on it, I regret that I was such a nightmare for them."

"You? I find that hard to believe."

"No, it's true. In high school, I fell in with the

wrong crowd because I was stubborn as a mule and determined to distance myself as much as possible from the Powell boys. They were all into sports. I hung out with the Iron Warriors."

Her brow furrowed. "No way."

"Yep. Probably would have eventually joined the motorcycle gang, but when I was seventeen, I got into a bit of trouble. After an argument with my uncle, I ran off. Met up with some of the Warriors. Decided it was a good idea to get drunk. They ended up trying to rob a strip club while I could barely stand on my two feet. I actually passed out in the middle of it. Anyway, the judge gave me a choice because I didn't have a weapon and my blood alcohol content had been off the charts and he considered me to be a Powell, which meant special treatment. Jail or the military."

"That's why Burk kept calling you *a Powell*," she said.

He nodded. "The rest of them got nine years in prison while I got off scot-free."

"You joined the military. Plenty of soldiers have died serving this country," she said, and he had gotten close himself more times than he cared to remember. "You still paid a price."

Matt didn't see it that way. He recognized the leniency shown and the opportunity he'd been given. "I got a GED and enlisted. The army straightened me out fast. By the time boot camp was done, I was a different person. My aunt and uncle were thrilled. Hopeful. Then Special Forces gave me a purpose that I committed to fully." He drained the last of the whiskey from his glass, surprisingly relieved that he'd finally shared the things he'd had bottled up inside all these years. "What about you? Why is your family your soft spot?"

Hannah didn't pull away or try to hide. She simply held his gaze. "In five words? My father is Edward Ressler."

Ressler? Why was the name so familiar? He'd recently heard it. Then it hit him. "The Neighborhood Killer…is your father?"

With grim eyes, she nodded. "I did have a picture-perfect family. At least, I thought I did. Dinners together every night. Church on Sundays. No fighting. My father was my favorite parent. We'd go hiking and fishing, and he'd take me for ice cream on a Tuesday just because. My mother was the bad guy, the one who made me clean my room and do my homework and criticized me for being a tomboy. My father's only rule, the one thing that he demanded, was that we not disturb him when he was in the garage, working on a project."

It was suddenly clear why her example of how Starkey's wife might not have known he wasn't home had been so specific. "Your father would sneak out, take a car that he had parked down the street and…" He let his voice trail off, not needing to say the words.

Sipping her whiskey, she gave a slow nod. "My father was my hero. I looked up to him. Thought he had a noble job, working for a big security company, keeping people safe. He installed security systems in houses. The same homes he later broke into after casing it and programming a backdoor code, murdering his victims."

"Foster said that you were the one to catch him."

"I went into the garage one day while he was out at work. I wanted to tinker around with his things. Be like him. I dropped something. A screwdriver. It rolled, and when I went to pick it up, I accidentally hit a baseboard that was loose. The piece of wood fell. I was going to fix it, but I saw things that he'd hidden behind it. Strange things. Small bundles of hair tied with red string. Driver's licenses that belonged to women."

"Did you understand what it was?"

"Not really. I mean, I was fourteen. At first, with the hair, I thought he had been sleeping with other women and he had keepsakes from them— but when I found the licenses, I knew something was wrong, that it was bad."

"What did you do?"

"I showed my mother. Explained how and where I found those things. For a long time, she sat at the kitchen table, thinking, staring at the stuff I had shown her. Eventually, she looked up the names on the licenses on the computer. She put it together that they were his victims. Then she packed a quick bag for each of us, grabbed food from the pantry and got me out of the house. We went straight to the police station."

He took her hand in his and held it. "That must've been unbearably hard. Grappling with the truth of what your father really was while dealing with the media frenzy at the same time."

She leaned over, resting her head on his chest, and he wrapped an arm around her. "It was devastating. Can't really explain it. Having my whole world collapse. But I guess you understand. Yours fell apart, too."

"It did but not like yours." There was no competition. He'd gotten lucky while she had gotten a raw deal.

"When we first went to the police, I kept telling myself it was a mistake and there had to be some reasonable explanation. Then they arrested him. I thought—as my life imploded and I discovered that my father, who I had idolized, who I thought I knew, became a devil, the true face of evil—that things couldn't get any worse. But they did. The police found a false-bottom space in the house where he stored sick drawings and kept newspaper clippings about the Neighborhood Killer. He confessed to the authorities. Boasted about what he had done. Told them that pressures of being a perfect father drove him to kill again."

"How could he do that to you?" If he had any love in his heart for her at all? "Did you blame yourself?"

"I did. To be honest, even after counseling, there's a little voice inside me that says if I had never been born, those other women never would've been murdered."

"You aren't responsible for his actions." He gentled his tone. "It wasn't fair for him to make you think otherwise." This explained so much about her: How guarded she was. Why she was always looking for a reason not to trust him. The way she so readily took the blame for things that weren't her fault. "You've saved countless people doing your job."

Atoning. For her father's sins and crimes. That's what she was doing, and his heart broke for her.

"The media claimed we must have known. No one believed that we hadn't. It seemed impossible, inconccivable, to them. Once we started receiving death threats, my mom filed for an emergency divorce. The court granted it with no delay. We moved, went by her maiden name after that. She added the h's to my first name to make it harder for anyone to figure out who I really was and dyed my hair blond." She sank against him, and he held her tighter. "Her health started to fail, and right after I graduated from the police academy, she died of a heart attack."

"I'm so sorry." He ached for her loss, for her grief, for the way she had to hide her identity and the worst experience of her life that had shaped her. "I'm glad you're telling me. Finally sharing it."

Knowing the truth of her past only made him that much more protective of her. Not that she couldn't defend herself—Hannah was a force to be reckoned with—but he wanted to shield her from the University Killer's mind games.

The ordeal with her father would only make her more sensitive to his manipulative tactics.

It made Matt long to show that murderer what ranch justice looked like. Where fiends didn't make it to court and were strung up instead.

But then he reminded himself he was a man of the law.

"I haven't been able to let anyone get too close." Her voice was low yet tense. "Not trusting my own judgment. Always waiting for some horrible reveal. But something about you made me wonder if it might be different with you, if I could understand you better. Do you see why I need to be certain that you aren't hiding something terrible about yourself?"

"Absolutely." He put a knuckle under her chin and tipped her face up to his. "You don't know every detail yet, like I leave the toilet seat up and

I'm a horrible cook and I've got a thing for beautiful women who rescue kittens," he said, and she cracked a sad smile. "Especially if they're in trouble. But you know everything big and important about me."

She pressed a palm to his cheek. "You swear no nasty surprises?" As she studied his face, a slight tremble went through her. "Because if we try to do this and there are, it'll break me."

His heart started pounding slowly in his chest. He couldn't explain it, how close he felt to her, the undeniable connection after only working on a case together twice. But for the first time in his life, he wanted to give himself completely, fully, to this…budding relationship. "I swear. You're safe with me."

Not taking her eyes from his, she slipped her hand to the back of his neck and lowered his mouth to hers. This time the kiss was savage and greedy. Unrestrained.

He wanted her. In his bed. Under him. Over him. Any way that he could get her. But he didn't want to bulldoze her into anything, either, if she needed to take this slowly. Mixing the physical with the emotional. A lot was on the line. He didn't want to blow it by rushing. So he pulled his mouth away.

She moaned, curling her fingers in his hair.

"It's been a long day, almost thirty hours with no sleep," he said, making his voice soothing. "If this is all you want right now, me holding you and kissing you, then I get it. I'm not expecting anything more than this."

Smiling and giving him a sexy, predatory look, she climbed onto his lap, straddling his thighs, and there was no hiding how aroused she made him. He groaned, clamping his hands on her hips.

She gripped the bottom of his tee and lifted it over his head. "Well, I'm expecting more, cowboy." Then she pulled off her tank top, tossing it to the floor, baring her full, exceptional breasts and pert nipples to him. "A lot more." She pressed the softness at the apex of her thighs down against the hard ridge in his pants and rocked her hips, making him throb for her. "And I'm willing to sacrifice sleep to have you. Right. Now."

Chapter Eighteen

Friday, September 20
Noon

Pushing up on her elbow in his bed, her leg draped over his, Hannah grinned down at Matt. "You realize we're going to be wrecks for the rest of the day."

"Complete toast." He lay limp and lax, looking sated, with his arm around her waist, keeping her close. Using his fingers, he drew circles on her hip. "But totally worth it. I didn't know how much I needed this."

She slid her palm up his taut washboard stomach to play in the curls on his chest. "How long has it been for you?" she asked softly.

His gaze flicked up to hers. "Four years."

Her eyebrows shot up. "Holy mackerel, that's a long, long time," she said, and he chuckled. She ran her fingers over his muscles, still exploring the lines and contours and every inch of his skin. "I needed it, too."

She had needed him. More than the physical release. A chance to unburden her secrets. To connect, for once. To enjoy this quiet intimacy that she usually denied herself.

But she kept those thoughts to herself. She wasn't ready to share everything quite yet.

He studied her for a long moment. "You deserve this. To be with someone who wants more than to sleep with you. Who wants to—"

"If you say *take care of* me, I'm going to gag."

His grip on her tightened. "I was going to say *care* for *you*."

And she realized that he did. "While we're working, we have to be just colleagues. Nothing else."

The look he sent her was inscrutable. "Nothing else," he repeated. Then he surprised her by reaching up and kissing her with a fiery hunger that stole her breath.

Fresh waves of desire and need equal in surprise washed over her.

"But later, though," he said, "when we're back in bed, we'll be much more."

She was looking forward to that. Although there was no telling when that would happen.

His cell phone chimed. He reached over. "It's Kent. You haven't responded to his texts."

She swore. "My phone is in the guest room. I should've thought to check it." But she'd been distracted, too busy enjoying Matt Granger and all he had to offer. "What does he say?"

"Foster didn't go back home last night. But he's in class, teaching. Kent has to go home and get some shut-eye. He'll resume watchdog duties this evening."

None of them were machines. She and Matt would probably regret not getting any rest once the adrenaline and endorphins faded.

"How did the handoff go with Logan?" she asked.

"I forgot to mention that my cousin texted while we were waiting for Forensics at your house," he said. "The crime lab at DCI is working on it now."

"Maybe we should hedge our bets. Have someone follow Starkey, too. Just to be sure. The University Killer isn't going to be prowling the parties on frat row tonight or the rest of the weekend."

He nodded. "I think you're right."

"Could you also send one to LPD to help the officer who's going through the DMV records?"

"How about you have your guy come down to the SWUPD?"

She pursed her lips. "Sure."

"We should swing by the ME's office on the way into the station. See if Norris has anything for us."

"Wish we could call the guy."

"Yeah. It'd be nice if he answered instead of

letting it go to voicemail. He must get lonely over there. Forcing folks to show up in person." Matt gave her butt a playful smack. "Come on."

MATT AND HANNAH found the medical examiner, suited up, over the body of Kyra Adams in the morgue.

"Hope you don't mind us popping in," Matt said, to be courteous.

Roger Norris always sent an email when he was ready for a visit. But Matt doubted the ME minded.

"Not at all." Norris waved them closer. Behind his forensic goggles, his green eyes were cool and hard. The ME was sharp, efficient and affable.

Matt only wished the guy would pick up the phone more often.

Music was playing; Norris rarely worked without it. Rather than listen to something somber and expected for work that required an admirable constitution, the bluesy, hard rock sound of Aerosmith came from the speakers.

"Here's what I know so far. She was nineteen. Best I can tell, five-three, five-four. Cause of death is the same as the other University Killer victims, except for Jessica Atkinson—strangulation. She was raped," Norris said.

Hannah shifted uncomfortably beside Matt. He didn't want to imagine what was going through her head. He only hoped she wasn't blaming herself.

"No signs of a struggle," Norris continued, "which would indicate she was heavily drugged and unconscious during the sexual assault and when she was murdered. I've ordered a tox screen. But my guess is, he used his preferred drug of choice, GHB, again. Like he did on Atkinson, with hers being the only lethal dose thus far. We'll know for certain soon enough. There are no secondary wounds or injuries."

Matt's phone rang. He pulled it from his jacket pocket. The weather had dropped about ten degrees, and he'd opted for a leather one. "Granger."

"Hey, Chief, it's Sergeant Lewis."

"Yeah, what's up? I'm at the morgue right now with Detective Delaney."

"Two things. First, the hospital called regarding Carl. He was poisoned with tetrahydrozoline hydrochloride."

"Tetrahydrozo-what?"

"Tetrahydrozoline hydrochloride?" Norris asked, looking up at him, and Matt nodded. "Eye drops. A common decongestant, like Visine or Clear Eyes."

"Did they say anything else?" Matt asked Lewis.

"His drink was spiked with a low dose."

"Could a higher dosage have killed him?"

"I don't know," Lewis said. "I didn't ask."

"Sure could," Norris said. "You know, there have been some recent cases in other parts of the

country where a couple of medical profession-
als used it to off their spouses. A nurse and an
EMT. Both caught. Tetrahydrozoline could also
give someone seizures or put them in a coma."

Good thing they were here with Norris.

"What was the second thing?" Matt asked Sergeant Lewis.

"We received a suspicious delivery a few minutes ago. You and Detective Delaney should get
back to the station as soon as possible."

Not only did a prickle flare down Matt's spine,
but his skin also began to tingle. "We'll be right
there."

Hannah was staring at him. "What is it?"

"Nothing good." Of that, he was certain.

SHOVING THROUGH THE front door of the SWUPD,
Hannah was right behind Matt.

The duty officer stood. "Sergeant Lewis is
waiting for you both in your office with the delivery, and an LPD officer is in the conference
room with Farran, going through DMV records
and the names of university personnel."

"Carl was released from the hospital?" Matt
asked.

"They only kept him overnight. He came in.
Says he feels awful about slipping up and wanted
to get back to work."

With a nod, Matt said, "Thanks. I need to
check on him when I get a moment."

They passed the front desk and headed back. Dennis Hill hopped up from his desk and hurried after them in the hallway.

"Whatever it is, can it wait?" Matt asked.

"I wish it could, but I held off yesterday."

Tension radiated off Matt. "What is it?"

"The bicycle-registration system is down. We can't print any new stickers."

"Students will simply have to wait," Matt snapped.

"You go through the effort of registering bicycles?" Hannah asked. She thought they would have their hands full with other things.

"Yes, we do," Dennis said.

Matt grunted. "Part of the job."

"Many bikes look alike, but identifying one with its serial number is the best way to protect property," Dennis said. "Speaking of which, we can't recover any lost or stolen bikes, either, because we can't access the serial numbers. Sergeant Starkey was working on getting the problem fixed until he left."

A groan rumbled from Matt. "I'll put Lewis on it."

"Thank you." Dennis turned around and went back down the hall.

Entering his office, Hannah spotted the delivery on his desk.

"What's urgent about a box of doughnuts from

the Wheatgrass Café?" Matt asked, taking off his hat.

"No one here at the department ordered it," Lewis said, standing in front of the desk. "I questioned the delivery boy. He said that a man came in first thing this morning right as they opened. Placed the order, specified the time of delivery as three thirty-three and told them to include a thank-you card, which he provided."

"Why was the delivery early?" Matt asked.

"There was a lull in customers at the café. The manager told the kid better early than late."

"Did you get a description of the man?" Hannah asked.

"Yeah," Lewis said. "White. Five-ten, five-eleven. Brown hair. Dark brown beard. Baseball cap. Thinks maybe he had a Southern accent. Possibly Texan."

"Sounds like our guy, wearing the same disguise from the hospital," Hannah said.

Lewis nodded. "That's what I thought. When I opened the box, this was inside with the doughnuts." Wearing latex gloves, he handed over a small white envelope with the same dimensions as the one left on Jessica Atkinson's body.

"Oh my God," Hannah said. "It has my name written on it, and this time it's sealed.

Matt moved closer to her. "He wanted to make sure you were the one to open it."

Hannah straightened her spine, bracing for

whatever tercet waited inside for her. Turning to the box of gloves, she grabbed some and handed a set to Matt. They both tugged on a pair.

She took the envelope, gingerly opened it and took out the card. Looking over her shoulder, Matt read the typewritten note along with her.

TO SAVE ZOEY WILLIAMS AND HAVE HER RETURNED UNHARMED,
    MEET ME AT THE ETERNAL HOPE CEMETERY BY THE OBELISK TO-NIGHT.
    7 PM. COME ALONE. OR THERE WILL BE CONSEQUENCES.

MATT CLENCHED A hand at his side. This madman was getting more and more personal with Hannah, dragging her deeper into his twisted games.

"Where is the Eternal Hope Cemetery?" she asked.

"Here," Lewis said. "In the middle of campus."

Confusion darkened her eyes. "Why would they build a graveyard in the center of a university? It's a bit somber for a college setting."

The explanation was a long story, which Matt had learned shortly after taking the job. "The graves were here first. When they decided to build the university, they relocated the bodies. As the school expanded, the graves were moved a second time to what is now the Eternal Hope

Cemetery. Deals were made with the town to keep building the university grounds, eventually around it."

"Any significance to the obelisk?" she asked.

Matt shrugged.

"I think the monument is dedicated to young villagers who had died in a skirmish in the late 1800s," Lewis said. "It symbolizes lives cut short."

"Where is it located in the cemetery?" she asked.

"At the center," Lewis said. "Can't miss it."

Matt shook his head. "No, you can't possibly be thinking about doing this."

"He's offered to return the girl unharmed."

"Sergeant Lewis, would you excuse us? And get with Dennis about the bike-registration-system malfunction."

The officer left, shutting the door behind him.

"You can't possibly think he'd simply give her back."

"She's not his type. He wasn't expecting her to be there. But it gives him an opportunity to use that as leverage."

"To what end, huh? Just to meet you?" He shook his head. "I don't think so. There's more to it than that, and you know it."

Looking in her eyes, he could see that she did and simply wasn't concerned with the risk to herself.

"And why at seven when it's still light out?"

Sunset wasn't until seven thirty, and the cemetery was a stone's throw from the quad. That early in the evening, the campus would have lots of activity, students walking about, though not through the cemetery. Most steered clear of it because of the ghost stories. "Why not at midnight? I don't like this. Not one little bit."

"Doing this is risky, yes, but if we have a chance to save an innocent girl's life, then we have to take it. *I* have to take it. Or I'd never be able to live with myself if something happens to her when I could've stopped it."

"Regardless of what happens to you?"

"Yes," she said, far too easily, like her life didn't matter.

He understood necessary sacrifice better than most, and this wasn't it.

The familiar prickle that warned him of trouble was now flaring hot. Felt like a live wire being raked down his spine. The last time the feeling had been this strong, his team had walked into an ambush, and he'd lost two buddies.

"This man is baiting you," he said, trying to get reason to sink in for her. "Using your guilt and compassion against you. It's some kind of a trap."

"Of course it is. But there's no other choice if we want to save Zoey."

"He's not going to give up something for nothing in return."

"A face-to-face with me is not nothing," she

said, refusing to back down. "You agreed to do this my way."

"But I didn't sign up to let you go kamikaze."

She heaved a breath like he was the one not understanding. "Step away from this case for a second and look at it in a different context. Have you considered that as we get closer to any moment of huge import—huge impact, huge challenge—that human nature tempts us to turn away from it? Sometimes that instinct serves us. But sometimes it's trying to protect what doesn't need protecting and instead is stopping us from taking that very risk we absolutely need to take."

Her point wasn't lost on him. In fact, there had been times in the military before embarking on a dangerous mission where it was easier to focus on why they shouldn't do it rather than why they had to. But she couldn't ignore how her instincts and choices were skewed, because they were going up against a monster that had been like her father. "I agree, but not about this. *You need protecting* when it comes to this guy."

If only she could see how her past made her more vulnerable.

"Why, because we slept together?" She put her fists on her hips. "Great sex isn't going to stop me from doing my job."

The barb stung. It had been more than sex to him. This was the start of something special between them that he didn't want to lose, even if it didn't mean the same to her. "I would never get in the way of you doing your job."

"If this guy wants to meet me in exchange for returning Zoey, then guess what? I. Will. Meet. Him. Getting her back alive is all that matters."

No, Hannah mattered, too. Every life did. But she was sharp and gutsy and made a difference in the world. He wasn't going to let anything happen to her.

"Fine. You'll go," he conceded. "But only over my dead body will you do it alone." His tone brooked no argument.

He would take every precaution conceivable to ensure her safety.

HANNAH WALKED DOWN the road that ran through the middle of the cemetery, the Avenue of Flags. At the center of the graveyard stood the obelisk, pointed toward the sky. It was quiet. No one was around except for the six officers in plainclothes, including Matt and Kent. Everyone had been given a section to cover. Since they had gotten Foster's DNA, Matt wanted to use Kent for this meetup.

The older detective was in his car, parked on the south side of the cemetery. Another officer was parked on the north end. Matt was concerned the University Killer would somehow lure Hannah to a vehicle, manage to get her in and take off. He was so worried, he'd insisted that she wear a GPS tracker.

No such thing as too careful.

At two inches in length by one inch in width and half an inch in height, the GPS tracker was smaller than a tape measure and fit tucked into her D-cup bra.

"I'm in position," she said into the two-way comms device in her ear concealed by her hair.

"I've got eyes on you," Matt said, his voice steady and husky.

She didn't know his exact location. Only that he had taken a discreet position behind a tree and was watching her through binoculars.

Part of her regretted telling him that it had only been sex for her and nothing more. The idea that their intimacy would change their working relationship had scared her, but she hadn't meant to hurt him. The other part of her understood Matt was a modern-day warrior. A natural protector. His instincts to safeguard someone he cared for would only be amplified, and the only way to prevent it would've been never to sleep with him.

There was no undoing it. Not that she wanted to.

Looking around, she spotted Sergeant Lewis dressed as a groundskeeper, pushing a wheelbarrow. Two more SWUPD officers, making up the rest of the team inside the cemetery, she couldn't see, which was a good thing.

Glancing at her watch, she checked the time. "It's four minutes past seven. Where is he?"

"Patience. He's out there somewhere."

A cell phone rang. But it wasn't hers.

Pivoting on her heel, she followed the sound. There was a burner phone at the base of the obelisk. Warily, she bent down and picked it up. The caller ID stated *Private*. She answered, "Hello?"

"Detective Delaney, how good of you to show up." The voice wasn't as deep as she had expected but was the same as the guy from Tuesday night. Slight Texan accent, barely perceptible.

"Where are you? I thought you wanted to meet."

"I wanted to send you proof of life first. Give me the number to your private cell phone."

"Why do you want my personal number? Send the proof to the burner phone you left."

"Don't give him your number," Matt said softly in her other ear.

"My game," the killer said. "My rules. Unless you don't want proof that Zoey is alive."

"No, I do." Hannah gave him her private number.

Seconds later, her cell phone chimed. A picture of the college student came through. She was seated in the front seat of a vehicle, sunlight filtering in through the window, trees behind her. The girl was dressed in a pin-striped pajama-shorts set that had strawberries on it. Tears filled her eyes. Her wrists and ankles were bound.

"See? She's fine. Not a scratch on her."

"I'd like to see her. In person. Why don't we finish this conversation in person? Isn't that what you want?"

"It is what I want. You were so, *so* close to setting sweet Zoey free," he said, and she cringed on the inside. "But you've hurt my feelings."

"What? How?"

"You're trying to trick me. Like I'm a fool playing your game and not the other way around. But I expected this from you, Hannah. Because you're deceitful and wicked."

"No, I'm not."

"Yes! You are. And now there must be consequences."

"I'm sorry. Please don't hurt Zoey."

"You're not sorry. Not yet. But you will be once you realize the unnecessary suffering you've caused." He disconnected.

No. What have I done? What will happen to Zoey?

There was no callback number. Still, she clicked on *Private*, trying to dial him back, and received a *not in service* message. Her gut twisted.

A gunshot cracked the air, making her flinch. The impact of the bullet spun Lewis forty-five degrees before he fell. Hannah drew her weapon as she spotted Matt lunge from his position, headed straight for her in a dead sprint.

No, no, no.

Another round whined in, this time hitting Matt, and Hannah's blood went cold.

Chapter Nineteen

Friday, September 20
7:40 p.m.

The EMT finished bandaging Matt's left arm in the back of the ambulance. "You're very lucky," she said. "The bullet went straight through the muscle. Didn't hit bone. Didn't nick an artery. No fragments left behind."

If only his other officers had been so lucky. Everyone in the cemetery hit had been shot except for Hannah. The murderer hadn't turned his sniper sights on her when he could've easily killed her. Kent and the officer parked on the north side of the graveyard had had their tires and windshields blown out, nothing more.

"Thanks," Matt said to the EMT, then climbed out of the ambulance.

As soon as his feet hit the ground, Hannah's gaze found his. The worry in her eyes was clear and unmistakable.

She was talking to Kent, who was wearing a

Kevlar vest. The two headed in Matt's direction, and he met them halfway.

"I'm glad you're all right," Hannah said, her voice soft and somber, and he could tell that she wanted to say more. But she glanced at Kent and took a deep breath. "Your three officers who were taken to the university hospital are going to be okay. Lewis was struck in the shoulder, the other two in the foot and hand."

Matt gritted his teeth, hating that his people had been injured and were in pain but also grateful that they were alive.

"Looking around, the only good sniper vantage from any of the surrounding buildings," she continued, "was the roof of the Animal Science facility and the Sweetwater Recreation Center."

"Laramie PD officers are checking out both now," Kent said, "since most of your guys are out of commission."

Matt shook his head. "This is on me."

"No, it's not," Hannah said. "The note was addressed to me. He gave explicit instructions that I was to come alone and if I didn't, there would be consequences." She was radiating more than anger, something like thundering self-blame. Her expression loosened for only a split second, but he saw what was beneath, how badly she hurt. "Now those men are in the hospital, and Zoey is still out there, trapped with monster."

The sharp-edged rage inside Matt shifted as he

realized that he had been so focused on protecting Hannah that he had forgotten to watch out for the rest of his team. "I knew this was some kind of trap or an ambush. I felt it in my bones."

"I wish someone would've given me the heads-up about that," Kent said dryly. "I would've brought my ballistic helmet."

Preparing for something like this used to be Matt's specialty. This failure rested squarely on him. "The cemetery was the perfect location for it. With him having the advantage of the high ground, perched on a rooftop, sighting through his scope, he could not only see all of us but reach out and touch us, too. Pick us off one by one."

"He's got to be a deadeye to shoot like that," Kent said. "Probably a proficient hunter or someone with tactical training."

"Might not be tactical training," Hannah said. "Aren't there a few places within a two to four-hour drive that offer long-range precision-rifle training?"

Kent nodded. "I can think of three. But they're not cheap, if someone wants to learn how to shoot farther than, say, six hundred yards. People spend six to seven grand a day on that kind of training. Won't be paid for in cash, either."

"So they won't be able to give us the runaround about not having records," Hannah said.

Kent tapped his nose with his finger. "They're closed now, but I can make some calls. See if anyone with a university affiliation has been through over the years. I might have to pay them an actual visit to get any real traction."

Matt's phone pinged with an incoming text. "I emailed Agent Nancy Tomlinson about what happened while I was getting my arm bandaged."

"That's the finest example of multitasking that I've ever heard of," Kent said.

"She wants a virtual meeting ASAP. She's emailing a link." The SWUPD had a secure video–telephone software program that was shared throughout the federal government. "She wants to know how quickly we can get started."

Hannah turned to Kent. "Will you take the lead with the LPD cops checking out the rooftops and forensics here?"

"Sure. I can handle it."

Her gaze flicked back to Matt. "Tell Tomlinson ten minutes."

On the walk back to his truck, he sent the text.

Once they reached his vehicle, she held out her hand. "Give me your keys."

"I'm okay to drive."

"Keys," she repeated, her voice firm.

He dropped the keys in her palm.

They climbed into his truck and took off. She switched on the red and blue flashing lights, which gave her the liberty to speed toward the SWUPD while he was seated in the passenger's seat. A first for him. And he didn't like it. But this didn't seem like an issue worth fighting over. Not after the tragic events of the night.

Hannah's mouth was set, her full lips compressed into a thin line of displeasure.

"Something you want to share?" he asked.

"You don't want to know."

Whenever she said that, he'd learned she was right. He probably didn't want to hear what was on her mind. Still… "Just spit it out."

"You were a fool out there," she snapped.

"Come again?" He had been foolish for not doing proper reconnaissance and anticipating a sneak attack, but he didn't expect her to say it, especially not after he'd been shot.

"Running toward me to protect me while a killer is taking potshots with a sniper rifle. *Foolish*. You know better. You're smarter than that. You should've been taking cover. Not further exposing yourself. Did you think my training wouldn't kick in? Did you assume I'd freeze and need you? You didn't charge toward anyone else, hell-bent on saving them. Only me. Yet I didn't get shot."

He exhaled relief over the fact that she was all right. "No, you didn't." He would've preferred to be the one to take the bullet if it meant she didn't have to endure the pain.

"If I had known that you would've acted with such disregard for yourself or that those officers would've gotten shot, I never would have listened to you. I would've gone alone."

"And that would have been a mistake."

"Tell that to the wives and children of your officers who are in the hospital." She whipped the truck into the garage, parked in the spot reserved for the chief and cut the engine. "I told you, when we're outside of the bedroom, we had to be colleagues only. Strictly business. You pretended like you got it. Like you were on board. You lied! I don't want you risking your life for me. I don't need you to do that. I don't need you at all." She reached for the door handle.

"Hold on." He grabbed her wrist, stopping her, and gasped from the lightning bolt of agony that sliced through his bicep.

She winced as though she'd been the one to feel the pain.

"I messed up." On multiple levels. "I did make a promise that I failed to keep. When the gunfire started, the line between colleague and someone I care for evaporated. I've never done this before. It's harder than I expected."

"That's why I don't sleep with people I work with. This was a mistake." In the light from the garage filtering into the truck, her eyes turned impenetrable. "Maybe after this case, we can reassess."

Mistake? Maybe reassess?

He reached over with his good arm, slipping

his hand around the back of her neck, brought her mouth to his and kissed her. Deeply. Until the tension drained from her and she softened against him. "I'm not running scared because I was shot. This—whatever it is—brewing between us is not a mistake. It's the first thing in my life that has felt right. Good. I don't need to reassess. Time is precious. People I care about have been ripped from my life without warning. Because they left or they were killed. I could've died today. We both could've but didn't. The fact that we're still breathing, not hospitalized, is a gift. We can't squander that. I don't want to waste one minute that I could be with you being apart instead."

Tears sprang to her eyes, and a shuddering breath left her lips. "I don't want you to die because of me."

"Well, me neither."

A hiccupping laugh came from her, and tears rolled down her cheeks. She wrapped her arms around his neck and tugged him close. "I just don't want anything to happen to you."

"Ditto. I don't want anything to happen to you, either." He pulled back. "No more talk about mistakes and reassessments. Let's just focus all our energy on catching this guy. Okay?"

Wiping the tears from her face, she nodded. "Yeah."

"You didn't mean it when you said that you don't need me, did you?"

She gave him a sad smile. "I don't want to need you. Because losing you would hurt too much."

He caressed her cheek and kissed her lips.

"Enough," she said, regaining her composure. "Agent Tomlinson is probably waiting by now."

She was right.

They hopped out, rushed into the building and hurried to his office.

He logged into his computer and clicked the link, dialing into the secure video conference. Hannah pulled up a chair and sat beside him.

A silver-haired woman with smooth ebony skin appeared on the screen. "Hello, Chief Granger and Detective Delaney."

"Agent Tomlinson," Matt said, "it's good to put a face with the name. Thank you for this virtual meeting. I'm glad you happened to still be at work."

"I'm always in the office. I keep promising my husband that I'll slow down so we can enjoy our golden years, but whenever I try, a pressing case finds its way to me. I wish I could've set up this virtual meeting sooner. The more information I receive from you, the clearer the picture. I appreciate the timely updates. Things have escalated far quicker than anything I've experienced in the past."

Hannah leaned forward. "What does that mean?"

"The problem is two-fold. Detective, you interrupted the UNSUB," Agent Tomlinson said, referring to the unidentified suspect, "during his ritualistic process. This has probably never happened to him before, angering and frustrating him. A major blow to his ego. Couple that with the fact that you look like his ideal victim. It's not only alluring to him but also quite vexing in a complex way. Based on everything that you have passed along to me, Chief Granger, I believe the University Killer has developed a fixation on you, Detective. A very dangerous one that he will go to extreme lengths to see satisfied."

Matt clenched his hand. "When you say satisfied, what do you mean?"

"Are you saying that he wants to kill me?" Hannah asked.

"Your death is no longer enough for him," Agent Tomlinson said grimly. "I wasn't certain of that until the unfortunate events of tonight occurred. But now I am. He wants to *eliminate* you in the same manner that he would one of his normal victims."

Disgust roiled Matt's gut. He was never going to let that happen. "We need more information in order to stop him. Why is he only taking his victims from campus? With the attention from law enforcement, wouldn't it be easier for him if he expanded his hunting ground?"

"Easier? Certainly," Agent Tomlinson said. "But he isn't interested in easy. He's interested in besting you. The campus is a place that he loves, enjoys, that makes him feel safe. He's definitely someone affiliated with the university."

"Every time we get a description of him," Hannah said, "he changes his disguise."

"This man is a master at deception. I believe he goes so far as to wear a mask on a daily basis. And I don't mean literally with a physical disguise. I mean not showing his true persona at work or even at home. It's only when he is dominating his victims in his environment, in his lair, that he lets his true self show."

How were they supposed to know what to look for? Matt shook his head in frustration. "You're saying if our killer quacks like a duck and walks like a duck, he might not be a duck."

"As confusing as that may sound," Tomlinson said, "yes."

"Have you found any clues or developed any theories about who he could be?" Hannah asked.

"After what the UNSUB did at the hospital, poisoning Officer—" Tomlinson glanced at her notes "—Farran and then killing Ms. Atkinson without violating her, I had a suspicion. However, it wasn't strong enough to share yet. Although tonight's events have convinced me of my theory."

The back of Matt's neck tingled. An itching prickle that made him rub at it. "Which is what?"

"He is someone who has a love–hate relationship with authority. Specifically with the police.

He could have used a lethal dosage of tetrahydrozoline hydrochloride, killing Farran. At the time, I realized it was also entirely possible that he may have guessed how much to use. That's why I kept my theory quiet. But tonight, he had your officers in his crosshairs. He made a choice not to kill any of you. The fact that he only inflicted relatively minor wounds was deliberate."

Matt had wondered about that, if the fact that they had been moving targets had thrown off the killer's aim. "But why, when he could have killed us?"

"I understand it may be hard to reconcile why, in your eyes, a cold-blooded monster who would take the lives of defenseless, innocent young women and not yours. There is a myth that serial killers don't love or care about others. The reality is that some of them often show loving and protective behavior over their own families and those in their inner circle even as they are slaughtering the children of others."

Hannah tensed, clasping her hands in her lap.

Matt knew that must be difficult for her to hear and wished the trauma of her past hadn't resurfaced, but he also knew it was impossible for her not to think of her father.

"That doesn't explain why he didn't kill us," Matt pointed out.

"But it does," Agent Tomlinson said. "You spare that which you care about, even if a part of you also holds it in contempt. His rage and disdain for the police—for the campus police, in particular—is exercised through his killings. Then the question becomes, how do you come to care about something, or someone, you despise? By being in close proximity. By pretending to care on a regular basis until he actually does on some level."

Hannah glanced at Matt before turning back to the screen. "Could it be a police officer? One high up in the ranks, who has been passed over for promotion to chief three times? Even if he passed a polygraph?"

"Most definitely," Agent Tomlinson said with a nod. "Sometimes serial killers are able to pass a polygraph because they don't view the world, the truth, the same way."

Hannah's phone chimed. She read the text. "It's Kent. Excuse me a minute." She got up and hurried out of the room, disappearing down the hall.

"That brings me to something else," Agent Tomlinson said. "Your guy has an obsessive compulsion around the number three. He's exhibited this in the timing of his kills, the number of his victims. Only choosing months that have exactly thirty days," she said, which was something Matt hadn't realized. "Asking for the doughnuts to be delivered at three thirty-three precisely. But I also strongly believe this will be exhibited in his personal life. Once you pinpoint the right man, it will become obvious on paper. He might have three cars. Three kids. Will use the number three in some deeply personal way that might not seem obvious at first glance."

"Thank you, Agent Tomlinson."

"Wait, wait, there's more. It's about his victims. His choice, blond and petite, is probably related to his mother, who was most likely an authoritarian figure for him. I suspect he tried to reconcile that in his dating life by choosing blondes. Then some woman—a girlfriend, between the ages of eighteen and twenty-one—hurt him, wounded his pride or ego in some way, and she was his first victim. It would explain why he didn't use a condom with his initial kill. He knew her. Violating her was his way of payback, and strangulation is a passionate, personal act. After that, he needed two more victims to fulfill his obsessive compulsion. And for him, there was no reason to use a condom at that point, since he'd already left his DNA on the first body. Look for a personal connection between him and the first victim. That link might not have been evident when he killed her. It's probably the reason he wasn't caught. You might have to go back three months, maybe even three years, from the time of her death to find the connection."

A spark of hope flared in him. "We'll go back over everything related to the first victim."

"Oh, I wish Detective Delaney hadn't left."

"Why?"

"Because I'm concerned for her welfare. Not only does she resemble the type of young woman he goes after and she interfered with his ritual, but she is also an authority figure. This makes her irresistible to him. Then there's the way he violated the sanctity of her home by taking his latest victim there. Raping the girl on the detective's bed," the agent said with a horrified look, "and then murdering her is alarming. Even more so was his elaborate ruse at the cemetery. It was a game. One specifically designed for Detective Delaney to fail."

"I don't understand. You mean he knew that she wouldn't go alone," he said, and as the words left his mouth, a chill snaked down his spine. Of course that monster had known. Otherwise, he wouldn't have been set up on the roof, already in position, waiting. "But why would he want her to fail? He wants to get up close and personal with her, and that was his chance."

"Once again, the answer is two-fold. He expected you and the other officers to be there. By shooting you, he effectively removed her protectors from the gameboard. Isolating her. Then she assumes the failure. The guilt. The responsibility. Not only for the lives of the officers but also for Zoey Williams. He wanted her to fail so that he could give her a chance to atone. To play his game on his terms. I believe Detective Delaney is in grave danger."

Chapter Twenty

Friday, September 20
7:55 p.m.
Ten minutes earlier

"Could it be a police officer?" Hannah asked Agent Tomlinson. "One high up in the ranks, who has been passed over for promotion to chief three times? Even if he passed a polygraph?"

"Most definitely." The senior agent nodded. "Sometimes serial killers are able to pass a polygraph because they don't view the world, the truth, the same way."

Hannah's phone chimed with a text. She glanced down and read it.

Say nothing to Chief Granger or anyone else about this or he dies. I swear it. Leave the SWUPD. Wait for my call. You have thirty seconds.

Her heart squeezed with terror. Pure fear for Matt. "It's Kent. Excuse me a minute." Not daring to look at him and give anything away in her eyes, she got up and hurried out of the room.

Once she had cleared the office, certain Matt couldn't see her, she ran down the hall, past the reception desk, ignoring the duty officer's quizzical stare, and shoved through the doors.

Her phone rang.

"I'm out of the SWUPD," she answered.

"Sixteen-year-old Zoey could still have a bright future. But that depends on what you do next. Do you want to save her?"

"Yes," she said without hesitation.

"Take off your badge and gun. Put both on the ground. If you don't, I'll know."

Glancing around the parking garage, she wondered if he was there, watching her. Hidden in one of the parked vehicles. The two entrances to the garage gave him a second exit so he wouldn't be boxed in. But there were cameras in here.

Instinct had her turning, looking beyond the garage. From where she stood, she could see the street and several parked vehicles. Which meant someone inside of one could also see her.

"Do it," he said, "or the kid will die screaming."

The last time she hadn't followed his rules, four men were shot, including Matt, and Zoey wasn't rescued. The only choice she had was compliance.

She did as he instructed, unhooking her badge

and service weapon and then setting them both on the ground.

"Good girl," he said, like she was a dog. "Now, I want you to run to Millstone Cemetery. It's 1.3 miles away. Once you're off campus, take Fifth Street headed west, not Grand Avenue. You have nine minutes, thirty-three seconds to be there, or Zoey dies. Leave your phone. Your time starts now. Run!"

Hannah dropped her phone, pulled Matt's keys from her pocket, letting them fall, and then her legs were moving, pumping as they propelled her through the parking garage. She darted down the road, skirting Fourth Street as she made her way off campus. Taking a right onto Eagle Avenue, she went in the opposite direction of Grand Avenue. She bolted down the sidewalk, her arms pumping, her heart hammering.

Hurry.

Faster.

You have to run faster!

An avid jogger, she was not a sprinter. A ten-minute mile was good for her. Nine was possible. But making it to the cemetery, 1.3 miles away, in less than ten would take everything she had.

The small GPS tracker still tucked in her bra rubbed her skin with each brutal stride she took. In the aftermath of the shooting, she hadn't thought to remove it in the whirlwind of cries, blood, the sirens and then there was Tomlinson's urgent request for a video conference.

Matt would be furious with her for taking off without him. But now she was in the crosshairs alone instead of him being in harm's way. He'd remember the tracker and could find her once she saved Zoey. She didn't care what happened to herself, so long as that young woman survived.

She reached the cross streets of Eagle and Fifth and tore around the corner. Racing down the sidewalk, she dodged pedestrians and darted through traffic, not even slowing for moving cars.

Her lungs were on fire. She could barely breathe. But the one thing that mattered, the only thing, was getting to Millstone in time.

She'd failed Zoey once. Not again.

Hannah's legs were noodles, but a steely determination drove her. The cool night breeze nipped her lungs. Sweat beaded her forehead. Her heart swelled at the sight of Millstone just up ahead.

She dashed across the last street, reaching the sidewalk in front of the cemetery, and suddenly, her legs gave up, bringing her to a teetering halt on the edge of the pavement. She took huge swallows of air, trying desperately to catch her breath and steady her pulse.

A cell phone rang somewhere in the graveyard. She ran inside, down the center lane, searching for the source of the sound, desperate to find it before it stopped.

There!

On top of a headstone was a cell phone. And a capped syringe.

Her mouth went dry, but she grabbed the phone. "Hello?"

"Good girl. You made it with three seconds to spare. I like that. Shows you're committed."

"Where's Zoey?"

"Not so fast. Saving her comes at a price."

She took several more ragged breaths, preparing herself, bracing. "I'll pay it."

"I know," he said, and she could swear she heard him smiling. "A life for a life. Yours for Zoey's. Pick up the syringe, remove the cap, insert the needle in your neck and depress the plunger fully."

Her heart turned to a block of ice.

"I'm watching you very closely. If you try anything funny, if you don't do exactly as I've commanded, Zoey's blood will be on your hands."

"How do I know that you'll let her live? That you'll release her?"

"I wouldn't enjoy a hookup with her. I wouldn't enjoy hurting her, either. She's not really my type. But *you* are."

The words curdled her stomach. "Give me proof that she's alive."

"Zoey, say hello to the pretty detective."

"H-Hello," a shaky, young voice said. "Please help me."

"I will," Hannah said, her heart pounding. "I swear it."

"Describe the detective and what she's wearing," he said.

"L-long blond hair. You're w-wearing a blue jacket and b-blue jeans."

Squeezing her eyes shut for a second, Hannah took a calming breath. She glanced around. A few vehicles were parked on the street adjacent to the cemetery, but no dark SUV that resembled the body type of a Tahoe or Yukon.

"There. You have your proof," he said. "Do as I command."

A cold lance of fear stabbed her, but she shoved it aside. Freeing Zoey was what mattered.

Hannah picked up the syringe with a trembling hand, flicked off the cap and injected herself in the neck.

"Good girl. Now, take off your handcuffs and put them on, wrists behind your back, and wait for me. I'll even let you see Zoey because you've pleased me."

She set the phone on the headstone, took the handcuffs from her belt. Putting her hands behind her back, she slapped them on, loosely enough to be able to slide her wrists free.

With the GPS tracker, Matt would find her in time.

I'll be all right.

No matter what this monster dishes out, you can take it.

I'll be all right. And I've still got the knife hidden in my belt buckle. Given the chance, one split second of opportunity, I'll kill him.

Her vision blurred but then came back into focus. She swayed on her feet, her head growing heavy, her thoughts clouding. The drug was already taking effect. Quickly.

A white van emerged from the shadow of a building and entered the cemetery, heading slowly toward her.

Squinting against the glare of the headlights, she wobbled, struggling to stay on her feet. Everything turned blurry, her limbs growing numb. A feeling of sludge in her veins slowed down her thoughts, her blood flow, her heartbeat.

The driver's-side door swung open. A man hopped out. It was him. Different wig. No beard. But he had a fuzzy mustache.

She longed to kick his butt, to stomp his face in and make him swallow his own teeth, but as she took a step, everything spun, and she realized her legs had given out and she was falling.

She hit the ground, her head smacking hard against the pavement.

The man opened the passenger door and pulled someone out.

Hannah's eyelids were heavy, so heavy, but

she needed to hang on. Long enough to see the girl was okay.

They walked toward her; the girl was crying and barefoot, wearing pin-striped pajamas with strawberries. He shoved her down to the ground on her knees.

Hannah looked up at Zoey's terrified face, and it was the last thing she saw before the darkness closed in.

A DEAL WAS a deal, and he was a man of his word. He picked up the cell phone from the headstone and handed it to Zoey. "Count to one hundred. Then I want you to make a phone call. There is one programmed number. Use it. Ask for Campus Chief of Police Granger. Tell him who you are and where to find you. He'll take care of you. Do you understand?"

"Yes." Sobbing and trembling like a leaf in the wind, the young girl took the phone.

"Fail to do as I command, and I will come back for you. Hurt you. Make you wish you were dead. Understand?"

"Y-y-yes."

"Now, say 'thank you.'" Young people had no manners anymore. He just spared her life.

Tears streamed down her cheeks. "Thank you."

He pulled an extra-long pushpin from his pocket that had a half-inch thick sharp steel needle and pricked the detective in her thigh to be sure she was out cold. Not so much as a twitch from her.

Good.

"Begin counting once I leave the cemetery," he told Zoey, and she nodded, clutching the phone to her chest.

He bent down and scooped up the detective into his arms. As he stood, he braced for the slight pain that flared up. An old leg injury from years ago. One that truly required him to wear a medical boot until it had healed. Sometimes it still bothered him. When it rained. When it snowed. When he had to pick up something heavy from the ground, like a body.

Adjusting her weight in his arms, he carried her to the van. A breeze blew through her hair, kicking up the scent of her shampoo. *Spicy.* Just like their hookup would be.

The detective was a feisty one.

He set her down in the passenger's seat. Then he opened the sliding door on the side. The crisp, powerful scent of bleach curled around his nose, comforting him. He grabbed the detective and tossed her into the van.

Climbing up inside, he looked her over and salivated. *Patience.* He removed her boots and patted her down, starting at the ankles, checking for any hidden weapons. This harpy was devious and wicked, and he wouldn't put it past her to have something dangerous concealed.

He ran his palms over her flat stomach and up to her breasts, giving them a nice squeeze. But he found more than supple flesh. Something hard.

What's that?

He pulled out a small, rectangular dark gray transmitter. A GPS tracker. He chained the detective up in the van. Instead of using GHB, he went for something different that wasn't as long lasting because he couldn't wait to party with her. She wouldn't wake up while he was on the road, but he didn't believe in taking unnecessary chances, either. Hence, the shackles.

Smiling, he took the tracker and placed it behind one of the rear wheels. He got into the driver's seat, threw the van in Reverse and rolled over the transmitter as he backed out of the cemetery with his prize secured.

Chapter Twenty-One

Friday, September 20
8:08 p.m.

"Thank you, Agent Tomlinson," Matt said, grateful for her insight. "But I don't think Detective Delaney can be persuaded to walk away from this case." He was almost certain of it.

"For her own safety, she must. The closer we get to the end of the month, the more aggressive and bolder the killer will become in his effort to achieve his goal. There's no telling how far he'll go. I would also recommend protective custody for her."

The one place he knew, without a doubt, that she'd be safe was the Shooting Star Ranch. "I'll speak with her." Although it would've been better for her to have heard it firsthand from a seasoned FBI agent. Then she might accept the gravity of this threat and not dismiss it as him being overprotective because of his personal feelings for her.

Where was she, anyway? Hopefully, Kent hadn't run into a problem.

"Good luck, Chief Granger. Liz was right to ask me to look at your case. Don't hesitate to reach out if you need anything else."

They disconnected.

Where was Hannah?

He left his office, going down the hallway in the direction she had gone. In the lobby of the station, he looked at the duty officer. "Have you seen Detective Delaney?"

"She ran out of here like the devil was chasing her. Then she stood outside the front door for a minute and bolted."

"What?" He started toward the entrance to see if she had taken his truck. Stepping outside, he saw his vehicle still there.

Then his gaze fell, landing on her gun in its holster, her badge, cell phone and his keys. Disbelief rattled through him as he bent down and picked everything up.

No. Please, no.

"Hannah!" But he knew, deep in his gut, that he was too late.

She was gone.

Fear surged through him, complete and deafening. He reeled against it, his heart stuttering.

He rushed back into the station. "Secure these." He handed the duty officer Hannah's badge and service weapon and slipped her cell phone into his pocket.

Give me the number to your private cell phone.

The University Killer had demanded her personal number so he could continue communicating with her. The text she had received in his office must have been from the killer.

"Call Sergeant Starkey's house," he said to the duty officer. "The landline number, not his cell. See if he's home." This was the quickest, easiest way to see if Sergeant Starkey was a real suspect. The man couldn't be in two places at once. Either Starkey was innocent and at home or he might be the killer and have Hannah chained up somewhere.

With a nod, the duty officer picked up the receiver.

Think.

Think.

The tracker. Maybe she still had it on. Hurrying to his office, he took out his cell phone and dialed Kent.

"Kramer."

"Did you text Hannah about ten, maybe fifteen minutes ago?" he asked, needing to be sure. He sat at the computer and toggled over to the tracking system.

"No, I didn't."

Rage seared through his veins, and he struggled to keep his emotions under control. "That

SOB took Hannah. He has her." The program was coming up.

"What? How? She was with you."

The words hit him like a dagger in the chest. "No time to explain. I need you to go to Foster's house. See if he's home. We have to find the killer. Tonight. Understand? We don't sleep. We don't rest. Not for a minute. Until we figure out where he's taken her and get her back."

"Yeah, okay."

Hanging up, he stared at the screen. No green dot. The GPS tracker she'd used earlier wasn't active.

He banged a fist on the desk. Taking a deep breath, he spun out of his chair and went to grab the file on the first victim.

"Chief," the duty officer said, poking his head down the hall, "Starkey's home. Now what?"

"Is he still on the line?"

"Yeah. But not for long. He's about to take his family for ice cream."

Matt raced down the hall and picked up the phone. "Victor, the University Killer shot three campus officers and me tonight," he said, bypassing any pleasantries and using Starkey's first name, to hit home that this attack on them was personal. "The others are in the hospital. I believe he's taken Detective Delaney. Your leave of absence is over, effective immediately. I need you here now. Uniform doesn't matter."

"On my way, Chief. I'll be there in ten."

Matt slammed the phone down on the receiver. As he was leaving to go grab the file, the phone rang.

The duty officer answered at the front and then called back to him. "Chief, it's for you. Sounds urgent."

Maybe it was him. The killer. Calling to gloat. To ask for something in exchange for Hannah. He put the phone to his ear. "This is Chief Granger."

"M-m-my name is Zoey Williams. He told me to call you. Only you. That you would make sure I was safe."

Grim calmness stole over him. "Detective Hannah Delaney. Did you see her? Do you know where she is?"

"He took her. The blond detective. He said 'a life for a life.'"

His stomach upheaved. Matt couldn't regret that an innocent teen had been released. But he also couldn't—wouldn't—accept this sacrifice that Hannah had made. He would do whatever necessary to get her back. "Where are you?"

"I don't know. A cemetery. Stone-something. I see a street sign for Grand Avenue."

"The Millstone Cemetery?"

"Yeah, I think that's it."

"I'm sending a cop to come and get you." While Matt would dig into the file on the first victim. "He'll be there in less than five minutes.

In the meantime, I'm going to put the duty officer back on the phone. He's going to talk to you
until you're in a patrol car. Okay?"

She sobbed over the line. "Thank you. Please
hurry."

HE PARKED THE van at the cabin in the woods,
which was only a thirty-minute drive from town,
and slung Delaney over his shoulder. Walking
past the front steps of the cabin, he went around
to the side of the house. He squatted, grimacing
against the ache in his leg. After removing the
padlock, he opened the door to the soundproof,
self-sealing concrete storm shelter. What he liked
to call "the party room."

Balancing her weight on his shoulder, he eased
down the steps.

Sometimes he brought his son out to the woods
to hunt deer and elk, but no one was allowed
down here. This was his special place, and only
he had the key for the padlock.

He flopped Delaney on top of the fresh sheets
and blanket covering the cot that was bolted to
the floor. A proper hookup always had to start
with clean white bedding. That way he could
enjoy seeing it get dirty.

Snickering, he uncuffed her. But she wouldn't
be unrestrained for long. He unbuckled her belt,
unzipped her jeans, peeled them off, removed her
jacket and T-shirt, undressing her down to her

underwear. He ran his hands over her body. She would do nicely. When she woke up, she would realize her place in this new world—his world, where he would be her god.

"FOSTER IS HOME," Kent said over the phone. "He's watching a cooking show. Drinking pinot noir. I'm headed back to campus. Almost there."

Matt slapped the file in front of him closed. "Thanks. I rechecked the case file on the first victim, Paige Johnson. She was nineteen when she was killed. I spoke with her father. He said Paige didn't have any boyfriends."

"Do you believe him?"

"Paige liked girls, according to her father. So yes. He also said she got along with everybody. Never had any negative run-ins with anyone." Matt sighed. "Agent Tomlinson was confident there is a personal connection between the first victim and the killer."

What was he missing?

He was peeling away layers of the puzzle, but he didn't have the core. Not yet. It was only a matter of time. He just didn't know how much Hannah had.

Starkey flung open Matt's office door and rushed in with Carl and the LPD officer.

"Did you find something?" Matt asked.

"Possibly," Starkey said, his face grave. "There are quite a few people working at the university who drive a dark Tahoe or Yukon. But Carl noticed something odd."

Matt put his cell on speaker so Kent could stay in the loop. "What is it?"

Starkey handed him the DMV records.

Looking over the list, he zeroed in on the one line that had been both circled and highlighted.

"Dennis Hill," Matt said, the hair rising on his arms.

"According to the records, he owns a twelve-year-old granite-crystal metallic Chevy Tahoe," Starkey said. "But he's never mentioned it and has never driven it to work. Like he's hiding it. He's already got a Jeep, and his wife drives a sedan."

"Three vehicles," Matt said. "Tomlinson said that there will be patterns of three's in the killer's life. Carl, grab his personnel record."

Farran hurried out down the hall.

"What do you know about Dennis?" Matt asked Starkey. "Anything involving three's in his life."

"Um, well, he married his wife three times. Does that count?"

"Why on earth would he marry her three times?" Kent asked.

"The first time was at the justice of the peace. Second was a big ceremony and reception. But his mother was sick or something. She's in the Silver Springs Nursing Home. The third time was over there so his mom could be a part of it. He's really proud of it, too. Celebrates three wedding anniversaries every year. His wife brags about how romantic he is."

Farran came back with the file.

Matt snatched it from his hands and opened it. Perusing it, he stopped midway. "He's got three kids, too."

"Oh yeah, he does." Starkey nodded. "Or did. I forgot. One of his daughters died. Meningitis, I think."

Matt looked for the date of death. "His daughter died three years ago. A month before the University Killer last struck. Hey, Kent. I need you to go to his house. Speak to his wife. See what she knows." He gave him the address. Hill lived in close proximity to the campus.

"Dennis has a son who attends the university," Starkey said. "Liam. We can find him at one of the frat houses. Alpha-something. He might know something, too."

Matt grabbed his hat and keys. "Let's find out."

Chapter Twenty-Two

Hannah stirred, her heavy eyelids lifting. Her throat was dry. Her mouth felt like cotton. She stared up at a low gray ceiling. Soft amber light came from a lamp somewhere. As she sat up, chains rattled. She realized she was on top of a bed. Full-size. Wrought iron frame.

Her wrists were now in front of her but still cuffed, with a long chain locked to the top of the bed frame. She gazed down at herself. Her clothes were gone, except for her bra and panties.

She stood, barefoot, more chains rattling, and swayed on her feet. There was an iron shackle around each ankle with a separate chain connected to one of the lower corners of the bed. Sickening awareness struck her that he'd restrained her in a manner to make spreading her legs easier.

Bile burned her throat, and her stomach clenched.

Where were her clothes? Her belt?

She looked around. The room was small. A cell, really. Made of concrete. Maybe nine by twelve. The bed took up most of the space.

In a corner sat a table no larger than a nightstand. With a lamp on top of it. Beyond the table was a door.

She shuffled forward, only to be snatched to a halt. The chain connected to her handcuffs wouldn't let her make it past the bed.

Kneeling down, she looked under the bedframe.

Her clothes—and a bucket, but she didn't want to think about what that was for. She reached for the pile of clothes and dragged it out. Everything was in tatters. He had cut her pants, jacket, top and belt into pieces. The only thing intact was the buckle.

The fool hadn't checked it. And she was going to use that mistake against him.

She pulled out the short blade and shoved everything else back under the bed.

As she stood, the room spun. Turning slowly, she gazed at the walls. When she faced the one behind the bed, she froze. Polaroid pictures of women, bruised and still—murdered—covered the concrete like some sick wallpaper. Her skin crawled.

Each photo was of a different blonde.

And there were more than twenty.

MATT STOOD INSIDE the foyer of the Alpha Theta Nu frat house alongside Sergeant Starkey, waiting for Liam.

His cell phone rang. "Granger," he said, answering.

"Bonnie Hill didn't answer the door," Kent said. "I looked around through the windows. Saw her unconscious on the couch. An open bottle of wine on the table. I kicked in the door. She's got a pulse, but I can't wake her. I think her husband drugged her. The ambulance is on the way."

"Okay. Search the house. See what you can find that might point to where he's taken Hannah."

"Will do. I'll keep you posted."

"What's up?" Starkey asked.

Matt was about to answer, but a tall kid—eighteen years old, with dark hair and dark eyes; a younger, fitter version of Dennis—came down the stairs.

"Hey, Sergeant Starkey." The young man looked at Matt. "Hi, I'm Liam."

"Chief Granger."

"I was told you needed to speak with me."

"Son, we're trying to locate your father," Matt said. "It's of the utmost importance that we find him. It's a matter of life or death."

"He should be at home. With my mom."

"We checked there," Matt said gently. "Your

mother was found unconscious and in need of medical attention."

"Oh my God. I'll call my dad." He reached for his phone.

"Please, don't." Matt raised a palm. "We're still piecing things together, and it would be best if we spoke with your father first."

Liam's brow furrowed. "Is he in trouble? You don't think he did something to my mom, do you?"

"We're not jumping to any conclusions," Matt said, not wanting to make the kid defensive, since they needed his help. "But it's imperative that we find him and speak with him in person." He kept his voice patient, his tone soft. "Is there any place that you can think of where he might go? A favorite spot? Somewhere he feels safe."

Liam nodded. "My grandparent's cabin. It's in the woods. In Wayward Bluffs." He gave them the address.

"Thank you." Matt turned to Starkey. "Take his phone and keep him at the station. No phone calls. Make him comfortable and give him updates on his mother's condition."

Matt turned and dashed out the door, running to his truck.

Hang on, Hannah.

His prize should be bright eyed by now and no longer groggy. He'd given her plenty of time to recover. Their first time together, he wanted her wide awake and fiery.

He removed the padlock, stuck the key back in his pocket and opened the door to the shelter.

Ducking his head, he climbed down and closed the door behind him.

Chains rattled as Hannah Delaney scooted back on the bed, bringing her knees up to her chest like she was scared. But fire burned in her eyes.

Was she up to something?

"Rise and shine," he said in a singsong voice.

Leaning forward a bit, she gaped at him. "You?" she asked, shock thickening her voice.

She didn't see the forest for the trees. Just like Granger and every other police chief before him.

No more disguises needed. He'd not only gotten rid of the wig, mustache and fake contacts but also the toupee he wore on a daily basis to hide his receding hairline.

He smiled. "These are the rules by which you live." And eventually die. "You will call me *Master*," he said, and she narrowed her eyes to slits. "Only by pleasing me during our hookups will you get food and water. If you make me angry, you will be punished. I own you now. The sooner you accept this, the better. For you." He waited to see what kind of response he'd get.

Sometimes they sobbed. Sometimes they argued. Sometimes they tried to bargain, promising that their parents would pay him money if only he released them. Inevitably, whether in the beginning or at the end, they all begged for mercy.

But Hannah didn't utter a single word. She just stared at him. If looks could kill, he would be ashes blowing in the wind.

He grinned.

She was strong and healthy and would last a long time. Longer than any other. Not mere hours or days but weeks. He was sure of it.

With her fighting spirit, he would have to hurt her. To teach her that she wasn't to try to hurt him. And in that lesson, she would also learn how glorious her pleasure could be after pain.

Like breaking in a wild horse, this would take a firm hand and patience on his part. He'd have to be careful, though. She was a threat, but only if he allowed her to be. Taming her would certainly be no easy task. He was up for the challenge.

She was special. Different. He would cherish her, even as he despised her.

Suddenly giddy, almost drunk with anticipation, he stepped to the foot of the bed. Watched her—his feral, quiet cat curled in on herself.

Grinning, he grabbed the chain connected to her right ankle and yanked it, forcing her leg to extend to the corner of the bed. He bent down and fixed one of the links on a hook on the floor to hold it in place.

As he stood, he sensed and then heard movement, the bedsprings creaking.

Hannah pounced forward like lightning and jammed something sharp in the back of his shoulder blade. Hot agony pierced him. But she didn't stop. She kept stabbing and slicing and drawing his blood while he tried to block her blows, howling and cursing in shock and pain.

He stumbled backward, away from the bed, out of her deadly reach.

Eyes full of rage, she was crouched, poised to lunge again, a blade in her hand covered in his blood.

Where had it come from? He'd been so careful.

"If you think I won't fight you until my last breath, then you had better think again! You took the wrong woman. Do you hear me, you sick, perverted monster?"

No. He took the right one. She was perfect. He liked it when they fought. When they struggled. "Breaking you will be that much sweeter. I think it's time for your first real lesson."

He stormed out of the shelter, leaving the door open. The cold night air would cool her off. He marched toward the cabin, realizing he'd forgotten to charge the cattle prod.

He swore to himself. While he had to wait for it to juice up, she would be that much weaker from the cold air, shivering, her teeth chattering, the deadly edge to her fighting drained.

But that wasn't enough punishment for Hannah Delaney. He was in agony.

Not only would he use the cattle prod, but he'd put her in a straitjacket, too. That would show her. Three days wearing that, and then she'd call him *Master*.

ABOUT A QUARTER of a mile down the road from the address Liam had given Matt, he pulled off to the side and shut the engine. From the back seat, he took a bulletproof vest, strapped it on and slipped his jacket over it. After he double-checked his Glock, he stuffed extra magazines, each containing fifteen rounds, into his pocket. He hooked two flash grenades on his vest, grabbed his night-vision goggles and flipped them down.

He set off into the woods, going the direction where the cabin should be. His shoulder ached something awful, but he ignored the pain.

Steadily, carefully, he moved, scanning for movement or anything that might give away his presence. Such as floodlights or security cameras. He spotted nothing. Kept going. Stayed alert. He slipped between the trees like a shadow.

In minutes, he came upon the back side of a cabin. He prayed that this was the right place and that Hannah was safe.

Footsteps pounded down wooded stairs at the front of the house.

Fifteen feet before the back porch, he cut quietly to the left, tracking the footfalls over dry leaves. He peeked around the side of the house.

A man stalked toward a mound.

Dennis Hill. Holding a straitjacket—the buckles flapping—and something else, like a metal stick, but then Matt noticed the familiar U-shaped tip. Sparks flared, tiny bright flashes on the faint green tinge of his screen.

A cattle prod!

Matt ripped off his night-vision goggles and took aim with his Glock.

But Dennis climbed down the stairs that led below ground, grabbing hold of the door to close it.

Right before it slammed shut, Matt heard Hannah swearing.

She was alive, and she was fighting. The icy fear that had squeezed his heart loosened its grip a little.

He rushed over to the mound. Took a flash grenade from his vest. Pulled the pin with his teeth. Cracked open the door. Tossed it in and shut the door.

A deafening boom erupted in tandem with a bright flash of light. It would incapacitate Hannah just as much as Dennis for a critical moment. But she would recover. The same couldn't necessarily be said about Dennis.

Matt threw open the door and hustled down the steps with his weapon at the ready.

The sight before him made his blood boil. Hannah was chained to a bed, writhing from the effects of the flash bang, bloody hands covering her ears and more blood splattered on her half-naked body.

Rage overwhelmed Matt. He charged Dennis, snatching him up from the floor, gritting his teeth through the sharp pain in his arm, and thrashed the man with his fist until blood ran from his nose.

Matt shoved him to the ground, face-first. Hard. He put a knee on his back, keeping him pinned, yanked Dennis's arms behind him and slapped cuffs on him tight.

Standing up, he spotted the straitjacket and cattle prod. He had half a mind to string Dennis up, use the cattle prod on him and then put an end to that brutal beast. But ranch justice, a quick death, was too good for him.

Matt kicked the cattle prod away. He looked up, and his gaze snagged on the concrete wall behind the bed covered in heinous photos. Renewed fury rushed over him, but he needed to help Hannah.

He went over to the bed, sat down and reached for her.

Still squirming, she lashed out with a blade that came dangerously close to his throat, but he'd been expecting anything and pulled back out of her reach.

He caught her wrists gently with one hand and pressed a palm to her cheek with the other. Her eyelids lifted, and her gaze found his.

Relief washed over her face. He hauled her up into his arms, the chains jangling, and held her tight to his chest. Her cold body shivered against him.

He pulled back, took off his jacket and wrapped it around her.

"You're right in the nick of time," she said, her teeth chattering.

"I try to be punctual." Matt dug out a handcuff key from his pocket and freed her wrists. "There's so much blood on you."

"None of it's mine. It's his."

He got to work on the shackles on her ankles and released her. "You take too many chances."

She stood and rubbed her wrists. "Only when necessary."

He ripped the blanket from the bed and wrapped it around her waist. "You scared the hell out of me." He tugged her back into his arms, determined to never let her go.

Tipping her head up, she looked at him. "You say the most romantic things."

Epilogue

Saturday, September 21
7:30 p.m.

Hannah leaned against Matt, her head on his chest, his uninjured arm curled around her as they sat on his sofa in front of a cozy fire. She sipped her whiskey, grateful she'd made it out of Dennis Hill's lair alive. Relieved Zoey Williams was unharmed. Happy to have Matt at her side, willing to go into hell and fight the devil—not only with her but also *for* her.

Matt picked up her legs and draped them over his lap.

"I still can't wrap my mind around how many women Dennis Hill actually killed," she said, her skin crawling as she thought about the photos on the wall.

Twenty-four in total had been murdered. Hill had a type, and he never deviated from the profile. Young, under twenty-two, blond, fair skin, petite.

"If not for you, we never would have found

his first twelve victims buried on the property of his cabin."

They'd thought Paige Johnson was his first victim, when in actuality, it was Nicole Noland.

"Agent Tomlinson was correct about the personal connection," Matt continued.

Nicole had dated Dennis when he was a kicker on the SWU football team. Number thirty-three jersey. Nicole had broken up with him after they got into a car accident, and he injured his leg and couldn't play anymore. He started dating Bonnie, his current wife, and waited three months to rape and kill Nicole. He'd used Bonnie as his alibi.

Hannah shook her head, horrified by what Dennis had done to his victims and his family. "For twenty years, he's been drugging Bonnie, making that poor woman think she has a drinking problem, so he could sneak out and kill women. The shame his wife must've felt when you questioned her about her husband's whereabouts the night Madison Scott was murdered. Too embarrassed to say she was drunk and had blacked out and couldn't remember, even though she had really been roofied."

"Dennis fooled everyone. He was so unassuming, lurking right under the nose of every campus police chief for the past twenty years."

After he'd graduated from SWU, Dennis tried to join the campus police department, but his leg injury prevented him from passing the physical, and he became the office manager instead, picking his victims from the students who came into the police station to register their bicycles.

He confessed that nothing in particular had triggered this latest murder spree. Only that he'd felt compelled to find a sense of release.

"Promise me something," Matt said.

"What?"

"That you'll never lie to me again," he said, referring to her telling him that Kent had texted her. "No matter how difficult. No matter how complicated. Not even to protect me."

She would always do whatever she could to protect him. But she'd never lie to him again. "I promise. I'm sorry. You understand why?"

He nodded. There was no judgment or anger in his eyes. Only warmth. The knowledge that he understood her and accepted her, flaws and all, meant everything.

Matt rubbed her legs before taking her foot and massaging it.

"I should be massaging you." She kissed him on the lips, loving the feel of his stubble against her skin.

"You should, and you'll get your chance later, in the bedroom." He winked at her.

She couldn't help but smile.

He picked up his drink, took a swallow and went back to massaging her foot. "The university administration is impressed that we caught two serial killers."

Foster's DNA matched that of the Emerald City Butcher. Following a hunch, Kent had cadaver dogs search the state park situated in between the two spots where Dr. Bradford Foster liked to fish. They'd found four more bodies.

"Sam Lee will finally be released from prison," she said. "But nothing can restore the years stolen from him."

"At least his name will be cleared, and he can enjoy his freedom while knowing that the real Butcher will get what's coming to him."

Her thoughts careened back to Dennis Hill and his plans for her in that storm shelter. "I feel for Hill's children." His son, Liam, and older daughter, Susie. "And his wife."

She understood the unique agony of being the child of a serial killer. A nightmare she wouldn't wish on her worst enemy.

"Foster had kids, too."

It was hard to believe such men loved their children, their families, when they would leave them that legacy of evil.

"I have no control over what Erica Egan prints, but I have some influence with the campus paper. They've agreed to make it clear that the families of Hill and Foster didn't know the horrible truth and will ask for people to respect their privacy."

"That was really thoughtful of you."

He was the sweet one in this relationship.

"Hey." He picked up her hand and kissed her knuckles, and the tenderness in his eyes made her breath catch. "This might sound nuts or too fast, but what do you think about moving in here? Us making a home together?"

Stunned, she looked at him, totally blindsided and speechless.

"It's fast, but we both put in crazy hours on the job, and I do a lot of work on the ranch. It might be the only way to see each other with any sort of consistency. I want to build on this. This connection. And you said you were never sleeping in your place again."

And she wasn't.

When she didn't respond, he said, "I'm not trying to push."

"No. I want you to push. Sometimes we need a nudge out of our comfort zone for our own good." Funny how coming inches from being tortured and dying had made her realize how much was lacking in her life. "I want to be with you. See what *this* can grow into." Happiness swelled inside her as she studied his face.

The side of his mouth curved up. "Even if you fall madly in love and end up needing me?"

"I'm already falling, cowboy," she said, not mentioning how hard she was falling, and he smiled fully. "And as for needing you? I've learned that's not such a bad thing."

She'd needed him throughout this entire case, as well as the one they'd worked on last year. But she hadn't realized that she also needed his warmth, his understanding, his intensity.

His strength.

He leaned over and kissed her with tenderness and heat. This new relationship, this remarkable joy and lightness of being, was scary but wondrous. And worth it.

She smiled at him. "I guess you better get me a set of keys, because this is home."

* * * * *

Mississippi Manhunt

R. Barri Flowers

MILLS & BOON

DEDICATION

In memory of my cherished mother, Marjah Aljean, a devoted lifelong fan of Harlequin romance novels, who inspired me to excel in my personal and professional lives. To H. Loraine, the true love of my life and best friend, whose support has been unwavering through the many terrific years together; and Carole Ann Jones, who left an impact on me with her incredible talents on the screen; as well as the loyal fans of my romance, mystery, suspense and thriller fiction published over the years. Lastly, a nod goes out to my amazing editors, Allison Lyons and Denise Zaza, for the wonderful opportunity to lend my literary voice and creative spirit to the Harlequin Intrigue line.

R. Barri Flowers is an award-winning author of crime, thriller, mystery and romance fiction featuring three-dimensional protagonists, riveting plots, unexpected twists and turns, and heart-pounding climaxes. With an expertise in true crime, serial killers and characterizing dangerous offenders, he is perfectly suited for the Harlequin Intrigue line. Chemistry and conflict between the hero and heroine, attention to detail and incorporating the very latest advances in criminal investigations are the cornerstones of his romantic suspense fiction. Discover more on popular social networks and Wikipedia.

Visit the Author Profile page
at millsandboon.com.au.

CAST OF CHARACTERS

Nikki Sullivan—A successful artist, living in Owl's Bay, Mississippi, who survived after being kidnapped ten years ago by serial killer Perry Evigan, who murdered her best friend, Brigette Fontana. Could the prison escapee come after Nikki again?

Gavin Lynley—A special agent for the Mississippi Department of Corrections, he is tasked with protecting Nikki while her former abductor remains at large. The assignment is made more difficult by the fact that Gavin blames Nikki for the murder of his then-girlfriend, Brigette, at the hands of Evigan. Can they bury their differences for a new beginning?

Brooke Reidel—A detective for the Owl's Bay Police Department, committed to solving a string of local murders that appear to be linked to the dangerous inmate on the loose.

Marvin Whitfield—Director of investigations at MDOC, he is resolute in recapturing the escaped convicts, with his own credibility and ambitions on the line.

Jean O'Reilly—An MDOC special agent who is as dedicated to locating the fugitive Evigan as he is to keeping Nikki out of harm's way.

Perry Evigan—An escaped serial killer, dubbed the Gulfport Nightmare Killer, he is determined to claim the life of the one who got away, whatever it takes.

Prologue

Nikki Sullivan was admittedly bored to death on this summertime Saturday night as she paced lazily around her cozy, minimally furnished third-story apartment in Gulfport, Mississippi. An artist, one year removed from receiving a Bachelor of Arts degree from the University of Mississippi, she wasn't especially in the mood to do any canvases. She was single again after kicking her cheating and financially strapped boyfriend, Felix Kovell, to the curb two weeks earlier and was the better for it. She debated whether or not to call her best friend, Brigette Fontana, to see if she wanted to hang out or something. Brigette was currently in a relationship with Gavin Lynley, whom Nikki found to be incredibly good-looking and otherwise drenched in masculinity, while ever attentive to his girlfriend. But one would never know these admirable qualities in the man, based on Brigette—who was stunning herself—seemingly taking him for granted while having a roving eye on other guys, be-

lieving there was more than enough of her to
go around. And around again whenever Gavin
wasn't looking. Or was otherwise preoccupied.
Though Nikki felt bad for him, she thought it
wasn't her place to come between them and expose Brigette. Much less suggest to him that he
could do better than her in a partner. Even if he
could.

*He'll find out sooner or later and then can
decide for himself*, Nikki told herself, fantasizing that maybe they could even wind up together
someday—assuming things didn't work out between him and Brigette. Before she could call
her friend, having lifted the cell phone from the
back pocket of her midrise skinny jeans, Nikki
received a call from Brigette instead.

"I was just thinking about you," Nikki confessed truthfully, feeling a tad guilty as well in
thinking about Gavin in romantic terms.

"Hopefully, good thoughts," Brigette joked,
none the wiser.

"Of course," Nikki claimed, sitting on her
leather sofa, folding her legs beneath her.

"So, what are you up to?"

"Not much. You?"

"I was supposed to go out with Gavin, but
something came up and he canceled." She muttered an expletive in displeasure.

"Sorry to hear that," Nikki said, and truly

meant it. But she knew that Gavin worked in corrections and sometimes, maybe more often than not, duty called. Even when he might have wished otherwise.

"Doesn't mean I need to sit here and mope about it," Brigette grumbled. "Let's go out and have some fun."

"What did you have in mind?" Nikki switched the phone to her other ear deliberately. "We could hang out here and watch some TV," she suggested. Or not.

"I'd rather do a few shots and some dancing," her friend countered. "Are you game?"

Nikki considered it for a moment or two before realizing how persuasive Brigette could be. Not to mention feeling antsy herself in wanting to get out of the stuffy apartment. Both were twenty-three, with Nikki having reached that age exactly two weeks ago. "Count me in," she agreed.

"Cool. I can be at your place in ten minutes or less."

"I'll be ready," Nikki promised and disconnected. She stood and shut her blue eyes for a moment as Nikki pulled her long light blond hair out of the low ponytail it was in, before changing into what she believed to be more suitable clothes for going out.

When Brigette arrived in her white Audi

A3—recently purchased after the Arkansas State University graduate landed a job as an event coordinator with a prestigious public relations agency—Nikki hopped in. Taking one look at her gorgeous friend, who had bold apple-green eyes, mounds of wavy raven hair and a stunning body to kill for, Nikki found herself somewhat envious and sad at the same time that Brigette never seemed to appreciate what she brought to the table as a person, and could lose if she wasn't careful.

"So, where are we going?" Nikki asked coolly.

"I know the perfect place," Brigette answered evasively, and took off.

Nikki chuckled, ill at ease. "You're scaring me." She wasn't sure if it was from the speed at which her friend was driving, the mystery of where they were headed, or both.

"Really?" Brigette laughed and seemed to go even faster down the narrow street. "Where's your sense of adventure, girl?"

"Guess I'm about to find out," she relented, sucking in a calming breath.

They drove to a nightclub on Pickford Street called Johnnie's Shack in a seedy part of town, again giving Nikki some fresh concern. "You sure about this?"

"It'll be fine," Brigette promised. "Relax. I've been here a couple of times. We won't stay long."

"Okay." Nikki followed her friend's lead this time and went inside, where they did some tequila shots and then stepped onto a small dance floor and danced together to an upbeat song, before a tall, muscular man joined them and danced with them. He was in his early thirties and not too hard on the eyes, with defined features, dark eyes, medium-length brown hair in a windblown pompadour and an aquiline nose. He wore a multicolored plaid shirt and black distressed jeans.

He flashed a crooked smile and said affably, "I'm Perry."

Brigette smiled back flirtatiously. "I'm Brigette and this is my friend Nikki."

"Nice to meet you ladies." He grinned again and continued to move his Chukka boots to the music. "Hope you don't mind if I dance with you?"

Though Nikki's radar suddenly went up that he was being a bit too friendly and getting in their space—or putting it simply, he was bad news—Brigette apparently felt just the opposite, seemingly forgetting all about the fact that she had a boyfriend in Gavin, and told Perry enthusiastically, "Why not?"

After leaving the dance floor ten minutes later, he joined them at their table for more drinks, but didn't try to put the moves on either of them.

Nikki still felt that something was off with the man, even if she couldn't quite put a finger on it in so many words, and convinced a reluctant Brigette that it was time to go. With no invitation for Perry to join them. When he thankfully put up no argument, remaining at the table as they left, Nikki thought they were home free of the potential threat. It was only when she began to feel light-headed in the dimly lit parking lot, and noticed the same with Brigette, that it became painfully obvious they had been drugged.

By who? Perry?

Nikki had her answer, as she watched the man in question picking Brigette up off the ground, where she had collapsed, and tossing her like a sack of potatoes in the back of a black Ford E-250 Super Duty cargo van. Then he did the same to her as, barely able to stand on wobbly legs, Nikki was unable to resist him before she passed out in his muscular arms. The last thing to enter her mind was whether or not she or Brigette would survive the night and the monster who had taken them against their will in a manner reminiscent of the serial killer who had been on the prowl in town.

PERRY EVIGAN COULDN'T help but chuckle with delight as he drove his latest captives back to the house he lived in on Robinson Road. Sitting on two acres of grassy land, it was far enough away from neighbors to allow him to come and go freely without attracting too much attention. He'd been planning on drugging and bringing back a single person for his trouble. He hadn't counted on two women for the price of one for him to have his way with before killing them and disposing of them as he had his other victims. But there they were, ripe for the taking like apples off the tree—for which he was only too happy to oblige.

Admittedly, he could tell that the one calling herself Nikki was suspicious of him from the start. For a minute there, he thought with her watching him like a hawk, he'd never get the chance to spike their drinks with gamma-hydroxybutyrate. Thankfully, her attractive friend Brigette was more amenable to them hanging out together—even to the point of allowing him to buy the next round of drinks and pick them up—which, unfortunately, would prove to be a big error in judgment, as both women would soon regret having ever laid their pretty eyes on him once he was done with them. Something told him they were already regretting this, as he glanced at the two still-unconscious women lying in the back of the van. It had been almost too easy to slip the GHB into the drinks and then watch coolly as they sipped innocently on them while laughing at his stale jokes to keep them occupied. All he needed to do was let the two leave of their own accord for all to see and then pretend to leave casually on his own afterward and abduct them as they passed out, with no one being the wiser. He would come back later for the vehicle they drove in to the bar.

Arriving at the two-story, two-bedroom Greek Revival-style house with a shed and woods out back, he carried the women, one by one, inside the residence, where he lived alone but always welcomed the right company. Soon, the fun would begin. At least for him. For them, he had to admit with a laugh within, not so much.

THE NIGHTTIME RAID by heavily armed FBI agents and Gulfport Police Department detectives and SWAT Team, supported by Harrison County Sheriff's Office investigators from the Criminal Investigation Division and K-9 Patrol dogs, on the house on Robinson Road, led to the arrest of suspected serial killer Perry Evigan. The nude body of a woman identified as twenty-three-year-old Brigette Fontana was discovered in a bedroom. She had been sexually assaulted and strangled to death, barehanded, by Evigan, according to the autopsy report two days later.

Another woman, Nikki Sullivan, who had been abducted by Evigan at the same time outside Johnnie's Shack nightclub, and was described as a good friend of Ms. Fontana's, survived the vicious attack. Upon her full recovery, Ms. Sullivan was expected to testify against her attacker, dubbed the "Gulfport Nightmare Killer," who was believed to have strangled to death at least ten women over an eight-month span within the city of Gulfport, Mississippi, Harrison County's co-county seat.

Chapter One

During a violent nighttime uprising at the Mississippi State Penitentiary in Sunflower County, Mississippi, three hardcore inmates seized on the opportune distraction to stage a dramatic getaway. After quickly overwhelming prison guards, the trio made a daring escape from Area I of the maximum-security prison on Parchman Road known as Parchman Farm.

The leader of the escapees, a convicted murderer, spotted a red GMC Sierra 1500 parked not far from the prison. Its driver, a lanky, thirty-something, baldheaded male, was talking on a cell phone, seemingly oblivious to his surroundings. Or the potential peril present. Once the inmates had his attention, it was too late for him to deny them what they wanted: his vehicle and the phone. Unfortunately, leaving behind a witness to their car theft wasn't in the cards. Strangling the man to death with his own leather belt was easy for the ringleader. After all, he'd had lots of experience using this method to kill others. And if things went as planned, he fully intended to pick up where he left off years ago.

Starting with the pretty one who escaped death before he could squeeze the life out of her.

The prisoners climbed into the pickup truck and headed west on Highway 32 toward the city of Ruleville, Mississippi. There, they would get a change of clothing, food, money and maybe switch cars, before fleeing the area entirely, ahead of the correctional authorities and other law enforcement personnel's determined efforts to recapture them. Or do whatever it took to prevent the dangerous fugitives from living in the free world again.

SPECIAL AGENT GAVIN LYNLEY of the Mississippi Department of Corrections, Corrections Investigation Division's Special Operations Unit, removed the FN 509 MRD-LE 9mm semiautomatic pistol from the tactical thigh holster as he cautiously approached the black Hyundai Sonata. It was parked outside a ranch-style home on Frinton Street in Vicksburg, Mississippi. A run on the license plate confirmed that the vehicle belonged to Titus Malfoy, a probation officer for the MDOC, who was wanted for embezzling money from probationers. The victims were working to pay off their debts to the court as required in the terms for regaining freedom. Instead, an internal investigation revealed that Malfoy pocketed what wasn't his to have at their expense, resulting in longer sentences for those victimized unsuspectingly.

Gavin glanced at the other side of the vehicle, where Special Agent Jean O'Reilly, her gun drawn, was also prepared to act should the suspect behind the steering wheel make the wrong move. Peering at the probation officer, who was talking on his cell phone, recognizing him, Gavin said with an edge to his voice, "Step out of the car and keep your hands where I can see them."

Looking surprised, Titus Malfoy cut the call short and complied with the order. He opened the door carefully and climbed out. "What's this all about?" he demanded as his brow creased in three irregular lines as though totally perplexed.

Gavin noted that they were about the same height of six feet and three inches. But he was in better shape than Malfoy, who was African American, a year younger at thirty-five than the man, had darker and shorter hair than the probation officer, who had a bleached high top and textured dreads, and was gray-eyed compared to the brown color of the suspect's eyes, which were shifting nervously. "Titus Malfoy, you're under arrest for embezzlement and abusing your position as a probation officer."

"What?" Malfoy cocked a thick brow of denial. "This has to be some kind of mistake."

"I don't think so." Gavin was confident that the monthslong investigation of his crimes was spot-on. He frisked the man and found that he didn't have a firearm or other weapon on him. "You messed up big time, Malfoy," he told him bluntly. "Now you'll have to answer for it."

Agent O'Reilly, slender and thirtysomething with long crimson hair in a tight bun, big blue eyes and fresh off a divorce, handcuffed the suspect behind his back and said skeptically, "If you're really innocent, you'll have ample opportunity to prove it. If not, you could be looking at decades behind bars. Sorry." Her tone indicated the apology was sarcastic rather than sincere.

As Malfoy muttered an expletive in response, Gavin told him tersely, "Let's go." He wondered just how many more bad apples they would discover in the probe of corruption within the ranks of the Mississippi Department of Corrections. It was troubling, to say the least, as he wanted to believe that this was just an isolated problem and not broad in scope for an organization that Gavin had been employed with for more than a decade. Or ever since shortly after he had received his undergraduate degree in Criminology from Mississippi State University, and followed the long tradition of family members who made careers for themselves in law enforcement.

Gavin led the suspect to the official CID vehicle they had driven to the scene, a dark ash metallic Chevrolet Tahoe SUV. Malfoy was put in the back seat, then Gavin sat in the front passenger seat, while Jean got behind the wheel and drove to the Vicksburg Police Department on Veto Street, where the suspect was turned over for processing.

Afterward, they took a mostly silent forty-five-mile drive to the Mississippi Department of Corrections Central Office headquarters on North Lamar Street in Jackson, where the report was filed on the arrest of Titus Malfoy, and Gavin settled into his office for some follow-up work. He was at a height-adjustable standing desk, glancing at his laptop, when the Director of Investigations at MDOC, Marvin Whitfield, strode in. He had an iPad in his hands.

Whitfield, African American, was in his forties, medium height and solidly built, with a short and tapered black Afro and sable eyes. "Good job, Lynley, with Agent O'Reilly, in taking Malfoy into custody without incident," he said, squaring his shoulders inside the jacket of his crisp navy suit worn with black plain leather Derbys.

"I wish it hadn't come down to that," Gavin said, twisting his lips in despair. He knew that the arrest indicated that one of their own had crossed the line, implicating the entire department to one degree or another by association. If not guilt.

"Yeah, I know what you mean." Whitfield pinched his broad nose. "But it is what it is... Unfortunately, we've got other problems to deal with." He paused, ill at ease. "Last night there was a riot at the Mississippi State Penitentiary."

"Yeah, I heard about it." Gavin recalled the news about an uprising at the prison related to conditions that had been described by some as deplorable. From what limited information he gathered, at least one inmate had been killed and several injured, before guards were able to bring things under control.

"While conducting an emergency head count at five this morning, it was discovered that three inmates were missing." Whitfield sighed noisily. "They took advantage of the melee and killed one guard—Stan MacGregor, age thirty-nine, who was married with four kids—while seriously wounding another, before the trio managed to flee the prison grounds. Along the way, the escapees stole a pickup truck after killing the driver, thirty-four-year-old Jason Ollero."

"Wow." Gavin felt terrible for the guards attacked, as well as the pickup driver, who was obviously in the worst place at the worst time. He hoped the injured guard pulled through.

"It gets worse," the longtime director muttered. "One of the escaped inmates is Perry Evigan..."

"What?" Gavin's heart sank into his stomach, even as Whitfield reiterated this disturbing news, and showed him Evigan's mug shot on the tablet. Seeing his chiseled face and foreboding hazel eyes, along with closely cropped brown-gray hair, gave Gavin the creeps.

"Yeah, freaks me out too," Whitfield muttered. He identified the other escapees as Craig Schneider and Aaron Machado, pulling their images up on the tablet.

Gavin glanced at Schneider, who was white, round-faced and blue-eyed, with a black crew cut and anchor beard. Machado was Latino, bald-headed, smooth-shaven, triangular-faced and had dark brown eyes. While noting their appearances, Gavin's focus was squarely on Perry Evigan. Ten years ago, Evigan raped and murdered Gavin's then-girlfriend, Brigette Fontana. She was strangled to death by him. Known as the Gulfport Nightmare Killer, Evigan had killed a total of ten young women by ligature strangulation in and around Gulfport. Brigette was his last homicide victim, who was abducted by the

killer along with Brigette's best friend, Nikki
Sullivan. Though she survived the kidnapping
and attempted rape, Nikki was left with a broken
jaw, busted lower lip, seriously sprained ankle
and a concussion—along with the psychological wounds she sustained during her victimization—before being rescued by the authorities
from Evigan's house.

Perry Evigan himself—a then-thirty-four-
year-old divorcé and journeyman, with a dark
fixation on such serial killers as the so-called
Boston Strangler, believed by many to be serial
rapist Albert DeSalvo, and cousins Kenneth Bi-
anchi and Angelo Buono Jr., known as the Hill-
side Stranglers—was taken into custody, in spite
of Evigan's resisting arrest. He would eventually be convicted for his crimes and sentenced
to spend the rest of his life in prison. Until now.

"Do we know where they are?" Gavin asked
the director tartly, hating the thought that Evigan was tasting freedom for even a second, after
what he'd done.

"Unfortunately, not at the moment." Whitfield
furrowed his forehead. "They made their way to
Ruleville and ditched the pickup. We're not sure
what they're driving now. We have the department's Fugitive Apprehension Strike Team and
K-9 unit trying to track them down, with assistance from the FBI and US Marshals Service,

along with the Jackson Police Department, Sunflower County Sheriff's Office and surrounding law enforcement agencies on full alert. We'll get them back," he said confidently. "But until such time, we need to protect the one woman who miraculously managed to survive Perry Evigan's attempt to sexually assault and murder her from being added to his list of fatalities. That's where you come in, Lynley—"

Putting aside his conflicting thoughts at the moment, Gavin met the director's eyes sharply. "You want me to be a bodyguard?" Even when questioning him, Gavin knew it was not nearly that simple.

"I want you to keep the person alive whose critical testimony helped put Evigan away, ensuring that he would spend the rest of his miserable life behind bars." Whitfield drew a breath. "At least that was our intention. Now he's out there somewhere, free as a bird, and just might try to track down Nikki Sullivan, insane as that sounds. But we can't put anything past Evigan, who, as I recall, singled out Ms. Sullivan as his one regret—not killing her when he had the chance."

"I remember," Gavin muttered painfully, knowing it was hard to forget, all things considered.

"Maybe he wants a redo." Whitfield jutted his

chin. "We can't let that happen. As a member of the Special Operations Unit, Lynley, we need to be able to occasionally provide protection, when warranted. This seems to be one of those times, with the prisoners' escape under our jurisdiction. As you and Ms. Sullivan share a common bond with Evigan's last murder victim, Brigette Fontana, this assignment should be right up your alley. Am I right?"

Gavin hesitated in his response. Normally, he would have agreed with this assessment. How could he not, given the situation as it were? But in this instance, he had an undeniable large chip on his shoulder where it concerned Nikki Sullivan. He blamed her for placating Brigette's reckless desire to go out that night, leading her right into the crosshairs of Perry Evigan. Though Gavin admittedly blamed himself just as much, considering he had to work the night in question, preventing him from being with Brigette and presumably saving her life—he was certainly glad that Nikki had come out on the other side and been given the opportunity to move on with her life. This notwithstanding, being around her right now would only remind him of what he lost in Brigette and any future they might have had. And everything that could have come with that package—like a family and home together. Wasn't that where they were headed? But that wasn't exactly an acceptable excuse for not being able to do his job effectively. Was it? Even if that job meant reuniting with Brigette's best friend, in order to keep her safe from the same serial killer who put Brigette in the grave at the young age of twenty-three.

Gavin nodded at the director, maintaining his cool in the process. "Of course, I'll do my best to keep Ms. Sullivan out of harm's way while Evigan is still at large." *Hopefully, that will be of short duration, or Evigan could be apprehended even before I have to come face-to-face with Nikki for the first time in years*, Gavin told himself, knowing that the sooner they located the three escapees, the sooner they could wipe the proverbial egg off their faces in having to account for the escape in the first place on their watch.

"Good." Whitfield flashed him a satisfied look. "Of course, we'll need to locate Nikki Sullivan first—assuming she hasn't remained in the same place—wherever she might be if she's still in Mississippi after a decade, before Evigan can, and warn her about the possible danger to her life."

"I understand." Gavin had not kept track of Nikki's whereabouts after Evigan's trial and conviction. There had been no need to with neither on particularly good terms with the blame game.

Both had gone their separate ways. But he had heard through the grapevine that Brigette's gorgeous, as he recalled, and talented artist friend had smartly moved from Gulfport and the dark memories left behind. Now he just had to find out where she was and make sure she remained safe till the escaped serial killer was back in custody where he belonged.

An hour later, after making a few phone calls and doing some double-checking, Gavin had his answer. Nikki Sullivan had relocated to Owl's Bay, a town in Yaeden County, about thirty miles down the coast from Gulfport and approximately one hundred and seventy miles from Jackson. Moreover, Owl's Bay was around three hundred miles from Ruleville, where Perry Evigan and the other escapees were last spotted. Though it seemed like a stretch that Evigan would try to make his way back to the area where he perpetrated his serial murders, if this were the case, he'd had a head start.

Gavin alerted authorities along US 49 South and I-55 South, leading into Owl's Bay from Ruleville, to be on the lookout, or BOLO, for the fugitives, who could be driving any type of vehicle while on the run. And that was under the assumption that they hadn't split up. For the moment, Gavin was more focused on Evigan, in particular, with his mug shot sent to the local law enforcement agencies. Should he be foolish enough to go after Nikki.

Against his better judgment, Gavin decided not to call Nikki, sure she'd hang up on his face. Freaking her out by leaving a disturbing message probably wasn't a good idea either. He assumed that she had heard about Evigan's escape and was taking precautions accordingly. *I don't want to spook her by leaving a text that her life could be in danger*, Gavin told himself, trusting that he could get to her in time to protect her. In the meantime, he would give the locals a heads-up on the situation as it related to Nikki Sullivan.

Gavin left the MDOC Central Office headquarters and climbed back into the Chevrolet Tahoe he had arrived in, then swung by his Louisiana-style house on a cul-de-sac on Heritage Hill Drive. He lived alone in the spacious two-story home that sat on two acres of land with mature landscaping and tall oak trees, but would gladly share it with the right person, were she to come into his life. He once thought that might be Brigette, but they were never allowed to put it to the test, before her life ended.

Stepping through the front door, Gavin headed across the vinyl plank flooring and up the straight staircase. He grabbed a few extra clothing items and toiletries, in case this assignment turned out to be longer than a day or two—

stuffing them into a black leather tote bag—then headed back downstairs and out the door.

With any luck, Perry Evigan and the other escapees would be back in custody and a prison cell before Gavin ever arrived in Owl's Bay. He only wished he could take luck to the bank, where it concerned a ruthless serial killer on the loose and a woman from Gavin's past who potentially had a target on her back.

NIKKI SULLIVAN SAT in a club chair in the circle of a support group for survivors of traumatic events in the large backyard of the vintage home in the small Mississippi coastal town of Owl's Bay. She had participated off and on ever since relocating there from Gulfport eight years ago. She considered it a security blanket of sorts to be around others who had been left with permanent scars on their psyche—and in some cases, the accompanying physical scars—as a result of experiences they could never forget. Even if they tried. This was certainly true for her, even as she tried to distance herself by moving away from the scene of the crime and the man who unfairly blamed her for it.

Nikki trained her ocean-blue eyes on Blair Roxburgh, a trained psychologist and the homeowner who started the group, which currently consisted of six women and two men. She and

Blair were both the same age of thirty-three and similarly slender in build, but Blair was a couple of inches shorter than Nikki's five-foot-seven-and-a-half height, and had a darker shade of blond in her short shag than Nikki's long and layered yellow locks that were fashioned in a blunt U-shaped cut. She listened as Blair retold her terrifying tale for the benefit of those new to the group.

"I was sexually assaulted as an eighteen-year-old college freshman," she said, her hazel eyes dampening as though thrust back in time to the moment the attack occurred. "My attacker was someone I thought I knew. Till he turned out to be someone entirely different—a monster hidden behind a handsome face. For the longest time, I blamed myself as many victims do when missing the warning signs that place you in danger, before gaining the courage to affix blame where it was due—squarely on the rapist himself." Blair took a moment to regain her composure. "We're all here today because of what we've been put through and are now survivors with a greater sense of self-worth and solace in knowing that we're not alone." She gazed warmly at Nikki and said even-toned, "Tell us your story, if you feel comfortable doing so."

Nikki smiled softly at her, having established a rapport that helped her feel at ease. "I'm Nikki

Sullivan," she told the group in a well-practiced and affable tone. "Ten years ago, I was the victim of a brutal attack by a serial killer named Perry Evigan. He sexually assaulted and then strangled to death ten women, including my best friend, Brigette, after he drugged us. I was supposed to die too, but the FBI and local authorities miraculously came to my rescue before he could finish the job. I got lucky—if you could call it that—ending up with a broken jaw in two places, that still aches on occasion, a concussion, badly sprained ankle and a bloodied lower lip." She winced at the thought. "In spite of my best efforts to the contrary, the regrets about what happened and what I might have done differently if I could go back in time have never gone away. Or the nightmares." She sucked in a deep breath as Nikki mused about Perry Evigan, hating that he still had a hold on her somewhat as a sexual predator, even after all these years, and knowing he was safely put away in prison for the rest of his life. "Anyway, that's my story," she said, lifting her chin defiantly, "and, like everyone here, I'm a survivor and proud of it."

With that, there was applause and Nikki smiled, while knowing that the strength in numbers was what kept each of them going when left to themselves. And that the ebb and flow between sadness and empowerment would continue as each person recounted his or her experience. The last to speak was one of the male survivors, Harry Rosen, a forty-three-year-old US Air Force veteran, traumatized from his experiences when serving in Afghanistan. It cost him one of his legs. He finished by saying courageously, "It's been tough some days, for sure. But right here, right now, I can tell you that I'd enlist all over again in representing my country in the military."

More applause came before it swung back to Blair. After the group meeting was over and they were alone in the backyard, Nikki was approached by the counseling psychologist, who had become a trusted friend. Blair said to her, "Are you free for lunch?"

Nikki shook her head. "I can't," she responded reluctantly. "My latest artwork won't paint itself, if I'm going to have it ready for the showing on Saturday."

"Understood," Blair said. "Not a problem."

"Rain check?"

"You've got it."

Nikki smiled gratefully. "See you at the next meeting."

Blair patted her hand. "Wouldn't miss it," she joked.

Nikki laughed. "Didn't imagine you would."

"If I ever did, you could always fill in for me."

"You think?"

"Absolutely." Blair nodded. "Everyone likes you and feels comfortable with you, which encourages them to talk about their ordeals."

"Hmm." Nikki flushed. "I'll keep that in mind."

She left the four-sided brick home on Aplen Avenue and headed for her car on this early afternoon with the sun shining brightly to remind her it was mid-July. She climbed inside the red Subaru Crosstrek and headed home, where she had her studio. Art had been her passion for as long as she could remember and Nikki had managed to turn it into a successful career over the years, specializing in landscape, still life and portrait oil paintings—with showings across the state and occasionally elsewhere.

She hadn't been nearly as successful with her love life. The few times she had dated someone over the years, Nikki had come up empty. That included a guy she had gone out on a date with exactly one time recently—a personal trainer named Kenan Fernández—only to find there was absolutely no chemistry whatsoever. He seemed to feel otherwise, but she had not seen him since, ignoring his phone and text messages.

The reality was that she had yet to find the right person to have a serious romance with. It left Nikki wondering if her standards were too high. Had her brush with death left her emotionally damaged? Or was it more about her unwillingness to take a chance on someone, only to fail and have her heart broken? Would that be more than she could take in only wanting a happy ending, after losing a friend to a serial killer?

Nikki's thoughts drifted away as her attention turned to the news brief on the radio. "According to the Mississippi Department of Corrections," the female broadcaster reported tensely, "in the midst of unrest at the Mississippi State Penitentiary, three inmates managed a brazen escape in the wee hours of the morning, killing a guard and the driver of a pickup truck along the way. The escapees, all lifers for serious crimes of violence, have been identified as forty-four-year-old Perry Evigan, thirty-six-year-old Aaron Machado and Craig Schneider, age twenty-seven."

Nikki's heart skipped a beat at the mention of Perry Evigan's name, even as she heard the newscaster say in dramatic fashion, "Evigan, once dubbed the Gulfport Nightmare Killer, strangled to death ten women—sexually assaulting them beforehand—before being captured a decade ago. One woman was able to survive an attack by the serial killer and testified at his trial nearly nine years ago, resulting in a conviction and life sentence. The escapees are described as armed and extremely dangerous…"

What? Evigan is out of prison and on the loose, Nikki thought, the very notion shaking her to the core as her fingers trembled around the steering wheel. How could that have happened? He was supposed to be locked away forever in a maximum-security facility. With no escape possible. She shuddered in recalling Perry Evigan's haunting last words to her during his trial.

I'll see you again someday, Nikki, and finish what I started. Trust me.

She had totally rejected his threat as the ravings of a defeated and defiant man on his way back to prison. Was he now in a position to make good on that threat? she had to wonder. *Am I in danger*? Nikki asked herself, worried. Did she need to go into hiding while that bastard remained free? Or would the authorities, who, according to the news report, had intensified their search for the escaped convicts, have them back in custody long before Evigan could seriously entertain tracking her down nine years later?

Nikki mulled over this troubling development and the potentially high stakes for her own life, security and future, as she pulled into the driveway of her custom-built, three-bedroom Creole cottage-style home on Waconia Way, outside the garage. With a stunning backside view of the nearby Jourdan River, the property was bordered by sugar maple trees, giving her some privacy.

Only when she got out of the car, did Nikki notice the dark-colored Chevrolet Tahoe parked across the street. Had it been there before? Did it belong to her neighbor?

A spasm of fear ripped through her, as the vehicle's driver-side door opened. Could Perry Evigan have already found her? Not that it would have been too difficult as she hadn't exactly tried to hide from him, per se, not believing she needed to. Picturing the smug face of the man who tried to kill her, Nikki's first instinct was to bolt for her front door, where she had a good security system inside that would protect her and alert the police. Short of that, she had a stun gun in her leather hobo bag to defend herself with. If that failed, she could always make use of the skills she'd learned in the self-defense courses she'd taken after her attack and refreshed herself with periodically.

When a tall and very fit male stepped out of the car, Nikki spied the somewhat familiar devilishly handsome face of a biracial man. One she never expected to see again, even if not necessarily her preference. Or maybe she had felt it was for the best, when considering the bad blood that had existed between them in the wake of Brigette's death. Now in his midthirties, he still had the taut oblong face, piercing gray eyes and slightly crooked mouth she had last seen right after Perry Evigan's trial ended. New was the five o'clock shadow beard and trendy style of his short raven hair in a midrazor fade. She stood there flatfooted as he quickly closed the distance between them in his boat shoes, to go with a light blue polo shirt and dark chinos. Her instinct to run away from him was stilled by curiosity, if nothing else.

"Nikki," he said tonelessly and paused. "It's been a minute."

"More like nine years," she said wryly to her late friend Brigette's former boyfriend, Gavin Lynley. Nikki fluttered her lashes. "What are you doing here?"

Gavin pinched his Roman nose and said without preface, "Perry Evigan has escaped from prison."

"I just heard it on the radio." Nikki's brow furrowed as she fought to maintain her composure. She was admittedly still piqued as to why Gavin needed—or even wanted, after the way they left things—to convey the news in person. Peering at him, she asked pointedly, "So, did you come to tell me that he's been recaptured?"

"I'm here to say I hope that will be a done deal shortly." Gavin glanced down at his shoes and then lifted his eyes to meet hers fixedly. "Until such time, I've been assigned to make sure Perry Evigan doesn't come anywhere near you."

Chapter Two

Gavin could tell that Nikki saw him as almost as much her enemy as Perry Evigan. Not that he could blame her any. The last time he had laid eyes upon her, they had parted as nothing but two people who had lost someone each cared about. They certainly hadn't moved in opposite directions on a positive note. Much less, as friends. Whether he cared to admit it or not, Gavin knew that he had to bear much of the blame for that. He had pushed Nikki away as the only person he knew with a direct line to Brigette when she was alive and, in theory, could have been a shoulder for Gavin to lean on. And vice versa.

But he had been too wounded at the time to think in those terms. All he wanted to do was try to put the past behind him—including Brigette's best friend, whom he'd been attracted to since the day they first met, but never acted on out of respect for Brigette in not wanting to cross any lines—and move on with his life. Clearly, this had been Nikki's intent too.

Till he unceremoniously reentered the picture. Thanks to their mutual foe: Perry Evigan.

Gavin studied her now, as Nikki glared at him with those enchanting royal blue eyes. They were beautiful, along with a delicate nose and generous mouth on a heart-shaped face, which had only gotten more attractive with time. The blunt cut of Nikki's long blond locks agreed with her. She was still appealingly slender and the perfect height in relation to his own, while wearing a peach-colored smocked-trim top, navy trouser pants and moccasin flats.

Now came the hard part. He needed to break the ice that had formed a thick barrier between them over the past nine years and at least try to remain cordial while keeping her out of harm's way.

"You're joking, right?" Nikki's eyes flashed hotly at him. "You've shown up out of nowhere to be my bodyguard? Maybe I'd be better off taking my chances with Perry Evigan. At least I know who I'm dealing with in him. As opposed to you, who outright accused me of being responsible for Brigette's death. My best friend. And never seemed to back down, as I recall. Now this?" Her lashes curled whimsically. "How did you expect me to react?"

Oh boy, this is going to be harder than I'd imagined, Gavin told himself, as he eyed her resting a hand on a slender hip. "Just the way you have," he had to confess. Or at the very least, he hadn't exactly expected a welcoming committee. He glanced about to assess the surroundings. Seemed pleasant enough, with mature cypress trees lining the streets and an otherwise peacefulness in the atmosphere. Unfortunately, this did little to make him feel at ease, fully aware that the facade would be perfect cover for a ruthless serial killer to go on the attack. Gavin turned back to Nikki and asked in a pleading tone, "Do you mind if we go inside and talk about this?" He looked over her head at the two-story cottage she called home.

Without uttering another word, Nikki turned and headed up the walkway, inviting him with her silence to follow, which he did. On the front porch, there were two black wicker chairs that they bypassed.

Walking through the door, Gavin stepped onto the travertine floor and took in the Spanish Cedar millwork and open concept with a high ceiling, cottage-style ceiling fan and symmetrical windows with vinyl Venetian blinds. There was a good-size living and dining area, wicker furnishings, floating staircase and gourmet kitchen with a marble countertop and breakfast nook. He took note of the security system, as well as the double-cylinder dead-bolt front door lock.

He gazed at Nikki and said sheepishly, "Nice place."

"Thanks," she responded tonelessly, her arms folded while waiting anxiously to hear more from him on the situation they found themselves in.

"Look, I know I'm probably the last person you expected to see show up at your house," Gavin conceded, "short of Perry Evigan. Truthfully, I wasn't expecting it either. But due to the circumstances..." He paused. "So, here's the deal..." Gavin knew there would be no sugarcoating this. So why try? "As a special agent with the Mississippi Department of Corrections, protecting crime victims and witnesses is part of my duties. Given that Perry Evigan was one of the escapees from our prison system and swore vengeance against you—and also happened to be responsible for the death of Brigette Fontana, my then-girlfriend—I suppose I was the obvious choice of my boss to keep you safe in the remote chance that Evigan manages to evade recapture and tries to make good on his threat."

"Obvious choice. Really?" Nikki pursed her lips skeptically. "Maybe not the best choice, given our strained history. To say the least."

Gavin found that hard to argue with on its merits. "I wanted to call to see if you were okay with this, but figured my best bet was to do it face-to-face," he said.

She reacted with a sneer. "I'm not so sure about that."

"Look, if having me around, even for a short while, really makes you uncomfortable, I can get the locals to assign an officer to protect you." Gavin met her eyes. "Until such time, I can wait outside till the officer arrives…"

Nikki seemed to weigh her options, before saying tentatively, "That won't be necessary. If this is your job, I suppose I can handle it, if you can."

He nodded in agreement. "I'm sure I'll be out of your hair in no time flat." Even in uttering the words, Gavin couldn't help but wonder what it would be like to run his fingers through that long luscious hair of hers.

"Fine." She took a breath. "Do you really think that Perry Evigan would risk his newfound freedom to try and find me after all these years?" she questioned.

It was something that Gavin had already asked himself more than once. Assuming Evigan still had a little common sense and even a little intelligence, it would seem improbable that he would roll the dice in coming for Nikki when he had to know that the risk would not likely justify the means. As it pertained to his staying on the lam successfully, it was a tough task under the best of circumstances. But something told Gavin that the psychopath in Evigan might well be driven by impulses beyond his own best interests. Or normal behavior.

Trying to keep it as diplomatic as possible, Gavin responded evenly, "Probably not. But the man is a serial killer and knows that with the high probability that he'll be caught sooner rather than later—he may feel he has nothing to lose and everything to gain, in trying to finish what he started ten years ago." Gavin reached out and touched her shoulder. He ignored the powerful sensation that this small gesture brought about, while telling her in earnest, "I won't let that happen."

Nikki gave a slow and grateful nod. "Thank you."

"Not a problem." Even if it had been, he wouldn't have admitted to this. He was on an assignment and owed it to her—and the shared memory of Brigette—to see it through, with minimal disruption of Nikki's life before walking away from her. Again. "So, are you still an artist?" The question was more conversational than anything. In the course of establishing her whereabouts and out of curiosity, Gavin had discovered that she had, in fact, made a name for herself in the local art world with prominent showings and paintings in high demand. Nikki had not used a pseudonym when relocating from Gulfport to Owl's Bay. Meaning that Evigan would likely have little trouble using social media or online news sources to discover her location, which concerned Gavin.

"Yes," she answered matter-of-factly. "Mostly landscape and still life, with some portraits."

"Nice." Gavin grinned, recalling how he had seen and admired some of her paintings back in the day when Brigette had insisted that he come along to check out a few that Nikki had laid out in her apartment. He imagined her work would be even more compelling today.

"Speaking of which—" Nikki broke into his thoughts "—I do need to get to my studio, down the hall, for some work. It will also keep my mind occupied on something other than Perry Evigan possibly trying to kill me…and—" she made an uncomfortable expression on her face "—sexually assaulting me beforehand, per his MO." She looked away. "Since you'll probably be here for a little while, I guess you can make yourself at home, Gavin. There are drinks and half an apple pie in the fridge, if you get thirsty or hungry. And the first-floor bathroom is just off the kitchen."

"Thanks." He appreciated the hospitality, even if Gavin didn't feel particularly welcomed and rightfully so. They'd had their differences and they wouldn't be resolved overnight. But that didn't mean they couldn't be nice to each other while occupying the same house. As soon as he got word that Evigan had been arrested and was no longer a threat to Nikki or anyone else, Gavin would get out of her life and they could each go about their business.

Or was this a good time to address the past and losing Brigette to senseless violence, once and for all?

He watched as Nikki walked away, before Gavin took out his cell phone and rang Marvin Whitfield. "I'm with her now," he told the director equably.

"No trouble?"

"Not yet," Gavin responded.

"Good. How's she doing with the news that Perry Evigan is out?" Whitfield asked.

"Probably as well as could be expected." Gavin glanced down the hall and saw that Nikki had gone into her studio. "Honestly, though she's put on a brave face, Nikki's spooked, and with good reason. Any word yet on the whereabouts of Evigan and the other escapees?"

"Reports have come in that the trio may have been spotted in Tennessee," Whitfield indicated.

"But others claimed to have seen them in Alabama." The director sighed. "Right now, we don't have a solid fix on their whereabouts. With the head start the inmates had before we realized they were missing, Evigan, Machado and Schneider could be anywhere, frankly. They are believed to be driving a black Chrysler Pacifica that was stolen in Boyle. According to the elderly owner, Donald Takeuchi, who wasn't home at the time, the trio also broke into his house and stole two legally purchased firearms—a Glock G43X subcompact semiauto pistol and a SIG Sauer P365 9mm pistol, along with ammo."

"That's not very comforting," Gavin told him bluntly, though hardly surprised that the escapees would arm themselves while on the run. "Evigan and his killer pals are not likely to turn themselves in peacefully and miss out on their one big opportunity to escape to greener pastures. They could've left the state—which would have been the smartest move—or chosen to lay low in Mississippi, traveling the back roads while trying to bypass roadblocks they would have to get past in whatever stolen vehicle they were driving."

"Yeah, desperate as they are, there's no telling what their mindset is while trying to avoid capture," Whitfield voiced. "All we know for certain is that they're still on the loose, armed and extremely dangerous."

Gavin muttered words in agreement. "Which makes the situation all the more aggravating and frightening."

"Just keep Ms. Sullivan safe," the director ordered, "till we can bring in Evigan, in particular, as well as Machado and Schneider."

"Will do," Gavin promised. Even if Nikki would probably still prefer another person to be her protector. Or had she begun to let her guard down a bit with him—and vice versa—in spite of the animosity between them spanning a decade, which he now regretted?

APART FROM FEELING most like herself in the studio, Nikki admittedly used it as a way to mask the strong physical awareness she unexpectedly had for Gavin Lynley's presence. Was it wrong to have romantic vibes for someone who hated her for allowing Brigette to talk her into going out that fateful night ten years ago? Was it just as wrong for Gavin to believe that Brigette walked on water as the love of his life—when in reality, she was anything but the faithful girlfriend with eyes only for him?

Telling him now would only make it seem like I'm rewriting history in knocking Brigette off her pedestal when she's no longer alive to de-

fend herself, Nikki mused sadly as she glanced about the art studio. With natural light coming in from a large picture window, there were canvases in various stages of completion on long wooden tables and lining the walls on the floor, along with pencils, brushes and multiple colors of paint ready to use. She liked to move back and forth between projects, tackling one or another whenever the spirit moved her. Aside from when she needed to prioritize for commissioned artworks. Or showings. She imagined painting Gavin, seeing him as the perfect human subject with his handsome, defined features and strong jawline. But his assignment would likely be over practically before it started—ending that fantasy where it probably belonged. In her head and now her heart.

The fact that she'd secretly had feelings for Brigette's boyfriend years ago but had wisely kept them to herself, not wanting to betray her best friend, did not change the reality that there was little chance that anything could happen now between Nikki and Gavin. Apart from the strained relations between them, she had no reason to believe he would ever be interested in her romantically. For all she knew, he was in a serious relationship—if not a marriage—with someone else, now that Brigette, his presumably first true love, was no longer around to give him the

family Brigette had indicated he wanted someday. Never mind that Brigette didn't necessarily
share his vision for her own future.

*I won't open up a can of worms for someone
who is merely here on assignment as a special
agent,* Nikki told herself as she headed to a canvas on an easel that she had started working on.
It was a painting of Mississippi wildflowers. It
was best not to go there and allow Brigette to
rest in peace and Gavin to keep her memory in
any way he saw fit. Just as Nikki chose to do,
knowing that Brigette would always hold a special place in her heart, flaws and all.

Not to mention that no matter who was responsible for their going out that night, it was
Brigette who made the ultimate sacrifice. Even
if that was never her intention. While Nikki
had somehow managed to escape her own date
with death, though not for lack of Perry Evigan's
wanting to see her suffer too, through a sexual
violation, followed by ligature strangulation.

And now, she feared, he may still come after
her, just as he promised, to deal her the same
fatal blow he dealt Brigette and nine other
women—all with the better part of their lives
still ahead of them. Until that was no longer the
case.

Nikki could only hope that Gavin was as committed to preventing this as he appeared to be,

their issues notwithstanding. Or that Perry Evigan was captured and put back behind bars, long before he could ever make his way to Owl's Bay.

GAVIN POKED HIS head into the art studio, where he had given Nikki a few uninterrupted hours to work and process the circumstances that brought them together again so suddenly. She was standing before a canvas, painting, and seemingly totally in focus. That didn't mean she had all but forgotten he was there. He was certain that she was just as ill at ease about it as he was. But no matter the second-guessing about the events that led to Brigette's death, it was necessary for him to occupy Nikki's space, as her safety was front and center. Not only as a matter of his directive as a special agent of the Mississippi Department of Corrections CID, but also on a personal level. Gavin hadn't been able to save Brigette from that monster. He would be damned if he allowed Evigan to harm her best friend as well.

He stepped inside the studio and said, to catch her attention, "Hey."

Nikki stopped painting the still life of wildflowers and turned to face him. "Hey." She flashed a tentative expression. "Any news on Perry Evigan?"

Gavin only wished he could tell her that Evigan and his fellow prison escapees had been recaptured and were no longer a danger to the public. Or her, in particular, where it concerned the serial killer. "I'm afraid that Evigan is still on the loose," he told her frustratingly.

She wrinkled her nose. "How have they been able to avoid capture? I assume law enforcement is on full alert on the prison escape?"

"They are," Gavin assured her. "Trust me, we're doing everything we can to find the escapees. How have they avoided capture?" He waited a beat while moving closer to her. "We're talking about hardened criminals here. They may well have planned their escape long before it actually happened and developed a strategy for staying hidden or otherwise circumventing the law. On the other hand, Evigan and his cronies may simply have gotten lucky, thus far, in evading the authorities. Either way, a BOLO has been issued for the trio, who are believed to still be together, along with the stolen vehicle they may be driving. It's only a matter of time before they're apprehended."

Nikki rolled her eyes. "Why doesn't that give me much comfort?"

"Probably for the same reason it doesn't me," Gavin told her in all honesty. "With Evigan's murderous track record—and Aaron Machado and Craig Schneider aren't any better, as they're also convicted murderers—we can't afford to let our guard down till Evigan's back behind bars."

"No, we definitely can't." A look of apprehension flashed across her face. "So, what now?"

"I stick around for as long as it takes while the man who attacked you and Brigette remains a fugitive." Gavin jutted his chin. "If that's all right with you—?"

Nikki nodded thoughtfully. "It has to be," she said in no uncertain terms. "I just want this over so I can get on with my life without needing to look over my shoulder."

Or having to deal with me and our shared and tragic history, Gavin mused. "I understand." He resisted the urge to touch Nikki's face, imagining how soft it would feel to his fingertips. "If you're hungry, how about we do takeout? It's probably best not to go to a restaurant at night right now," he indicated, knowing that exposing themselves under the cover of darkness could well be playing right into Evigan's hands, assuming he was able to continue to dodge the dragnet.

"Actually, I'm starving," Nikki said. "And, yes, takeout is good. And quicker than cooking something, as I wasn't, umm…prepared for a guest. Short of day-old apple pie."

Gavin grinned sideways. "I had a piece," he told her. "It was tasty."

"Glad you liked it." She showed her teeth,

which brightened her good looks that much more. "Brigette taught me how to make one. Before then, I was pretty useless when it came to desserts."

He remembered Brigette being good with apple, cherry and pecan pies—and even chocolate and caramel cake—having been taught the art of making delicious desserts from her own mother. It was one of the things that attracted Gavin to Brigette, given his sweet tooth and all. If only he didn't have to work that fateful night, forcing him to cancel their date. Then Brigette would still be alive and neither she nor Nikki would have ever been victimized by the likes of Perry Evigan.

This was something Gavin would have to live with. Even if he wished Nikki had been stronger in pushing back against Brigette's greater risk-taking ventures.

THE ESCAPED CONS traveled down the back road in the stolen Chrysler Pacifica. They were armed, antsy, hungry and looking for a way to keep the journey to freedom going for as long as possible. In fact, none of them relished the thought of going back to prison. On the contrary, each was willing to do whatever was necessary to avoid doing just that. Having managed to circumvent their pursuers only emboldened them to continue fleeing from them and let the chips fall where they may.

If that meant taking out anyone who stood in their way, then so be it. With nothing to lose, all options were on the table. That included taking hostages and making sure that any and all of their demands were met. Or else.

At least one of the escapees thought that Mexico might be a good option. It would be relatively easy to disappear once there and start over in some small town where each person's business was his own.

Another saw that as a stupid idea, knowing from experience that living south of the border with the authorities in full pursuit would be no walk in the park. Just the opposite. For his part, he would rather remain on the lam in the United States, moving from state to state if necessary. There were plenty of places to hide where one might never be found. Staying one step or two ahead of the law might be challenging, but possible with determination and ingenuity.

The other escapee and self-appointed leader of the group, Perry Evigan, had his own agenda, but kept it to himself. No need to ruffle any feathers at this point when not in a position to speak his mind in a way that would not potentially blow up in his face.

Sitting in the front passenger seat, he gripped

tightly the Glock G43X subcompact semiauto pistol in his hands. He saw it as not only protection, but also a means to an end for his desire to achieve his objectives in picking up right where he left off a decade ago as the Gulfport Nightmare Killer.

The one who got away had haunted his dreams, and only she could allow him to be himself again. He wanted that—*her*—more than anything. But before he could even seriously begin to think in those terms, Perry knew he had to figure out a way to survive, with the walls closing in on them, he sensed.

He hadn't come this far in his quest only to be denied. Not when his quarry was out there, waiting for him, more or less.

The pretty face of Nikki Sullivan filled his head. He couldn't help but crack a grin at the thought of her. If he had his way, Perry was sure they would meet again. But the forces working against him could prevent that from ever happening.

Or not.

Chapter Three

In the dining area, Gavin sat in an upholstered side chair across a pedestal table from Nikki and decided it was time to address the elephant in the room. At least this was what he sensed during the mostly quiet and clearly strained eating of their take-out dinner consisting of country-fried steak, mashed potatoes and garden salad, along with coffee. Gazing at her, he said in an earnest tone, "Look, I think we need to clear the air…"

Nikki stopped eating, staring back at him. "The air in here is pretty clear, last time I checked," she spoke wryly.

"I'm sure you know what I mean." Or was this trip down memory lane only one-sided?

She dabbed a paper napkin to her mouth and said thoughtfully, "Well, go on, say what's on your mind."

Gavin took a breath and put down his fork, before responding apologetically, "I shouldn't have taken my frustrations about what happened to Brigette out on you."

"But you did," Nikki said with an edge to her tone. "For the past ten years, you gave me a guilt complex—made me believe that I somehow should've stopped Brigette from wanting to go out. As if." Nikki rolled her eyes at the absurdity of it, with them both knowing just how headstrong Brigette could be when she made up her mind to do something. "And that I was responsible for putting us in harm's way—or the crosshairs of a serial killer—by not insisting that she stay put on a Saturday night after you bailed on her. So, why the change of heart now?" she challenged him.

His shoulders slumped as Gavin was forced to look squarely at his own culpability in not only Brigette's death, but Nikki's suffering at the hands of Perry Evigan. Not to mention being present when he killed her best friend. "You're not going to make this easy for me, are you?"

"Nope." Nikki gave him a firm expression. "Did you want me to?"

"I guess not," he answered, knowing full well that going light on him would only be a cop-out. Which he didn't deserve. Gavin collected his thoughts and said, "The truth of the matter is, on some level—actually, more than that—I've always known that you weren't to blame for what happened to you and Brigette. You were twenty-three-year-olds, just wanting to do what most

young people liked to do on a Saturday night—
go out and have fun. Neither of you could have
anticipated that you would run into Evigan at
a club. Or that he would spike your drinks and
victimize you further."

Gavin picked up his fork and moved the salad
around, as his own guilt took center stage. "If
anyone deserves blame for what you were put
through—besides the creep who perpetrated the
attack—it's me. I've kicked myself more than
once over the years, wishing I'd not canceled
the date with Brigette. At the time, I was still
getting my feet wet on the job and didn't feel I
could afford to slack off when duty called. Had
I stuck with getting together with Brigette, it
probably would've saved her life and spared you
what Evigan put you through."

"You can't know that for sure," Nikki countered and lifted her mug of coffee. "Even if
Brigette and I hadn't gone out that night, we
could have still ended up being targeted by Perry
Evigan another night. Maybe that's how the universe works. Fate. Or whatever. Point is, there
may have been nothing you or I could have done
to prevent what happened—no matter how many
times we replayed the what-ifs to try and rewrite
history. Or at least reimagined it."

"You're right," Gavin said, somewhat surprised that she had come to his defense, after he

had wanted to assuage his own feelings of guilt by putting it on her, to one degree or another. He could only wonder how their friendship would have evolved had they been on the same page years ago in putting the tragedy behind them. "It does no good to rehash everything that went wrong that night. But I'm still sorry that it took me so long to come to this place."

"Me too." She favored him with a tender smile, sipping the coffee. "I know that Brigette—as the person who brought us together—would have wanted us to at least remain friends over the years. So, better late than never, I suppose."

"Yeah, agreed." He grinned at her, believing that having Nikki in his life, even from a distance, was something he needed. The fact that she seemed to feel the same was just as pleasing.

They resumed eating and Gavin considered that the one positive that came from the ordeal was that Evigan was stopped in his tracks—preventing him from victimizing others down the line. That was something to take solace in.

Except for the fact that the serial killer had escaped from prison. And was still on the loose. Meaning that Nikki was in danger for as long as Evigan remained free.

NIKKI COULD HARDLY believe that she and Gavin had just had a heart-to-heart discussion in confronting the albatross that seemed to hang around their necks for the better part of a decade. She could only imagine Brigette scolding them both for taking so long to bridge the gap as two people important in her life, to one degree or another.

In the process, Nikki realized she'd had to come to terms with the fact that, on some level, she had blamed Gavin for her own victimization. Had he chosen Brigette instead of his job that night, Nikki would have likely stayed home, even if bored out of her mind—thereby sparing her from being almost raped and strangled to death by Perry Evigan. She realized now how foolish that was to think. Gavin had a right to reschedule his date with Brigette to work, not knowing what would go down by virtue of this. He was no more guilty of being responsible for what happened than Nikki was in not trying to talk Brigette out of going out on the town for drinking and dancing.

Agreeing on this was definitely a good thing, Nikki told herself, as she cleared the table with Gavin's help. She welcomed the opportunity to come away as friends, after the dust resettled with Perry Evigan once again behind bars. Or dead, if he resisted arrest.

They sat back at the table with a slice of apple pie for dessert and a glass of red wine. After a few minutes of keeping things light, Nikki decided to be brave and asked Gavin out of curiosity, "So, are you seeing anyone these days?" She hoped she wasn't being too forward, prying into his personal life. But they were on friendly terms again, right?

"No," he responded over his wineglass and without prelude. "I've dated off and on over the years, but nothing stuck."

"I guess Brigette was a hard act to follow, huh?" Nikki said, a twinge of envy coursing through her, knowing that her late friend's feelings weren't entirely reciprocated toward him.

Gavin kept a straight face as he sipped wine and answered coolly, "I did care about Brigette a lot, but I moved on, having no choice but to do so. As for her being a hard act to follow, she was certainly a handful at times as a girlfriend. The truth is, I'm not sure where things were headed between us. Maybe nowhere over the course of time. Regarding being single right now, I guess I'm still waiting for the right person to come along and see what happens—"

"I see." She tasted the wine, while wondering just how long it would take for that right person to come along. Or was he just as picky as she was?

"What about you?" Gavin caught her attention. "Anyone in your life these days?"

"Can't say there is," she told him honestly.

"Like you, I've dated people from time to time since moving to Owl's Bay—including, most recently, a guy named Kenan Fernández, a personal trainer—and struck out, unfortunately, insofar as finding my soul mate, if you believe in that type of thing."

"Actually, I do believe it to be true," Gavin surprised her by saying. "When it happens, you just know it."

"Perhaps you're right." She wondered if he thought of Brigette as his soul mate when they were together. And, if so, would any other woman ever measure up?

He used his fork to cut into the slice of apple pie and said, "So, do you have family? I seem to recall from Brigette that you grew up in what, Clarksdale?"

"Yes, I did." Nikki smiled. "My mother and stepdad still live there. I lost my dad when I was five. I'm an only child. How about you?" Didn't Brigette once mention to her that he had a younger sister?

"I have a sister, Lauren, two years my junior," Gavin confirmed. "She and her husband, Rory, live with their two cute little girls, Ellen and Miley, in Cape Cod. My parents passed away a few years ago, though separately," he said sadly.

"Sorry to hear that." Nikki considered Gavin's pain with having to deal with their losses coming after Brigette's death. Had that also destroyed any plans to have children of his own someday?

"Both had been dealing with some health issues off and on," he noted, "and went pretty quickly at the end. Apart from Lauren and Rory, I had a lot of support in dealing with it from cousins that I'm close to. They all happen to also be gainfully employed in law enforcement careers."

"I remember Brigette mentioning something about that." Nikki tasted the pie thoughtfully. "I'm sure they probably have something to say about the brazen prison escape by Perry Evigan and the others."

"Yeah, whether I want to hear it or not," Gavin quipped. "Seriously, they've got my back and definitely want to see Evigan behind bars again where he belongs."

She sipped her wine musingly. "Where do you think he is right now?"

Gavin put the wineglass to his mouth and then said bluntly, "Running scared and wondering just how much time he has left before his taste of freedom comes crashing down like a house of cards—one way or another…"

Nikki took solace in that assessment, while feeling even greater comfort in Gavin's presence as the last line of defense should Perry Evigan someway, somehow, still show up at her door. Only to have a second crack at her.

BRUSHING SHOULDERS AS they removed the dessert dishes and wineglasses, Gavin once again felt a spark when touching Nikki. Surely, she felt it too? Was there something between them that he had missed a decade ago? Had he hedged his bet wrong when turning his attention to Brigette, when Nikki was just as attractive? And perhaps a better fit for him, character-wise?

"If it's okay with you," Gavin asked Nikki evenly, "I'd like to camp out on your living room sofa for the night—while Evigan is still at large. Or, if that's cramping your style too much, I can sleep out in my car. Not a problem."

"Don't be silly." She dismissed that last notion with a wave of her hand. "No need to spend the night in your vehicle, Special Agent Lynley, in keeping me safe from a dangerous man. Or, for that matter, sleeping on my sofa. It's comfortable, but only to a point." Nikki smiled at him. "As it is, I have a guest room upstairs that you're welcome to stay in, as long as needed. It has an en suite as well, if you want to shower or anything."

"Thanks. I'll take you up on that." Gavin grinned while also feeling an underpinning of desire as he imagined her in bed in another room not far from the spare bedroom—and him in it with her. "I'll just step outside to get my bag."

As he did just that, Gavin scanned the perimeter, looking for any sign of Evigan, while keeping a hand close to the 9mm semiautomatic pistol in his holster. He saw nothing out of the ordinary or otherwise suspicious and so Gavin continued on to his Chevrolet Tahoe. *If Evigan dares to show up here, I'll arrest him and he'll be back in prison where he belongs in no time flat*, Gavin told himself, while grabbing his tote bag and heading back inside the house.

"I set some fresh towels on the bed," Nikki told him.

"Appreciate that." He smiled and they both climbed the stairwell and Gavin was led to the guest room.

"Here you go," she pointed out.

Gavin glanced inside the room and saw rustic furniture, including a log bed. He thanked her again for the hospitality. "This will do just fine," he said nicely.

Nikki gave a nod. "If you need anything, let me know."

"Will do."

"Good night."

"Good night," he told her, watching briefly as she walked away, while wondering how he could have wasted a decade blaming her for something that was entirely on Perry Evigan. And no one else. At least Nikki didn't seem to hold it against him after they had talked this through. Gavin saw that as a positive step forward for both of them.

After closing the door, he removed his firearm, setting it on the wicker nightstand, along with his holster. Then Gavin pulled out his cell phone and fell onto a rattan armchair, where he reached out to the Owl's Bay Police Department to make sure they were on the same page in terms of the BOLO for Perry Evigan and the other escapees. That seemed to be the case, which gave Gavin comfort, wanting there to be as many sets of eyes keeping watch in town for the prisoners as possible. Even if it appeared to be a long shot at face value that the trio would show up in Owl's Bay as a group. Gavin only wished he could feel as confident where it concerned Evigan operating alone, still envisioning the serial killer's smug face after his arrest, during the trial and upon his conviction. It was obvious that Nikki remembered this too.

Gavin called his cousin, Scott Lynley, returning a voice mail he'd left earlier. An FBI special agent and cold case specialist, working at the field office in Louisville, Kentucky, he and Scott, who was a few years older, were always cool and supportive of each other's careers and personal trials and tribulations.

Scott answered the video chat request, his oblong face appearing on the screen. "Hey."

Gavin gazed at Scott, who had gray eyes and thick black hair in a comb-over pomp, low-fade style. "Hey."

"I heard about Perry Evigan's daring escape from prison."

"Who hasn't by now?" Gavin pursed his lips.

Scott furrowed his brow. "Are they any closer to catching him?"

"I'd sure as hell like to think so," he told him. "But as of now, Evigan and his prison buddies, Aaron Machado and Craig Schneider, are still roaming free."

"That's too bad."

"Tell me about it." Gavin sighed, jutting his chin.

"No doubt your old girlfriend, Brigette, and the other women Evigan murdered are spinning in their graves, wondering how this could have happened."

"They seized on the distraction from the uprising," Gavin muttered. "Which shows there's still a major flaw in the system that the three were able to pull it off."

"They won't get very far," Scott said. "The

FBI is doing its part to help track them down as soon as possible."

Gavin nodded. "I know and am grateful for the support."

Scott paused. "Have you contacted the surviving victim of Evigan? I know you had your differences..."

"Nikki's been alerted about the escape and is safe," Gavin reported. "I've been assigned to stick with her till Evigan is back in custody."

"Really?" Scott cocked a brow. "How's that working out?"

"Better than expected." He sat back thoughtfully. "We're good," he told him. "Or at least have found a better way to deal with Brigette's death without pointing fingers."

"That's good to hear."

"Yeah." Gavin listened as Scott briefly talked about his own latest investigation and recent second marriage, before they disconnected.

After taking a shower, Gavin hit the sack, falling asleep, while thinking about Nikki.

An hour later, he awakened to the sound of a woman screaming.

Nikki. She was in danger.

Jumping out of bed, wearing only knit pajama shorts, Gavin sprang into action. He grabbed his pistol off the nightstand and ran out of the room and down the hall toward Nikki's bedroom.

Stepping inside, Gavin expected to see Perry Evigan looming over Nikki, in the process of trying to strangle her. At which point, he would stop the serial killer escapee by any means necessary.

Instead, Gavin was quickly able to establish that Nikki was in the room by herself, restless on the platform bed from what appeared to be a bad dream. Evigan had not managed to disengage the security system and enter the house with murder on his mind.

Moving past traditional furnishings to the bed, where Nikki was squirming and moaning beneath a patchwork bedspread, Gavin sat on it and grabbed her gently by the shoulders and jostled her awake as he called out her name.

"Get off me!" Nikki shrieked, as she flailed at him as if he was attacking her. She half sat up and out of the bedding, wearing a red chemise lingerie nightgown.

"Nikki, it's Gavin," he said gently, blocking her attempts to strike him in the face.

"Gavin?" Nikki opened her eyes and settled down upon gazing at him. "What are you doing in my bedroom?"

"I heard you scream," Gavin explained, releasing her. "I thought you were in serious trouble. But it looks like you were just having a bad dream."

"Oh." Her tone quieted.

"You're safe."

"I remember now," she said, ill at ease. "I was dreaming that Perry Evigan was trying to...well, do everything he wanted to do before—" She drew a breath. "Thank goodness it was all in my head."

"Do you often have nightmares about him?" Gavin wondered, feeling bad that she'd even had one.

"I used to. Especially in the years right after it happened. Not so much lately." Nikki looked up at him. "Guess the fact that Evigan escaped triggered a return to the nightmares. Sorry if I woke you up."

"No apologies necessary," Gavin stressed. "I'm sorry that Evigan being on the loose triggered the bad dream. Hopefully, the dream and his freedom will be short-lived."

"I hope so too."

"Try to go back to sleep." Gavin felt a strong need to protect her at all costs. "I'll be just down the hall, if you need me."

"All right." Nikki touched his hand. "Thank you for coming to my rescue. Even if it turned out that I didn't really need rescuing in this instance."

"Actually, I think you did," he begged to differ. "Nightmares can be just as frightening as real life. I wouldn't have sat back and allowed you to be victimized again by Evigan, even within your subconscious mind."

Against his desire of wanting to stay the night in her room to make Nikki feel more secure, Gavin left and went back to his own room, knowing that the longer Evigan remained out of prison, the more he would be able to wreak havoc on Nikki's psyche, along with his own.

Chapter Four

"Were you able to get back to sleep last night?" Gavin asked as they ate breakfast the following morning.

"Yes, surprisingly," Nikki told him across the table, where she spooned cereal, to go with toast and coffee, while fully dressed. She had figured that, after the nightmare, she would stay awake all night, freaking out over the likes of Perry Evigan. But perhaps knowing that Gavin was just down the hall and committed to keeping her from harm made the difference. "How about you?" She hoped he said yes, hating to think that his guard duty included pulling all-nighters.

"Yeah, I pretty much slept like a baby," he claimed with a straight face. He added, "But kept one eye open, just in case."

She chuckled. "That must have been challenging."

"Not so much." He grinned. "Comes with the territory sometimes."

Nikki colored. "You mean you jar awake other

witnesses or victims having nightmares, as a routine thing?"

"Not really." Gavin laughed and bit into a piece of toast. "But in this business, you have to be ready for everything. Including needing to get out of bed at a moment's notice in the wee hours of the morning."

She tasted the coffee and, eyeing him, asked curiously, "So, where do you live when you're not on bodyguard duty?"

"I'm based in Jackson," he said matter-of-factly.

"I see." She lifted her spoon. "I've visited Jackson a few times. There's a thriving art scene there."

"Really?" Gavin titled his face as though totally shocked. "Can't say I've been much into the art world—I'm more of a college-football-and spy-novels–type guy—but after seeing some of what you bring to the table, I'm becoming a true fan of your works."

Nikki blushed. "That's sweet of you to say." She would gladly invite him to her showing next week, but assumed he would be long gone by then. The notion of such was already depressing, even though it would also mean, presumably, that Perry Evigan had been captured. But then again, wasn't that why Gavin showed up at her house in the first place? No one said anything about him extending his time there. Much less moving beyond that by getting to know one another better. "Speaking of art," she said, shifting thoughts, "I need to step out for some supplies this morning." She assumed she wouldn't need to put her entire life on hold while Evigan was out there somewhere as a free man.

"No problem," Gavin spoke smoothly. He sipped coffee. "I'll drive you."

"Okay," she agreed, and bit into a piece of toast.

Shortly, they were in his vehicle and Nikki was still trying to come to grips with the fact that they were sharing the same space and no longer at each other's throats. She could only imagine what Brigette might think if she could see them now. Would she encourage them to cultivate their newfound camaraderie after years of animosity that centered squarely around her? Be jealous that there seemed to be a romantic connection of sorts forming between them? Or might Brigette have actually felt relieved that she could be single again and pursue someone other than Gavin, who might be more suited for her style and character?

"Have you always known you wanted to be an artist?" He intruded upon Nikki's thoughts.

"I suppose I have," she admitted, "ever since I was a little girl and spent much of my spare time with crayons and coloring books with all types of interesting pictures that I envisioned drawing or painting from scratch."

"Looks as though your instincts and talents have paid off for you."

"I do all right for myself," Nikki uttered modestly.

Gavin grinned. "Yeah, I think you have, and more."

"How did you end up working for the Mississippi Department of Corrections anyway?" She looked at him curiously. "As opposed to the FBI, DEA, Homeland Security, or a local police department?"

"It's a good question," he said, switching lanes as they approached an intersection. "Well, while I was a senior majoring in criminology at Mississippi State, their Career Center helped me land a job with the MDOC. I went with it—in separating myself from an uncle and cousins in law enforcement—and have been at this ever since. Overall, it's been worthwhile helping to deal with inmate issues inside and outside the penitentiary, as well as investigations involving corrections personnel who cross the line. Then there's special assignments, such as protecting crime victims or witnesses."

"Like me?" Nikki smiled at him.

"Yeah, exactly." Gavin glanced at her. "In this

instance, there was the added incentive of not wanting to see history repeat itself."

"Definitely wouldn't want that," she had to agree, while feeling maudlin thinking about what happened to Brigette—even more than what Nikki went through herself—in destroying her friend's life. And any chance she might have had of happiness, with or without Gavin.

GAVIN PULLED INTO the parking lot of the Owl's Bay Art Shop on Quail Street. As they got out of the car and headed for the store, he was keen on checking out the surroundings. There had been no sightings this morning, thus far, of the escapees. Least of all, Perry Evigan. Gavin had no reason to believe he had come to town, but kept a lookout for him nonetheless and remained armed to that effect.

Once inside, he took a sweeping glance at the main area with art supplies, then looked into two aisles with various arts and crafts, before deciding it was safe for Nikki to go about her business. Gavin watched as she grabbed a basket and said to him, "This shouldn't take long."

"Take your time," he said evenly, knowing he was committed to her well-being, wherever she happened to be while Evigan continued to circumvent the authorities. When his cell phone rang, Gavin removed it from the back pocket of his twill pants and saw that the caller was Special Agent Jean O'Reilly. Probably miffed that he left her hanging. Or appeared to. "I need to get this," he told Nikki.

"Please do." She offered him a grin. "I think I can manage on my own for a while."

He smiled. "All right."

Walking away, Gavin stepped outside, passing a shorter, solid-in-build Hispanic male in his forties, with shoulder-length brown hair parted on the side, who was entering the art shop. He was wearing workout clothes and white sneakers. His dark eyes met briefly with Gavin's, before looking away.

Gavin waited until the man had gone into the building before taking a few steps and accepting the video chat request. He watched Agent O'Reilly's face appear on the screen. "Hey."

"You might have given me a heads-up that you'd been reassigned, Lynley," she snapped.

"I had to leave on short notice," he said by way of apology. "Besides, technically speaking, I haven't exactly been reassigned, per se." He glanced at the art store window. "I'm sure you've heard about the prison break?"

"Of course. And Director Whitfield filled me in on your assignment of protecting serial killer escapee, Perry Evigan's former victim, while he remains on the prowl. I just don't get why it had to be you—with the FBI and US Marshals fully capable of keeping her safe."

"Maybe the director failed to mention that the victim, Nikki Sullivan, was the best friend of my then-girlfriend, Brigette Fontana—who was one of the ten women murdered by Evigan." Gavin wrinkled his nose, still feeling guilty for not being around to protect Brigette from him. Or Nikki, for that matter. "Nikki barely survived the ordeal herself. Anyway, between the two, it gave me added incentive to accept the assignment, along with the fact that it will be of short duration, in all likelihood—meaning that I should be back in Jackson in no time flat to continue mop-up work on the Titus Malfoy investigation."

"I didn't realize you had a personal connection to Evigan's crimes." Jean's face reddened. "Sorry about your ex—and for coming down on you."

"Don't give it a second thought," Gavin said. "I should have called you and explained why I had to leave town abruptly."

"So, how's Ms. Sullivan holding up?"

"Not that well, considering," he responded in all honesty. "Last night, she woke up screaming from a bad dream about Evigan."

Jean frowned. "That's understandable, given what he put her through."

"True." Gavin gazed again at the store, while

wondering just how many supplies Nikki needed to buy. "She's better today. But of course, until we can get Perry Evigan and the other escapees back into custody, Nikki's likely to have more restless days and nights."

"Their taste of freedom won't last long," she reassured him. "We've got people searching everywhere and anywhere the prisoners were allegedly spotted—or may have gone or be en route toward. Needless to say, the Mississippi Department of Corrections has some major egg on its face for allowing this escape to take place. As such, we're pulling out all the stops to make up for it—hopefully, before the inmates can hurt anyone else."

"Good to know," Gavin told her, still feeling anxious till it was a done deal.

"If you need any backup there, let me know," Jean said. "I'm sure the case against Titus Malfoy can wait, especially now that he's been arrested."

"I've got it covered, for now, with the locals on full alert."

"All right."

"I have to go," he told her, wanting to get back inside, in case Nikki needed help carrying out her supplies. "See you when I see you."

"Ditto," she said.

Gavin closed down the conversation and glanced around, before heading toward the door of the art store.

"WHAT ARE YOU doing here?" Nikki asked, wide-eyed, as she stared Kenan Fernández in the face.

The personal trainer, whom she had made the mistake of going out to lunch with a week and a half ago, after meeting at an Owl's Bay fitness club, narrowed his eyes and said in a perturbed tone of voice, "Why haven't you returned my calls and text messages?"

She shuddered, sensing the hostility in him as someone who apparently didn't take rejection very well. "I thought I'd made it perfectly clear that I wasn't interested in anything further with you, Kenan," she spoke sharply, glancing over his shoulder for any sign of Gavin. "Responding to the calls and texts would only have encouraged—or upset—you. I didn't want either."

He lowered his chin. "Maybe if you just give us another chance, it can work out between us," he pleaded.

"I don't think so." She regarded him warily. "How did you know I was here?"

"I didn't," Kenan claimed, peering back at her. "I just happened to see you through the window when passing by."

"I don't believe you," Nikki said straightforwardly, switching the basket she was carrying from one hand to the other. She didn't believe in these types of random encounters. Not even in a relatively small town.

"It's the truth." Then, abruptly, he reversed the denial. "Okay, so I followed you from your place."

"You what?" She flashed him a hot stare while contemplating his chilling words. How did he know where she lived? "You're stalking me?"

"Not exactly." Kenan shuffled his feet. "When you never answered my calls or texts, I had my ways of discovering where you stayed and went there this morning—hoping we could talk. Then I saw you leaving with some dude. Who the hell is he to you...?"

As Nikki fumbled with a response, while considering the question at face value, recognizing the metamorphosis of her relationship to Gavin, she read the irrational jealousy in Kenan's glare. What gave him the right to pry into her personal life after one meaningless date?

Before an answer to his demand escaped her lips, Gavin walked up to them and looked from one to the other, then asked in a commanding voice, "Is there a problem?"

"Not unless he chooses to make it one," she answered tensely, and faced her stalker. "I think Kenan was just leaving. Isn't that right?" Nikki challenged him to say otherwise as he and Gavin stood toe to toe.

Gavin, taller and clearly the more intimidating of the two men, added more fuel to the fire in putting Kenan on notice, by saying boldly, "She's with me. Or I'm with her, whichever you prefer. I'd leave it at that, if I were you."

While Kenan seemed to be considering his options, Nikki was struck by Gavin's characterization of their *being together.* Though she was sure that it was meant more to send Kenan a message that she was unavailable in romantic terms than in Gavin's official capacity as her protector from Perry Evigan—Nikki almost found herself wishing that the former was true. Even if it may have been unreasonable to wish for, given their stressed history and association with Brigette.

Abruptly, Kenan made a noise that sounded like growling, eyeing Nikki sharply once more, and walking off like a defeated man.

She and Gavin waited till he was out of listening distance, after which Gavin said observantly, "So, what was that all about? I only caught enough of the conversation to gather that the man wasn't welcome company."

"He definitely was not," Nikki confirmed without prelude, as she suddenly felt the weight of her loaded basket. "That was Kenan Fernández, the personal trainer I mentioned going out with once. He followed us here from my house, wherever he got the address from. Looks like he doesn't know how to take no for an answer, even when calls and texts have gone unanswered."

Gavin frowned. "Sounds like the classic stalker. If you think he failed to get the message loud and clear, I can have a talk with him. Or make a call to local law enforcement about him…"

"Thanks, but neither should be necessary at the moment," she told him, though Nikki welcomed Gavin's coming to her aid outside his mandate. "I don't want to blow this out of proportion. Whatever his problem is, I doubt that he wants the police on his case," she stressed. "Hopefully, this will be the last I'll ever hear from him."

"Hopefully. But should that change while I'm still around, let me know," Gavin told her, an edge to his tone. "In my experience of dealing with inmates who were involved in intimate violence that included stalking and worse, this oftentimes escalated into more stalking and other criminal behavior."

"Hmm…" Nikki furrowed her brow, clearly uncomfortable. "Not exactly what I need at this time in my life—with Perry Evigan still on the loose," she admitted.

"I know. Just keep your guard up," Gavin cautioned, running a hand along his firm jawline. "Everything will be fine."

She nodded, taking him at his word. "If you say so."

"Why don't I grab that basket for you," he said, removing it from her hand before she could object, "and we can get out of here—if you have everything you need?"

"I do," she told him, offering a grateful smile. Other than perhaps peace of mind that was certainly reduced when having to deal with a potential stalker and a definite serial killer.

Chapter Five

Nikki was back in her art studio, putting away supplies, feeling like she was in her comfort zone. At least to the extent possible, with a ruthless serial killer potentially targeting her again—Gavin's strong presence in the other room notwithstanding. Beyond that disturbing reality of Perry Evigan still very much on the loose, it really irked her that Kenan Fernández knew where she lived, further encroaching upon the safety net she had established since moving to Owl's Bay. Perhaps she hadn't moved far enough away from Gulfport and the dark memories that had hung over her there like a cumulus cloud.

Could she have ever run far enough away from something that was bound to stay with her for the rest of her life, to one degree or another? Maybe not. But the fortitude that had empowered her over time would need to carry her through the present danger. And even afterward, when Gavin Lynley was no longer around to protect her from the bad guys. As much as Nikki had quickly gotten used to having him around, the man had a life of his own that didn't include her. Or Brigette, for that matter, as Gavin had obviously moved on from their short romance.

It was only brought back to the forefront with the prison escape of Perry Evigan. Would Gavin just as easily be able to put the genie back in the bottle—and Nikki with it—once the serial killer was safely back behind bars? As if their bonding on one or more levels since Gavin had come to town had never occurred?

Being on her own these days had suddenly no longer seemed like the way to go. Nikki truly did want someone in her life. Could Gavin fill that void? Or was the specter of what happened to Brigette anything but water under the bridge?

"Hey," Gavin's voice penetrated her reverie.

Nikki turned to see him standing there, close enough to touch. She had to fight herself not to do that very thing. "Hey."

"Are you all right?"

"I'm fine," she told him with a straight face.

He smiled at her. "We'll get through this—together."

Nikki liked the sound of that: together. "Okay."

"So, what are you working on right now?" Gavin gazed over her shoulder at the painting covered by a sheet and over a canvas drop cloth on the floor. "Or is that a trade secret in your world, till your latest masterpiece is finished?"

"No trade secrets, I'm afraid." She laughed. "Not sure I would call the oil painting a masterpiece, but here it is…" Nikki lifted the sheet to reveal a landscape that showed off Owl's Bay, complete with open land, loblolly pine trees, housing and a snippet of the Jourdan River for good measure. "It's still a work in progress, but I'm just about there, as part of my showing on Saturday." She looked up at him with a curious slant of her eyes. "So, what do you think?"

"I think it's amazing," he responded without preface. "You really know what you're doing in giving art lovers something to work with."

She blushed. "Is that so?"

"Yes, most definitely." He paused, rubbing his chin. "Brigette was always gung-ho on your talent—maybe even jealous in a way. I think she'd be applauding you now."

"Hopefully, she would be applauding us both," Nikki put forth contemplatively. "And we'd be applauding her in return, knowing that, as a go-getter, she would be a big success in whatever she chose to do."

Gavin gave her a thoughtful look. "I agree."

Nikki couldn't help but wonder if the two of them would have ended up together—no matter

Brigette's preference for playing the field without Gavin being the wiser. Or would he have realized that they weren't right for each other at the end of the day and given someone else a chance to make him happy?

Nikki regarded Gavin keenly and gave an honest assessment when she put it out there by saying, "It would be great if I could paint you someday." She was sure this was an implausible scenario, given the time limit of his presence in town.

"Me?" Gavin cocked a brow. "Not sure I'd make a very good subject."

"Are you kidding? With your classic features and good looks, you'd make an excellent subject for a portrait."

"Thanks for saying that," he uttered. "I'm flattered."

Nikki toned down her enthusiasm. "Of course, I realize that you won't be around much longer, once Evigan is tracked down and sent back to prison."

"That's true," Gavin admitted. "But that doesn't mean I couldn't come back…to sit for the painting, that is…"

"That would be nice." She smiled at him, while trying hard not to read anything else into the suggestion. Such as wishing to do a return visit to spend more time with her as someone he was interested in seeing again.

I won't put unspoken thoughts into his head, Nikki told herself, even if she found appeal in the notion of extending this new comradery between them beyond his role as her special agent bodyguard.

Gavin's cell phone rang. He lifted it from the back pocket of his pants, gazed at it and said, "I better get this—"

Nikki nodded and watched as he turned away and took the call. "Lynley," he spoke routinely into the phone. His body language and tone of voice while responding to the caller told Nikki that something was up regarding the status of the escaped convicts.

GAVIN WAS TENSE as he listened to the MDOC Director of Investigations, Marvin Whitfield, who said in a heated voice, "There's been a major break in the investigation… We think that Evigan, Machado and Schneider are holed up inside an abandoned farmhouse in St. Clair County, Alabama—"

"Really?" Gavin glanced at Nikki, who was watching him intently, undoubtedly sensing that the call pertained to the prison escapees.

"Yeah, deputies from the St. Clair County Sheriff's Office spotted a black Chrysler Pacifica matching the one the prisoners stole in Boyle, Mississippi," the director said. "They changed the plates, but a neighbor reported seeing three men matching the physical descriptions of the escaped cons running from the car and inside the farmhouse. We were able to determine through the VIN and DMV that the vehicle in question was, in fact, the one belonging to and stolen from Donald Takeuchi, in Boyle."

"So where do things stand now?" Gavin asked anxiously.

"The farmhouse is surrounded by our Fugitive Apprehension Strike Team, US Marshals, FBI agents and the St. Clair County Sheriff's Office's SWAT Team," Whitfield reported. "We also have on hand a Mississippi Department of Public Safety crisis negotiator—with the aim of getting the escapees to give up and end this thing peacefully."

"Any indication that they have hostages inside?" Gavin wondered.

"Not at this time. If that is the case, we'll deal with it."

"Keep me posted on how this goes down," Gavin told him after being briefed a bit more on the logistics of the operation underway.

Once he was off the phone, Nikki moved closer to him and, with eyes narrowed, asked eagerly, "What's happening?"

"It appears that Perry Evigan and the other two escapees are surrounded inside a rural farmhouse in Alabama. They're trying to get them to surrender. That hasn't happened yet."

Nikki breathed a sigh of relief. "As long as the escapees are at least contained, it means Evigan can't get away to come after me—or anyone else," she stressed boldly.

"True." Gavin could see how much the prospect of the serial killer who victimized her being apprehended took a giant load off Nikki's shoulders. He suddenly found himself taking her into his arms for comfort. "It'll be okay," he maintained, feeling her heart beating fast, along with maybe his own. "Evigan is far away from here and has his hands full. He can't hurt you. I'll see to that."

When Nikki lifted her chin and peered into his eyes, Gavin sensed that she wanted him to kiss her as much as he wanted to do just that. He hesitated for a moment, questioning if it was wise to give in to desire, given their history— before tossing caution to the wind for what felt right. He lowered his head and claimed her mouth. The kiss was slow and steady, soft and hard, sizzling with intensity, rattling his bones while they held on to one another.

Gavin caught his breath after pulling back. He didn't want to ruin a good thing. Mislead.

Or be misled. "Do you want to go grab a bite to eat?" he asked her. "With the threat of Evigan as a fugitive apparently being neutralized even as we speak, it shouldn't pose much of a risk to dine in a public place."

Nikki nodded as she touched her swollen lips. "All right."

He resisted the urge to touch her while offering a soft smile, even as Gavin wondered where things were headed—or not—for them, when he no longer had an excuse for being in her world once Perry Evigan was again out of the picture.

MARVIN WHITFIELD SAT edgily at his walnut L-shaped corner desk at the Mississippi Department of Corrections Central Office headquarters. His raven eyes flashed between the laptop before him and a picture window that provided a respite from the pressure he felt. As the Director of Investigations in the Corrections Investigation Division, it ultimately fell on him to spearhead the recapture of the escaped prisoners from the Mississippi State Penitentiary. Beyond that, he needed to learn what weaknesses in the system allowed Perry Evigan, Craig Schneider and Aaron Machado to exploit the prison riot to successfully engineer their escape.

Frankly, it drew the ire of Whitfield that this had happened under his watch. It wasn't exactly what he wanted on his résumé when the opportunity to move up the ladder of the MDOC presented itself. He would make damn sure to hold the MSP superintendent, Crystal Rawlings, and warden, Zachary Livingston, accountable for the melee and escape. Including, as a result, the death of correctional officer Stan MacGregor, with another guard, Stewart Siegfried, still listed in critical condition.

Right now, Whitfield was most interested in getting the inmates back behind bars where they belonged. Particularly Perry Evigan. He had been following the investigation into the serial killer's strangulation murders, and Whitfield was elated when they were able to apprehend, convict and incarcerate Evigan. The fact that Gavin Lynley had been involved with Evigan's last homicide victim, Brigette Fontana, and was acquainted with a surviving victim, Nikki Sullivan, made it all the more urgent that they recapture Evigan. Then both Gavin and Nikki could try to put this behind them again and get on with their lives.

At least that was the plan as Whitfield saw it. With Evigan and the other fugitives cornered in the farmhouse, it now seemed only a matter of time before their violent escape came to an end—through one means or another. The director grabbed his cell phone off the desk and called the leader of the FAST at the scene and crisis negotiator for an update.

NIKKI FELT NERVOUS excitement over the prospect of Perry Evigan being arrested again and put back in prison for the rest of his life—facing charges on at least two more homicides to add to his killings. *Who knows how many others he might have strangled to death or otherwise murdered the longer he had remained a free man?* she thought. Still, she was so glad that he and the other fugitives were nowhere near Owl's Bay, forcing her to have to relive a nightmare. Not that she didn't have help warding off danger in Gavin, who was just as affected by the serial killer's being a free man as she was. They both needed this to be over so Brigette could once again be able to rest in peace.

She glanced across the wooden table at the Owl's Bay Country Restaurant on Talridge Avenue, where Gavin was eating pan-seared Atlantic salmon with collard greens, as she had a tuna and butter bean salad. In the moment, Nikki couldn't help but think about kissing him. Or was it the other way around? Whichever—apart from the tickle she felt from her face touching the hair on his chin—the kiss had sent lightning shooting throughout her body like nothing she'd ever felt before. Then, just like that, it was over.

Neither of them said a word afterward, as if to do so would imply that it meant something. Or not. She felt confused and had some clarity at the same time, knowing that she was beginning to develop feelings for the man. Even if it was one-sided and destined to go nowhere, all things being equal with their history and separate lives and locations presently.

"About the kiss..." they both voiced at the same time.

"Yeah, that..." Nikki colored, deciding to protect herself by taking the lead. "It was nothing," she suggested. "We were both just caught up in the moment. No worries."

"I was thinking the same thing," Gavin contended, dabbing a paper napkin to a corner of his mouth. "You're a great kisser though," he threw out, as though to lessen the awkwardness of the moment.

"So are you," she had to admit, and forked her salad musingly.

"We're good, then?" He met her eyes coolly, his face tilted to one side.

"We're good." Nikki was happy to leave it at that. Or maybe not, but felt it was for the best. Nothing to be gained by getting in over her head for the special agent whose mission and presence in her life were just about up.

As though to relieve the tenseness of the moment, Gavin asked her, "Aside from being an artist, which obviously can be time-consuming, what else do you like to do for fun or whatever?"

"Well, I teach an art class once a week at the local community college," she told him. "I wouldn't necessarily call it fun, but it's certainly rewarding in helping others learn the proper techniques in their own artistic pursuits." Nikki didn't need to give it much thought beyond that as she said, "On the fun front, I like to go to the gym, play tennis, swim, dance—though no style in particular—and read romance and thriller novels."

"Sounds pretty well-rounded to me."

"I suppose. And how about you?" she asked, lifting her glass of water. "What do you do for fun outside of working as a special agent for the Mississippi Department of Corrections?" Given what great shape he was in, Nikki could already imagine some pastimes.

"I like to work out," he confirmed evenly. "I jog, bicycle, listen to jazz and what else—oh, sing in the shower when no one else is listening." He laughed. "I'm not very good at it."

"Do you still go dancing?" She gazed at him thoughtfully. "I seem to recall that you and Brigette loved to hang out at dance clubs." Nikki tried to put out of her mind that Brigette was just as content to dance with any other guy who asked her when Gavin wasn't around.

"Every now and then," he responded. "Maybe if I had the right dance partner these days…"

Nikki refused to draw anything from that, though she too felt the same way, as she imagined them ballroom dancing together. Or slow dancing, cheek to cheek.

Gavin broke into her reverie when he asked, "Do you like to travel?"

"Yes," she said. "I've been to Mexico, England and Italy, along with typical hot spots in the US, like Las Vegas, Los Angeles, Miami and New York City—all with booming art scenes. I'd love to go on a cruise someday."

"Yeah, a cruise does sound like it could be fun." He sat back, thoughtful. "Can't say I can match that as far as overseas travel, but I have been to a law enforcement conference in Singapore, visited the Bahamas and a couple of places in Canada. Like you, I've made my way around the country, here and there, for both business and leisure—but always find myself back at home in Mississippi."

"Me too." Nikki smiled. Honestly, she had pondered moving elsewhere once or twice. Especially right after the ordeal with Perry Evigan. But she refused to allow him to drive her away from her home state, giving that monster more power over her life.

Gavin's cell phone rang. He met Nikki's eyes and her heart skipped a beat as she sensed that there was news on the standoff between the escaped cons and the authorities surrounding them.

Chapter Six

"Hey," Special Agent Jean O'Reilly spoke to him over the phone. "Just got word that the standoff is over."

"Really?" Gavin perked up as he gazed across the table to Nikki, who had an equally vested interest in this. He put it on speakerphone. "Tell me more…"

"Well, according to Matt Baccarin from the Fugitive Apprehension Strike Team, there was a shootout between the escaped convicts and our side," she said. "Whether something ignited accidentally or was started deliberately, the farmhouse caught on fire, trapping those inside. They were apparently determined to fight it out till the end—refusing to surrender."

Gavin shifted on the seat and asked, "So, they're all dead…?"

"Yeah, I'm afraid so," Jean confirmed. "Once the fire was put out by members of the St. Clair County Fire and EMS Association, three bodies were removed by the St. Clair County Medical Examiner and Coroner's Office."

"Have they been able to confirm that Perry Evigan is, in fact, one of the deceased individuals?" Gavin had to ask, eyeing Nikki again, knowing this was important for her peace of mind too.

"Not yet," the special agent told him. "The victims of the fire were burned beyond recognition. Dental records for Evigan, Machado and Schneider will be examined by forensic dentists to positively identify the deceased. Shouldn't take too long to confirm the identities, but all signs point to the dead being the three fugitives—Perry Evigan included."

"Okay," Gavin told her. He added, though knowing that Director Whitfield would fill him in on further details of the investigation, "Thanks for the update and keep me posted on any new developments."

"Will do." Jean sighed. "For what it's worth, if it turns out that Evigan is dead, both you and Nikki Sullivan should be able to breathe a little easier in knowing that the Gulfport Nightmare Killer will no longer be around to terrorize anyone he decides to target or who gets in his way."

"It's worth a lot, Jean," he assured her, and hung up, then identified her to Nikki for the record as Special Agent Jean O'Reilly of the MDOC.

Nodding, Nikki wasted no time in saying with a catch to her voice, "So, it looks like Evigan's evil deeds have finally caught up with him."

"Yeah, looks that way." Gavin gave her a little grin, then turned serious. "We'll know soon enough."

"For all his faults—and they seemed to be endless—Perry Evigan is still human," she stressed. "If he was truly inside the farmhouse, I'm pretty sure that he didn't develop wings and somehow fly away to evade capture and continue his evil ways."

"I agree. Evigan's definitely not superhuman. Or an invincible extraterrestrial." Gavin chuckled and ran a fork haphazardly through what was left of his collard greens. "Still, until we get the official word that he truly is dead, if it's all the same to you, I'd like to stick around." Gavin wasn't quite ready to return to Jackson and his own life full-time. Not with the passionate kiss they shared that still resonated with him, in spite of going along with the notion that it was merely a moment of weakness and nothing more. For his part, he wanted to put that theory to the test. If the kiss did mean something, didn't they owe it to themselves to explore this further? Or was his point of view entirely different from hers?

"I would like that," Nikki told him, flashing a nice smile. "What's that old saying about never counting the chickens before the eggs hatch? I think we should continue hanging out till Perry Evigan's death has been verified through forensic dentistry and the coroner, or any other means..."

Gavin grinned. "Then it's settled."

Even as he said the words, though happy to extend his stay at least a little while longer, per his assignment, internally, Gavin wasn't quite sure that was true where it pertained to his growing attraction to Nikki and where it could possibly lead down the road.

"HEY," NIKKI SAID to her mother and stepdad on a laptop video chat, while she sat in an Adirondack chair on the rear deck of her cottage. She had delayed phoning them as long as possible, knowing how freaked out they would be in learning that the man who tried to rape and murder her had broken out of prison and would possibly come after her again. Normally, Nikki might have assumed they had already heard the news. But she knew that the prison escape coincided with their long-awaited vacation to the Cayman Islands in the Caribbean. It was highly unlikely that the news would have traveled there, nor would she have wanted this to cast a shadow on their holiday. But now it didn't have to, with what she could tell them.

"Hi, honey," Nikki's mother said, a bright smile lighting up her pretty face. A retired middle school teacher, Dorothy McElligott was in her sixties, slender, blue-eyed behind horn-shaped glasses, and had blondish-silver hair worn in a pixie cut.

"Hey, there," William McElligott said, sitting beside her on a black leather sofa in their hotel room. Also in his sixties, big and strong, with slicked-back salt-and-pepper short hair, a hipster beard and gray-brown eyes, Nikki had always considered the pharmacist her mother married more than two decades ago to be her father, while barely remembering her real dad.

"How are you enjoying the Cayman Islands?" she asked them cheerfully.

"It's everything we thought it would be—and so much more," her mother gushed.

"Wish you could have joined us," William pitched in.

"Me too," Nikki said sincerely. "Maybe next time." She waited a beat before saying, "I have to tell you something—"

Dorothy's brows lowered, showing concern. "What is it?"

Nikki drew a breath and said, "Two days ago, Perry Evigan broke out of prison…"

"What?" Her mother cringed. "How?"

"He and two other violent prisoners managed to escape during a prison riot," she reported to them.

"And we're just finding out about this now?" William's thick brows knitted.

"I didn't want to worry you guys," Nikki explained, "putting a damper on your trip."

"We're your parents," Dorothy snapped. "It's our job to worry—no matter how old you are."

"She speaks for me too," her stepdad said earnestly.

"I'm sorry." Nikki almost felt as though she were living back at home under their protective thumbs again, but understood why they would be upset. "Anyway, the good news is that it appears Evigan and the other escapees were trapped in an Alabama farmhouse that caught on fire—killing all three."

"Well, that's a relief," her mother said, her features relaxing a bit, "even if you never want anyone to die that way."

William wasn't quite as magnanimous when he said bluntly, "When you break out of a penitentiary, whatever happens afterward is on you."

"Dental records will be used to positively identify the remains," Nikki told them. "But the authorities believe it's merely a formality at this point."

Dorothy said feelingly, "I'm so sorry this happened, Nikki, dredging up painful memories for you."

"I know." Nikki agreed wholeheartedly, but was forever grateful she'd had their unwavering support throughout the ordeal. She was reluctant to tell them about the recent nightmare she had that forced her to relive the victimization in much too vivid detail for her comfort. But Gavin had brought her out of it and she hoped there would not be a repeat performance now that the threat Evigan presented seemed to be over. "Something positive has come out of it though," she indicated.

"Oh…?" Her mother favored her with a curious look.

Nikki told them about her protector during the crisis being none other than Brigette's former boyfriend, Gavin Lynley, now a special agent with the Mississippi Department of Corrections. They had been made aware of the acrimony at the time between Nikki and Gavin surrounding Brigette's death. Nikki would never have imagined that they would ever break the ice—and more…

"Really?" Dorothy touched her glasses. "Who would've thought?"

"How's that worked out?" William asked cautiously.

"You mentioned positive…?" her mother questioned.

"Yeah, we've made peace with the past," Nikki was happy to report, offering them a genuine smile. "Turns out that all we needed was a face-to-face to air out our grievances surrounding Brigette's death and find a way to work around them."

Dorothy smiled. "I'm so happy to hear that. You both lost someone you loved. Nothing can bring her back, but the fact that you and Gavin are on speaking terms now is a good thing in moving forward."

"I agree," her stepdad said.

"Thanks, guys," Nikki told them, and couldn't agree more herself. She thought about the kiss she and Gavin shared and couldn't help but wonder if there was more of their story to be told, in spite of the very real possibility that they were living together on borrowed time.

KNOWING THAT NIKKI was on the back deck speaking with her parents, Gavin thought it might be a good time to step out on the front porch and catch up with his ecologist sister, Lauren Nolden. Though they lived in different parts of the country and didn't get together as often as he would have liked, he still felt close to her and loved his nieces, Miley and Ellen, like they were his own children. He hoped one day to start a family, believing he had what it took to be a great father. The trick was bonding with a person who could be good marriage and mother material. He once thought that Brigette might fill those shoes, in spite of wondering if this was truly something she was made of. The fact that Nikki came to mind in that moment left Gavin wondering if it was possible that what he had been looking for had been staring him in the face all along, minus nearly a decade of time apart.

"What's up?" he said casually with a grin when his sister appeared on the screen of Gavin's cell phone for a video chat.

At thirty-three, Lauren was attractive with voluminous black hair in a Rezo cut and their mother's brown eyes. "I'm good," she said, smiling. "How about you?"

"Well," he began thoughtfully, "the man who murdered Brigette broke out of prison recently." Gavin recalled how Lauren had been there to help him pick up the pieces when he was still trying to make sense of it all.

"You're kidding?" Lauren's mouth hung wide in disbelief in what was obviously news to her. "How did I miss that?"

"With all the info on cable and social media on violent crime and violent criminals across the country these days, it wouldn't have been all that hard," he told her in all honesty. "But the good news is that it seems as though Perry Evigan is dead, having been located hiding at a farmhouse in Alabama, along with two other inmates who escaped."

"That is good to hear." Lauren's features softened. "Having him on the loose, even for a day, must have had you climbing the walls," she voiced.

"Yeah, that about sums it up." Gavin furrowed his brow pensively. "There's more..."

"What?" his sister asked nervously.

He hesitated before replying, "I've gotten back in touch with Brigette's best friend, Nikki Sullivan." Gavin had shared his feelings at the time with Lauren on Nikki, in finding fault with her regarding Brigette's death. He knew now that this had been a big mistake and only wished he could take it back. But Nikki had forgiven him, more or less. Now he just needed to forgive himself.

"Oh, really?" Lauren gave him a long look. She had firmly rejected his position at the time, calling him misguided and unreasonable. "You're finally ready to bury the hatchet and acknowledge that Nikki was no more to blame as a crime victim than you were that Brigette fell prey to a callous serial killer?"

"Yeah, it's been buried," he told her happily.

"Or at least we're getting there." Gavin glanced at the cottage, expecting Nikki to step outside. "I actually had my hand forced, so to speak, to make peace, in being assigned by the MDOC to protect Nikki while Evigan was still at large."

"I see." Lauren tilted her face to one side. "And now that the coast is clear...?"

He thought about the kiss they shared and general feeling of closeness developing between them. "We're going to keep in touch," he said sincerely, while thinking that could be an understatement when all was said and done.

"Good to hear. Something tells me that Brigette would believe it's the right way to go."

"I think so too." Even then, Gavin wondered if his former girlfriend would be on board as well were anything to develop with Nikki that moved more deeply into the romantic realm. Or would Brigette somehow view it as a betrayal from her boyfriend and best friend, even from beyond the grave? "Say hi to Miley and Ellen and Rory," Gavin said before disconnecting, only to find Nikki standing there. He wondered how much she had heard and what it might mean, if anything, moving forward.

NIKKI HAD OVERHEARD Gavin talking on the phone to his sister, Lauren. Though they had never met, Nikki sensed that they might have become friends had the opportunity presented it-self back in the day—before disaster struck with Brigette's murder and Nikki's own brush with death. Along with Gavin's hostility toward her, lessening only slightly during her gut-wrench-ing testimony during Perry Evigan's trial, only to resume afterward. But things had taken a dra-matic turn between her and Gavin since they got beyond their differences with his bodyguard du-ties. Didn't hurt matters any that they'd kissed. Or that he had been there when she'd had a re-currence of a nightmare involving Evigan try-ing to kill her.

Now, from what Nikki gathered, it appeared as though Lauren was in her corner—and had been all along—in believing that bygones should be bygones and Gavin and Nikki should have a camaraderie in modern times. At the very least.

"Hey," Nikki said evenly.

Gavin grinned easily at her. "Hey."

"Was that your sister?" she asked innocently.

"Yeah. Between work, marriage and two young kids, Lauren has her hands full these days."

"I'm sure." Nikki admired his sister for being able to juggle work and home life, as so many women did these days. She hoped to emulate this by becoming a wife and mother someday.

Gavin was thoughtful. "How are your parents doing?"

"Great! They're having the time of their lives in the Cayman Islands."

"How did they take the news about Perry Evigan?"

Nikki wrinkled her nose. "They were shocked to learn he had escaped from prison," she told him. "But were annoyed even more that I hadn't shared this with them sooner."

"Parents will be parents," he remarked understandably. "I'm sure they were relieved to know that the indications are that Evigan will no longer pose a threat to you or others."

"They were," Nikki conceded, just as his sister was. "Actually, on that note, I belong to a support group for survivors of disturbing events. We have a meeting this evening. In light of the recent events, I'd like to go as planned."

"Of course." Gavin stepped closer, meeting her eyes. "Mind if I tag along?" He paused. "Might do me some good to hear, outside of law enforcement, from others who have survived tragedies."

She nodded. "You're welcome to attend, Gavin." Nikki wondered if he might even wish to talk about what he went through with Brigette's murder, knowing that their perspectives were slightly different. Even if both arrived in the same place and suffered the same sense of loss.

He smiled. "Great. Hopefully, we'll both soon have closure with the official confirmation of Perry Evigan's death that you can share with the group at the next meeting as part of coming to terms with what happened to you."

"I hope so too." But for now, Nikki took solace in coming out on the other side of their shared experience and finding constructive ways of dealing with it.

Chapter Seven

Gavin was admittedly a little uneasy about attending the support group meeting, as he sat in the circle in the backyard surrounded by Japanese maple trees. Outside of family and a few friends, he had chosen to deal with his grief on his own. On the other hand, now seemed like a good time to, at the very least, show his support for Nikki as the group had obviously helped her deal with the victimization she'd gone through and also with what Brigette had experienced, paying the ultimate price by falling into the crosshairs of Perry Evigan.

After listening to Air Force vet Harry Rosen recount the horrors of war that resulted in the loss of a leg, Gavin watched as the host, Blair Roxburgh, went through her trauma, followed by a slender woman in her late twenties named Miriam Broderick. Running thin fingers nervously through her short, choppy brown hair with blond highlights, she blinked her green-brown eyes and recounted how her year older brother, Quint, had been the pedestrian victim of a hit-and-run driver a year ago. The driver had been under the influence of alcohol and antidepressants.

"Seeing Quint's life and bright future taken away in such a senseless fashion by an out-of-control driver who should never have been behind the wheel, shook up my whole world," Miriam expressed painfully. She wiped away tears and said, "Being in a support group like this has helped me to better process my loss and focus more on the good memories I have of my brother rather than the end of his journey."

Nikki, who sat next to her and sought to comfort her, then picked up where Miriam left off. She seemed to go back in time as Nikki's lower lip quivered when summarizing her ordeal at the hands of Perry Evigan, which included his brutal attack on Brigette.

While avoiding eye contact with Gavin in the chair next to her, Nikki uttered solemnly, "Honestly, I wasn't sure I'd ever make it out of Perry Evigan's house alive. Quite the opposite. When he murdered my best friend, I felt I was sure to follow." She sucked in a deep breath and now regarded Gavin feelingly. "But somehow, someway, I must have had an angel on my shoulder, as rescuers came before Evigan could make me another victim of a sexual assault and homicide by strangulation." Another deep sigh. "And here I am, able to tell my story. Including the fact that my attacker escaped from prison two days ago, before apparently meeting his fate in a fiery death. Karma can work for you and against you. This time, it seemed to have worked out right for society itself, by and large."

Though resisting any show of affection, Gavin was deeply moved by her heartfelt trip down memory lane, bringing him back to his own perspective of that fateful day a decade ago. He wished he had been there for Nikki when she needed him most as someone who could relate to what she was going through. Now, as fortune would have it, he was given a second chance to make up for lost time, if she let him.

Blair, who sat across the circle, leaned back in her chair and said, "Gavin, why don't you tell us a little about yourself—and anything else you feel comfortable sharing regarding what you've gone through…"

Feeling put on the spot, Gavin felt ready nonetheless to get off his chest something he probably should have a long time ago. He eyed Nikki, whose expression was one of encouragement, and said equably, "My name's Gavin Lynley. I currently work as a special agent for the Mississippi Department of Corrections, Special Operations Unit. And, no," he joked to lighten the mood, "I'm not here to haul anyone off to jail." He got a chuckle or two in response, including one from Nikki. "Ten years ago, I was still a correctional employee, but also the boyfriend of someone who was a victim of a sexual assault before being murdered." He choked back the words, as the image of her final moments was hard to digest. "I was supposed to hang out with Brigette that night, but had to go into work at the last moment and, as such, was forced to cancel the date…"

Gavin paused and felt the empathetic hand of Nikki's on his. "Needless to say, it's haunted me ever since, to one degree or another, knowing that if I had only made different choices back then, Brigette would almost certainly be alive today—" He favored Nikki with an emotional gaze and said, squeezing her hand, "But through some means, Brigette's best friend—Nikki— was able to survive being a victim of the same psychopath and serial killer." He took a breath, looked away and then back at her. "I admit that there was a time when I tried to blame Nikki for something that obviously wasn't her fault. I deeply regret that now. The fault for what happened to her and Brigette lies entirely with the man who drugged and attacked them. I can't express enough how glad I am that Nikki didn't suffer the same fate as Brigette—and has found a way to get past that time in her life and make something out of it."

"Thank you for saying that," she whispered to him, her eyes watering.

"It's been long overdue," he returned with sincerity.

Blair smiled at him and said, "Owning up to past mistakes, while sharing your own story of loss, regrets and moving forward, is commendable, Gavin."

He grinned sideways. "It's a step or two in the right direction anyway," he allowed, knowing it would take more to make things right with Nikki—and himself, for that matter.

The host then invited another survivor to speak as Gavin listened, while focusing largely on Nikki and wanting to see her gain greater closure once they knew that Perry Evigan was indeed dead and soon to be buried.

AFTER THE SESSION was over, Blair pulled Nikki to the side and said, "It was good of you to bring Gavin along, seeing that you two have so much in common with the ordeal you both went through."

"I'm glad he came too," Nikki admitted, not at all sure that would happen. She supposed he needed to let out what was bottled up in him all these years to a wider audience.

"Having your tormentor escape and then be stopped in his tracks must have sent you on a roller coaster of emotions."

"Yes." Nikki made a face. "I'm afraid my stomach is still tied up in knots as I process everything."

"I'm sure." Blair put a hand on her arm. "Staying in touch with Gavin should do wonders to get you over the hump."

Nikki glanced at Gavin, who was chatting with Harry Rosen. "That's the plan," she told her. Even if she was unsure to what extent. "Hope you can make it to my art exhibit tomorrow?"

Blair flashed her teeth. "You couldn't keep me away if you tried."

Nikki laughed, happy to have her busy friend in attendance. "I was hoping you'd say that."

They joined others and made small talk, before Gavin asked Nikki, holding her elbow, "Are you ready to head out?"

She felt his touch and warmed to a grin playing askew on his lips, responding accordingly, "Yes, I think so."

The drive back to the cottage was mostly quiet. Nikki was sure that Gavin was getting back in touch with his feelings for Brigette, now that he had bared his soul in talking about the crime and losing his girlfriend. For her part, Nikki felt grateful that Gavin had gotten past accusing her of not doing enough to keep Brigette from going out that fateful night, as he seemed to acknowledge that Brigette was old enough to make her own choices in deciding what she wanted to do in her life from one day to the next.

The same had been true for Nikki. She had been restless that Saturday night and relished the opportunity to have some fun with her best friend. Especially when not that far removed from having ended things with her disastrous boyfriend at the time, Felix Kovell. How could she or Brigette have known that they were headed into a hornet's nest when they went to Johnnie's Shack nightclub, where Perry Evigan lay in wait like the evil vulture he was, lulling them into a false sense of security?

Obviously, she should have relied on her instincts that told Nikki that Evigan was very bad news and they should never have invited him back to their table for another round of drinks. But she rejected this in favor of trying to make her best friend happy—at least for the moment—in the absence of Gavin, whom Brigette didn't seem the least bit put off about that he'd left her hanging.

I can't change history, Nikki told herself candidly. She glanced over at Gavin behind the wheel and wondered if it was possible to change the future. Or their future, by taking a step back to the past. Or would they do more harm than good were she to spill the beans about Brigette to the man who clearly had never gotten over her? Spoiling his fantasy, perhaps, about the one whom he missed his chance with by virtue of a serial killer.

After having a nightcap, during which they spoke mainly about the near certainty of Perry Evigan's timely demise and the weight that would be lifted off their collective shoulders, Nikki and Gavin went to their separate rooms with just a simple good-night.

To Nikki, this was the best way to go. Even if she was undeniably interested in Gavin— whether it was wise or not—a one-night stand with someone soon on his way out the door was simply not in the cards. She doubted it was something he wanted either. And since a steady relationship seemed unlikely, why do anything they both would likely regret?

That night, Nikki tossed and turned in bed. Only this time, she wasn't having a nightmare about Perry Evigan, the Gulfport Nightmare Killer. Instead, she found herself dreaming about Brigette and the different faces of guys other than Gavin that she was cozying up to. Seemed as though her best friend had made a habit of two-timing Gavin right under his nose. That was so not cool, Nikki knew. But it wasn't her place to expose Brigette then.

And what about now?

That last thought was enough to wake Nikki from the deep sleep and disturbing dream. Though she felt her heart racing and was perspiring, she must not have made any sounds that resonated, as Gavin never showed up in her room to snap her out of it. She was glad, as Nikki wasn't sure how she would have responded had he asked about the dream. How might she have come across to him, in tarnishing what was obviously someone he had placed on a pedestal?

Climbing out of bed, Nikki went downstairs barefoot for a glass of water. Part of her wished Gavin would come down too, if only to talk. But he never did. She drank the water and went back to bed. It took a while, but she finally fell back to sleep. In the process, she'd debated whether or not to be honest with Gavin, as she would have wanted him to do with her had the shoe been on the other foot, before an answer came as clear as day.

WHEN GAVIN CAME down in the morning, he saw that Nikki had made breakfast. He noted that her hair was in a high ponytail and she had on jogging clothes and running shoes. Unlike last night, when she was probably wearing something similar to the red chemise lingerie night-gown she'd had on the previous night, conjuring up intimate images in his head. He'd heard her come downstairs and actually considered joining her for perhaps a nightcap, but decided against it. He'd invaded her space enough by his very presence, which, for better or worse, was close to running its course.

"Hey." He gave her a grin.

"Good morning." She returned the smile. "Hope you're in the mood for blueberry waffles with orange juice and coffee?"

"Sounds great," he said, stepping closer in his bare feet, while wearing tapered jeans and a casual shirt. "Can I help?"

"Feel free to take your plate to the table," she said, handing it to him with the steaming waffle.

Gavin did just that as he studied her. Seemed like there was something on her mind. He'd picked up on this ever since the support group gathering. Or, more specifically, ever since he had chosen to speak about his own ordeal ten years ago. So what was it? Had the trip down memory lane, mixed with the fall of their nemesis, Perry Evigan, messed with her head? Or was bringing Brigette back to the forefront a bad idea?

He waited till they were both seated across the black-and-pecan wooden corner breakfast

nook table, before Gavin asked Nikki straightforwardly over his coffee mug, "Is there something you want to talk about…?"

She sliced the knife perfectly into her waffle,
stuck the fork in and held it there, and gazed at
him for a long moment, then said tentatively,
"I've been debating whether or not to say anything…"

He cocked his brow curiously. "Regarding?"

"Brigette." Nikki set her fork down and tasted
the orange juice.

"What about Brigette?" Gavin asked, but had
a feeling he knew where this was going.

Hesitating again, Nikki responded, "First, let
me just say I loved her like the sister I never
had, in spite of our differences in personalities
and styles…" She swallowed thickly and looked
him in the eye. "I know you loved Brigette too,
which makes this all the harder to say."

"Just get it out, Nikki," he pressed, resting his
arms on the table in wait.

"All right." She sighed. "I hate to speak ill
of the dead, especially after your impassioned
thoughts about Brigette and how her life ended.
But now that we've gotten to know each other
better—along with the fact that I might not get
another chance to be perfectly honest with you
once you leave Owl's Bay—I think it's only fair
you know that Brigette was not the loyal girl-

friend you may have believed she was in plotting a future with her at the time…"

Gavin knitted his brows and raised a hand to stop Nikki from going further. "I know that," he said flatly.

Her eyes widened. "You do?"

"Yeah, of course." Whether he wanted to face up to the truth or not, Gavin knew it was high time he did just that. Especially if he had any hope at all of beginning something with Nikki without the specter of Brigette coming between them. Holding Nikki's intent gaze, he continued thoughtfully, "I caught her once making out with another guy. I knew then that she'd likely gone even further with him or others. On some level, I think I always knew she wasn't faithful to the relationship or took it as seriously as I did—but I chose to ignore this, believing I had what it took to make her see things my way." Gavin sat back, ruminating. "Guess it was just an ego thing. No one ever wants to accept defeat in a romance, no matter how challenging. When Brigette was murdered, I was at the point of ending things with her, realizing that we just weren't right for each other. But I never got that chance. Feeling guilty that I hadn't been there for her at the end, I chose instead to blame you for what happened. Along the way, I managed to push out of my mind the reality that Brigette and I were through, for all intents and purposes. Perry Evigan—that bastard—deprived me of the opportunity to ever tell Brigette."

"I'm sorry," Nikki expressed sincerely. "Sorry I ever brought this up."

"Don't be," he argued in earnest, forking a slice of waffle and coating it with maple syrup off the plate. "It needed to be said. If you hadn't done so, I would have, sooner rather than later. We both cared for Brigette and that can never die. But we also owe it to ourselves to put those feelings and the times that they represented to rest properly—especially since it appears that Evigan is no longer around to keep the dark memories alive and poisoning the atmosphere."

"You're right. It still feels a little weird though."

"For me too." He met her eyes musingly. "But it feels more right to get it out in the open and recalibrate our lives beyond Brigette—wherever that takes us—accordingly."

Nikki showed her teeth, indicating they were on the same page in that respect. "Okay."

He smiled back, feeling as though they had turned a corner, no matter what might be around it. "Good."

They finished eating and then she told him nonchalantly, "I'm going out for a run."

"I'll go with you," he said, knowing that until it became official that Evigan was no longer a threat, Gavin wasn't about to take any chances in making her a target of the serial killer.

"Think you can keep up?" Nikki challenged him.

"I can try." He expected he would do more than that, in spite of jogging not being his forte, per se, as an exercise option. "Let me get into my running shoes."

NIKKI FELT A huge sigh of relief that Gavin hadn't thought she was overstepping by spilling the beans about Brigette. Not only did he believe it was the right thing to do, but he'd also already known that Brigette was not as into the relationship as he was. Gavin had planned to break up with her, but had been deprived of this by Perry Evigan.

So where does that leave us? Nikki asked herself bewilderingly as she ran in front of Gavin down the tree-lined sidewalk, with him keeping pace like running was as natural for him as it was for her. She wouldn't deny having feelings for the good-looking special agent. She sensed it was more than a one-way street. Might they be able to turn it into a real romance, now that everything was out in the open? Or would their shared past continue to stand in the way of any type of future—with Evigan seemingly now out of the picture and Gavin no longer having a legitimate excuse for remaining in town much longer?

"Remind me why I agreed to this?" he quipped, catching up to her and breaking the reverie.

"Because you're in great shape and working those long legs comes with the territory in your business. Piece of cake," Nikki added with a smile.

Gavin breathed out of his nose. "Then it's a good thing I have a sweet tooth for tasty desserts, including caramel cake and lemon cake— or need I remind you of that?"

"How can I forget?" She faced him while recalling how he went to town on her leftover apple pie. "As for those cakes, I'll have to look into that." Nikki wondered if he planned to stick around long enough to give her a reason to accept his kitchen challenge.

"Fair enough." He brushed shoulders and asked, "Is that a hill I see up ahead?"

"Afraid so." She chuckled as they approached it. "Is that going to be a problem?"

"I think I can manage," Gavin told her with a laugh. "I'll wait for you up there." He suddenly took off, leaving her in the dust.

It took Nikki only a moment to recover before she went after him, while feeling she could get used to these mini challenges. And more, should it come to that.

When she got to the top of the hill, Nikki saw that Gavin was on his cell phone. From the gist of it, she gathered that he was talking to his boss. Between Gavin's disturbed expression and switching the phone to his other ear, she knew it was not good news.

But just how bad it truly was registered when Nikki heard him voice sourly, "You mean Perry Evigan is still alive—?"

Chapter Eight

"It sure as hell looks that way," Director Whitfield stated on the cell phone, as Gavin listened
while eyeing Nikki, who had clearly picked up
on the conversation once she caught up to him
on the hill.

As it was, Gavin saw no benefit in keeping
the disturbing news from Nikki that Perry Evigan was not in the farmhouse when it caught on
fire, leaving three bodies charred. But he could
at least delay this till they got back to her cottage. He asked Whitfield to hold that thought.

After surveying the area and seeing no signs
of trouble, Gavin led the way in a quick and
steady dash down the hill, while both he and
Nikki stayed close to each other, a tense silence between them. For his part, Gavin was
still caught up in seeing Brigette's betrayal in a
new light, his growing feelings toward Nikki and
how Perry Evigan's being seemingly still on the
loose might impact their ability to move forward.

At the cottage, Gavin got Whitfield back on the phone, letting his boss know he was on speaker, and after meeting Nikki's keen gaze he said to the director in a straightforward tone of voice, "You were saying about Evigan and the farmhouse fire—"

"As you know, we pulled out three bodies— or what was left of them—from the burned-out location," Whitfield said intently. "Working with the St. Clair County Medical Examiner and Coroner's Office, a forensic dentist, Dr. Allie Tagomori, compared the dental records of the three escapees to the teeth belonging to the charred corpses. Well, two of the victims were officially identified as Aaron Machado and Craig Schneider. The third victim's teeth were not a match for Perry Evigan's dental records," the director lamented.

"How is that even possible?" Gavin furrowed his forehead, but he knew the answer, in spite of the improbability of the decedent being someone other than Evigan.

Whitfield responded knowingly, "Well, it looks like Perry Evigan was never even at the farmhouse, as shocking and disappointing as that is. He must have decided at some point to separate himself from the other escaped cons. Turns out to have been a good move on his part," the director admitted. "As arson investigators sifted through the charred wreckage, indications are that the fire was set deliberately by someone inside the farmhouse. Apparently, one or all of the fugitives had no intention of going back to prison alive."

The fiery ending at the farmhouse notwithstanding, to Gavin, it was less about Evigan making a good move or being smarter, per se, than the other fugitives from justice, and more a matter of being much luckier than them when he needed this most.

"So, who was the other victim of the fire?" Gavin asked, gazing at Nikki, who was undoubtedly just as curious as him.

"Turns out, it was an ex-con named Merrill Carlyle," Whitfield said. "Dr. Tagomori was able to create a DNA profile from the decedent's teeth that was entered into CODIS and came back with a hit on Carlyle. He was the cellmate of Aaron Machado. Carlyle was serving time for armed robbery before being released four months ago. Apparently, he and Machado kept in touch and rendezvoused at some point during the escapees' journey, and Carlyle chose to stay with them."

Gavin set his jaw, again turning to Nikki and her stunned reaction. "Any clue on the whereabouts of Perry Evigan?"

Whitfield made a sighing sound, then replied

without elaboration, "We have reason to believe that Evigan may be attempting to evade capture by heading to Mexico. Information was found in his cell about Guadalajara. He could be driving a white Chevrolet Malibu. Someone matching Evigan's description was reported stealing such a vehicle from a shopping center parking lot in Blytheville, Arkansas. We're looking into it."

"With all due respect, that's not very reassuring as to Evigan's whereabouts," Gavin offered candidly, believing there was still a good chance that the escaped serial killer had no intention of leaving the country. "I'm still worried that Evigan may try to come after Nikki Sullivan." Gavin met her unreadable eyes. "For that reason—" and others he chose to keep to himself, such as wanting to remain in Nikki's company while they sorted out their feelings for one another "—if it's all the same to you, Director Whitfield, I'd rather stay with her as long as Evigan remains on the loose." *And who knows how long that could be?* Gavin told himself, seeing how resourceful the fugitive had proven to be at eluding capture, thus far.

Without prelude, Whitfield was in agreement. "Yeah, that's probably a good idea. You can stay with Ms. Sullivan for now." The director waited a beat, then warned, "Just don't get too comfortable with this arrangement, Lynley. You do have other assignments," Gavin was reminded. "Wherever he's holed up, Perry Evigan has probably heard by now about his fellow escapees' fiery demise. Not to mention having every law enforcement officer in the country on the lookout for him. As such, he's likely not to want to go anywhere near her while on the lam with the authorities in hot pursuit. If it becomes necessary, we'll see to it that Ms. Sullivan has a personal protection detail to keep her safe."

"That's good enough for me," Gavin told him, sure that he was skating on thin ice in wanting to continue as Nikki's primary bodyguard while Evigan remained at large. But he would take whatever the director was giving him in allowing Gavin to use their time together to protect her and bond with her further.

"ARE YOU KIDDING ME?" Nikki's eyes narrowed at Gavin as they stood in the living room, where he had just ended his phone conversation with Marvin Whitfield. "I can't believe that Perry Evigan has managed to remain free while the two other convicts he escaped from prison with are dead—"

"I know." Gavin turned to her sympathetically. "It's just one of those things. He played his cards right this time. The next time, he might not be so lucky."

"And I'm supposed to put my life on hold till Evigan runs out of luck?" she complained, arms crossed petulantly, even as Nikki knew that the chances the serial killer would actually get his bloody hands on her again were nil at best. Particularly when Gavin had talked his boss into allowing him to stick around as her armed, much of the time, protector. She certainly wasn't complaining. Quite the opposite, in fact. Having him around for a while longer was just what Nikki needed to see what flames might erupt from the smoke that seemed to be swirling around them at every turn and was given room to grow now that the air had been cleared regarding Brigette.

In her reverie, Nikki barely realized that Gavin had drawn her very near to his body as he said attentively, "You should definitely keep your life going as normal as possible, with only some minor adjustments temporarily. Such as sharing your lovely cottage with me. And, of course, being aware of your surroundings and who might be lurking about. Or not." She felt his warm breath on her cheek as Gavin added, "Of course, I'll be around to make sure Perry Evigan doesn't get any wild ideas and try to act upon them in targeting you again for his sick impulses."

"That's nice to know," she had to admit, even

if just how long it would last was unsettling, to say the least. She regarded him. "So, do you really think Evigan could show up here, even with all the heat he's facing, constantly needing to look over both shoulders and then some?"

"You never know," Gavin said with a straight face, still with his hands at her waist. "I gave up trying to figure out serial killers with a pathologically warped mind a long time ago. What I can tell you though, is that I don't want you to spend too much time worrying about the likes of Perry Evigan. Though he's still on the loose, the man is basically yesterday's news where we're concerned."

Nikki wasn't sure he truly believed that, considering Gavin's very—and strong—presence in her life. But she was happy to go along with it on both fronts. "In that case," she told him casually, "I suppose I can feel free to stick with the exhibition I have for this evening at an art gallery downtown?"

"Absolutely!" Gavin said smoothly. "No reason to cancel what you've been planning in showcasing your amazing talents," he insisted. "I'd love to see your art on display—and maybe I'll even buy a piece to put on the wall in my great room that's pretty barren."

"Hmm…" She smiled, trying to imagine the layout of his house. Would he ever invite her there, once his time in Owl's Bay was up? "In that case, I'd better head to my studio to put the finishing touches on one more painting to be in the exhibit."

"All right. And one more thing…" He cast his eyes upon hers, tilted his face, and Gavin moved slowly toward her lips as though to give Nikki an out in case he was overstepping his bounds. But she had no desire to do such a thing, and raised her chin just enough to accept the kiss.

Shutting her eyes, Nikki took in his hard mouth, opening her own slightly to perfectly contour with his, as she clung to him like he was all hers—at least while they kissed. But as her senses came back and Nikki realized she needed to restrain her desire for the man, she pulled their lips apart and, meeting his gaze, asked, "Is this another caught-up-in-the-moment show of weakness…?"

He held her stare and, tasting his lips, said frankly, "I think we both know it goes beyond that."

"Just checking." She grinned at him while acknowledging, "I think so too. But I still needed to hear you say it."

"I'm saying it," he affirmed solidly.

"Good." Nikki left it there, knowing she still had some work to do before the showing. And she also wanted to give them time to assess where this could lead and just how far and wide, once a serial killer was truly left in the rearview mirror once and for all.

ON A DIRT ROAD, Perry Evigan was driving a stolen gray Buick Encore, having ditched the Chevrolet Malibu he had stolen earlier in Blytheville, Arkansas, after making his way back to Mississippi. With unfinished business, a decade in the making, he was on a mission and would not be denied.

He considered the unfortunate deaths of his fellow escapees, Craig Schneider and Aaron Machado, along with Aaron's former cellmate, Merrill Carlyle. Perry couldn't honestly say that he was surprised. He knew that the authorities were gunning for them. He also knew that none of the fugitives—himself included—had any intention of going back to prison. Which was precisely why he separated himself from the others, as Perry believed his will to survive was far stronger than theirs.

As was his determination to get the one who managed to survive the power of his hands meant to strangle her to death. Just like her friend, Brigette. And his other conquests.

Nikki Sullivan.

Perry thought back to when he first spotted the news about the object of his desire to kill while accessing the prison's library services. The piece was entitled, "Prominent Local Artist to Showcase Work at Owl's Bay Art Gallery."

That artist was none other than Nikki Sullivan, the near victim he could never quite get out of his system. Now he was free and had another chance to go after her, to do with as he pleased. Before strangling her to death like the others. The mere thought excited him no end.

The exhibition was tonight in Owl's Bay.

If lucky, maybe he could make it on time to rain down on her parade.

Perry laughed at the thought, but then turned dead serious, knowing that it was anything but a laughing matter. At least not until the deed was done.

WHILE NIKKI WAS upstairs getting ready for her big art exhibit, Gavin took a video call from his cousin, Russell Lynley. He watched as Russell's square face appeared on the cell phone screen. Gray-eyed and black-haired, in a high, tight cut style, they were the same age. Like Russell's brother, Scott, he was an FBI special agent, working out of the field office in Houston, Texas, while specializing in serial killer and domestic terrorist cases.

"Hey," Gavin said evenly.

"Hey." Russell gave a little grin before turning serious. "Heard that Perry Evigan has some-how managed to dodge the fate of his fellow escapees."

"Yeah, looks that way." Gavin leaned back as he sat on a wicker accent armchair in the living room. "The man seems to have nine lives—as if to add up to the number of women he mur-dered plus one."

"He only has one life," Russell said firmly. "And its shelf life is hardly inexhaustible. FBI agents are working overtime with your guys to nab him, or otherwise stop him in his tracks."

"I know and I'm sure it's only a matter of time before we get him. But it's the wait that's driv-ing me crazy—not knowing where he is at the moment and what he's up to..." Gavin drew a breath as he pictured the creep killing Brigette and damned near ending Nikki's life as well.

"I hear you," Russell put forth, his thick brows knitting. "I know you're concerned that Evigan might try to come after the surviving witness, Nikki Sullivan—"

"The thought has crossed my mind," he re-sponded wryly. "Which is why I'm doing guard duty as long as Evigan stays a fugitive." Gavin knew that his interest in Nikki had moved well beyond a professional obligation, but there was no reason to go there just yet. So long as the threat remained for her safety, first and foremost.

"It won't be long." Russell narrowed his eyes thoughtfully. "Have you two been able to reconcile with everything that went down with Brigette?"

"Yeah." Gavin nodded. "Nikki was every bit as much a victim of Evigan as Brigette," he acknowledged. "I get that now and only want to make sure she gets to live the life she's entitled to and that was taken away from Brigette."

"She will," Russell sought to reassure him, before they spoke briefly about a case he was working on as part of a task force that included Russell's wife, Rosamund, a Homeland Security Investigations special agent.

When Gavin got off the line, he spotted Nikki coming down the stairs. Taking one look at her in a figure-flattering, floral surplice jersey dress, worn with strappy black sandals and her long hair in a plaited bun, made his jaw drop. "Wow! You look amazing," he told her, getting to his feet.

Nikki blushed. "Why, thank you." She eyed him. "You're not so bad yourself, mister."

He grinned at the compliment but downplayed it nonetheless. "Guess it was a smart idea to bring along a set of nicer clothing," he said, wearing a crisp lilac dress shirt, navy slacks and black loafers. "Anyway, this evening is all about you, Nikki. I'm only along for the ride." *And to keep my eyes open for any signs of Perry Evigan*, Gavin told himself.

"I'm glad you could come," she told him, meeting his steady gaze. "That's good enough for me."

"Same here."

Both ignored mentioning the part where an escaped serial killer threatened to cast a dark shadow over the art exhibition.

Chapter Nine

At the Owl's Bay Art Gallery on Fellows Street, Nikki was ecstatic over having her art works on display. Though this wasn't her first merry-go-round, she did feel a little extra burst of adrenaline in having Gavin there to see what she brought to the table. It was also comforting to know that the special agent for the Mississippi Department of Corrections had her back, just in case Perry Evigan did decide to make an appearance.

Even if a part of her felt this was unlikely, given that the search was on to recapture the escaped con, Nikki wasn't about to let her guard down as long as he was still out there somewhere. *I can't let him get to me*, she told herself with determination, while surveying her portrait, landscape and still-life oil paintings with Gavin.

"So, what do you think?" she asked, gazing up at him as they both held flutes of champagne.

"I think you're incredible," he told her. His eyes lit up as he peered at a landscape work of art and then shifted his focus to look at a painting of a bowl of red and green apples.

Nikki laughed. "I bet you say that to all the girls." One she knew for a fact he did once upon a time.

Gavin chuckled. "Trust me, I don't. I know talent when I see it—and so much more." He met her gaze and she could tell that the compliment went beyond her artistic skills.

"That's nice to know." She flushed and tasted the champagne. "Hopefully, there will still come a time when I can paint you," she threw out, already imagining the thrill of getting him on canvas.

"Count on it," he said confidently as Gavin sipped his own champagne.

They moved on and were joined by Blair Roxburgh and her boyfriend, Oliver Pascal, a tall, fifty-something chiropractor with shoulder-length, swept-back salt-and-pepper hair and a matching egg-shaped full beard. He touched his octagon glasses while turning blue eyes on Nikki, and said, "Your paintings are stunning."

"I told you they were out of this world," Blair marveled, holding a flute of champagne.

"We're all in agreement there," Gavin pitched in.

"Thank you all," Nikki said, grinning from ear to ear. Getting praise from people she knew gave Nikki all the validation she needed that this was what she was meant to do with her life. She told them humbly, "I'm still forever a work in progress as an artist, but I'm honing my craft with each painting."

"That you are, indeed." Blair smiled at her and raised her flute glass in toast, with everyone joining in.

"So this is where you've been hiding in plain view…"

Nikki heard the lyrical voice and turned to see the gallery owner, Jillian Yamaguchi. In her late sixties and a great artist in her own right, she was frail and had fine white hair in a chignon bun. "You found me," Nikki joked, and introduced her to everyone.

"Good." Jillian's brown eyes crinkled. She cupped an arm beneath Nikki's and said, "Hope you don't mind if I steal her away for a bit? I have some people I want to introduce Nikki to, while playing up her exhibition."

Nikki looked to Gavin, in particular, for his approval and he nodded. "Please, go mingle with your audience. I'll try to stay out of your way."

She knew that meant he wouldn't go too far, in case she needed him. "Okay."

"We'll just check out more of your works," Blair told her, holding hands with Oliver.

"I'll find you later," Nikki told them, and headed off with Jillian.

GAVIN WATCHED NIKKI walk away with the gallery owner before he began wandering around, looking this way and that for any indication that Perry Evigan had made his way to the art gallery. Admittedly, it seemed like a giant leap to believe that the fugitive serial killer would actually have the wherewithal to track Nikki down in this location, at this time. But Gavin had been in law enforcement and corrections long enough to know that hardened and tenacious criminals could never be underestimated. That was certainly true for Evigan, who had managed to strangle to death ten women without being caught, before he finally had the hammer dropped on him.

The man had walked away from a maximum-security prison farm and remained on the loose for days, while his fellow escapees had perished in a fire. That alone told Gavin that Evigan was not one to be taken lightly, no matter the odds against his taking another shot at Nikki.

As a result, Gavin found himself checking out anyone and everyone who was anywhere near Nikki, while maintaining a good enough distance to allow her to bask in her success as a local artist. *I don't want to see Evigan spoil her showing by trying to take Nikki out*, Gavin told himself. She'd paid a high enough price for her earlier victimization by him. Not to mention, witnessing the sexual assault and murder of her best friend. Gavin would not allow Nikki to go through that again—so long as he was able to stick around and protect her while her attacker was out there.

He moved beyond the perimeter to see if anyone else matching the serial killer's general description came into view. Nothing. Breathing a sigh of relief, Gavin continued to walk around and took out his cell phone. He called Special Agent Jean O'Reilly. She picked up immediately. "Hey," he told her. "Any news on Perry Evigan and his whereabouts…?"

"The assumption is still that he's headed for Mexico," she reported. "But I'm not so sure about that. Evigan, who thinks he's smarter than everyone else—and seemed to spend much of his time in prison educating himself even more— doesn't strike me as someone who would be happy spending the rest of his life south of the border."

Gavin had the same thought, but asked, "What about the material on Guadalajara found in Evigan's cell?"

"From what I understand, it belonged to his cellmate, José Contreras, another convicted murderer, who came to this country as an illegal immigrant sex trafficker, by way of Guadalajara."

"Hmm…" Gavin muttered. "So, Evigan could

pretty much be headed or hiding anywhere."
Even in Owl's Bay, Gavin thought, but tried to
push that notion away.

"True," Jean said, "but it appears that he might
be moving toward the Midwest, or farther away
from Mississippi. The white Chevrolet Malibu
Evigan was believed to have been driving was
found abandoned in Arkansas. Someone matching his description was reportedly spotted in Indiana."

Maybe he isn't anywhere near Owl's Bay,
Gavin thought, glancing about at the art lovers
who showed up. Could be that he was giving Evigan far more credit than he deserved. Or maybe
there was good reason to feel uneasy for as long
as the escaped killer was not back behind bars.

"Keep me in the loop for anything else you
find out," Gavin told her, knowing that he was
just a bit preoccupied to be in the midst of the
hunt for the Gulfport Nightmare Killer.

"You've got it," Jean promised, and Gavin
hung up, realizing he'd managed to lose sight
of Nikki and needed to find her in a hurry, to
make sure she was all right.

"THIS IS KENAN FERNÁNDEZ." Jillian introduced
the man she had described as an art lover.

Nikki cocked a brow with dismay as she

stared at the personal trainer she thought she had seen the last of. "Kenan..." she gasped.

Jillian looked from one to the other. "Do you two know each other...?"

"We've crossed paths," Kenan responded, a smug grin on his lips.

"Something like that." Nikki peered at him, then told Jillian, "Can you give us a moment...?"

"Of course." Jillian flashed her a mildly concerned look. "Find me when you're through."

"I will." Nikki offered her a gentle smile and watched Jillian walk away; then Nikki scanned the room for Gavin, who seemed to have disappeared. But something told her that it wouldn't be for long. She glared at Kenan and snapped, "You shouldn't be here."

His brows joined. "Why shouldn't I? You invited me to your showing, don't you remember?"

Nikki had forgotten this and wished she could take it back. "That was before I realized that we weren't right for each other," she told him candidly. "You know it, I know it." She had blocked him on her cell phone. "Now I'd like you to leave, Kenan."

He scowled at her. "You can't get rid of me that easily," he spat. "I think there's still something between us. If you'd only get off your high horse and let it happen."

She shot him an icy stare. "Are we really

going to do this—here? I have an art exhibition underway with lots of people around. Be smart, Kenan. Stalking is a crime, whether you want to believe it or not."

"Believe it!" Gavin's voice boomed as he came up from behind her. He got in Kenan's face and said, "I thought we understood each other?"

Kenan held his ground as best he could. "You thought wrong."

Gavin pulled out and flashed his identification. "I'm a special agent with the Mississippi Department of Corrections. One phone call and I'll have you arrested and charged with aggravated stalking," he asserted. "If convicted, you could serve five years in prison. Believe me, you don't want to end up there." Gavin allowed that to sink in and asked toughly, "So, what's it going to be? Will you leave Nikki alone?"

Kenan set his jaw. He eyed Nikki like a man who seemed still obsessed with her, but appeared to know when he was outnumbered and backed into a corner. Throwing his hands up, he muttered, "Yeah, whatever."

Nikki watched him storm off and said under her breath, "Hope he's finally gotten the message this time."

"So do I." Gavin frowned. "But in case he's still bent on harassing you, I think you need to take out a protective order against the man. If

Fernández tries to circumvent it, he'll get himself further into hot water that won't end well for him."

"I'll do it," Nikki was quick to agree. "I've about had it up to here—" she raised her hand to her chin "—with him. If it takes a restraining order for him to back off, so be it." *And having you around as my bodyguard is certainly an extra deterrent*, Nikki told herself thankfully.

"Good." Gavin smiled at her warmly. "Anything else interesting happen since I left...?"

"Only that everyone seems to love my artwork," she answered, but sensed that he was referring to any sign that Perry Evigan had decided to pay her an unwelcome visit too. "No sighting of Evigan, thus far, knock on wood."

"I doubt that he'll show his face around here," Gavin spoke confidently. "He's got too much to lose by coming after the one living—and protected—witness to his serial crimes. Besides, Evigan's allegedly been seen in Indiana in his quest to evade recapture."

Though feeling relieved to hear this, Nikki still had to ask, "Do you think that's true?"

He hesitated before responding. "Perhaps. But we won't really know till Evigan's back in custody and we can interrogate him and see exactly what path he took to avoid capture."

"Well, that time can't come soon enough," she declared anxiously.

Gavin nodded. "I'm with you there."

"How's everything going?" Jillian asked when joining them.

"We're good," Nikki told her, glancing at Gavin.

"Yeah, she's all yours." He grinned as he looked at the art gallery owner.

Jillian smiled. "Actually, this evening, Nikki is not just mine, but everyone's artist extraordinaire."

"I couldn't agree more." Gavin flashed Nikki a devastating smile and she took it in, while masking her growing desire to be with him in ways that had nothing to do with his safeguarding role in her life.

WHEN THEY GOT back to the cottage, Gavin double-checked the perimeter for his own peace of mind that there was no indication it had been broken into, that they had been followed, or otherwise suggested that Perry Evigan had been there. Or even Kenan Fernández, for that matter. Though both men had more reasons for staying away than coming there, at risk to their freedom, Gavin wasn't convinced that common sense and logic would overcome obsession, irrationality and stupidity, where it concerned the two men.

I have no problem going the extra mile to protect Nikki from any potential predators, Gavin thought, knowing full well that this had become personal, as much as his duty for the MDOC. He needed Nikki to stay alive and well, so they had the opportunity to take what had been given them in each other and run with it.

They entered the house and Nikki punched in the code to the security system, after which Gavin took a quick walk-through with Nikki close by, before he told her levelly when they were back downstairs, "Looks like the coast is clear."

"That's nice to know," she said. "I would hate to think of this cottage as ground zero for a serial killer on the prowl. But thanks for checking."

"Not a problem." *Not yet anyway*, he thought, and wanted to keep it that way. Gavin turned his attention away from threats to her big art exhibit. "It was fun seeing you in your element this evening. Your paintings, on full display, were incredible. And so are you."

Nikki blushed. "I try my best. Sometimes even that falls short, but what can you say?"

He grinned. "Not everything needs to be said. There are things that speak for themselves."

"You're quite the philosopher," she said with an amused chuckle. "So, I guess I'll allow my artwork to do the talking for me—and add my two cents every now and then."

Gavin laughed. "Seems like a pretty good plan of action."

She smiled and headed into the kitchen. "Would you like a glass of wine?"

"Sure, that sounds good."

He followed her and watched as she took the bottle of white wine from the stainless-steel fridge and removed two wineglasses from a cabinet. After filling each halfway, she handed him a glass and, after sipping from her own, said, "It's been nice having you here and getting reacquainted."

"I feel the same way," he made clear, putting the glass to his lips. "I wish it had been sooner to reach this point in time, but getting to know you now has been well worth the wait."

"I agree wholeheartedly." She beamed. "That is, getting to know the man you are today."

Gavin stared into her entrancing blue eyes and knew instinctively that this was the right moment to kiss her again. He cupped her chin and went for it, pressing their lips together for a stirring kiss that upped his desire for her a few notches.

As though she were reading his mind and matching it with her own, Nikki met his eyes and cooed sotto voce, "I want to get you into bed."

His libido soared even more. "I'd like nothing more than to make love to you, Nikki," he told her with a sense of urgency.

"Then what are you waiting for?" she challenged him. "Make love to me—now..."

In his head, Gavin imagined ripping her clothes off, lifting her onto the countertop and engaging in primordial sexual relations. But as he imagined that might be a bit uncomfortable for her, he showed restraint and uttered, "Let's go to your bedroom."

"Yes, let's..." she agreed, taking him by the hand and leading the way, as they brought the glasses of wine with them.

KENAN FERNÁNDEZ FINALLY decided to drag himself from the Hawthorne Bar and Grill on Burnsten Street before they kicked him out. He finished off the Alabama slammer whiskey shot and headed for the door, still miffed that Nikki Sullivan had decided he wasn't worth her time. Without even giving him a chance to show what he was truly made of, she'd essentially kicked him to the curb. That included blocking his calls and texts, adding insult to injury. She had apparently taken up with this other dude—a special agent—who had threatened to have him charged with aggravated stalking if he didn't back off his pursuit of Nikki.

Kenan muttered an expletive as he stumbled across the small parking lot toward his red BMW 228i Gran Coupe. He had admittedly never taken rejection well. And he wasn't quite ready to start now. But how could he compete in a fair fight against someone who seemed equally determined to keep him away from the gorgeous woman Kenan had a thing for?

He climbed into the vehicle, buckled up and headed home to the nearby beachfront condominium he owned.

Caught up in his thoughts, Kenan was oblivious to the fact that he was being followed. It was only when another vehicle—a gray Buick Encore—pulled up alongside his on the driver's side with the passenger window rolled down, that he took notice. But by the time Kenan became aware that someone was pointing a gun at him through his own open window, it was too late to do anything about it, as a shot rang out, hitting Kenan squarely in the face.

His world had already gone dark by the time a second shot hit the mark, for good measure. Kenan Fernández's car veered out of control, crashing into a light pole.

The Buick continued on down the street as if nothing tragic had happened.

Chapter Ten

"Do you happen to have any condoms?" Gavin thought to ask Nikki as they stood in her primary bedroom, still fully clothed while they were between hot kisses. She had let down her hair.

She was happy that he was responsible in wanting to protect them from an unplanned pregnancy, but told him to ease his concerns, "I'm on birth control." Nikki added, "But if you'd feel more comfortable using a condom—"

"I'm good," he told her in a relaxed manner, indicating that Gavin was confident that neither of them had any sexually transmitted diseases and was ready to carry on.

"So am I," she let him know coolly, eager to be with him in intimate relations.

"Then let's do this." Gavin put his hands on her cheeks and they started kissing again.

Nikki felt as light as a feather as she inhaled his manly scent and fantasized about what was to come, a decade after her earlier fantasies about him. They pulled apart and stripped off their clothing. It took her only an instant to realize that Gavin's firm body in the nude and rockhard abs were everything she had imagined and then some.

"You're perfect," she gushed, unable to resist saying it, even while he was perusing her admiringly.

He laughed. "Not sure about that, but I am sure where it concerns just how gorgeous you are from head to toe…and everything in between…"

"Hmm…" Nikki basked in the words every woman wanted to hear before making love. "Come here, handsome—"

Gavin obeyed, gave her a mouthwatering kiss, then scooped her up in his arms and carried her to the bed. Just as Nikki sought to take the lead in their foreplay, he told her smoothly, "Relax. And enjoy this…"

She did as she was told, closing her eyes, when Gavin used his mouth and masterful fingers over the expanse of her entire body to whip Nikki up into a frenzy. Unable to take it anymore, needing him as she had never needed anyone like this, she uttered demandingly, "I want you inside me—now!" She sighed and softened her tone, but not the fervent desire she had. "Please, make love to me, Gavin."

"I'm more than willing to do as you ask," he responded, his voice lowered an octave to reflect his own overpowering needs. "I want you too—more than you could ever know..."

He climbed atop her and Nikki lurched as Gavin plunged deep inside her. She wrapped her long legs around his hard back and moaned as the feeling of sexual satisfaction gripped her like a fever. The instantaneous nature of the climax shocked Nikki in a way, but was quite expected in another, as the pent-up needs were brought to the surface by Gavin and his determination to please.

It was only after this that she gave him the go-ahead to complete their lovemaking by reaching his own apex of fulfillment. Their slickened bodies clung together like second skins as Nikki had a second orgasm and cherished it, before things settled down and they lay side by side on the satin sheet, catching their breaths.

"Did we really just do that?" she had to ask with a nervous laugh while regaining her equilibrium.

He raised a brow. "Uh, if you mean red-hot sex, then the answer is yes, we did."

"Okay." Nikki colored. "I know what transpired—and I agree, it was mind-blowing—but was it because you truly wanted me or someone you could no longer have?" she questioned openly, as Brigette entered her head, perhaps unwisely.

"Definitely you," Gavin made clear, seemingly picking up on the insinuation. "What I had with Brigette was then—painful as it was to deal with her murder while knowing the escaped killer is still on the loose—and this is now and all about us as two people attracted to each other, who needed what happened between us and acted upon it."

She smiled, feeling relieved. "Good answer."

"I meant every word," he assured her. "I'm not looking to go backward in time—only forward to wherever that leads us."

"Me too." Nikki wondered just where that might be. She vowed not to overthink things, such as what would happen after the Perry Evigan episode had ended, and let it play out in real time.

Gavin cozied up to her. "Good. Now that we settled that, might a second round be in the cards?"

She chuckled. "Are you sure you have the energy?"

He laughed. "I think I can manage when I'm with someone who is a total turn-on."

Nikki felt him caressing her, causing her own need for him to be reinvigorated. "Works both ways," she promised, then upturned her mouth to meet with his in a passionate kiss.

GAVIN TRIED TO sit still on the wooden stool in Nikki's studio the following morning. He had let her talk him into posing for an oil painting. As she had been persistent enough, the least he could do was capitulate and let her go to work, even if he didn't necessarily see himself as worthy of being the subject to be shown in a future art exhibit. Or even hanging on the wall surrounded by an expensive frame. But if Nikki felt otherwise, who was he to argue? Not to mention, he was flattered to be seen in a way beyond his professional life in corrections, zeroing in on his physical appearance that he had grown to take for granted through the years.

His mind shifted to making love to Nikki well into the wee hours of the morning. Gavin knew that she saw him as well in a more carnal sense that delved into both their basic instincts and natural attraction toward one another. He pictured her small but full breasts, taut body and perfect streamlined figure—even her small feet and cute toes did it for him. As did her pleasing scent and the way she laughed and blushed.

It made Gavin imagine what it would have been like had he connected with Nikki on this level a decade ago—instead of Brigette—and been allowed to build a relationship over the years. Maybe they would be married today, with children. How had he missed the boat then in not clearly recognizing what was staring him right in the face?

I was too blinded by my stubbornness to look past Brigette's unwillingness to commit to a serious relationship and my foolish attempts to get her to see things my way, to end things between us and look elsewhere for happiness, Gavin chided himself. But it was well past time to move on from past mistakes, and he had, with Nikki, who had come back into his life and helped him to see the light. Much of which shone all around her.

"You're not too deep in thought over there, are you?" She caught his attention as Nikki stood before the canvas, paintbrush in hand, a little paint having found its way on to her white bib apron.

Snapping to attention, Gavin gave a chuckle, realizing he had been caught in reverie. "You got me," he confessed.

She regarded him curiously. "Care to share?"

"I was just thinking that I'm so glad you reappeared in my life."

"Uh, I think it's the other way around," she said wryly.

"How about both?"

"Deal." Nikki studied her subject. "Any complaints?"

"None whatsoever," he promised her. *Both in and out of bed*, Gavin thought truthfully.

"Me neither." Nikki drew a breath. "Can you turn your head just slightly to the right for me?"

Gavin obeyed, then quipped, "Well, now that you mention it regarding complaints, it's anything but easy trying to stay still or keep the smile off my face when I'm desperate to do just the opposite."

She chuckled. "You're doing just fine. I promise, it won't be too much longer."

"Isn't that what all artists tell their subjects?" he questioned.

"Only the ones who whine too much," she tossed back, causing them both to laugh.

"Point well taken." Gavin made a straight face. "No more whining, I promise."

It was this easygoing banter between them, among other things, such as her beauty and their intimate connection, that told him he wanted her in his life well beyond the time when Gavin's special agent duties had come to an end. Were they on the same wavelength here?

When Nikki's cell phone rang, she took the call and listened in, before her expression changed as she blurted out, "What?" Gavin tried to read between the lines, but waited till Nikki's next words were uttered forlornly. "Thanks for letting me know. Bye, Blair."

"What's up?" Gavin asked immediately, detecting the tension in her posture.

Nikki approached him, looking as if she had seen a ghost, and said tonelessly, "My friend Blair just told me that Kenan Fernández is dead."

"Dead?" Gavin got to his feet, meeting her gaze. "How?"

"He was shot to death while driving in his car," she said, a catch to her voice. "The killer is still at large—"

By the uncertain look in Nikki's eyes, Gavin knew that the murder of Kenan Fernández was for her, just as much as for him, a cause for concern. On its face, this may have been entirely coincidental as it related to Nikki. Or could this be connected in any way to the escaped con who was still on the loose as far as Gavin was aware, and potentially targeting Nikki?

HONESTLY, NIKKI WASN'T quite sure what to think as she sat beside Gavin while he drove them to the Owl's Bay Police Department. Had Kenan, whom she barely knew, been involved with some bad people? Was he targeted accidentally?

Or could Perry Evigan have somehow come after him in some sick form of revenge against her? This admittedly seemed like a hard pill to swallow. After all, how would Evigan have known about her one date with Kenan? Never mind the fact that she had absolutely no interest in the personal trainer. But stranger things had happened, hadn't they?

Of course, to believe any of this would mean that Perry Evigan was actually in Owl's Bay. And not in Indiana. Or wherever.

"You all right over there?" Gavin asked, breaking the silence between them.

"I will be, once we can get to the bottom of Kenan Fernández's murder," Nikki responded forthrightly. "Not that I have any vested interest in his death, per se," she pointed out. "Seriously, I never wanted to see him again—"

"But you didn't want to see him dead either, especially as a homicide victim." Gavin turned onto Vandeer Street. "I get that."

"Do you?" She eyed him, but knew they were very much in tune with one another in terms of the possible nature of the murder that neither could ignore.

"Of course." He drew a breath. "Let's not jump the gun though, in making any assumptions that may fall flat, till we see what the police have to say about Fernández's death."

"All right." Nikki yielded to his rational sense of logic. She glanced out the passenger-side window. Getting flustered over what-ifs would do her no good. And only feed into the paranoia she once had regarding Evigan. She couldn't allow him to play with her psyche again. Not unless there was good cause.

INSIDE THE POLICE STATION, Gavin and Nikki met with the homicide investigator assigned to the case, Brooke Reidel. The fiftysomething, slender detective was blue-eyed and had layered strawberry blond hair in a medium cut.

"Nice to meet you, Agent Lynley, Ms. Sullivan," Brooke told them, as she shook their hands in her corner office and then offered a seat in two faux leather guest chairs next to her L-shaped wood desk. She leaned against it and asked, "You wanted info on the Kenan Fernández case?"

Gavin looked up at her from the chair and replied candidly, "Whatever you can share." Knowing it was an ongoing investigation, he added, "Nikki had a run-in with Fernández yesterday at her art exhibition."

Brooke gazed at her intently. "Did you know the victim?"

"We went out once," Nikki said tartly, fidgeting in the chair. "It was a dead end, as far as I was concerned. But Kenan seemed to believe otherwise. He showed up at my showing at the Owl's Bay Art Gallery."

"So, you're saying Fernández was stalking you?"

Nikki glanced at Gavin and back. "Yes, it seemed that way."

"I confronted Fernández at the exhibit and told him to lay off—threatening to have him charged with aggravated stalking," Gavin told her. "Fernández left at that point."

"And you never saw him again?" the detective asked, shifting her eyes from one to the other.

"No, and we were together till this morning." Gavin was more than willing to acknowledge their involvement with one another as their alibi, realizing that the encounter with Fernández technically made them suspects in his murder.

"Okay." Brooke took a breath. "From what we know thus far, last night, Kenan Fernández was at the Hawthorne Bar and Grill on Burnsten Street, before leaving at approximately ten p.m. Shortly thereafter, he was shot to death in his BMW by someone in another vehicle on Shaw Boulevard. We currently have a BOLO alert out for that vehicle, which is believed to be a gray Buick Encore, that was picked up on surveillance video around the estimated time the incident occurred."

"What can you tell us about the weapon used to kill Fernández?" Gavin asked her with interest.

"According to the medical examiner and ballistics, the victim was shot twice with 9mm Luger ammo that came from a SIG Sauer P365 9mm pistol," the detective said. She added, "Our Crime Scene Investigations Unit was able to collect the shell casings near the crime scene to corroborate this finding." She gazed at Gavin. "Why do you ask?"

"Nikki was a witness and the victim of an escaped serial killer, Perry Evigan," Gavin told her, glancing at Nikki, whose shoulders slumped understandably. "One of the weapons Evigan and his fellow escapees stole was a SIG Sauer P365 9mm handgun," he recalled, making him fearful that Evigan could be in Owl's Bay.

Brooke reacted to this revelation by creasing her brow. "Yeah, I heard about Evigan's escape and the farmhouse fire that took the lives of the other two fugitives and another ex-con." She eyed Nikki. "Sorry you were put through that. It must have been awful."

"It was," she confessed. "But that was a long time ago. I'm over it." Nikki sighed. "Or at least I was, before Evigan broke out of prison—"

"I get that," Brooke said sympathetically. "But from what I've gathered, Perry Evigan has gotten out of Mississippi."

"We'd like to believe that," Gavin said musingly. "However, given that Fernández was shot with the same type of pistol that Evigan may have in his possession, along with his unnatural desire to go after the only victim to survive his serial murders, I'm not prepared to leave anything off the table where Evigan is concerned."

Nikki's voice shook when she uttered, "I'm a bit spooked as well with the prospect that he might have murdered Kenan as some sort of psycho calling card to let me know he's back and coming for me…"

"I understand both of your concerns," Brooke told them. "It's certainly worth checking out. But we think that Fernández's death may be related to a drug deal gone bad."

Gavin cocked a brow. "Really?"

"Yes. The Hawthorne Bar and Grill has been a hot bed for drug use and trafficking in recent years," the detective said, leaning forward. "Moreover, a witness reported seeing Fernández having a heated exchange with an African American male, described as being in his mid- to late-twenties, shortly before Fernández left the bar. For now, this unidentified male is our primary person of interest."

"All right." Gavin had heard enough. He looked at Nikki and could see her strained features relax with the prospect that Fernández had been murdered by someone other than Perry Evigan. This too gave Gavin comfort, as the last thing he wanted was for the serial killer fugitive to have tracked Nikki down, with sure intent to do her bodily harm. He stood, prompting her to do so as well. "Thanks for your time," he told the detective.

Brooke nodded. "I know the BOLO for Perry Evigan is still in effect, as long as he remains free. If we get any credible information that suggests he has come to this town, you can be sure that the Mississippi Department of Corrections will be informed, Agent Lynley."

Gavin offered her a small grin. "Fair enough."

They walked out of the Owl's Bay Police Department with a renewed sense of safety. But in the back of his mind, Gavin still had an uneasy feeling that danger could well lurk around one corner or another as he knew there would be no rest as long as the Gulfport Nightmare Killer remained on the loose somewhere.

Chapter Eleven

Nikki was happy to resume the portrait of Gavin, if for no other reason than to take her mind off the unexpected death of Kenan Fernández. It may have been a big mistake when she agreed to go out with him, and he could be a real jerk in his persistence, but he certainly didn't deserve to die. Even if he was into drug dealing, as the police suspected, which she still found hard to believe. It seemed to her that, as a personal trainer, he prided himself on staying healthy and fit. Neither went well with drug use, which often accompanied those who were in the business of trafficking drugs. But what did she know?

"Now, if you could just bend your head ever so slightly to the left, that would be perfect," she told Gavin, who complied with a handsome grin playing on his nice lips. He was not only an excellent subject, with great bone structure and a flawless complexion, but he also didn't complain like some of her other subjects. Come to think of it, he checked a lot of the boxes for her—not only as ideal for painting, but as great relationship material as well. Not to mention, he was a good lover whom she could never imagine tiring of.

"If there's anything else I can do to make your job easier, just say the word," Gavin told her smoothly.

"Hmm…" Nikki flashed her teeth with a naughty thought. *Be careful what you agree to*, she mused. "I'll certainly keep that in mind." She worked on his gray eyes with her brush, feeling that they were something she could drown in, so enchanting they were. Her thoughts turned back to the murder of Kenan and how relieved she was that apparently this was not the work of Perry Evigan. So why did she still feel uneasy? As if his presence still loomed large? *Get your mind off this and focus*, she admonished herself, peering at Gavin, not wanting to allow her victimizer to ruin a good thing they had going. For however long it lasted.

"So, how are we looking over there?" Gavin asked patiently, his hands resting on his lap.

"Just about done," Nikki told him as she applied the finishing touches around the eyes, before changing brushes to work a bit more on his chiseled chin. "Hope you like it…"

"How can I not?" he expressed confidently.

"I've seen your artwork. I'm more than honored to become a permanent part of it."

She blushed. "I'm equally honored that you agreed to sit for me." Not to mention break the ice in coming to her rescue with an escaped killer on the loose. "There," she voiced. "Done, save for a few touch-ups here and there once it dries. Come have a look."

"All right." Gavin got up, stretched his long legs and came over to her.

Nikki waited with bated breath to see what he thought, as he stared at the painting in utter silence. "Well… What do you think?" she asked nervously.

"I love it!" he declared. "You've done an incredible job in capturing the best parts of me."

"You think?" She smiled.

"Unquestionably. I never thought I could look so good on canvas. But you've made a believer out of me, Nikki."

She flushed. "Glad you approve."

He grinned at her. "Oh, I approve of a lot of things about you, Ms. Sullivan."

Her lashes fluttered coquettishly. "Is that so?"

"Yeah." Gavin wrapped his arms around her waist and drew her close. "Such as the sweet taste of your lips."

"Hmm…"

"Mind if I try them on for size?"

"Be my guest." She happily gave in to him.

They kissed for what seemed like a few minutes that definitely left Nikki all hot and bothered, before coming up for air. "I'd better get cleaned up," she told him, knowing she had managed to get paint on her face and hands.

"Okay, if you insist." He favored her with a sexy grin. "But just for the record, even with a few smudges, you still look great."

She laughed. "I'll take your word for that." Along with reading between the lines, which Nikki admittedly felt gave her hope for bigger and better things with him down the line. She headed upstairs to wash her face.

GAVIN WATCHED HER leave the studio, then he turned back to the portrait of himself. He really did appreciate it and wondered if it would find its way into her next art exhibition, before he could take it home. Actually, truth be told, he would rather bring Nikki back to his place, see how comfortable she felt there and see which way the wind blew in enabling them to seize this point in time for establishing a real romance. *Let's see if she's amenable to that when this Evigan business is behind us*, Gavin told himself with optimism, before removing the cell phone from his khaki pants.

He checked his messages and saw a text

from Marvin Whitfield, who was following up on their earlier conversation regarding the current whereabouts of Perry Evigan, which made Gavin nervous. He called the director with a video request and asked tentatively after Whitfield accepted it, "So, where do things stand with Evigan?"

Whitfield's brow furrowed. "We seem to have lost track of his possible whereabouts at the moment," he said disappointedly. "There've been a few sightings here and there, but nothing that has been substantiated."

"What about the last known vehicle Evigan was believed to be driving?" Gavin thought about the gray Buick Encore that the unsub in Kenan Fernández's murder may have been driving.

"That's just it," the director said, "we don't have a credible lead on that right now. Could be that he's driving around in a stolen car that had already been stolen by someone else. Hence, no report of it. If I had to make a guess, I'd say that Evigan is probably changing vehicles every chance he gets—trying to remain one step ahead of the law."

Gavin didn't disagree with that assessment. It still left open the door that Evigan could have shown up in Owl's Bay and was able to locate Nikki, while waiting for the right time and place to strike. He brought up the SIG Sauer P365 9mm pistol that was used to pump two rounds into Fernández's head. "Could be the same SIG Sauer firearm Evigan stole in Boyle from Donald Takeuchi," Gavin pointed out.

"Yeah, we're checking into that," Whitfield told him. "We've asked the Owl's Bay Police Department to submit the firearm casings to the National Integrated Ballistic Information Network to see if any matching bullets have been used and, if so, where. Of course, getting ahold of the murder weapon would be very helpful if we're to link the homicide to Evigan."

"I know." Gavin resigned himself to the fact that without possession of the SIG Sauer P365 9mm pistol—in the absence of a positive identification of Perry Evigan in Owl's Bay—he couldn't know for sure if Evigan was the shooter. Or if, in fact, it was a drug-related hit and a local unsub actually carried it out.

"Is she doing okay?" the director asked.

"Nikki's holding up fine," Gavin said, but knew there were limits as to how long that would last. He was glad that Nikki had her art to keep her preoccupied while Evigan continued to elude authorities.

After ending the video chat, in which Whitfield made no mention of withdrawing him from the assignment for now, Gavin gazed again at his oil portrait. He used the cell phone to take a picture of it and then sent it to his sister, followed by his cousins, knowing that they would all enjoy seeing it. If he had his way, Gavin hoped that someday they would all be able to sit for their own portraits. This, of course, would mean that he and Nikki's relationship had become just that—evolving into something that would warrant get-togethers both ways with his family. As well as hers.

ON MONDAY AFTERNOON, Nikki drove to teach her art class at Owl's Bay Community College. Gavin came along for the ride, sitting in the passenger seat, looking at his cell phone. Neither had brought up Perry Evigan today, but she was certain that Gavin was mindful that the serial killer had still not been brought to justice and, consequently, they would remain on edge till such time.

She glanced at Gavin and couldn't help but wonder what his thoughts were for their future. Or had he given much thought at all to whether or not what they had between them was lasting? As opposed to taking a wait-and-see attitude? She wouldn't push him one way or the other— even if in her heart, Nikki knew that what she was starting to feel for Gavin was very real. And not at all subject to misconception. Or time-limited. But that was just her. He would need to decide for himself if he wanted a life with her firmly planted in it or not.

She pulled off Praceson Road and into the parking lot, where Nikki found a spot right in front of the Department of Fine Arts and Design. "Here we are," she told Gavin with a smile.

He looked at her and grinned. "Let's go."

They went inside the building, where Nikki's class was on the first floor. "You're welcome to come in, if you like," she invited Gavin, though suspecting he would decline.

"Thanks, but I'll wait out in the hall," he said. "I need to make some calls and give you your space at the same time. At least in the classroom."

Nikki would have been just as comfortable to have him in her space, but understood that he needed his own, while remembering that he was still on duty as a special agent and surveillance was part of that. So long as Evigan remained even the slightest threat.

"All right." Nikki smiled again at Gavin. "See you in a bit." Carrying a black leather satchel with art materials, she headed inside where students awaited her. She greeted them, including her newest student, Miriam Broderick, who walked up to her, and also happened to be a member of Nikki's support group. It was there that Miriam expressed a strong interest in developing her art skills and working her way past the tragic death of her brother a year ago.

"Hey, Nikki." She flashed a generous smile. "Thanks so much for inviting me."

Nikki's eyes lit up. "Thank you for wanting to come. Hopefully, you'll get what you need to improve your craft and I'll be here to help in any way I can."

"I appreciate that and I'm excited about the opportunity."

"Me too." Nikki grinned and walked toward a kidney-shaped laminate table, where she set the satchel and eyed various works of art lining the walls, and imagined others yet to come, before turning to the students to begin the class.

"I HAVE NEWS…" Jean O'Reilly told Gavin over the phone.

"Hopefully, it's good news," he said, while moving farther down the hall, away from Nikki's classroom.

"I wish," she moaned. "Two days ago, there was an unauthorized use of an ATM card in a town about a hundred and fifty miles from Owl's Bay. This led to a welfare check of the card owner, a fifty-five-year-old male veterinarian named Richard Pelayo. He'd been stabbed to death in his garage. The medical examiner believes Pelayo was killed at least twenty-four hours before his body was discovered."

"And this relates to Evigan how?" Gavin asked tensely.

"A man fitting his general description, and wearing a hoodie, was picked up on surveillance video outside the house," Jean replied matter-of-factly. "We're still trying to determine if it was Evigan or not by finding his DNA or fingerprints at the crime scene, or other means of identification."

Gavin swallowed thickly, switching the phone to his other ear. "Do you happen to know if Pelayo owned a car?"

"A Buick Encore was registered in his name," she responded. "We think it was stolen by whoever killed Pelayo—"

Gavin frowned. "It's the same make and model as a car involved in the shooting death of a man named Kenan Fernández here in Owl's Bay," he told her bleakly. "If Evigan is the man in the surveillance video footage, then he's likely responsible for both deaths."

"Hmm…" Jean hummed. "I can understand killing Pelayo in the course of a home invasion, but why Fernández?"

"It may have something to do with his interest in Nikki," Gavin said, and explained the convoluted scenario.

"Wow," she voiced afterward. "Seems like a stretch, insofar as motivation. Not to mention the high risk versus uncertain reward for Evigan, should he have been able to fit these pieces together in Nikki's life and times."

"I agree," Gavin told her, when it was put that way. "Maybe I have it all wrong about Perry Evigan. But my gut instincts tell me that I can't rule out anything in regard to what the escaped serial killer may be capable of. Which is why we need to find him ASAP."

"We're doing everything in our power to do just that," Jean assured him. "The Fugitive Apprehension Strike Team and our partners in law enforcement are all over this, looking at every lead regarding Evigan, whether he's still in the state or elsewhere."

"All right." Gavin took a breath. "Let me know what forensics comes up with on the Pelayo murder crime scene or otherwise."

"I will." She paused. "You'll get through this. So will Nikki Sullivan."

"Yeah. I hope you're right." After disconnecting, Gavin walked back toward Nikki's art class and peeked in the door window. He could see her. The need to protect her from the likes of Perry Evigan was stronger than ever. As were the feelings for Nikki that had begun to fill Gavin's heart in ways he couldn't have imagined just a few short days ago. Now it was something he would never want to turn his back on, no matter where things went with them.

He stepped away from the door and called Detective Brooke Reidel, informing her about the possible connection between the murders of Kenan Fernández and Richard Pelayo, with the potential common denominator being wanted fugitive, Perry Evigan.

PERRY HAD ADMITTEDLY grown restless in his intense desire to pick up where he left off as a heartless strangulation serial killer. Time had only increased his appetite for death of those deserving. Though he knew without question that the big prize would be Nikki Sullivan, he had been unable to get to her just yet, thanks to the presence of her bodyguard. Perry assumed he was law enforcement in some capacity, determined to keep Nikki alive.

This was the polar opposite of Perry's own quest and desire. He had waited this long; he could wait a little longer to achieve his ultimate objective. In the meantime, he needed a warm-up to get him back in the game in a way that could get him excited. And he had already latched on to the perfect target for his deadly craving. Now it was just a matter of luring her into his trap, for which there would be no escape.

Tilting the brim of the beige bucket hat he was wearing to help disguise his identity, along with dark cat-eye sunglasses and the stubble he'd allowed to grow on his face and neck, and a fresh set of clothing and boots, Perry walked inconspicuously away from the Owl's Bay Community College's Department of Fine Arts and Design building. Shortly, he arrived at the latest vehicle he had stolen—a blue Toyota Corolla Cross—having believed that the Buick Encore had become too hot now.

Climbing inside, he drummed his fingers on the steering wheel fretfully and waited.

Chapter Twelve

"Mom, Dad, this is Gavin Lynley," Nikki introduced him to her mother and stepfather, Dorothy and William McElligott, via a video chat while holding a tablet in the living room. They were back in Clarksdale after their visit to the Cayman Islands. Now seemed as good a time as any to have them meet Gavin, knowing the bad blood that had once existed between her and Brigette's former boyfriend. So much had changed since then—as it related to Nikki's evolving relationship with the handsome special agent—that it was incumbent upon her to share this with those she was closest to.

"Hi, Gavin," her parents spoke in unison in friendly voices.

"Hey." He looked over Nikki's shoulder. "Good to meet you both."

"You too," her mother said, smiling.

"Same here," her stepdad added, and after a beat, asked, "So, where do things stand on Perry Evigan? I've heard conflicting stories on his whereabouts and even whether or not he's still alive—"

So have I, Nikki thought unnervingly, while considering the latest news that the escaped serial killer may have been involved in an identity theft and home invasion turned deadly in a town a hundred and fifty miles away. The suspect's head was covered with a hood, but he seemed to match Evigan's description and apparently stole the victim's Buick Encore—the same type of vehicle believed to have been used by someone in the murder of Kenan Fernández. Were the culprits truly one and the same? Had her tormentor finally found her?

Gavin, who had managed to keep her grounded while doing his best to downplay the threat, even while being much more guarded against being confronted by the fugitive, responded candidly, "I believe Evigan is still alive. As to his whereabouts, we haven't been able to pinpoint this definitively as yet, but we're working night and day to apprehend him."

Dorothy frowned. "After what that man put my daughter through, I worry that the longer he remains on the loose, the greater the chance that he will find his way back to her for more terrorizing…and worse…"

"I will not let Evigan hurt your daughter," Gavin said firmly, trying to reassure her. "I'm not letting Nikki out of my sight till Evigan is back in custody. Or dead, so he can't ever come after her again."

"Listen to Special Agent Lynley," William said comfortingly to his wife. "Nikki's in good hands. He won't let anything bad happen to her."

"I do feel safe with Gavin nearby," Nikki pitched in, flashing him a smile of support, while knowing that the nature of their involvement had gone well beyond potential victim and protector. "Wherever Perry Evigan is, he's running out of time to remain free. We're okay here."

Her mother's blue eyes crinkled. "I'm happy to know that."

"Love you both," Nikki uttered sweetly, promising to keep them abreast of anything new to report about the wanted escapee. Beyond that, she was eager to apprise them of where things were headed between her and Gavin, once Nikki knew herself in no uncertain terms.

After ending the video conversation, she gazed at Gavin, who grinned back and said thoughtfully, "Hope I made a good impression on your folks."

"You did," she said knowingly. "I'm sure they approve of you being here."

"Yeah?"

"Of course." She smiled, reflective. "If you get to meet them in person, they will surely fall head over heels for you." *Just as I have*, Nikki told herself.

Gavin blushed. "In that case, I look forward to getting together with your mom and stepdad. And for what it's worth, if my parents were still alive, they definitely would have been happy to meet you and get to know you as someone who's in my life. I'm sure Lauren and her family will be quite taken with you when they get to meet you."

"It's nice to know you feel that way." Even more comforting to Nikki was hearing him say that she was in his life—and wanted to extend that to those he was closest to—giving them both something to build upon.

The trick though, was to not allow Perry Evigan to find a way to come between them as someone who still wanted to see her dead.

AFTER HER OFFICIAL shift had ended on Monday evening, Detective Brooke Reidel received the call that an adult female had been found deceased under highly suspicious circumstances at a residence on Willow Lane. Knowing that her job for the Owl's Bay PD didn't give her the luxury of picking and choosing hours that worked best, Brooke grabbed her Glock 26 Gen5, holstered it and left her dog, an Irish Setter named Mandy, in their Craftsman bungalow, and hopped into her white Ford Explorer to head to the scene.

En route, Brooke got more info on what she was coming upon. According to a first responder, the dead female had been identified by her townhouse neighbor as Miriam Broderick, a twenty-seven-year-old product line supervisor for a trucking company and divorcée who lived alone. Brooke couldn't help but wonder about the other aspects of the victim's life that led up to it ending prematurely. Was it a happenstance victimization? Wrong place, wrong time-type circumstance? Or a terrible situation she put herself in by bad choices or a misguided association?

Truth was that Brooke had seen them all. Even in a relatively small town like Owl's Bay, where she had put in more than twenty years as a detective and more than a decade in homicide. Take, for instance, the death of Kenan Fernández two nights ago. It had all the earmarks of a drug hit. Except for the fact that Fernández was not a known player in the drug use and drug dealing sphere. Nor did he have a criminal record to suggest he was involved in this illicit activity.

On the other hand, Fernández had been accused of stalking. Had that been a factor in his death, as the search continued for the gray Buick Encore believed to have been used in his execution, as well as trying to track down the current person of interest in the case?

Complicating matters was the possibility that the vehicle was stolen and Fernández's killer might be responsible for the murder of another man a hundred and fifty miles away. Brooke considered that the unsub could well be fugitive serial killer Perry Evigan. Nikki Sullivan had managed to come away alive from her ordeal with him, after being drugged and kidnapped by Evigan. Had he shown up in Owl's Bay to take another crack at her?

Brooke left that one to ponder as she pulled up to the Cetona Townhomes complex on Willow Lane. After getting out of her car and by-passing onlookers, in what had clearly become a crime scene, she ducked under the yellow tape and made her way up the stairs to the victim's townhouse, where Brooke was greeted in the foyer by Officer Lester Hu. She flashed her identification at the twentysomething, slender Asian man, who was brown-eyed and had black hair in a faux hawk style, and asked him routinely, "What do we have?"

Lester furrowed his brow. "It looks to be a homicide," he spoke bluntly. "It's not pretty. See for yourself." He turned away from her.

Brooke stepped inside the contemporarily furnished great room and saw that it had been ransacked. Lying face up on the bamboo floor behind a coffee-colored love seat with flared arms was the nude body of an adult female with short, choppy brown hair with blond streaks. Her green-brown eyes, wide-open, were devoid of any signs of life. A scarf was wrapped tightly around her neck in a way that made it clear that this was no fashion statement.

A chill ran through Brooke as her mind went straight to the so-called Gulfport Nightmare Killer—whose calling card in a series of ligature strangulations included a scarf asphyxiation. Was he back in business—only now as the Owl's Bay Nightmare Killer?

GAVIN GOT A phone call from Detective Brooke Reidel. He assumed she had an update on the unsub and/or vehicle believed to have been used in the deadly attack on Kenan Fernández. Knowing that Nikki would want to hear this too, and feeling a need to keep her informed, he put it on speakerphone—even if he would rather shield her from any unsettling news pertaining to Perry Evigan. Especially with the promise made to her mom and stepdad about protecting their daughter at all costs. It was something Gavin stood by, as much for his own desire for a long-term future with Nikki in it, as doing right by Nikki and her folks.

"Detective Reidel," Gavin said apprehensively. "What do you have for me—or us?" he amended as he let her know she was on speaker, and gazed at Nikki, as they stood inside her art studio.

"I'm afraid it's not good…" Brooke sighed. "I'm at the scene of a homicide. The white female victim, age twenty-seven, was found by a neighbor. In a preliminary examination, the Yaeden County medical examiner believes that the decedent, Miriam Broderick, was strangled to death with the scarf wrapped around her neck…"

"Did you say Miriam Broderick?" Gavin asked, recognizing the name.

"Yes—do you know her?"

He turned to Nikki, whose expression dampened as she responded solemnly, "Miriam was in my support group for trauma survivors. She also attended an art class I taught today at Owl's Bay Community College." Nikki's voice shook as she asked the detective timorously, "Do you think this was the work of Perry Evigan?"

Brooke wasted no time in replying straightforwardly, "It fits the MO of Evigan's previous strangulation murders. Of course, we won't know for certain till we see if his DNA or fingerprints were left at the crime scene," she emphasized. "We're looking at surveillance video as well."

Nikki's eyes narrowed. "If it was Evigan, then he knows where I am and will try to come after me," she argued.

"If Evigan wanted to announce his presence, all he's done was bring more heat on him," Gavin stressed, placing his hand on the small of her back supportively.

"Agent Lynley is right," Brooke said firmly. "We'll be working overtime to solve Ms. Broderick's murder—whoever the perp is…"

"Anything more on the gray Buick Encore?" Gavin asked the detective. With its possible connection to the murders of Kenan Fernández and Richard Pelayo, there was also good reason to link the vehicle to Perry Evigan, now the chief suspect in yet another homicide.

"We're still trying to locate the vehicle," she told him, sounding irritated. "It's only a matter of time before we do, then we'll have a better idea of where we stand on the multiple investigations."

Gavin gritted his teeth. "Keep me posted."

"Of course," she promised. "In the meantime, we can put patrols around Ms. Sullivan's house, if you like?"

"Sounds like a great idea," he responded, but knew that this might still not be sufficient, if Evigan was intent on coming after her.

Once Gavin was off the phone, he faced

Nikki, who uttered with watery eyes, "If Miriam was killed because of me—"

"You weren't responsible for her death, no matter who the killer was," he wanted to make clear, even if Gavin knew how easy it was for Nikki to blame herself, were Evigan behind it. "There was no way for you to know that Evigan would break out of prison and find a way to remain on the loose for days—killing anyone who stood in his path. Or otherwise, was ripe for the picking."

"You're right." She twisted her lips acquiescently. "But that doesn't make me feel a whole lot better."

"Come here." He brought her up to his chest, wrapping his arms around her. "You'll get past this, Nikki," he promised. "We both will."

In that instant, Gavin couldn't help but think about Brigette and how—through fate, by design, or whatever—her tragic death had brought him and Nikki together and given them a chance to come to terms with the past and see the light that a future could bring them. So long as the darkness of an escaped serial killer didn't snuff it out.

IN SPITE OF a mostly restless night's sleep, for all the wrong reasons, Nikki was up bright and early the next morning. She was still trying to square with the reality that her fellow survivor of a traumatic time and art student, Miriam Broderick, was a victim of a homicide. What was that all about? *Was she targeted because of me?* Nikki had to wonder, even when she knew that things did happen in life or the universe itself happenstance, with no one at fault, per se.

On the other hand, she knew that someone was most definitely at fault for Miriam's death. Was it Perry Evigan? Or someone else as perhaps payback for a drug deal gone bad?

As she wrestled with these thoughts, Nikki found Gavin sitting at the breakfast nook table, gazing at his computer. Beside him was a mug of hot coffee. He looked up at her and grinned, giving her the once-over, as she'd thrown on one of his button-down shirts—it was light green and oversize on her, but surprisingly comfortable. "Hey," he said.

"Hi." She blushed under his perusal.

"I don't imagine you slept much better than I did."

"I think you're right."

"Sorry about that." Gavin furrowed his brow. "Coffee's ready."

"Thanks." Nikki was happy that he seemed to have made himself quite at home in her kitchen and elsewhere. Sign of the times? Or future? She poured herself a cup of coffee and studied him, fully dressed for the day. "What are you doing?" Her voice rang with curiosity, knowing the uneasiness in the air with the latest revelations.

He hesitated. "I was just taking a look at the autopsy report on Miriam Broderick."

Nikki cringed while imagining her horrific death. "What were the results?" she asked, taking a seat across the table on the side bench.

"I'll spare you the details," he said protectively.

"Don't." She peered at him. "I'm a big girl, Gavin. I also witnessed firsthand someone being strangled." Brigette's once beautiful face appeared in Nikki's head, before it was forever tarnished by that maniac. "If this is the work of Perry Evigan, I need to know what he's up to, no matter the chilling nature of it…"

"All right." Gavin nodded understandingly. He took a breath, glanced at the screen and stated, "According to the Yaeden County Medical Examiner Flora Ueoka, Miriam was the victim of ligature strangulation, with the actual cause of death being asphyxia. She was also sexually assaulted by her killer…" Gavin paused and gazed at Nikki. "Do I need to go on…?"

"No." She'd heard enough and did not need more explicit information from the report on the suffering Miriam had been put through, before death came mercifully. Nikki sighed and asked pointedly, "Do you think it was him?"

Gavin tasted his coffee musingly and responded with candidness, "We need to be prepared for that distinct possibility."

Her eyes grew wide and her mouth hung open distraughtly. "How does one prepare for the reality that a monster is out there—back in force in picking and choosing which women to rape and strangle to death next?"

Reaching out and taking her hand, Gavin said composedly, "By steeling ourselves against falling into his trap of feeling helpless. Or a bad sense of inevitability. Wherever this thing goes, we control our own destiny. I'll be damned if I allow Evigan to dictate that for you or me. And I won't let you feel that way either."

Nikki wrapped her fingers around his large hand, with her pulse racing, but her heart telling her that having him on her side was more than she could ask for against a common enemy. Even if Perry Evigan was not the one responsible for Miriam's death, his sheer presence as an escaped serial murderer could not be dismissed. So long as the menace of him remained a serious thorn in Nikki's side for her health, well-being and longevity.

Chapter Thirteen

Gavin watched as Nikki headed upstairs to get dressed. If he had his way, he'd love to see her completely undressed and spend as much time as possible with her in bed. She had that kind of effect on him these days. Probably would have a decade ago as well, had he given her half a chance instead of his misguided belief that Brigette was *the one*. Clearly, she was not. He had already come to that painful realization, more or less, when she was killed. But by then, it was too late in the game to see if he and Nikki might have made a connection before someone else won her heart.

This is a whole new beginning for us, Gavin thought, tasting his second cup of coffee. He could live with that and see where it went. All that mattered for the time being was that they couldn't allow Perry Evigan to put a halt to their progress by victimizing Nikki as he wanted to do, in following what he did to Brigette.

Gavin phoned Brooke Reidel for a video chat as he paced around between the living and dining areas, returning her call from a couple of minutes earlier. When her face appeared on the cell phone screen, he said cautiously, "Hey. What's up?"

"We located the gray Buick Encore linked to the murder of Kenan Fernández," Brooke said, running a finger across a thin brow. "It was abandoned behind a vacant building on Tuffas Road. We dusted it for prints and were able to retrieve some that belonged to Evigan. He was definitely in that car at some point," she stated matter-of-factly. "And he has to be considered the number one person of interest in the murder of Kenan Fernández."

Gavin jutted his chin and, before she could continue, asked her, "What about the Buick itself—was it…?"

"Yes, the car belonged to Richard Pelayo," Brooke confirmed. "As such, there's every reason to believe that Evigan killed him too, before taking his car and driving it a hundred and fifty miles to Owl's Bay to continue the murder spree…"

As Gavin digested this, it left the obvious question in his head and the anticipated answer. "Are you saying what I think you are regarding the death of Miriam Broderick?"

Brooke furrowed her brow and nodded affirmatively. "DNA removed from the victim as a result of being sexually assaulted was sent to CODIS. It came back with a match of Perry Evigan's DNA. Moreover, his fingerprints were also left at the scene of the homicide, leaving little doubt that he murdered Ms. Broderick and is still at large."

"And coming after Nikki." Gavin uttered what the detective was surely thinking.

"We've alerted the relevant authorities about this and Owl's Bay is now front and center in the search for the escaped con," Brooke said with concern in her voice. "In the meantime, the police department will assist in any way we can to keep Ms. Sullivan—Nikki—safe."

"All right." After he ended the call, while considering his options and waiting for Nikki to come down, Gavin wasted little time in phoning Marvin Whitfield to confer on the news that Perry Evigan was almost certainly still in Owl's Bay and, as such, a clear and present danger to Nikki.

Whitfield muttered an expletive and snorted, "How this bastard has managed to evade the law while resuming his murderous ways is beyond me."

"I'm in total agreement," Gavin told the director respectfully, in assessing Evigan's amazing ability to dodge recapture and add more notches to his belt as a serial killer and sociopath, "but that doesn't change the fact that by his mere presence in town, Evigan is threatening the very person you assigned me to protect. That's problematic, to say the least."

"I hear you." Whitfield took a breath. "So, what do you suggest?"

"I need to move Nikki out of Owl's Bay, to be on the safe side." Gavin took nothing away from the ability of the MDOC's Fugitive Apprehension Strike Team and other law enforcement agencies involved in the hunt for Evigan. Or, for that matter, the benefits of sheltering in place at the cottage with a good security system and him being armed. With the Owl's Bay PD providing adequate backup. But honestly, none of that gave Gavin comfort right now that the escaped killer might not still find a way to breach that safety net and place Nikki in harm's way.

I couldn't live with myself if I let Evigan have a repeat performance in victimizing Nikki again, Gavin thought, determined not to let that happen. He hoped the director was on board with this.

"Where to?" Whitfield asked.

"A lakefront cabin in the woods just outside of Gulfport," he said to him. "A friend of mine named Jake Kendrick owns it. I've spent time there. It's secluded and has plenty of windows to give me a 360-degree view of who's coming and going. I'm sure he won't mind letting us borrow it for a day or two, if necessary, while Evigan is being tracked down and ultimately taken into custody."

"Okay, then go for it," the director said. "If you're sure about this?"

"I'm just going with my gut here," Gavin told him frankly. "I think it's better to err on the side of caution by temporarily relocating Nikki." The thought had crossed his mind about taking her back to his house in Jackson as a safe refuge. But given the distance and high likelihood that Evigan would be recaptured shortly, Gavin opted against making a move that might seem a bit premature and presumptuous as it related to things evolving in their personal relationship sooner than Nikki might have desired. The last thing he wanted was to rush her. Or otherwise mess things up between them by jumping the gun. "Having lost someone to Perry Evigan ten years ago, I don't want to give him even the slightest opportunity to come for Nikki again— in a place that he may well have already sized up."

"I understand. Get her out of there, then, Lynley. We'll do everything in our power to recapture Evigan and put him back where he belongs.

Hopefully, that will come sooner rather than later. Until then, Nikki Sullivan—and you— deserve some peace of mind while the serial killer remains on the loose."

"Thanks, Director Whitfield." Gavin took a calming breath, but knew there would be no comfort as long as the threat to Nikki's life remained real.

"As an added measure of security, we'll send along a US marshal to escort you and provide an extra set of eyes for your destination," Whitfield said.

Gavin thanked him again and disconnected, only to find Nikki standing there with a hand on her hip and a scowl on her face.

Nikki had overheard some of Gavin's conversation with the Director of Investigations at MDOC. They were talking about moving her out of Owl's Bay, to a cabin in the woods, while Evigan remained free and a threat to her life. She cringed at the implications, but needed to get the scoop from Gavin on exactly why she needed to leave the cottage.

"Hey," Gavin said evenly, though his hardened expression gave away the uneasiness he felt about the current situation.

"What is going on?" she asked straightforwardly, peering at him. "Why the need to relocate me…?"

He drew a breath and, meeting her gaze directly, replied in an acerbic tone of voice, "It's been confirmed that Perry Evigan is in Owl's Bay. His DNA was found on Miriam Broderick and his prints were also found at the crime scene…"

Nikki gasped and put a hand to her mouth as the gravity of Evigan doing to Miriam what he did to Brigette hit her like a ton of bricks. Suspecting something was bad enough. Having it verified was so much worse and left Nikki speechless.

Gavin placed his hands on her shoulders and said knowledgeably, "Beyond that, Evigan's prints were also found in a stolen vehicle believed to have been used by the shooter in the death of Kenan Fernández and another man. Why Evigan would go after Fernández is anyone's guess. But I do know that while Evigan is still on the loose, you're not safe here, Nikki." Gavin's warm breath fell onto her face. "I want to take you to a friend's log cabin, where I can put some distance between here and Evigan's reach. Now that his location has been pinpointed, I expect our Fugitive Apprehension Strike Team and supporting law enforcement to close in on him at any time. But even that's not soon enough to want to wait around and give him a target—you."

"I don't want that either," Nikki said in a hushed voice. "I'll go pack some things."

"Good." Gavin flashed her a sideways grin. "Make it quick. We don't want Evigan to have any time to make his move."

She nodded. "Right."

Having Gavin at this cabin with her would certainly make it easier for Nikki to temporarily relocate from what was supposed to be her comfort zone, after leaving Gulfport eight years ago. Now Perry Evigan had managed to turn her world upside down. And make her cottage a place she could not feel safe in while he was on the prowl, having already murdered two people she was acquainted with in Miriam and Kenan.

The last thing Nikki wanted was to join them—and Brigette—in an early grave. But was there truly anywhere that she could escape the serial killer's wrath against her as the sole survivor of his onslaught?

HALF AN HOUR LATER, Nikki was meeting with her friend, Blair Roxburgh, at Calyne's Coffee Café on Foulter Way. She didn't dare go to Blair's house, potentially placing her in danger. But given the murder of Miriam Broderick, Nikki felt a need to reach out to the support group founder before she left town temporarily. A café in a public space made it unlikely that a wanted fugitive would show his face there. If he were to, Gavin, who was seated at another table to give them a little space and trying to keep a low profile while on the lookout for the serial killer, would nab Evigan in a hurry, as per his role as her protector.

Nikki waved Blair over as she spotted her entering the café. The two women hugged and Nikki cried, "I'm so sorry about Miriam."

"So am I," Blair uttered. "She didn't deserve to go that way."

"I know." Nikki pulled away, wiped her eyes and they sat at a square wooden table away from the window, where she had taken the liberty of ordering them both iced lattes and cinnamon rolls. "Perry Evigan killed her."

Blair lifted a brow. "Are you sure about that?"

"I only wish I weren't." Nikki frowned. "It gets worse. The police believe that Evigan killed Kenan Fernández too."

Blair's eyelids fluttered wildly. "What?"

Nikki told her what she knew about the crimes and the massive search for Perry Evigan underway in Owl's Bay. "Seems like he's been fixated on me ever since he escaped from prison, along with anyone I'm associated with…" She glanced over at Gavin, who was shifting his gaze this way and that for any sign of trouble, and turned back to her friend. "I never imagined that—"

"Stop it." Blair leaned forward, touching her hand. "You're in no way to blame for someone else's actions, Nikki. Least of all an escaped serial killer's. The fact that Perry Evigan has somehow been able to carry out more crimes while on the run is not your fault. You're as much a victim as anyone. But you're also a survivor—and don't ever let him or anyone else take that away from you."

Nikki grabbed a cinnamon roll, nibbled off a piece defiantly and then declared, "I won't." She couldn't give in to Evigan's tactics, even if from a distance. Hadn't the years since the attack made her strong enough to withstand the psychological manipulation? She would not backtrack on that now. Especially with Gavin supporting her. And Blair too. "You're right," she told her. "I can't control what a fugitive serial killer chooses to do, no matter how vile."

"Exactly." Blair favored her with a tiny smile and picked up the latte, taking a sip. She glanced over at Gavin. "Does he want to come and join us?"

"Probably not," Nikki said. "He's fine keeping watch over me while trying not to crowd me. I'm good with that." Not that she had a problem with their spending lots of time together, as they had. The bigger issue still was how they fared once the threat to her life was over, one way or the other.

"Well, I'm glad he's got your back," Blair said. "And I'm sensing it's even more than that."

Nikki blushed. "Let's just say we're in a good place right now."

"Sounds like a nice place to be in."

"It is." She eyed him, and Gavin grinned and lifted his mug of coffee in an approving toast. "But right now, his focus and mine is on averting a confrontation with Perry Evigan. Which is why I'll be leaving town temporarily with Gavin, as the authorities try to close in on Evigan."

"I see." Blair sipped her latte. "I'm sure you feel it's better that I don't know where you're going?"

"Correct—for your own safety," Nikki pointed out, biting off a chunk of the cinnamon roll.

Blair's mouth tightened. "I can take care of myself, always have, ever since the attack back in college," she spoke bravely.

"I know." Nikki understood that, like her, Blair had taken self-defense classes to better protect herself from villains. But even that could only go so far, should the perp catch them off guard. Or otherwise be relentless and lethal in an attack. She smiled at her. "If all goes right, I'll be back before you even start to miss me."

"I'll hold you to that." Blair chuckled, grabbing her cinnamon roll. "In the meantime, let's keep our fingers crossed that the man who ended Miriam's life will be brought to justice in no time flat and you can get back to your life."

Nikki nodded, while crossing her fingers on that thought and hoping for the best, even as something inside her still feared the worst when it came to the maniacal serial killer.

GAVIN LIFTED HIS mug of flat white coffee and took a sip, as he turned his eyes to Nikki and Blair at their table. He was sure that they were commiserating over the senseless loss of their survivor support group member, Miriam Broderick. Gavin knew that the only way the pain would be eased was with the capture or elimination of the person responsible for her death. Though he was certain that was imminent, and he would like nothing better than to slap the cuffs on Brigette's murderer himself, Gavin's number-one priority had to be protecting Nikki at all costs. He would defer dealing with Perry Evigan to his colleagues.

I need to get her out of here to a safe place where he can't find her, Gavin told himself, assuming Evigan, against all odds, managed to slip past the tracking operation well underway in town. He owed it to her to not give the escaped con an opportunity to replay the terror he'd instilled upon her a decade ago.

Lifting his cell phone, Gavin called his friend, Jake Kendrick. The two had known each other since they attended Mississippi State University and lived in the same residence hall. Jake now lived in Winnipeg, Manitoba, in Canada, where he owned an upscale restaurant and was happily divorced. He kept his cabin as an investment property and for occasional getaways.

Jake accepted the video chat request. Thirty-six, with a medium build and dark hair in a side-swept undercut, and bearing a crooked grin on his round face, he said, "Special Agent Gavin Lynley. What's up, dude?"

Gavin grinned. "I'm good. How about you?"

"Busy as ever. That's the restaurant business for you. No rest for the weary, but I can't complain."

"Then you're in better shape than I am," Gavin said wryly.

"I seriously doubt that," Jake countered. "At least physically speaking."

Not going there, Gavin got to the point. "Say, I have a big favor to ask of you…?"

"Name it."

"I need to borrow your cabin for a day or two—it's important," he emphasized without going into the details. Jake had been there for him during his darkest hours, but now was not the time to relive the past or address the future. "I promise to leave it the way I find it."

"No problem," Jake said without prelude. "It yours for as long as you want. I don't expect to be back in Mississippi for the foreseeable future."

"Thanks. I owe you one," Gavin told him.

"And I won't let you forget it." Jake laughed. "There's some beer in the fridge, but not much else."

"That's a pretty good start," Gavin quipped. "I'll take it from there."

"Cool. And in case you've forgotten, the key is still under the mat."

"I remember."

"Have fun or whatever. Or with whomever."

Gavin smiled, looking at Nikki. He disconnected and briefly thought about Brigette and how the two women were so different. If only he had been able to better read the tea leaves back in the day, he might have been able to save Brigette and build something much sooner with Nikki. But he had now to turn the page and welcomed the opportunity to do so.

He stood and went over to Nikki's table. After acknowledging Blair, he asked Nikki, "Are you ready to go?"

"Yes." She smiled at him and rose. "All set."

Blair got up as well. Putting her hand on Gavin's elbow, she looked him in the eye and said sharply, "Take care of her."

"I will," he promised, while knowing it was something he didn't take lightly. Not by a long shot.

Chapter Fourteen

As Nikki waited in his car for the drive to the cabin, Gavin conferred outside it with the MDOC's Fugitive Apprehension Strike Team Commander, Eddie Prescott, telling him calculatingly, "Evigan's here, lurking in the shadows, daring us to find him and take him down."

Prescott, fortysomething, built like a brick, with graying hair in a buzz cut and a dimpled chin, narrowed his brown eyes and declared decisively, "If he's still in Owl's Bay, we'll find him—one way or the other. You can be sure of that."

Gavin only wished he could be. As it was, the fact that Evigan had skillfully eluded capture thus far, made the escaped serial killer that much more formidable an opponent. "I want to believe you can track him down, once and for all," Gavin told his friend. "With all the manpower we have in the pursuit, along with any help from the public, it should be a given that Evigan's days as a free man are numbered. But if it's all the same to you, I need to put some distance between Evigan and Nikki Sullivan, the one person who came out alive after crossing paths with that monster."

Prescott glanced at Nikki in the Chevy Tahoe and said understandingly, "Do what you need to do. Keep her safe till this is over."

"I intend to." Gavin shook his hand. "If this goes sour, don't hesitate to reach out to me."

"I won't," Prescott promised. "Now, get out of here."

"Okay."

Gavin walked away and over to the gray Chevrolet Blazer that belonged to US Marshal Everett Ulbricht, who was in the driver's seat. The marshal, who was in his midthirties, was assigned to follow them to the cabin and make sure they weren't being followed or threatened in any other way. He had on a black cap over curly brown hair and wore dark shades.

"Ready to hit the road?" Gavin asked him.

Ulbricht nodded, touching his sunglasses. "Yeah, let's do it."

"Okay," Gavin said, and glanced around before returning his gaze to Ulbricht. "If you see any sign of Evigan—"

"I'll let you know," the marshal told him in earnest.

"All right." Gavin went to his own car and got

behind the wheel. He smiled at Nikki, trying to make this seem like a vacation getaway, rather than running and hiding from an escaped convict who had her in his crosshairs. "I think we're good to go now."

"Great." She smiled back, putting up a brave front, masking what Gavin was certain was an uncomfortableness in having her life put on hold. And all because Perry Evigan had not been taken into custody—keeping the danger he presented alive and well.

If there was a silver lining to the dark cloud the serial killer represented, Gavin saw it as another opportunity to bond more with Nikki in a neutral and relaxed woodsy environment. Even if short-lived, it could be just enough to make a difference in what they were starting to feel for one another.

AFTER A LARGELY silent ride down US Route 49 North, Gavin turned onto Blane Lake Street, an unpaved road in Osweka County. He waved at US Marshal Everett Ulbricht, indicating that the marshal was no longer needed as an escort the rest of the way. Nikki watched him give Gavin the thumbs-up and continue down the highway. She felt somewhat relieved that there had been no indication from Marshal Ulbricht that they had been followed from Owl's Bay, suggesting that Perry Evigan had no idea where she'd gone, as the authorities closed in on him.

Driving a short distance past groves of broad-leaf and conifer trees, Gavin pulled up to the red log cabin. Nikki took one look at the two-level lakefront property and couldn't help but utter in awe, "When you said your friend had a cabin in the woods, I was just assuming it was a typical campground-type cabin—not this!"

"Yeah, it is pretty cool." Gavin chuckled. "Jake got a good deal on it, borrowing money from his folks to pay for it. Though he's living in Canada now, he wisely decided to hang on to the place, which is a perfect hideaway for us to lay low for a little while. Why don't we go take a look inside?"

"Okay."

Nikki wanted to forget about this being more about Perry Evigan threatening her life than building a future life with Gavin. Or were the two inexorably linked? How could they not be? Hadn't her shared experience with Gavin led to this point in time, with Brigette's killer still able to effectively mess with their heads?

But the unintended tugging at their heart-strings and what it might foretell was something that Nikki clung to as what she hoped to be the most important thing to come out of this ordeal, whenever it was over.

Upon grabbing their bags, they headed down the stone walkway and onto the wraparound deck, where Nikki watched as Gavin dug the key out from beneath a white-and-black-striped welcome mat and unlocked the door. "Here it is," he said, as they stepped inside.

Setting her things down, Nikki took a sweeping glance of the first level. It had a cathedral ceiling with exposed beams, laminate wood flooring, floor-to-ceiling windows throughout, offering breathtaking views of the lake from different angles, and rustic pine wood furniture. There was a full-size chef's kitchen with granite countertops. And a security system.

"Nice," Nikki had to say, admitting that if she had to relocate temporarily with barely a moment's notice, this might have been the place she would have chosen to be sheltered with Gavin. "Very nice."

"Yeah." He grinned at her. "Want to see the rest?"

"Sure." She followed him up the wooden U-shaped staircase to the second floor and took in the well-appointed main bedroom, with barn-wood furniture and a built-in sunroom. The thought of them making good use later of the rustic king bed excited her. Or did Gavin not have that in mind in his capacity as Special Agent Lynley? "I like the way your friend has decorated the place," she said, sending her thoughts in a different direction.

"Me too."

They finished the tour, which included an up-stairs deck with more magnificent views, for which Nikki was glad she had brought along her sketch pad to draw for a future painting, before heading back down to the first level.

Gavin drew her near to him and said, "Sorry to have to pull you away from Owl's Bay and your life, but I prefer to go with the better safe than sorry philosophy than not."

"It's fine," she told him, smiling. "There are worse things in life than having to be tucked away in a lovely cabin by the lake with a won-derful man."

He gazed longingly into her eyes. "I feel the same way—only turning that around to being here with a gorgeous and sexy woman."

"Hmm…" Nikki felt a flutter of desire, but kept it in check. "So, we're even, then?"

"Yeah, you could say that." Gavin flashed her an askew grin. "Better yet, we're compatible in every way that counts, making what we have that much more compelling."

Her lashes fluttered. "You think?"

"Don't you?"

She answered without preface, "Yes, I believe we are very compatible."

"That really seems to fit when it comes to kissing," he told her.

"Oh…?"

"Yeah." He cupped her cheeks and laid one on her lips, as though to prove the point.

Nikki lost herself in the kiss for a long moment, taking her away from the peril that Perry Evigan had brought upon them in forcing them to escape to a place beyond his reach. When Gavin pulled back, he grinned and said lightheartedly, "Proves my point."

She touched her stinging mouth. "Guess it does."

They went into the kitchen, where Gavin opened up the refrigerator and Nikki saw that it was empty, aside from a bottle of ketchup and three bottles of beer.

"Jake wasn't kidding when he said there was nothing here," Gavin remarked musingly. "Even though we're likely only going to be here for a short while, I suppose we should've stopped at what was probably the only grocery store in town that we passed along the way to pick up a few items."

"There was a pizza place across the street from it," Nikki remembered, feeling her stomach start to growl.

"Why don't we head over there now and get what we need to wait this out," Gavin said, closing the refrigerator, "till the threat that Evigan poses has been brought to a close."

"All right." She wondered just how long that would take, wanting this to be over for good, even while she was happy to make the most of the time away with Gavin.

NIKKI WONDERED IF it was her imagination running wild. She could've sworn she saw Perry Evigan peering at her down the aisle at the supermarket. Or at least someone who resembled him. Granted, she hadn't seen Evigan face-to-face in nearly a decade and only had a mug shot and a photograph shown on television that was taken of him from a court hearing a few years ago when he'd gotten into trouble after a prison fight. But the way the man seemed to be looking at her made Nikki uncomfortable, caught her attention and left her shaking.

She turned to Gavin, who was grabbing a bag of potato chips from the shelf to put in the cart, and said almost in a whisper, "I think Perry Evigan has found us—"

"What?" Gavin tensed and she could see him nearly go for the firearm that was inside his concealed carry holster, tucked within Gavin's waistband.

"At the end of the aisle..." she stammered,

bravely angling her eyes in that direction. Only to find him gone.

"No one's there—" Gavin said, gazing in that direction. He faced her. "What makes you think it was Evigan that you saw?"

"It was just his general appearance and the way he seemed to be studying me, as if sizing me up for the kill…" Nikki swallowed the lump in her throat. "Maybe I was mistaken," she suggested, suddenly questioning her own interpretation.

"Maybe, or maybe not…" Gavin pursed his lips thoughtfully. "Wait right here where I can see you…"

"Okay," she obeyed.

Nikki watched as he hurriedly headed down the aisle and past an elderly female shopper. Gavin kept his hand close to his weapon, without removing it. At the end of the aisle, she saw him look in both directions, before quickly making his way back to her. "Stay put," he directed, and went down the other way to the end, where Gavin peered one way, then the other, before rushing back to her and stating evenly, "I didn't see any sign of anyone who resembled Evigan. But that doesn't mean he wasn't there."

Again, having second thoughts, she wondered out loud, "How would he have found us? Even as he was at the same time trying to avoid re-capture?"

"Those are good questions, and there are no easy answers." Gavin rubbed his chin while contemplating this. "My guess is that you saw someone else and thought it could have been Evigan. If he had followed us out of Owl's Bay, I'm pretty sure that either I or Marshal Ulbricht would have noticed a car that was trailing our vehicles."

Nikki wrinkled her nose. "You're probably right," she conceded, feeling foolish in causing him to panic unnecessarily. "Guess I just got spooked for no reason..."

"You had a very good reason for being spooked," Gavin said, wrapping his hands around the cart's handle. "I'll never fault you for that. Let's pay for these items and go get that pizza."

Nikki nodded and they headed down the aisle, still feeling a bit strange about the entire episode, as if there was an itch that wouldn't go away where it concerned the escaped serial killer.

THOUGH GAVIN WAS fairly certain that Perry Evigan had not found their location and was stalking Nikki as a prelude to kidnapping her again, it still made him nervous about the fugitive, while Evigan remained on the loose. The fact that Nikki had been freaked out at the grocery store in what appeared to be an unprovoked and unreal sighting of the escapee, told Gavin, if nothing else, that Evigan still loomed large in her psyche. That was not likely to change for the time being, in spite of them being thirty miles away from Owl's Bay. And presumably far enough from Evigan's crosshairs to be in a safe space.

Still, Gavin found it incumbent upon himself to reassure Nikki that she needn't worry about the serial killer while they were at the cabin. He wanted the worry to fall on his shoulders instead. "Don't let him get to you. Why don't we just try and relax and enjoy this, to the extent possible," Gavin told her in a gentle tone as they sat in ladder-back side chairs across a pine solid wood trestle dining table from one another in the cabin, eating pizza with soft drinks.

"I will if you will," Nikki countered, lifting a slice of the pizza topped with cheddar cheese, ground beef, onions and green peppers.

"Deal." He gave her a convincing grin, wanting to shift the mood to one that was more agreeable—as if they were on vacation together, which he hoped to turn this outing into.

"Good." She bit into the pizza. "Mmm, this is delicious."

Gavin took a bite from his own slice and had

to concur. "It is." *But not even close to being as delicious as you are to kiss and make love to,* he told himself, knowing it was coming as much from the heart as his libido. He only needed to show her that more and more, so she knew he meant business in wanting what they had to continue to progress into something truly special when this was over.

While Nikki was clearing the table, Gavin checked the windows and front door to make sure they were locked, then went upstairs, where he called Jean O'Reilly for an update on the situation. "Hey."

"Heard you had gotten out of Dodge," she quipped.

"Seemed like the smart thing to do, with Evigan proving to be so difficult to pin down and take into custody," Gavin said honestly.

"You're probably right about that."

"What's the latest on the search for the fugitive?"

"We haven't captured him yet, if that's what you're asking," Jean told him.

"Didn't think you had." Otherwise, Gavin would know that Nikki was finally out of harm's way for the long-term. "Anything at all I can work with…?" Before she answered, he added ruefully, "Nikki thought she might have seen Evigan at a store in town. Though I never laid eyes on him to confirm this and am thinking it was a case of mistaken identity, I'd like to know that all signs point toward him still being holed up in Owl's Bay..."

"The signs do suggest that to be the case. But we both know they can be misleading at times."

"How so?" he pressed.

Jean paused. "Surveillance video footage from yesterday picked up a man we believe to be Perry Evigan getting into a blue Toyota Corolla Cross outside of a strip mall in town. We got the license plate number and saw that the car had been reported as stolen. Evigan never bothered to switch plates. There's no reason to believe he's not still driving the vehicle—when out on the road at all—and we've issued a BOLO on it and him."

"All right." Gavin hoped they were that much closer to nailing the bastard and putting an end to the nightmare he'd put Nikki through. "If you get anything at all on his whereabouts or his capture—"

"I'll definitely keep you abreast on all fronts," Jean promised him, before Gavin disconnected.

Nikki had come upstairs and regarded him suspiciously. "Everything okay?"

"Yeah," he said in a calm voice. "We're good."

Chapter Fifteen

"I was thinking that we should make the most of this situation," Gavin uttered erotically to Nikki, while resting his hands on her hips as they stood in the main bedroom.

"Oh, really?" Her lashes fluttered coyly. "And just what did you have in mind?"

He grinned, turned on by her in every way. "Well, this…" Gavin kissed her right cheek. "And this…" Next came the left cheek. "And, of course, there's that—" He went for her abundant mouth, and she reciprocated in kind, letting him know she was more than amenable to what he was suggesting.

"I'm all yours, Agent Lynley." Nikki tsked, wrapping her arms around his neck and bringing their mouths together again for a passionate kiss.

"Since you put it that way, let's see what we can do about that," Gavin teased her.

They wasted no time undressing and he took her to bed, getting cozy atop the matelassé bedspread, where Gavin went to work making sure that he tapped into every sensitive spot on Nikki's perfect body and shapely breasts to give her the hands-on treatment she deserved. Only after the undulating tide of satisfaction came for her amid deep sighs and quivering, did he let go and complete the overwhelming joy of their lovemaking. It sent them both to new heights of ecstasy that was only solidified by their circumstances.

Catching his breath as he lay beside her still and slick body, matching his own, Gavin kissed Nikki's soft shoulder and said truthfully, "I wish we'd had the chance to experience this long ago."

"So do I," she cooed, draping a silky-smooth leg across his thigh. "But it wasn't our time then. I guess it is now."

"Yes, I'd say so." Gavin was in complete agreement. He couldn't very well argue with fate as it were. Maybe they weren't meant to be together ten years ago. Or maybe they were, but were prevented from doing so by forces beyond their control. He wouldn't overthink it. Instead, he was grateful that the universe gave them a second opportunity to find each other and they had. If he had his way, they would never let this slip away.

As soon as the danger that Perry Evigan posed had subsided, Gavin wanted nothing more than to work on a future with Nikki. After all, wasn't that to be expected when two people had fallen in love? Not that he could speak for her, but he could for himself. And when she was ready to tell him how she felt, he would be there to listen.

For the moment, all Gavin wanted to do was hold Nikki, listen to their heartbeats synced and see what tomorrow brought in the hunt for a serial killer escapee.

NIKKI IMAGINED THAT she had known from the moment she first saw Gavin Lynley that she had fallen in love with him. She hadn't exactly been in denial about being in touch with her feelings. It was more that she couldn't act on them with Gavin seeming to be totally hooked on Brigette. Now it was clear that this hadn't been the case. At least not to the extent that he wouldn't have been open to giving someone else a chance.

The problem had been more of going after someone that her best friend was involved with. Nikki would never have tried to come between Brigette and Gavin—no matter the serious cracks in their relationship—as long as they were together. But now, somehow, some way, Gavin had come into Nikki's life a decade later and things had heated up between them, in and out of the bedroom, telling her that what they had was real. And, from her point of view, it had the potential to be lasting, if she was reading Gavin correctly in his body language and mentality. Now, if only they could put the saga of a dangerous serial killer on the prowl in the rearview mirror.

Slipping from beneath Gavin's protective arms as the morning sun filtered in the window above the cellular shades, Nikki allowed him to get a bit more shut-eye, as she got up and left the room quietly. She hoped to take advantage of this time of the day to sketch the magnificent landscape and breathe in the fresh air.

After washing her face and pulling her hair together into a messy pineapple ponytail, she threw on a white scoop neck tunic tank top, some dark blue shorts and her running shoes. Downstairs, she had a glass of water and then grabbed her sketch pad and drawing pencil from her straw tote bag. Peeking out the window, Nikki saw nothing that alarmed her. She had decided earlier that Perry Evigan had not followed them to the cabin after all. It was just her panicking, unreasonably so. As such, it was likely safe for her to step onto the wraparound deck, where she would do the sketching, before having breakfast with Gavin.

No sooner had she gone out on the deck and began to sketch, observing some ducks and rabbits out and about by the lake, than Nikki heard a sound that she couldn't quite decipher. Realizing it was the cedar deck boards creaking, she turned in that direction only to come face-to-face with her worst nightmare.

Perry Evigan stood there with an eerie grin playing on his lips and sporting a patchy beard, as he said coldly, "Nice to see you again, Nikki. We have some unfinished business to take care of…"

"No, we don't!" she shot back with defiance, glaring at the man who was unmistakable, in spite of being ten years older.

Just as she attempted to use a self-defense technique, then make a run for it and scream at the same time, Nikki was grabbed roughly and felt a needle pierce her neck. Before everything went black, she heard the Gulfport Nightmare Killer remark smugly, "Don't fight it, Nikki. The ketamine I injected you with will make you mine as we get out of here and go to a safe place where we can get down to business uninterrupted."

GAVIN AWOKE WITH a start when he thought he heard the sound of screeching tires. Expecting to find Nikki beside him—in a dreamy sleep after making love much of the night—he instead realized her spot on the bed was empty. For whatever reason, his gut instincts kicked in that something wasn't right. He shot out of bed, slid

into some slacks and went in his bare feet looking for her. But he couldn't find her in the cabin.

Where was she? Why didn't she wake him
up? How could he have not heard the creaking
of the stairs?

Gavin resisted the urge to panic, hoping that
Nikki had simply gone outside while not going
too far. Hadn't she talked about wanting to
sketch the scenery? Maybe she had fallen and
hit her head? He opened the door and walked
out onto the wraparound porch. At first, he saw
nothing that got his attention to suggest Nikki
was in trouble. But then, near the side of the
deck, he spotted what looked to be…her sketch
pad and drawing pencil lying there.

Would she have left them there voluntarily?

Gavin called out to her, "Nikki!" He went
around the entire deck on the chance that she
was there somewhere and hadn't heard him.
But she was nowhere to be found. He called her
name again. No answer. Would she really leave
him hanging if she were able to speak?

Now it was time for panic to set in.

He stepped off the deck and checked the perimeter of the cabin, but saw no sign of Nikki.
Realizing that without his firearm and shoes on,
he was at a disadvantage, should she be in danger.

Sprinting back into the cabin, his heart racing, Gavin hurriedly scaled the stairs, finished dressing and grabbed his loaded FN 509 MRD-LE 9mm semiautomatic duty pistol. He went back outside and started to look for Nikki, calling her name, while holding out hope that she wasn't in jeopardy.

But when he reached the dirt road and saw fresh tire tracks, Gavin recalled thinking he'd heard tires screeching when he awoke. It hadn't been his imagination after all. Someone had taken Nikki.

No, not someone.

Perry Evigan had her.

The mere thought that the bastard had kidnapped Nikki made the hairs curl on the back of Gavin's neck. He needed to regroup and find the woman he'd fallen in love with. Before Evigan was able to murder someone else Gavin cared for.

AT FIRST, Nikki thought she was in some weird dream where everything was fuzzy and nothing was as it seemed. She was trapped under water and sinking fast. As she tried to scream, her mouth filled with muddy water and death seemed imminent. Then she opened her eyes and saw nothing but darkness and felt herself lying in a fetal position in a tight space. She realized she wasn't dreaming at all. She was caught in a living nightmare.

Though groggy, she came to the conclusion that she was trapped inside something... A trunk. And the car was moving.

Everything began to come back to her. She was on the wraparound deck of the log cabin of Gavin's friend—about to sketch the surroundings—when she was accosted by Perry Evigan, who injected her with a date-rape drug.

It was the last thing she remembered. Till now.

He'd kidnapped her and was taking her somewhere. Nikki quickly realized that the trunk emergency release lever had been ripped out. She tried to push and kick open the trunk lid, to no avail. And though she wanted to scream, nothing seemed to come out of her sour throat and dry mouth but a whimper.

Where were they going? Was Gavin aware that she was missing? Or was he still asleep, oblivious to what had happened to her?

Am I going to be able to get out of this alive? Nikki asked herself fearfully. Or would Evigan make good on his pledge of revenge, doing to her whatever ghastly things he had in mind? Finishing with strangling her to death and maybe burying her where she could never be found. And leaving Gavin and her parents to mourn her death, just as they had Brigette's. While their killer remained free to go after other young women, with no end in sight.

This frightening scenario chilled Nikki to the core and was one that she needed to do everything in her power to avoid. Now if only she could overcome the dizziness and trouble breathing in the enclosed space to formulate a plan of action.

PERRY EVIGAN COULD barely believe his good fortune. First, he executed a timely escape from the Mississippi State Penitentiary—dodging every close call in the effort to recapture him. Then, he managed to avoid the fate of fellow escapees, Craig Schneider and Aaron Machado, who literally went up in flames rather than go back inside.

And now, Perry had gotten hold of his prized possession, Nikki Sullivan. He'd found his way to her in Owl's Bay, where she had thought she was safe from him. She had become his for the taking—and he fully intended to do just that— before ending her life once and for all, as he had intended to do a decade ago. He could hear her squirming inside the trunk, hoping to find some miraculous way of breaking free. He was confident that wasn't going to happen.

Perry glanced at the rearview mirror to make sure he wasn't being followed. There was no one behind them. Good. He had dumped the Toyota Corolla Cross he had stolen for a green Dodge Charger GT. By the time they figured out it had been carjacked by him, he would have done what he set out to do with Nikki Sullivan and moved on.

So much for her protector Special Agent Gavin Lynley keeping her safe from harm. Perry laughed at the thought. He remembered learning that Lynley had been dating Brigette Fontana ten years ago—only to come up short in preventing her death. Now he was about to go 0 for 2 in the saving a damsel in distress department.

You lose again, Perry mused wryly, as they neared the destination for his latest kill. He salivated at the thought, knowing it would be even more of a thrill when the deed was done.

"NIKKI'S MISSING," Gavin spoke glumly over the speakerphone to Marvin Whitfield while driving.

"What do you mean she's missing?" the director asked, ill at ease.

"He took her," Gavin hated to say, feeling nauseated picturing Nikki in the clutches of the serial killer. "Somehow, Perry Evigan managed to lure Nikki out of the cabin. Or she went out unsuspectingly and he was waiting for her…and kidnapped her."

Whitfield spat out an expletive. "I thought we had him boxed in," he groaned, "if not in custody."

"Instead, Evigan's outfoxed us in being able to slip out of Owl's Bay and track down Nikki." Gavin frowned and sucked in a deep breath, blaming himself for placing her in harm's way and allowing the escaped con to nab Nikki under his watch. "I don't know where he's taken her, but they couldn't have gotten very far," Gavin said, driving in the direction the tire tracks suggested Evigan went. "Only a few minutes passed before I realized that Nikki was gone."

"Tell me exactly where you are and we'll have the Fugitive Apprehension Strike Team and other law enforcement converge on the area and try to cut Evigan off."

Gavin gave his GPS coordinates and said, "If Evigan is still driving the Toyota Corolla Cross, we should be able to narrow down—"

Whitfield cut him off by saying forlornly, "We found the Toyota a few hours ago. It had been abandoned by Evigan. He's obviously using another vehicle right now."

"Figures," Gavin muttered sarcastically, then remembered Nikki believing she had seen him yesterday at the grocery store, as he approached it. "Let me get back to you. I may be able to pin down what Evigan is driving…and has Nikki inside against her will."

The director sought no explanation as he deferred to Gavin's potential new lead, while both moved into high gear, trying to find Nikki alive, before it was too late.

PACING IN HIS OFFICE, Marvin Whitfield was on pins and needles as he contemplated the dire situation with Perry Evigan. In no way should it have gotten to this point, where this serial killer seemed to be calling the shots. And not him as the Director of Investigations at MDOC. He couldn't let this stand, as the buck stopped with him. Last thing he needed was to have Evigan do to Nikki Sullivan what he did to her friend, Brigette Fontana. Not to mention give Gavin Lynley another reason to shoulder the blame, should this go south on him.

Whitfield wondered if it was wise to send Gavin to do bodyguard duty of the artist. Maybe this was a little too close to home for him, causing the special agent to lower his guard just enough to allow Nikki to slip through his fingers for Evigan to nab. And now had them all at a disadvantage in a race against time to stop him from killing her.

But as the director reconsidered this, he knew deep down that Gavin Lynley was where he needed to be. He had every right to confront the enemy—no matter the cost. And to play a role in rescuing Nikki Sullivan from the grasp of Evigan and his evil intentions.

Whitfield was determined to do everything in his power to stop the escaped convict from continuing to circumvent the law by remaining free to wreak havoc in their state and flaunting this in their faces. He got on his cell phone to speak with the Fugitive Apprehension Strike Team Commander, Eddie Prescott, to talk strategy in converging on Osweka County and holding Perry Evigan accountable for his crimes and bringing him to justice.

Chapter Sixteen

Nikki felt the car driving onto gravel, before coming to a stop. She heard Evigan get out and approach the trunk. Holding her breath, she waited for it to open and have to face her tormentor again.

When the trunk lid was lifted, Perry Evigan stood there smugly, wearing a dark blue fleece pullover hoodie and jeans. His short brown-gray hair was uncombed and his face had become weathered after a decade.

"I see you're awake," he said with a laugh, while holding a gun. She wondered if it was the one he'd used to shoot to death Kenan Fernández. "Good to see I didn't overdo it with the ketamine." She sneered but said nothing as he grabbed her with one hand and pulled her out of the trunk. "Welcome home, Nikki."

It took her a moment to recognize the setting. It was the same two-story Greek Revival house on Robinson Road that he had first brought her and Brigette to ten years ago, after also being drugged. Only now it was overgrown with weeds and looked more dilapidated. Was anyone actually living there these days?

"I see it's all coming back to you now," Perry expressed, grinning wickedly as he clicked together his scuffed brown Chelsea boots. He kept the gun on her and pushed her toward the house. "Get inside and I'll try to make this as painless as possible."

Yeah, right, Nikki told herself doubtingly. She expected it to be just the opposite, knowing that, based on his history—including the rape and murder of Miriam Broderick—the serial killer got his kicks out of inflicting pain and humiliation on his victims, before he strangled them to death with ligatures. Or even his bare hands.

I have to play along for now, Nikki thought, biding her time till she struck back. Or died trying. Assuming Gavin was unable to come to her rescue in the nick of time.

"You won't get away with this, Perry," she spat, if only to try to reach his sense of self-preservation.

He chuckled, shoving her again. "Watch me."

As they neared the porch, Nikki took a quick glance at the shed and then nearby woods, and tried to map out an escape route, should the opportunity present itself.

That thought had to be put on hold as Perry Evigan forced the front door open and made her go inside.

GAVIN FLASHED HIS identification as he said to the grocery store manager in an official tone of voice, "Special Agent Lynley."

Sarah Yarborough, fortysomething and petite, with red hair in an angled short cut and blue eyes behind oval glasses, asked, "How can I help you, Agent Lynley?"

"I need to take a look at your security footage from yesterday, inside and out." He gave her a time frame to work with. "We have reason to believe that an escaped prisoner may have been seen in the area…"

"Sounds scary."

"And for good reason—if it's him," Gavin told her point-blank, while trying to hold it together, knowing that every second counted where it concerned Nikki's survival.

Sarah furrowed her brow uneasily and said, "Follow me."

She led him through the store to a back room with surveillance equipment. Standing before a laptop, the store manager pulled up security video footage at the store's entrance.

Gavin waited till he saw what—or whom—

he was looking for and asked her to stop. "Can you zoom in on that man?"

"Sure." Sarah did just that, giving Gavin a closer look. "Do you recognize him?" she asked.

"Yeah, I'm afraid I do," Gavin muttered, his nose wrinkling in disgust. The man was clearly on edge, his big hazel eyes shifting this way and that, for fear of being recognized, even with the hood of his dark-colored sweatshirt over his head. It was him, undeniably. "His name's Perry Evigan."

Though years removed from when Gavin confronted the serial killer in court, he would recognize Brigette's killer anywhere. Nikki had been right in believing she spotted Evigan at the store yesterday.

I should have trusted her judgment and been better prepared to deal with it when he came for her, Gavin told himself, knowing that if Evigan laid one hand on Nikki, he would never forgive himself.

"I heard about him," Sarah confessed. "Can't believe he was actually here."

"Believe it." Gavin jutted his chin. "Let's switch to the outside surveillance camera…"

"All right."

She pulled up the footage from just after the time Evigan was inside the store and Gavin spotted him walking to a green Dodge Charger GT. He got inside and started to drive away.

"Stop it there!" Gavin ordered her, and asked her to zoom in on the license plate. He took a photo of it on his cell phone and said, "I've seen enough." He knew that with Evigan having a head start on him with his deadly plans for Nikki, there was no time to waste in going after the serial killer before the damage done was irreversible.

MINUTES LATER, Gavin was in his car as he passed along to Jean the license plate number of the green Dodge Charger GT that Perry Evigan had sped off in from the supermarket parking lot the day before.

"Got it," she said and was able to quickly run the plates and determine that the vehicle had been carjacked. "The thirtysomething owner of the Dodge Charger, Karl Shimomura, who was also robbed but not physically harmed, had reported the car stolen at gunpoint by a man wearing a hoodie."

"Perry Evigan," Gavin thought out loud, recalling the hoodie Evigan was wearing at the store, coupled with him being the one who fled in the stolen vehicle.

"We'll issue a BOLO immediately on the Dodge Charger GT," Jean stated, "which shouldn't be too difficult to track down—if Evigan is still in the area—with the tremendous amount of manpower that's out in full pursuit of the escapee."

Gavin twisted his lips. "I've heard it all before," he voiced cynically. "Evigan knows we're onto him—making him all the more dangerous and desperate, as his kidnapping of Nikki was conniving and deliberate."

"If he had wanted to kill her right away, Evigan would have done so," the special agent surmised cautiously. "That tells me Nikki Sullivan is probably still alive."

But not for much longer, unless I can find her in time, Gavin told himself, trying hard not to panic at the thought of being too late. He only needed something to go on for a sense of direction in discovering where Evigan was headed with his captive.

"If the BOLO alert comes up with anything," Gavin told Jean as he drove, "hopefully, I'll be close enough to get to Nikki." Before Evigan could put into action the horrible ordeal he'd put Brigette through, culminating in her death.

THE PLACE HAD a musty smell that suggested it hadn't been lived in for a while, along with the dusty contemporary furnishings and even a few cobwebs that Nikki spotted in corners and hanging from the ceiling. As she was pushed forward across the dark hardwood flooring on the main level, she knew she had to buy time before the escaped serial killer went on the attack.

Rounding on her kidnapper, who was still brandishing the firearm and sizing her up like a piece of meat, Nikki asked point-blank, "It was you who killed Kenan Fernández, wasn't it?"

Evigan cracked a grin. "Yeah, I confess—little good it's going to do you."

"But why?" Not that she needed to know what went on inside the head of an obvious psychopath. However, she was still curious as to what had prompted him to go after Kenan.

"Why? Because I could tell that he wanted you too," Evigan argued. "I saw him through the window at the art gallery. The way he was all up in your face and the way you reacted, told me that the man was a problem. You were mine and I had to eliminate the competition."

Nikki sneered. "Kenan wasn't competition. I rejected his advances and wanted nothing to do with him."

Evigan laughed. "I don't think he saw things that way. Kenan Fernández got what he deserved." Evigan's brow wrinkled. "So too would've Brigette's former boyfriend, Special Agent Lynley, who really rubbed me the wrong way at my trial—just as you did—except for the fact that I wasn't able to get the jump on him without putting my own life at risk. Lucky dude."

Nikki was given a start at the thought that Evigan had wanted Gavin dead apparently as much as he wanted to kill her, in spite of the fact that Gavin had every right to be angered at the sexual assault and murder of his then-girlfriend by Evigan. Nikki could only feel relief that the escaped inmate hadn't succeeded in killing Gavin and destroying his life in the process. Even if she was unable to avoid this fate, with Evigan clearly planning to finish what he started ten years ago.

"Why did you go after Miriam Broderick?" Nikki shot him a hard look. "Was it because of me?" She needed to know if his obsession with her caused Miriam to lose her life, no matter how the forces of fate might work in death.

Evigan threw his head back and roared with laughter. "Sorry to have to tell you this, but the world doesn't just revolve around you, Nikki. The truth is I had sized her up for the kill when I spotted her walking on campus. Miriam fit the bill as someone who met my criteria as a fresh victim—young, attractive, naive and unsuspecting, till it was too late to change what I had in store for her. Much like the predicament you're in now, Nikki—again." He chortled, giving her a lascivious look, ogling her from head to toe, then turning demonic in his facial expression.

I'll see you again someday, Nikki, and finish what I started. Trust me.

She recoiled at the threatening words he'd said to her during his trial and his intentions of making good on his vow, even as she took solace in learning that Miriam's death hadn't been preventable, per se, as Nikki related this to herself and the prison escapee.

I can't give up fighting for my life, Nikki thought resolutely, while eyeing the demented killer and trying to find the slightest chink in his armor.

As though he was reading her mind, Evigan knitted his thick brows and said meanly, "In there."

Nikki looked toward a downstairs bedroom and back at him, her heart pounding. "I know you want to make up for lost time with me, but can't we just talk about this, Perry...?"

"I'm afraid the time for talking is over, Nikki." He made a menacing sound. "Time to get this over with. Now move."

She weighed whether or not to comply. He was still holding the gun on her and seemingly daring her to try to take it from him. Having the serial killer shoot her on the spot and still likely carry out his other sick plans, Nikki thought better of it.

She would obey him while knowing the will to survive was just as strong as ever. Meaning that she would need the courage to do whatever it took for that to happen. Assuming that Gavin would not be able to swoop in and save her—even if Nikki sensed that he was moving heaven and earth to try to do just that.

WITHOUT PREAMBLE, the director said with an edge to his voice, "Fifteen minutes ago, a traffic camera picked up the Dodge Charger GT stolen by Evigan, headed toward Gulfport."

"Gulfport?" Gavin repeated into the cell phone, pensive. It was where Perry Evigan had abducted and taken Nikki and Brigette a decade ago. Why go back to the scene of the crime?

"Yeah," Whitfield confirmed. "With the walls closing in on him, I'm guessing that Evigan may be headed to familiar territory to hide out."

"Not just familiar to him," Gavin remarked, as a light bulb suddenly went off in his head. "Evigan's taking Nikki back to the house where he did his dirty work—and where she was rescued by FBI and other law enforcement."

"Hmm... I'd heard that the house had gone into foreclosure a few years back," the director pointed out. "Don't know what's happened to it since."

"Whoever owns the property or doesn't—my gut instincts tell me that's where we'll find Nikki—and the serial killer," Gavin said worriedly.

Whitfield responded sharply, "I'll notify the Fugitive Apprehension Strike Team, Gulfport Police Department and the rest, along with the Mississippi Department of Public Safety crisis negotiator, to head there."

Knowing he couldn't afford to put Nikki's life solely in their hands, Gavin told him with a sense of sheer determination, "I'm only a few minutes away from Gulfport. I'll meet them there."

"All right. Just be careful, Lynley," he warned. "I don't think I need to remind you that Evigan can be considered armed and dangerous—meaning it puts Nikki Sullivan at that much greater risk as both a victim and human shield."

"I know," Gavin allowed, as he pressed down on the accelerator. "Which is precisely why I need to do this. I won't let Evigan have his way with another woman I want in my life when this is over."

He disconnected and put on even more speed in what had literally become the race of Gavin's career and life, knowing that the life of the woman he loved now hung unsteadily in the balance.

Chapter Seventeen

Nikki was shoved into the room. It was barren, aside from a platform bed with only a soiled mattress, as if left for this moment in time. Dusty faux wood blinds were drawn on the windows. She obviously didn't like where this was going, but had no way out, as he had her at a decided disadvantage.

I need to get him talking more, Nikki told herself, believing that this might be her last chance to not only buy time—that she hoped to sell to Gavin and the others in law enforcement, who were undoubtedly doing everything in their power to locate her and Evigan—but get him to lower his guard somewhat, taking away his inflated sense of invincibility and superiority.

"Take your clothes off, Nikki," Evigan ordered her snappily.

"Okay, okay," she said, turning toward him and seeing that he was still pointing the gun at her. While delaying this demand as long as possible, Nikki stared at her kidnapper and asked curiously, "Just let me ask you a question, Perry... How is it that you didn't end up with the other escaped prisoners at the farmhouse that caught on fire?"

Evigan regarded her thoughtfully and laughed. "I'm a hell of a lot smarter than they were," he said unashamedly. "They didn't want to separate—strength in numbers and all that silliness. Whereas, that's all I wanted, to go it alone and stick to the game plan I had all along, which was to come after you and take what I was deprived of ten years ago when the cops showed up at my door."

I'll see you again someday, Nikki, and finish what I started. Trust me.

His chilling words once again resonated in her head. Nikki's knees nearly buckled under the weight of his lascivious gawk. Instead, she stood her ground and, peering at Brigette's killer, asked flippantly, "So, now that your wish is about to come true, what happens after that, Perry? Do you intend to go on, sexually assaulting and strangling other women? Or will you simply sail off into the sunset and rest on your laurels? Better yet, maybe you'll turn yourself in, knowing that the authorities will never stop looking for you—wherever you go or try to hide."

Evigan chuckled. "Hadn't really thought that far ahead, to be honest. But if you must know, as a natural-born serial killer, chances are that I'll keep at it for as long as I can—handpicking new victims to go after, feeding my thirst for what I can get from them." His eyes narrowed. "Enough of the questions and answers. Now, take your clothes off! Or I'll rip them off myself."

Nikki pretended that she would voluntarily remove her tank top before stopping. "Maybe you should do it," she dared him. "Or are you afraid to drop the gun and handle me with your bare hands?" She knew this was taking a big risk by incurring his wrath even further and challenging him to get rough with her. But it was better than trying to fight someone who could shoot her at any time.

Evigan took the bait and tucked the gun inside his waistband. "Okay, if that's what you want, you've got it." He pushed her down hard on the filthy mattress. "This is going to be fun—at least for one of us. I'll even strangle you afterward with my bare hands. Just like I did your friend, Brigette."

He tossed out a sickening laugh as if to really rub it in just how cold-blooded he was as a serial killing monster. The thought of what he did to Brigette and intended to do to her the second time around, only fueled Nikki's anger. Along with her strong will to not give in to victimization again from the same perpetrator. When he relaxed his body while overconfident, and started to bend his knees to lower himself onto the bed, Nikki used the self-defense class mechanism she had been taught. In one quick motion, she lifted her right foot in a running shoe and slammed it as hard as she could against the side of his left knee—immediately dislocating it.

As the leg buckled badly, Evigan screamed an expletive at her and tried to grab his leg to keep from falling. The momentary distraction was enough for Nikki to use her other foot to thrust it with all her might smack-dab against his aquiline nose. The wicked crunching sound told her she had broken it.

While Evigan wailed like a wounded animal as he raised his hands to his bloody face, he lost his balance and fell onto the floor. Not taking any chances of a quick recovery, Nikki wasted no time in jumping off the mattress, knowing she needed to get out of there. She started to race toward the bedroom door, when she felt her leg being grabbed from behind. It was twisted just enough so she lost her balance and tumbled to the floor.

Before she could recover, Nikki was dragged toward Evigan, who said acrimoniously, "You're going to pay for this, bitch, and I'll enjoy every second of it."

Nikki's pulse raced wildly as she tried to fight

off the serial killer, who was now more intent than ever to make her suffer, before strangling her to death.

GAVIN DROVE UP to the Greek Revival-style home on Robinson Road. He spotted the carjacked green Dodge Charger GT parked in the driveway haphazardly. It appeared to be empty. Meaning that most likely Evigan had already forced Nikki inside the house.

I pray I'm not too late, Gavin mused worryingly, as he climbed out of his Chevy Tahoe. Taking the FN 509 MRD-LE 9mm semiautomatic pistol from his tactical thigh leg holster, he checked the Dodge Charger and then approached the foreclosed property cautiously. He refused to believe that Nikki was already dead. There was too much left unsaid for their journey to end prematurely. Evigan could not take away everything that had become most important to Gavin—the chance at love and a lifetime of happiness.

Resting on that optimism and having faith in Nikki's ability to hang in there as long as she possibly could, Gavin stepped onto the porch, which squeaked. In spite of being fearful that he had tipped his hand in warning Evigan that they had company, this didn't prevent him from going full steam ahead as Gavin went inside the broken door that was left partially ajar.

With his pistol out in front of him, he saw signs—such as footprints in the floor dust—that indicated someone was in there. Just as he was about to head up the stairs, Gavin heard Nikki's voice as she called out for help. It was coming from a downstairs bedroom.

He raced toward it and stepped inside, where Gavin saw Perry Evigan halfway atop Nikki on the floor. The serial killer's nose was a bloody mess and one of his legs was awkwardly bent. When Evigan grabbed a handgun from his waist and pointed it at Nikki, Gavin never gave him a chance to use it.

He aimed his pistol and fired twice, hitting Evigan both times in the head, causing brain matter to spray out. The dead man slumped over, falling off Nikki, who was still clothed and appeared unhurt, but clearly shaken as she sat up.

Looking at Gavin, she said softly, "You found me."

"Yeah." He stepped over to her and grinned, helping her to get to her feet, and then hugged her, happy to be able to touch her again. "Are you all right?"

"I think so." Nikki hugged him back for a long moment, then glanced over at Evigan. "Is he...?"

"Yes, Evigan's been neutralized," Gavin spoke confidently. "He won't hurt you or anyone else, ever again."

"That's good to know."

Gavin regarded the serial killer. "Looks like you did quite a number on him before I showed up."

"He really didn't leave me any choice," she said matter-of-factly. "Either fight back or give up. That wasn't an option."

Gavin gave a satisfied smile. "Glad to hear it."

Nikki paused. "He wanted to come after you too."

He arched a brow. "Excuse me?"

"Ever since the trial, Evigan has apparently been caught up in some vindictive vengeance mindset against both of us," she informed him. "But as an armed special agent, you were harder to corner. Though he would likely have never given up trying."

"Wow." Gavin let that roll around in his head for a moment. The idea that Evigan wanted to put him and Nikki in the grave, alongside Brigette, only made it more comforting that he had been stopped cold, before carrying out the rest of his agenda. "The man was obviously the worst kind of human being. Neither of us have to watch our backs anymore, where Evigan's concerned."

Nikki's voice broke as she uttered, "It's a relief, for sure." Her eyes watered. "I thought I might never see you again."

"That wasn't going to happen," Gavin assured

her with a straight face. Never mind that, at times, that frightening thought had crossed his mind too. "Not if I had anything to say about it."

"He was waiting for me outside the cabin when I went onto the wraparound deck to sketch the landscape," Nikki explained.

Gavin nodded. "I gathered as much." He only wished he had gone out there with her. And had been able to take out Evigan sooner.

"Before I could react, Evigan had injected me with ketamine and thrown me into the trunk of his car—and brought me here." She looked at Gavin curiously. "How did you figure it out anyway?"

He turned to Evigan and what was left of his head, before Gavin decided that Nikki didn't need to see any more of the man who kidnapped and tried to kill her. "I'll explain in a moment," he told her, taking Nikki's hand to lead her out of the room. Then he said, "You were right about seeing Evigan at the grocery store. After he abducted you, I had a hunch and went back to the store to take a look at their surveillance video. I saw not only Evigan inside, but outside—where he got into a green Dodge Charger GT. Found out that it was carjacked. The vehicle was picked up heading toward Gulfport. I was able to put two and two together that he was taking you here—the scene of the original crimes against you…and Brigette."

"Your instincts were spot-on," Nikki declared.

"In his warped mind, Evigan wanted to try and re-create what happened ten years ago—only this time succeeding in his plans to finish me off. Just like he killed Brigette."

"But Evigan failed again," Gavin told her, with a catch to his voice. "He overplayed his hand and lost. Brigette can now have the peace she has long sought. And so can we, Nikki."

She nodded with teary eyes, and said quietly, "It's what I'd always hoped for."

"Same here." Gavin gazed into her eyes soulfully as they heard the sounds of sirens approaching. "But there was always something else I'd always wished for—"

"Oh…" Nikki met his eyes. "What's that?"

"To truly fall in love with someone and be able to tell her that."

"Oh," she repeated. "Is that what you're saying to me?"

"Yes, it is." Gavin's voice fell an octave. "I have fallen in love with you, Nikki Sullivan. Not just young love like I may have felt for Brigette," he made clear, "but adult love for a beautiful and talented artist, who gets me and made me get her. I never thought it would happen this fast, but it has and you need to know that."

"There's something you need to know too," Nikki said, and took his hands, her own trembling. "I think I've been in love with you for

the past ten years—or since we were first introduced. But I tried to ignore it for obvious reasons.
I felt all along that there was a real connection
there, even if your attention was on someone
else. After Brigette's death and being blamed
for it by you, I thought our moment had passed.
That seemed even more the case after the trial,
when it seemed like I would never see you again.
Then, just days ago—which somehow seems like
a year—you showed up at my house..."

"And the rest, as they say, is history," Gavin
finished, while looking squarely toward the future, elated to hear that she loved him too and
had for some time.

"Yeah." She flashed her teeth. "Something
like that."

"And like this," he said, as Gavin cupped her
cheeks and they kissed, before putting everything on hold when the Fugitive Apprehension
Strike Team and support team showed up and
took over the crime scene.

THREE MONTHS LATER, Gavin was driving his
Chevrolet Tahoe, with Jean O'Reilly in the passenger seat. They were en route to the Mississippi
Department of Corrections Central Office headquarters to discuss with the director of investigations an ongoing probe into gang violence and
narcotic violations in the state's prison system.

"Director Whitfield will be happy to know we're making serious progress in getting to the root of the problem and offering constructive solutions," Jean said.

"You think?" Gavin suspected that making progress and really rooting out the dual problems of gangs and drug-related offenses among inmates were two entirely different things that Whitfield, a stickler for actual results, likely wouldn't have much trouble differentiating.

"Hey, have you forgotten how we nailed Titus Malfoy to the wall and made Whitfield look good in the process?"

"I remember." Gavin considered that the probation officer they had investigated for embezzlement and other crimes had pleaded guilty and implicated another probation officer and a parole agent for the bargain. Whitfield had used this to tighten procedures and accountability for those working in these fields in the MDOC.

"Then there's Perry Evigan and the other escapees that came to a satisfactory conclusion under the director's watch," she mentioned.

Gavin thought about Evigan and just how close he came to murdering Nikki—to add to the eleven other women he strangled to death and the four men he killed as well for good measure. The fact that Evigan was now dead and buried gave Gavin only a limited amount of placation.

His death could never bring back Brigette or the other victims. But it could bring closure to survivors, such as Nikki, who had gotten an added measure of payback in shattering Evigan's nose and messing up his leg, before the serial killer's time on Earth ran out.

A firearms examiner was able to positively link the SIG Sauer P365 9mm pistol Perry Evigan tried to shoot Nikki with to the murder of Kenan Fernández, to tie up one loose end. Another was to hold those responsible for the prison escape of Evigan, Craig Schneider and Aaron Machado accountable—with Whitfield reassigning Mississippi State Penitentiary superintendent, Crystal Rawlings, and warden, Zachary Livingston, in an effort to reduce the chances of this from happening again in the future. Whitfield went public with this to show both his commitment to prison reform and to take credit for the fugitives being taken off the streets.

"I take your point," Gavin told Jean, with a slight grin. "Maybe we can score some points with the director—and vice versa."

"Yes, I'm game for a basket or two, if you are." She laughed. A minute later Jean asked him, "So, when do you plan to pop the question?"

Gavin glanced her way. "Pop the question?" he asked, as though befuddled.

"Uh, ask Nikki to marry you?"

He didn't need to give this any thought. "As a matter of fact, I plan to do it today."

Jean's eyes widened. "Seriously?"

"Yeah. It's time." Gavin knew, and already felt giddy about tying the knot with the woman he was in love with. "I just hope she says yes."

"There is that." Jean gave a chuckle. "From what I've seen of you two, the *yes* part is a mere formality, Lynley."

He grinned crookedly, while eager to put that to the test.

AT THE OWL'S BAY FITNESS CENTER on Tenth Street, Nikki was on a treadmill, enjoying a good workout. She welcomed being able to do one of the things she loved most in staying fit, without the ominous shadows of Kenan Fernández and, even more, Perry Evigan, hanging over her. She was still coming to terms with the fact that the serial killer who murdered her best friend and was on the verge of sending her to an early grave as well—had Gavin not intervened—was now dead himself. Meaning that he wouldn't get the chance to escape from prison again to wreak havoc on her life or the lives of other innocent people.

Justice was definitely served here, Nikki told herself, as she turned toward her friend, Blair Roxburgh, who had been there for her throughout the ordeal that included them losing another friend to Evigan, Miriam Broderick.

"Having trouble keeping up, are we?" Blair joked, as Nikki had inadvertently slowed down her pace during the reverie.

"Sorry about that." She laughed, while picking it up again. "I'll try not to drift off any more."

"You're entitled," Blair said. "Especially if you're fantasizing about that hot boyfriend of yours, Special Agent Lynley."

Nikki colored. "Maybe I was," she confessed, at least to some degree. "Can you blame me?" She knew that Blair, who had recently gotten engaged to her boyfriend, Oliver Pascal, was hoping Nikki and Gavin would follow suit. Though they were rotating spending long weekends at her place and his, the subject of marriage hadn't come up. For her part, Nikki was more than ready and willing to walk down the aisle with the man she loved. But pressuring Gavin to want the same wasn't in her nature. Should it be?

"Not one bit." Blair grabbed her water bottle and took a sip. "You know, you could just go out on a limb and ask Gavin for his hand in marriage. I'm guessing that he would never want you to get away."

"Hmm…" Nikki drank water thoughtfully. Was Gavin ready for that? Or was he content to keep things as they were for now, while still expressing his love for her? "We'll have to see about that," she told her friend noncommittally. "All I know for certain at the moment is that I never want to let Gavin slip away from me."

"That's never going to happen," Blair reassured her. "Whatever else I may think of your special agent, he definitely knows a great thing when he sees and touches it."

"Ditto." Nikki cherished the thought of a future together with Gavin, in whatever form both could live with.

WHEN GAVIN SHOWED up at Nikki's cottage that evening with a dozen long-stemmed red roses, it was fully intended to woo her. "For you," he said coolly.

She blushed. "Thank you." Her nose took in the fragrance. "They're lovely."

"So are you." Gavin grinned, resisting the urge to kiss her for the time being.

Nikki smiled. "I'll go put these in some water."

"Before you do—" he lifted one rose from the bouquet that held something hidden in a leaf and removed it "—you might want to see if this ring fits…" Falling to one knee, Gavin held up the 2.5 carat princess-cut engagement ring with a diamond band in platinum and said affectionately, "Nikki Sullivan, I don't think it's any secret that I've fallen madly in love with you. That's only grown these past few months. I'd like nothing more than to make it official by becoming your husband and father to any children that come our way. Will you marry me and make my happiness level off the charts?"

Without ado, Nikki cried, "Yes, yes, I'll marry you, Gavin Lynley. I love you too, just as madly!" She put a hand to her mouth at the joy of the moment, then stretched it out for him to slide the ring onto.

"I'm delighted to hear that," he professed, and put the ring on her finger. "How does it feel?"

"Like it belongs," she uttered, gazing at the engagement ring admiringly. "Like we belong."

"We do." Gavin got to his feet, finding it difficult to take the smile off his face. "For the rest of our lives," he swore.

"Yes, the rest of our lives," Nikki repeated blissfully. She tilted her face upward. "Kiss me and we'll make this official."

"With pleasure." He puckered his lips and brought them upon hers that opened slightly in anticipation for that sweet kiss, which was stirring and gave Gavin something to definitely look forward to time and time again. He broke their lip-lock just long enough to say sweetly, "I think that definitely makes our engagement to marry and live happily thereafter official."

Epilogue

Gavin watched as his sister, Lauren, and her husband, Rory Nolden, along with their two little girls, Ellen and Miley, appeared on the laptop screen for a Zoom video chat.

"Hey, everyone," Gavin said evenly.

Ellen and Miley, seven and eight, respectively, both with long curly dark hair and brown eyes, and resembling both parents, said in unison, "Hi, Uncle Gavin."

"What's up, man," Rory said merrily, wearing round reading glasses over brown eyes. His brown hair was styled in a spiky quiff cut.

Lauren, who had already picked up on his closeness to Nikki during other conversations, still looked on with anticipation, behind her own geometric-shaped glasses, when she said wryly, "It's so nice to visit with my big brother. Anything special happening in your life these days?"

Gavin laughed. "As a matter of fact, there is…" He took a breath while standing over the marble countertop in Nikki's kitchen. "I wanted you all to be the first to know that I've asked Nikki to marry me…"

"Did she say yes?" Miley asked animatedly.

"Yeah, did she?" Ellen pressed impatiently.

"Come on, out with it," Lauren demanded.

Gavin chuckled. "I thought I should let Nikki tell you herself."

Nikki, who had been standing just out of view of the laptop's camera, moved beside him. "Hey, guys!" She flashed a brilliant smile and stated enthusiastically, "I said yes!" She lifted her hand to show off the engagement ring for everyone to see.

"Congratulations," Lauren said lovingly. "I'm so happy for you both and applaud you, Nikki, for finally being able to make an honest man out of my brother."

Nikki chuckled. "Believe me when I tell you, the pleasure is all mine. Well, maybe a little bit is left over for Gavin."

He laughed, kissing her on the cheek and giving them an opportunity to get to know one another better now that they were about to become family.

ON HER WEDDING DAY, Nikki had butterflies in her stomach with the wonderful anticipation she felt in knowing that she would be spending the rest of her life married to Gavin Lynley. She only wished in an odd way that her first best friend, Brigette, were alive to be there. Though Brigette and Gavin were once an item, Nikki was certain that Brigette would have wanted them both to be happy in her absence.

The wedding was held outdoors on a gorgeous and sunny day in Jackson, Mississippi, where Nikki and Gavin would live. They had already begun home shopping, in search of a property that both could put their stamp on as a place to raise a family. Nikki was thrilled that Jackson was also a wonderful place for artists. She'd already begun to establish herself there with a few pieces on display at various art galleries.

Nikki felt honored that her stepfather had agreed to give her away and was already bonding with Gavin—as both were into jazz music and such great artists as Billie Holiday, Duke Ellington and Sarah Vaughan. Blair was Nikki's maid of honor and the bridesmaids were Gavin's sister, Lauren, and his equally beautiful cousins, Madison and Annette. With Lauren's daughters, Miley and Ellen, serving as the flower girls. All had been very welcoming in having Nikki join their family.

Gavin had asked his college friend and log cabin owner, Jake Kendrick, to be his best man, while choosing his handsome cousins in law enforcement, like Gavin—Scott, Russell and Caleb

Lynley—to be his groomsmen. Nikki was elated to be on the threshold of becoming a Lynley herself and hoped to have at least one son to carry on the family name for the next generation, joining their cousins.

As her stepfather walked her down the aisle, Nikki felt beautiful in a white floral lace, V-neck sleeveless mermaid gown with a side cut and white peep-toe high heel sandals. When she stood before her fiancé, Nikki was enamored with him, as he was resplendent in a black tuxedo and matching patent leather Oxfords.

"You look incredible," Gavin told her, a generous grin on his handsome face.

Her teeth shone. "So do you."

"You ready for this?"

"I've never been more ready," Nikki told him, meaning it with all her heart.

"Same here," Gavin promised her.

They brought their own vows to read and did so without missing a beat, while gazing into each other's eyes. When they were finished and exchanged diamond wedding bands, the female pastor pronounced them husband and wife and gave them permission to kiss one another. It was short, sweet and satisfying to Nikki as her husband took her by the hand and they headed down the aisle joyously. Nikki stopped briefly to give her mother a hug.

"I'm so proud of you, Nikki," she told her tear-fully. "And Gavin too."

"Thanks, Mom." Nikki received a kiss on the cheek from her parents and then proceeded on with the man she intended to have a great life with as Mrs. Gavin Lynley.

Their wedding night was everything Nikki could have asked for and so much more. It felt like both the first time and a comfortable sense of familiarity that she looked forward to relishing for years to come.

FOR THEIR TWO-WEEK HONEYMOON, Gavin surprised Nikki by fulfilling her dream of going on a cruise. He wanted to make the start of their marriage a memorable occasion and a shared adventure that could propel them to further outings in keeping the romance alive through the years.

As the riverboat cruised the Upper and Lower Mississippi River, its ports of call included fas-cinating small towns in multiple states including Missouri, Tennessee, Minnesota, Louisiana and, of course, Mississippi. In each place, they en-joyed the cuisine, culture and music of the locals, all while discovering more about each other.

Halfway through the voyage, Gavin and Nikki stood on the private veranda in their stateroom, while appreciating picturesque landscapes and astounding views of the Mississippi. They were sipping Manhattan cocktails, when Gavin had to ask, "So, is this everything you thought a riverboat cruise would be?"

"How could it not be?" Nikki beamed. "Getting married and then taking this journey with the man of my dreams is more than I could ever have asked for."

"Really?" Gavin was delighted to hear her say that, eager to please in every way he could.

"Well, actually, there is one other thing I could think of that just might truly make it complete."

He tasted the cocktail and gazed curiously into her lovely eyes. "And what might that be?" he asked nervously.

"Only this—" Nikki stood on her tiptoes and laid a mouthwatering kiss on his lips that left Gavin breathless and wanting for more.

"Oh, was that all?" he quipped once their mouths had separated.

"Hmm…" She licked her lips. "Well, maybe there is one last bit of business to absolutely make the cruise unforgettable…"

Gavin regarded her keenly. "Name it."

"In that case," Nikki said flirtatiously, "here's precisely what I had in mind…"

She whispered sweet and sensual words in his ear and the rest spoke for itself.

* * * * *

INTRIGUE

Seek thrills. Solve crimes. Justice served.

Available Next Month

Conard County: Covert Avenger Rachel Lee
Colorado Kidnapping Cindi Myers

....

The Killer Next Door Amanda Stevens
What Lies Billow Carol Ericson

....

K-9 Defender Julie Miller
Hometown Homicide Denise N. Wheatly

Larger Print

Available from Big W, Kmart and selected bookstores.
OR call 1300 659 500 (AU), 0800 265 546 (NZ) to order.

Visit **millsandboon.com.au**

6 brand new stories each month

INTRIGUE

Seek thrills. Solve crimes. Justice served.

MILLS & BOON

Keep reading for an excerpt of a new title
from the Romantic Suspense series,
VANISHED IN TEXAS by Karen Whiddon

Chapter 1

The instant Willow Allen caught sight of her grandmother's white-frame ranch house, something inside her unclenched. West Texas might be flat, the earth dry and desert like, and the weather in July hotter than most people would consider hospitable, but no matter where Willow currently lived, she'd always consider it home.

For the past five years, Willow had lived in California, with its perfect weather, palm trees and beaches. She'd taken a job there right out of college, working as an actuary for a large insurance company. The work was not particularly glamorous, but she'd always loved numbers and considered it a good fit.

But then her grandmama had mentioned going to the hospital with chest pains and, after returning home, had refused to discuss her health further. She'd steadfastly said she was fine, claiming nothing was wrong. Alarmed, Willow had immediately put in for some of her accumulated PTO and made the long drive back to Getaway, Texas. She'd decided not to tell her grandmother, aware Isla would tell her not to come.

She hadn't been home since Christmas. Seven months ago, her grandmother had been just fine. At least, as far as Willow had been able to tell. But Isla lived alone, and despite expressing happiness with her new relationship with a local rancher, Willow worried. The woman she considered her mother had single-handedly raised her and loved her without reservation after Willow's birth mother, Isla's daughter, had died of a drug overdose. She was and would always be the most important person in Willow's life. Willow couldn't wait to surprise her. She planned to wrap her arms around her grandmother's tiny frame, breathe in her unique patchouli scent and spend the next three weeks catching up.

Parking her shiny, new red Ford Bronco in the driveway, Willow got her suitcase out of the back and pulled it up to the front door. She used her own key and entered, calling out to alert her grandmother to her presence.

Nothing but silence answered her. Just her luck. Grandma mustn't be home. She dug out her phone and called her. Immediately, a phone in the master bedroom started ringing.

That was odd, to say the least. Willow hurried over and, sure enough, spotted her grandmother's cell on the nightstand next to the neatly made bed.

Concerned, Willow began searching the house. What if Isla had experienced another chest pain episode and fallen? She might even now be lying unconscious. Heart racing, Willow went through every room, checking in the closet and shower, the kitchen pantry and laundry room and, finally, the garage.

Her grandmother's silver Toyota Corolla still sat parked inside.

What the…? Willow backtracked to the master bedroom and opened the closet. While she wasn't an expert on Isla's wardrobe, it didn't look like much, if anything, was missing.

Maybe her grandma's new beau had picked her up and taken her out somewhere, and she'd simply forgotten her phone. That had to be it. Willow would simply call him, make sure her grandmother was okay and wait for her return.

She grabbed Isla's phone and realized she didn't know the passcode. Despite trying several combinations, from her grandmother's birthday to her own, she couldn't get in. Frustrated, she went back to her own phone and scrolled through the texts between the two of them, trying to find the guy's name. Finally, she located it. Carl. No last name. And while Willow knew most of the families in town, without more information, she had no idea who Carl might be.

Still concerned, she called her friend Amanda. Unlike Willow, Amanda had never left Getaway. After graduating from cosmetology school, Amanda had opened her own beauty salon right on Main Street. No one had better access to the local gossip than the proprietor of Hair Affair. But the receptionist who answered said Amanda was with a client and offered to take a message.

Instead of leaving her name and number, Willow hung up. No way did she intend to sit around aimlessly and wait for Amanda to return her call. Patience had never been one of her virtues.

She grabbed her car keys and decided to head downtown. She might as well ask Amanda in person. That way, she could go directly to this Carl's house and see if her grandmother was there. If not, maybe Carl might know where Isla had gone.

While she hated to take such drastic measures, Willow didn't see how she had a choice. None of this was like her mom. Even if Isla hadn't been aware her daughter was coming to pay her a surprise visit, she had her self-imposed routine. Ever since becoming an empty nester, she'd filled her days with various activities, all scheduled. She attended yoga on Tuesdays, book club on Thursdays, and she volunteered at the local animal shelter on Friday afternoons. She'd taken up knitting and gardening and took great pride in her rose bushes. By her own unvarying schedule, Isla should be home right now, making something for the noon meal.

Pushing away her niggling worry, Willow went back outside to get in her SUV to make the short drive back to town. But before she could even start the engine, a large dually pickup pulled up in front of the house.

Maybe her grandmother had arrived home. Excited, Willow got out of her SUV and started toward the huge truck. As she approached, instead of Isla, a tall man wearing a black cowboy hat got out. He wore well-fitting Wranglers and boots. Ignoring her, he started for the front door.

"Excuse me," she said, causing him to break stride. "No one's home."

This finally caught his attention. He turned, muscles rippling under his tan Western shirt. His handsome, rugged face seemed vaguely familiar, as if she might have seen him on a television show or in a movie.

She froze, her first thought *rodeo cowboy*. But then again, maybe not. He had a strong profile and chiseled features. And he moved with a kind of easy grace that she found somehow sensual. A true West Texas specimen brimming over with masculinity. And absolutely everything that she'd once found unbearably sexy and now abhorred in a man.

Or thought she did, right up until this very moment.

"I'm looking for my father," he said, his husky voice tinged with the familiar West Texas drawl. "Carl Johnson. His, er, lady friend lives in this house."

Crossing her arms, she took a deep breath. "My grandmother lives here. And she's gone. I just arrived in from out of state. I was hoping she was with him."

Now she'd caught his attention. "Gone?" His narrow gaze swept over her. "Where is she?"

"I don't know. Her car is in the garage. And she left her cell phone in her bedroom. I have no idea where she might be. In fact, I was heading into town to see if I could find out where your father lives so I could check there."

"His truck is still at the ranch too," the man mused. "I wonder if they had friends pick them up."

"What about your dad's cell? Did you try calling it?"

Slowly, he nodded. "I did. He left it behind too." Moving a few steps closer, he held out his hand. "Rey Johnson."

"Willow Allen." She took his hand and shook it, hiding her amazement at how easily his large hand engulfed hers. "I need to find my grandmother. And since your father is missing too, maybe we can team up to make the search easier."

"I wouldn't say missing," he began, then shrugged and shook his head. "Though I guess you could call it that."

With that, he turned to go.

"Wait!" Stunned, she rushed after him. "What are we going to do about it? We have to find them."

"We?" He turned and stared.

Deciding to continue pushing, since she had no idea what else to do, she nodded. "Yes, *we*. Two heads are better than one, don't you think? And since our parents are likely together, it only makes sense."

When her plea didn't appear to convince him, she continued. "I grew up here. And while I don't live here now, I know enough about Getaway to know all of us stick together and help each other."

"Did you go to school with my younger brother, Sam?" he asked.

It took her a moment to put the name together. "Sam Johnson?" Stunned, now it was her turn to stare. "I did. I had no idea my grandmother was dating his father."

"Our father," he corrected. "But, yes. The two of them have been seeing each other for several months."

She took a moment to fully digest this. When she and her grandmom had talked on the phone, Isla had been uncharacteristically giddy about her new relationship. Willow had been happy for her. After all, her grandmother had been alone for as long as Willow could remember. She'd dated, certainly. But she'd also cultivated a wide circle of friends, and between social activities and her volunteer work, her life had seemed full.

Until the health scare. The mere fact that Isla refused to talk about it, when she and Willow kept no secrets from one another, had been really concerning. This, more than anything else, had made Willow drive home.

Right now though, she needed to find her grandmother. "What about their other friends? Do you think they might be out somewhere with another couple?"

He shrugged. "I have no idea, but since neither of

them took their own vehicles, that has to be what happened. I just got back from Colorado, where I picked up livestock. Since my dad was really excited about them, and he knew when I'd be back, I was surprised when I couldn't find him. Sam has been busy repairing fence all day, so he didn't know anything."

The undercurrent of worry she thought she heard in his voice gave her pause. "Do you think something might have happened to them?"

When he met her gaze, his brown eyes seemed kind. "Let's not jump to conclusions. I'm sure there's a rational explanation."

She wanted to believe him. Yet she couldn't seem to shake the feeling that something was wrong. "I'm going to go into town and ask around. One lunch at the Tumbleweed Café should catch me up on all the local gossip."

This comment made him laugh. "Truer words have never been spoken."

"What about you? Would you like to join me?" she asked.

"Maybe another time," he replied, holding her gaze. The warmth in his expression made her mouth go dry. "I need to head back to the ranch. How about I give you my number and you can text me so I have yours. That way, if either of us gets any new information, we can let the other know."

She entered his number into her phone contacts and then sent him a text so he'd have hers. Then she watched as he strode to his truck, an unfamiliar ache warring with the worry inside of her.

Just as he reached for his door handle, he stopped and turned. "I changed my mind," he said. "If you still want to, let's go grab lunch. I haven't eaten since sunrise and could go for one of the Tumbleweed's burgers."

"Sounds great." She hurried to join him before he changed his mind.

To her surprise, he went around to the passenger side and opened the door for her. "Thanks," she said, realizing she'd almost forgotten what it was like to live in small-town West Texas.

Buckling up, she waited for him to get in and start the engine. Now she could only hope they'd run into both their parents, so she could put this sense of foreboding behind her.

Damn. Drumming his fingers on the steering wheel as he drove, Rey Johnson tried to reconcile his admittedly vague memories of the teenaged girl who'd hung around with his younger brother with the stunning woman in his passenger seat.

He'd known, of course, that his father's girlfriend had a daughter who lived in California. Sam had mentioned bitterly several times how much he envied Willow for having the courage to get out of West Texas and start a new life somewhere better. For all his talk, Sam seemed awfully content to stick around the family ranch and do the bare minimum to help keep the place running.

Both Rey and their father humored him. Carl because Sam was his youngest son, aka the baby, and Rey because he understood what made his brother tick. While Sam might be a dreamer, he hadn't yet made the connection between dreams and the hard work necessary to accomplish them.

Shaking off these thoughts, Rey glanced at Willow.

"I'm guessing it's been a while since you visited your grandmother?"

"Christmas," she answered, clearly distracted. "Just about seven months ago. I work in LA. I usually save up my vacation days so I can come home. Though my grandmom and I talk on the phone at least once a week. Sometimes more."

"LA?" He could understand why she'd gone to California. Whether her dream had been to model or to become an actor, someone who looked like her would be sure to get noticed. "Do you act?"

"Act?" Frowning, she eyed him as if he'd suggested she'd taken up cliff diving as a hobby. "No. I work in insurance. I'm an actuary. My job is to analyze the financial costs of risk and uncertainty." She took a deep breath and then smiled. "I absolutely love it."

Her smile lit up the inside of his truck and made his heart beat just a little bit faster.

"An actuary," he repeated, trying not to show his surprise. "I take it you must also love math."

"And spreadsheets," she countered, still smiling. "But yes. Math is my jam."

Not sure how to respond, he nodded.

"What about you?" she asked. "Since you're a rancher, I'm guessing you work around the place with your father."

"And brother," he added. "Sam works there too. We raise cattle, though recently we expanded to include bison. That's what I was doing in Colorado."

"Yet neither of you noticed when your dad left? Why wouldn't he have mentioned he was going somewhere?"

"That's just it," he replied, frustrated. "He's been really looking forward to seeing the bison we purchased.

He knew what time I'd be getting back. I actually expected him to be there to help me unload."

Turning onto Main Street, he noticed the way Willow sat up straight. "The Tumbleweed looks busy as always," she said, her lips curving. "I think out of all the places to eat in Getaway, I missed this one the most."

Since he'd never even once wanted to live anywhere else besides the town where he'd grown up, he simply shrugged. "Some things never change."

He found a parking spot close to the entrance. When he and Willow walked in together, several patrons sent interested glances their way. Which meant they'd be talking about him later.

The hostess, a quiet girl named Barbi who looked like a college student, led them to a booth close to a front window. Busy scanning the restaurant, Willow nearly ran her over when she stopped in front of their seats.

"I'm so sorry," Willow said. "I'm just looking for my mother or even some of her friends. Maybe you've seen her? Isla Allen?"

Barbi stared and then shook her head. "I'm new," she replied. "This is only my second day. I'm home from Tech for the summer. So if she's a regular here, I wouldn't know her. I can ask around though, if you want."

"I'd appreciate it." Willow slid into the booth and accepted the menu.

A moment later, Rey did the same. He'd barely glanced at the menu when an older man wearing a Western shirt, Wranglers and boots walked up. "Afternoon, Rey."

Rey pushed to his feet and held out his hand. "Good to see you, Walter. You haven't happened to have seen my father around town today, have you?"

"Nope. I haven't seen much of Carl ever since he went and got himself a lady friend." Walter eyed Willow curiously. "And who's this here pretty young thing?"

"My name is Willow Allen," Willow said, smiling. "I'm Isla Allen's daughter."

Walter's faded blue gaze sharpened. "Nice to see you back in town. I remember when you were just knee high."

"We're looking for them both," Willow continued. "As you seem to know, his father, Carl, and my grandma, Isla, are a couple. We're hoping someone around here might have seen them."

"You can't find them?" Walter asked. "Are you saying they're missing?"

"Not at all," Rey said, aware he needed to step in before Walter started a panic over the gossip grapevine. "Both of us just got back in town—separately—and we're thinking maybe the two of them are out doing something fun together. Willow here wants to surprise her grandmother. That's all."

"Oh." Clearly disappointed, Walter shrugged. "If I happen to see them, I'll let them know you're looking for them." Dipping his chin at Rey, the older man left.

The waitress appeared. "Can I get you something to drink?"

"Iced tea, please," Willow responded. Rey seconded that.

"Are you two ready to order or do you need another minute?"

"I'm ready," Willow said, sliding her menu across the table so the waitress could grab it. "I'll have the mushroom Swiss burger with fries."

"Bacon burger for me, please." Rey handed over his

menu as well. Once the waitress left, he leaned over and spoke quietly so he wouldn't be overheard. "I know you've been gone for a while, but I know you have to remember how quickly the gossip spreads around here."

"I do." She sighed. "And you're right. My grandmom wouldn't be happy if I started rumors about her. I just can't help but be worried. She's never done anything like this before."

"Like what?" he asked. "From what you've told me, she had no idea you were even coming to visit. I really think she and my dad are out somewhere enjoying themselves with friends. They'll show up eventually."

Expression enigmatic, she eyed him. "You sound awfully certain."

"I am." He sat back in his seat to make room for the waitress with their tea. He waited until she'd left before continuing. "Seriously, what are the alternatives?"

She sighed. "You're probably right, but I tend to have an overactive imagination. I worry."

"I get that. But give it until tonight. If she doesn't return home by then, we'll talk again."

Some of the tenseness seemed to leave her expression. Slowly, she nodded. "Sounds like a plan." For a moment, she studied him. "How is it that your dad is around the same age as my granny? You don't seem to be more than a couple of years older than me, and I know Sam and I are the same age."

"Carl is actually my uncle. He and my father ran the ranch together. When my mom died giving birth to Sam, he became like a second father to us." He took a deep breath, since he hated dredging up the painful past. "I was five when my father died during a bull-riding incident out in Cheyenne. He'd taken up rodeo when Sam and I were both toddlers and left us with Carl most of the time. He's Dad to us now and has been for a long time."

Her sweet smile contained a hint of sadness. "Same with my grandmother. She raised me up and is the only mom I ever knew. I don't know what I'd do if something happened to her."

Their food arrived then. Though his burger made his mouth water, he found himself watching as she picked hers up and took a bite. She ate with gusto, which he appreciated, and yet there was somehow something sensual about the way she enjoyed her meal. His body reacted immediately, and he busied himself with eating to get it back under control.

When he looked up again, he realized they'd finished at the same time. Each of them had a few fries remaining, but nothing more.

"You must have been hungry," she said, touching her napkin to the corners of her mouth. "I know I was."

"Starving," he agreed. "Maybe once our folks reappear, we can all go out to dinner together."

"Definitely." Her quick answer made him exhale. "And Sam should come along. He and I have a lot to catch up on."

Since there was no way to counter that suggestion without making himself look bad, he nodded. While he hadn't meant a date, not really, he was actually hoping to get to know her a little better. At least until she went back to California.

Just the thought was enough to put a damper on the moment of brief foolishness he'd allowed himself to entertain. Willow might be beautiful, she might be the most interesting woman he'd met in a long time. Sexy too, he definitely couldn't forget that.

But she wasn't going to stay. Which, in years past, might have made her a perfect woman with whom to indulge in a hot and heavy, no-emotional-baggage relationship. Not anymore. While he loved his life, he'd reached the stage where he thought he might be open to something more.

In addition, her mother and his father wouldn't appreciate their offspring indulging in a no-holds-barred erotic fling. That alone would be enough to counter any temptation.

"Are you okay?" she asked, interrupting his musing.

Blinking, he looked up, glad she couldn't read his mind. "I'm good," he replied, his voice a bit husky. "Lunch is on me."

Just as Willow started to protest, the waitress arrived with the check, as if on cue. They both reached for it at the same time, their fingers colliding. Somehow, Willow managed to come away with it.

"My treat," she insisted. "After all, you drove. And took pity on an exhausted, overly stressed stranger. I appreciate that more than I can say."

Her words touched him. Dipping his chin in a rancher's way of saying thanks, he abandoned any further effort to convince her to let him pay.

"The next one's on me," he said instead.

She considered him for a moment. "Deal."

On their way out, several old-timers stopped them to talk. Unfortunately, none of them had seen his father or her mother in the last couple of days.

He and Willow walked out to his truck without speaking.

After helping her in, he went around to the driver's side and got in. When she looked at him, he swore he could see the worry in her eyes.

"They'll show up soon," he said, feeling quite certain. "And we'll all have a good laugh over this later."

"I hope so." Finally, she sighed. "I'm exhausted. It's a long drive, and now that I've eaten, I can barely keep my eyes open. When I get back to the house, I'm going to take a nap. Hopefully, when I wake up, my mother will be back."

Don't miss this brand new series by
New York Times bestselling author Lauren Dane!

THE CHASE BROTHERS

*Ridiculously hot
and notoriously single*

One small town.
Four hot brothers.
And enough heat to burn up
anyone who dares to get close.

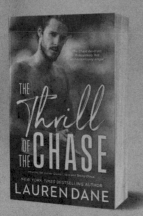

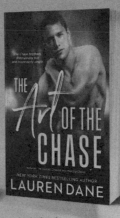

Includes the first two stories
Giving Chase and *Taking Chase*.

Available September 2024.

Includes the next stories
Chased and *Making Chase*.

Available December 2024.

MILLS & BOON

millsandboon.com.au